Praise for

CHILD *of* VENGEANCE

"[A] superb depiction of samurai culture." —*Kirkus Reviews*

"Kirk's spare portrayal of the way of life of the samurai, whose duty it is to protect, defend, and avenge and for whom dying is nothing and winning is all, proves remarkably compelling."
—*Booklist*

"A swashbuckling good read, laced with wisdom.... Worthy of its own samurai film." —*National Post*

"A fascinating, exciting book, beautifully observed. Kirk avoids clichés at every turn, and creates characters of great depth. An absolute gem." —Conn Iggulden,
New York Times bestselling author of
Genghis: Birth of an Empire

"The book I've been waiting for! Razor-sharp samurai action coupled with a brutally realistic vision of life in sixteenth-century Japan, a real find." —Anthony Riches, author of
Wounds of Honor

David Kirk

CHILD of VENGEANCE

David Kirk first became interested in Japanese history when his father gave him a copy of James Clavell's *Shogun*. Years later he would be inspired to write his dissertation on samurai cinema. Kirk now lives in Japan, where he works as an English-language teacher and is currently at work on a second Musashi Miyamoto novel.

CHILD *of* VENGEANCE

David Kirk

Anchor Books

A Division of Random House LLC

New York

FIRST ANCHOR BOOKS EDITION, DECEMBER 2013

The Library of Congress has cataloged the Doubleday edition as follows:
Kirk, David.
Child of vengeance / David Kirk.—1st ed.
p. cm.
1. Miyamoto, Musashi, 1584–1645—Fiction.
2. Japan—History—Azuchi Momoyama period, 1568–1603—Fiction.
3. Japan—History—Tokugawa period, 1600–1868—Fiction. I. Title.
PR6111.I74C48 2013
828'.92—dc23
2012015187

Anchor ISBN: 978-0-345-80300-9

Book design by Maria Carella

www.anchorbooks.com

146122990

A novel of fathers, for my father, Frank.
I'll work an Uzi into the next one somehow, I swear.

Many people claim that
the resolute acceptance of death
is the way of the samurai.
However, these people are wrong;
warriors have no monopoly on this virtue.
Monks, women and peasants too
can face death bravely.
No; the true distinction of a samurai
lies in overcoming other men
and bringing glory to himself.

—Musashi Miyamoto, *Go Rin No Sho*
(The Book of Five Rings), 1645

CONTENTS

AUTHOR'S NOTE

All names are
presented in the
Western fashion of
given name before
family name—e.g.,
Munisai Shinmen
rather than the
technically correct
Shinmen Munisai.

Part One

GHOSTS

The armor sits, as it has done for eight years, empty. The boy stands at the edge of the room looking at it, clenching and unclenching his fists. He loathes and he loves what is before him.

The house around him is dark and silent. It is big enough for a dozen, but the boy alone lives here. He is the son of samurai, and so he is tended to by the peasants of the village. He wants for nothing—the house is cleaned, the garden pruned and raked, food always within chests and barrels—but he never sees his custodians. They are fearful of him and of this house, and he is cared for as if by phantoms.

The boy is called Bennosuke. The armor is his father's. His father is not dead, but gone. In his absence the armor must be maintained, but the peasants cannot permit themselves to touch such a thing. Thus it falls to the boy to clean it, and he has done so for almost as long as he can remember. He bows to the suit as he would to the man, and then approaches on his knees, his eyes downcast.

The armor is magnificent. The body of it is a rounded lacquer cuirass, its black smoothness without flaw. From this, hanging from the shoulders and the waist are large square panels to guard the legs and the arms. Narrow rectangular layers of metal and wood lap over one another like fish gills, each strip hidden beneath a rich base cloth of light blue over which threads of gold and silver have been woven into pattern.

It is the helmet that is the most striking. It has a large copper crest that rises off the brow in burnished brilliance, shaped after leaves and the whiskers of mythical beasts. The bowl of the helmet is etched with interlocking patterns and within the lines of these the most delicate of prayers to bring fortune and victory are carved. It begs the face of some shining hero, but where that should be is only empty darkness.

Bennosuke feels that darkness looking into him as he begins to clean. His hands move with years of practice, picking grime and motes of dust from within the crevices of the armor. He rubs fine oils into metal where it is exposed, ensures each link between the pieces still holds strong whether it be steel hoop or tough cord. Then he takes a cloth and a small bowl of wax, and begins to polish the cuirass.

It is this he hates the most. As his hands rub in small circles, slowly the lacquer becomes as a pool of dark water, as clear as any mirror. The boy begins to see himself reflected, and his blush begins. He is a gangly boy of thirteen, as tall as any man in the village where he lives already, but without poise or grace. He looks awkward, but that is not what shames him.

Across his face and neck, and then down onto his body hidden beneath the kimono, are sickly red welts and scabs. It is not called plague only because it has not killed him, nor will it, but he knows that this is why he is alone. He knows this is why the peasants fear him. He imagines them coming to this house as a funeral gang, cloths across their faces and incense burning as they quickly fulfill their tasks.

The image is warped across the curve of the stomach of the armor, twisting his body further and taunting him; the boy dreams of wearing this suit, but what he sees reflected in it shows him that this could never be. Still he dreams of it, though, for he wants to be a samurai above all else. The boy awaits the unknown day his father must return with longing and dread. He imagines the man teaching him to be a strong and proud warrior beloved of the light, and at the same time knows the samurai who wore this armor would be disgusted with the wretch his heir has become.

He feels his face burning in shame, feels all that twisting in his heart, but the boy continues to polish. Though he hates this task, he knows that this is his duty, and that diligence in duty is the first tenet of a samurai. He perseveres, his hand going in spirals until it is done. Then he folds the cloth, shuffles back on his knees, and bows once more, his brow upon the woven rush mats of the floor.

The boy holds it for a respectful amount of time, and then rises. He is careful not to let his eyes look upon the name stitched stark white upon the foremost lap guard of the armor, as though the reading of it might somehow summon his father and bring the day he yearns for lurching hideously forward.

He is careful not to read the name Munisai Hirata.

CHAPTER ONE

The battle was over, but still Kazuteru ran. He had duty to fulfill. The young samurai ignored the howling of his lungs and the ache within his muscles and bore forth his sacred burden: a dagger the length of his hand. His lord awaited it on the valley top above him.

It had rained all day yesterday and most of the morning too, an anomaly in the high summer. The sun shone bright now, but too late. Hundreds of feet and hooves had trampled the sodden slope and churned it into a swamp. Kazuteru's armor and underclothes, which had once been a brilliant blue, were now a mottled gray, and his legs were heavy with plastered clay and turf.

His hands alone were clean, protected as they had been under gauntlets and gloves. Bared, the flesh had remained immaculate enough to hold the dagger. But the humidity and the layers of metal, cloth, and wood he wore had made his entire body slick with sweat. It stung his eyes and he could taste it on his lips, and when the ground gave suddenly beneath him as he ran, he felt it on his hands also. His wet palms fumbled, and the dagger slipped from his grasp.

The blade caught the light as it fell. It winked white once at him, and then plunged into the slimy dirt and vanished with a sad little sound. Kazuteru let a smaller, sadder whimper escape him. His waiting lord had a thousand swords and spears with him already, but they would not suffice. They were not ceremonial and pure. The dagger, which had been, was now sullied.

He fell to his knees and plunged his left hand into the muck. It vanished up to his wrist. He began to grope blindly, hastened by desperation but slowed by fear of the blade's edge.

Something to his right moaned suddenly, a pained voice so pitiful that it stopped Kazuteru. He saw a man twisted where he had fallen, one leg so shattered and bent that his toes almost touched his hamstring. The samurai had no mind left for words; his eyes pleaded with Kazuteru to kill him, and for a moment he thought to oblige.

But then Kazuteru realized that the man wore the red of the enemy, and for that he left him. The man's agony was but one voice in dozens.

Hundreds.

His fingers touched blunt metal. He pulled the dagger free, and filth came with it. Kazuteru tried to wipe the blade clean as best he could. Once when he was a child—too young to know about sacrilege—he and his friends had hidden a small cast-iron Buddha in an ox's feed just to see if the beast was too stupid to notice. It had been, and three days later they had found the Buddha again. Looking at the dagger now, he was reminded of that serene, shit-smeared face.

Water. He needed water.

But there was none here, save for that which had soaked into the ground; this was where the fighting had been. There was no time to return to their distant camp, where he had just run to collect the blade in the first place. The only place he could look was up the slope, toward the valley top they had stormed not one hour ago.

He began to run toward the hilltop once more, skidding and stuttering in the mud, dagger in his filthy left hand with his right hand held high and free of any contamination. Ahead of him, overlooking the entire valley, Lord Kanno's castle burned. One of the smaller curved roofs groaned loudly, and then collapsed inward. A ragged cheer carried on the distant breeze, and a fresh billow of black smoke erupted into the sky.

There, in the corner of Kazuteru's eye—a mangled man lying against a barricade of bamboo stakes, seemingly drunk as he fumbled about himself. His numb hands were trying to put a canteen to his lips. Clear water dribbled from the mouth of the ray-leather bladder, catching the light.

Kazuteru hesitated, his conscience caught, but it was clear the man was beyond any help that water could possibly bring. He squelched to his knees beside the samurai, and tried to take the canteen. The man held on stubbornly.

"I need that water, friend," said Kazuteru gently.

"W'tr?" mumbled the man, his eyes distant. Still he tried to remember how to drink, still his hands corpse-tight upon the canteen.

"Our Lord Shinmen requires it," said Kazuteru.

"F'r Lord Shinm'n," the man said. Out of instinct alone, he obeyed that name and released his grip. His eyes closed, something that wasn't blood or water bubbled out of his mouth, and then he died.

Kazuteru muttered his thanks to the man's departing soul as he began to slowly pour the water on the dagger. It was not quite enough, one clod of black mud remaining. There was nothing else to do but stick his tongue out and lick it clean, and then he knew the taste of the battlefield. He spat, and then the dagger was as clean as it was going to get. Back it went into his pristine right hand, and then he ran once more.

The ground up on the valley top was not so bad, some solid green turf remaining. Nothing slowed him as he weaved his way through the groups of surviving samurai toward where the lords and generals awaited. A cadre of exhausted foot soldiers, all as dirty as Kazuteru, knelt in a clustered circle around their superiors, facing inward to bear witness to this final act. Lungs were still panting, open wounds being treated.

Kazuteru dropped into a walking crouch as he drew close to the mock court, holding the dagger above his head respectfully. Men parted for him until he came to where his lord, Sokan Shinmen, sat on a small stool. He dropped to one knee and waited.

The lord was sitting in his underarmor of toughened cloth. During the battle an arrow had thumped into the plate of his chest armor almost directly over his heart, and he had removed the heavy cuirass to nurse the bruise it had left. The narrow escape had given the lord a spark of manic joy in his eyes that he was unable to conceal.

Shinmen took the proffered dagger and examined it. Kazuteru held his breath. The lord raised an eyebrow for a moment at the drops of water upon the blade, but he said nothing. He shook it dry and nodded appreciatively at Kazuteru. The samurai bowed low, and then backed away on his knees to melt into the crowd. The taste of mud still in his mouth, relief and pride flooded him; he had done his duty.

"Lord Kanno," said Shinmen, turning back to the three who

awaited in the center of the gathering, "do you know what follows now?"

Lord Kanno was the defeated enemy, and he had nervous tears in his eyes as he knelt. Regaled in a full set of miniature armor, he could have escaped from some comedy theater. He was nine years old.

"I think so," the boy lord said. "I have to perform seppuku. But . . ." the boy began, then faltered.

"But?" said Shinmen.

"But I don't know how, Lord," Kanno said sadly. His small shoulders wilted. "I was never allowed to see. I wanted to, but Father said I was too young."

An affectionate laugh rippled through the crowd of samurai. Only two men remained silent. One was Kanno's General Ueno, who knelt beside his lord. He was an old man with thinning gray hair that hung disheveled around him. It was he who had been truly in command of the enemy, and he who had lost the day. His eye was bruised, his nose was bleeding, and he bristled with futile venom.

The other stood behind the kneeling pair, his face emotionless for it would be obscene to show joy in front of defeated enemies, and it was he above all the men there who had defeated the Kanno clan. His armor was plain and practical, without any mark of garish boasting save for perhaps the dents and scrapes that spoke of how much fighting he had seen and yet still stood. He was Munisai Shinmen, commander of the lord's foot soldiers, and so trusted and beloved was he by Lord Shinmen that the lord had bestowed the honor of his own name upon him. Now he waited for command patiently, one hand upon the swords at his hip.

The mirth subsided, and then Lord Shinmen spoke on. "Seppuku is not difficult, Lord. It is what we are bred for."

Kanno still looked nervous. "My brothers told me that you put a sword in your belly. Is that right?" the boy said.

"They were right, Lord."

"But doesn't that hurt?" asked the boy.

Shinmen smiled at the innocence. "I should imagine it does. But not for long, Lord. A moment of pain, and then your honor is restored and your spirit is free to wander the heavens and be reborn. It is a good death," he said.

"But I never lost my honor! It was my father, Lord! It was he who declared war on you!"

"The clan is as the lord," said Shinmen. "This is the way of nobility. The body changes over the years but in you is your father and your grandfather, as my father and my grandfather are in me, all the way back through to the start of time. In you all of their honor rests—will you disappoint them?"

"No! I'm not afraid . . ." said Kanno, panicking because he could not explain himself and like all children feared looking small in front of adults. "It's just . . . I . . . I don't know!"

"Well then, perhaps your general could show you how it's done?" said Shinmen. The kneeling Ueno raised his maddened eyes.

"If you think I'm going to give you cowards the honor of that, you dogs can—" He began snarling, spit flecking from his lips.

"Where is your dignity?" snapped Munisai, speaking for the first time. "Your lord needs your help, and you act like this? Are you samurai, or did someone dress a shit-tossing peasant in the general's armor this morning?"

"A cunning ruse, perhaps," said Shinmen.

"You're one to talk of ruses, Shinmen! Accepting our gold and feigning peace like some demon fox! And you"—the general growled, jerking his head toward Munisai—"you are one to talk of samurai! Instead of standing on the field like any true warrior would have, you sneak around our rear like some common thief!"

"That rear was where I found you hiding," said Munisai.

"I was protecting my lord!" Ueno shouted.

"A fine job you did of that," said Shinmen, and laughter rippled around the gathered men. There was no warmth this time. Ueno could do nothing but glower at the ground and try to endure the humiliation, but it was much too great to bear.

"To the hells with you all!" he spat. "Very well, I will show him! Give me the blade!"

"What of your death poem?" asked Shinmen.

"I have nothing I want to say to you. Tossing coins to stray cats," said Ueno, as he unbuckled his armor, hands furiously jerking the clasps open. He placed the cuirass on the ground before him and rose into a dignified kneel.

"The blade," he commanded. Shinmen wrapped the dagger in a length of white silk, and then it was conveyed respectfully to the general, who took it wordlessly.

"I suppose I will have the honor of the great Munisai Shinmen taking my head?" Ueno sneered as he placed the tip of the dagger to the side of his stomach.

Munisai looked to Lord Shinmen, who nodded once. He moved to the side of the general and drew his longsword. The elegant weapon was dulled with use, and so it did not gleam as Munisai held it high, ready to flash the killing stroke.

"I am ready, General," he said simply.

"Are you watching, my lord?" asked Ueno. The boy uttered a small affirmative. Ueno took a few deep breaths, licked his lips, and steeled himself.

"This is how a samurai dies," the old man said, and suddenly threw himself backward at Munisai.

It was impressively fast for an old, exhausted man. He had sprung onto his feet and thrust the bulk of his weight upward into Munisai before the samurai had a chance to react. Munisai was knocked off balance, and barely managed to catch the dagger as Ueno spun and stabbed it downward, seeking the gap in the armor at his neck.

Munisai was staggering and encumbered with holding his sword, and there was a hanging second where it seemed to the onlookers that the tip of the blade would surely split his throat. But he found his footing once more, and then it was simply a matter of age and but the work of a moment to roll himself around and throw Ueno over his hip. The general landed heavily, and before he could rise Munisai had stabbed savagely downward with his sword, impaling him through the chest.

It was a brutal blow, deliberately crude as to be insulting. The two locked eyes as the general lay dying, and Munisai knew Ueno understood the affront. But the old man did not make a single sound. He merely mouthed wordless curses at Munisai as his strength left him. Eventually his lips ceased to move, his eyes glazed over, and then Ueno was still.

"Disgusting," said Munisai in the silence.

He withdrew his sword, wiped the blood off the blade, and then sheathed the weapon. Only at that signal did the bodyguards release Lord Shinmen; they had thrown themselves around him as a human shield as soon as Ueno had pounced. Munisai had trained them well.

"He hated you," said Lord Kanno quietly. He hadn't moved from where he knelt. "You killed his son last summer, Munisai."

"Then he let that cloud his judgment," said Munisai. "What of his honor? His son died well, in equal combat. He did not. We gave him the chance of an honorable death, and . . . That was not the way it should be done, Lord Kanno."

"Then what is?" asked the boy. Munisai hesitated, but then he saw the look of worry in the child's face. The earnestness of it sparked something within him that he had not felt in many years, and slowly he began to speak in a soft tone.

"We are samurai, Lord. Death defines us. We must become a master of dealing it to our enemies, yes, but most of all lose all fear of our own. Seppuku is the ultimate test of this. You must draw the blade across your stomach. Some rare men will complete the ritual in its entirety, turn the blade, and draw it back across. But rare men indeed, for there must be complete silence. If you whimper or cry out, it proves that you are afraid, and thus not samurai and never were. If you are too cowardly to force the blade up, or if you lose yourself to blind emotion like Ueno, then all the worse."

He cast another scornful gaze at the general's body, and then nodded for the boy to take in the ugliness of the thing—the way it lay twisted in the mud, the hatred still upon the face, bestial and fragile and spiritless. After a few moments Munisai turned and gave another gesture. A brush, ink, and a scroll of silk affixed to an easel were brought forth and placed before Lord Kanno.

"Ueno hated me?" said Munisai. "Then he should have damned me in his death poem. The ritual must have dignity. The ritual must have calm. To write the death poem is to cleanse yourself of all emotion. Put all your fear, or your anger, or your sadness into the poem, and then you are empty and free to do the act as it should be done."

"A poem?" said Kanno. "I've never written a poem."

"It is not difficult, Lord," said Munisai. "It does not have to be a poem proper, no rhyme or rule . . . Just say what you want."

Kanno thought for some long moments. All watched silently as the boy dipped the brush into the black ink and began to slowly write. His brow furrowed in concentration as he did so, taking care to be perfect.

Kazuteru watched Munisai as the boy wrote. He had never heard his commander speak more than curt orders, let alone give a speech. Now the man was staring at the child with a strange intensity. It looked almost like longing.

Eventually the boy sat back on his knees and placed the brush aside. Munisai looked over his shoulder.

"Is it good?" the boy asked anxiously.

Munisai nodded. Kanno smiled happily, proud of his work. He withdrew his clan's centuries-old seal and stamped it below the letters. Then the silk was folded and sealed, placed into a lacquer box, and whisked away. It would be joined, after the ritual, by a lock of the lord's hair and sent to the boy's mother as proof that he died well. She would smile as she wept.

A sheet of white hemp was laid on the muddy ground while Lord Kanno stripped out of his armor. The ceremonial blade was pried from Ueno's death grip, cleaned in a pail of water, and then given to Kanno. It seemed the size of a sword in his hands. He knelt, and pointed it toward himself.

"From one side to the other?" he asked.

"Yes," said Munisai. "It won't hurt for long, I promise, Lord."

Munisai drew his sword once more, and this time, because it was the boy, he dribbled water along his blade also. A pure blade for a pure young soul, the weapon glistened in the afternoon sun as he raised it now, a bar of light almost. He nodded at Kanno.

"Your ancestors depend on you, Lord. So be brave," he said.

"Thank you, Munisai," said the boy.

He turned and bowed deeply to Lord Shinmen and the gathered samurai one last time, rose to his knees, and then thrust the dagger into his belly. He doubled over and his eyes went wide.

Of course they did not expect a child to force the blade across himself. Munisai heard the boy's sharp intake of breath, and before Kanno could cry out and shame himself, he slashed the sword down perfectly and struck the boy through the neck. There was a dull thump as the head rolled free, and then the small body toppled sideways. The white hemp turned red.

The gathered samurai, whether lord or common soldier, bowed deeply to the corpse, and a sigh of admiration ran through them all. Such immaculate bravery from one so young.

"What did his death poem say, Munisai?" asked Lord Shinmen.

"That is not for me to say, my lord," said Munisai, and though Shinmen could have ordered him to do so, he gave his lord such a look that Shinmen questioned him no further.

When the bleeding stopped, they took Kanno's head and his body and cleaned them. Then they wrapped them in a white funeral shroud, anointed them properly, and cremated the boy. They spread his ash on the wind so that it might travel to the ends of Japan, and then his name was added honorably to the centuries of names on his clan's gravestone. It would be the last to ever be chiseled. Years later a tree had sprung from near the spot of the seppuku, and the local peasants knew their brave lord must have returned to them. They wove a sacred rope and tied it around the tree so that Kanno's spirit might never leave again, and for centuries after pregnant noble-women would visit the place and pray that their children might have the same courage as the young lord.

General Ueno, however, was left for the crows.

The war had been the fault of the old Lord Kanno. The summer before, the old man had suddenly decided to try to recapture his youth and play soldier again. Lord Shinmen was engaged in a war with a neighbor to the north, and so Kanno reasoned that Shinmen could not protect the valuable paddy fields on his eastern border. He was right, for a while.

Kanno's mistake was to go riding in winter. Buoyed by the successful annexation of the paddy fields, the old lord felt twenty in his heart again. In his knees, however, he was still very much his seventy years, and the frozen mountain paths were treacherous at the best of times. Borne from the bottom of the canyon where it was found, his corpse was anything but regal.

Kanno had been a lecherous old goat. He had fathered many sons to many embittered women, and he harbored a great fear that his boys loved their mothers more than him. Not one of his four previous heirs had lived beyond nineteen, by accident or design, and now his fifth would not see ten.

The newly installed boy lord's advisors had offered a truce in the springtime. Shinmen had feigned acceptance of the ridiculous terms—no mention of returning the stolen land—and so two days ago, with the coming of the summer, Shinmen had launched a lightning raid. His small force had overrun the watchtowers and outposts with such speed that Kanno's army had barely had time to rally here in the very heart of their domain.

Were it not for the rain the day before slowing them, there would not have been time at all for Kanno's men. But those few bogged-down hours had given Ueno time to entrench his army around the castle and force Shinmen into a bitter uphill fight. Hundreds of men had died simply because of the vagaries of weather.

But what was victory without sacrifice? Blossom without fragrance, nothing more.

Munisai sat down among the flowers. He held a man's hand as the samurai oozed his last breaths out. He had been run through by a lance, the blade entering at his collarbone and exiting at his pelvis. Skewered entirely, but somehow the man had lingered this long with the wood of the shaft still wedged through him. He gurgled and writhed. His eyes met Munisai's for a moment, desperate and pleading.

"It'll be over soon," said Munisai. "You did well. We won."

There were many like this man here where the healers worked their art, a mass of mangled men encircled by a ringed white palisade fifty paces across. The air was rent with moaning and the stench of purifying herbs burning as doctors dashed from man to man, trying to do what they could. Healthy men knelt or stood by as friends died, the filth smeared across their faces slashed by the path of tears.

Munisai had been here many times before. It was strange to him how the land partitioned to the healers was always worse, always more frantic after victory. After all, if you ceded a battlefield, you ceded every man left there upon it. Loss brought silence and contemplation, triumph only misery and despair and guts in your hand.

Blossom and fragrance, he told himself. The man whose hand he held hacked up a fresh shower of petals.

Munisai was in a strange mood. Something was different this time. He had never felt joy after victory for more than a few vital, visceral seconds, but neither had he felt lingering doubt like he did now.

The samurai looked up and saw the smoke from Kanno's castle drifting lazily across the evening sky. Memories came to him. He saw his home village on fire, the night aglow the color of persimmon peel, and then the charnel stink in the morning as thick, greasy plumes hung low across the valleys.

But that was not it entirely. He had seen fire before on the battlefield, and he remembered that terrible day of his past more than he cared to admit.

The eyes of the boy lord, Kanno. Determined and innocent. Those were what haunted him, for in them he saw another boy, one whom he had left behind and tried to forget about, a boy who was through no fault of his own the bane of his life.

He wondered what the face around those eyes looked like now, many years since he had seen it last. Children, boy or girl, were feminine; the father did not truly show until adolescence. Hatred coursed through him at that thought, both for the face he imagined and for himself. But still he imagined it, for the unanswered ache within him knew that he needed to see.

"Bennosuke," murmured Munisai.

"His name is Aoki," said a healer, gesturing at the man with the spear through him who lay by Munisai's side. "*Was* Aoki."

Munisai barely heard him.

He let go of Aoki's hand. He dropped to both knees and bowed to the corpse as a mark of respect, and the men watching quivered with pride as they saw their commander humble himself so.

When he stood, he saw that atop the slopes alongside the inferno of Kanno's castle a great palanquin had arrived to pomp and fanfare and waving banners. It was decked in burgundy and it shimmered like a peacock. Munisai looked at it with disgust. Dozens of men had carried it—dozens of men who could have carried spears and helped in the battle instead.

The clan Nakata had arrived.

There was a dull, throbbing pain underneath his left shoulder that he did not want to think about, but the very sight of the palanquin made it pulse anew. He would be expected to visit that gaudy thing, to bow and prostrate himself before men he hated, and the thought filled him with loathing.

But the Nakata were allies of his Lord Shinmen, so he would have to endure it. This was duty, he knew, and duty was distraction. Duty meant that he did not have to feel or think of wounds of both the flesh and the heart.

He looked around once more. Those warriors who could bowed to him as his eyes passed across them. The doctors, shaven-headed and sweating, were too frantic to worry about him. Saying nothing, he rooted around in a wooden chest and took some bandages and a small envelope of what smelled like salve, and left them to tend to their macabre and glorious garden.

ON THE WAY to the palanquin, Munisai found himself giving commands that did not need to be given, dallying to supervise that which needed none. But he could not avoid it forever, and when he finally arrived he stood before it for a few moments. Night was all but here already, and the burgundy silk glowed from lanterns lit within. A mobile palace brought to reign over a place that other men had fought and died for. He had to force the scowl from his face before he ducked his head and passed through the curtains.

As soon as he entered, he was hit by the smell of incense. Wisps of it hung in the air, no doubt to mask the stench of the battlefield. He held back in the shadows of the entrance and looked inward.

All was silk or lacquer wood painted in gold leaf. When it was carried, the hall was big enough for perhaps a half dozen to sit in comfortably. But set down, the palanquin's hidden panels and curtains could be opened and unfurled so it grew, and now it was big enough for Lord Shinmen and the Nakata to sit on a raised dais while a few ranks of bodyguards and courtiers from either clan knelt around them. A woman plucked quietly on a koto harp in the background, the music lilting and soothing.

Lord Shinmen's wound had been treated in a way that Munisai did not know how to describe without talking ill of his lord. The bruise where the arrow had struck certainly didn't warrant a sling, but now the lord's left arm was tightly bound to a body swathed in bandages, and he made a show of having difficulty drinking.

There were two of the Nakata with him. Both wore rich kimonos in burgundy, patterns traced upon the garments in threads of silver. The man closest to Shinmen was Lord Nakata; an old, squat man with a doughy, round face and eyes that were constantly pinched into a squint. The jokes ran that he was always looking for the last coin in the room, so scared was he of missing wealth.

Munisai recognized the other man as Nakata's eldest son and heir, Hayato. He was burning the incense, idly poking stick after stick to stand in a small bowl of sand. He looked little like his father, being a slight man with a long face. His eyes were wide and dulled, the incense holding him in its sway.

Indeed, Hayato seemed oblivious to anything but the smoke. He ignored his father and Shinmen as they spoke. The pair of lords had chosen a polite, inoffensive topic as etiquette required.

"It is believed the slaughter was great, that the enemy were dashed to pieces upon the rocks of your brave men like a great wave of filth and pestilent vermin, Lord Shinmen?" asked Lord Nakata, eyes blinking around blindly.

"Indeed, Lord. Were guessing required, it is not unreasonable to think that even their distant descendants will still have nightmares of this day," replied Shinmen.

"Quite so, quite so. No wonder, if even one such as a lord should sustain such a grievous wound as you have. Would it be rude to inquire of the combat, my stalwart ally? It is trusted the wretch who struck you paid with his life?"

"Unfortunately not, Lord. He was but a cowardly archer, so his fate is unable to be ascertained. But with this sword alone, three enemy were sent to their graves. The last one was barely worth calling a man! Have you heard the cry a pig makes as it dies, Lord? The cry this man made was not dissimilar!"

"Regrettably that pleasure has yet to be experienced, Lord. Were it only that all our enemies could suffer such a fate, gorging on their own entrails and drowning in their own blood."

"If that were so, Lord, one might be happy. But then what would we do? We are samurai. It is our nature to slay our enemies. Peace is only the gasp of breath before we can plunge back into that rapturous ocean known as war."

"Quite so, Lord. Quite so!" said Lord Nakata, and raised his cup of sake politely. Shinmen returned the gesture.

Munisai saw what he had feared—his lord had changed again. Gone was the man from the battlefield of today, confident and trustworthy and the one he had followed for five years. Here now was the new Lord Shinmen, who had been seeping in more and more these past months, the closer he drew to Nakata and his promise of wealth.

Ambition, they said, was a virtue. Once it had been, when Shinmen's was a desire for honest struggle, for he and his forces to prove themselves upon the battlefield, as samurai ought. But now it had festered, rotted him from within, and drew him instead to shrines of affluence like the one he sat in now. Munisai could not bear seeing the man behave like this.

No one here would stop them, though, for it was regal mouths speaking and so all had to acknowledge it as profound rather than what it was—ridiculous. His face unreadable, Munisai made as if he had just arrived, swinging the curtain aside wildly and ensuring his armor rattled. He approached the dais and then dropped to his knees before Shinmen, placed his forehead to the floor, waited the respectful length of time, and then rose.

"My lord, forgive my lateness. There is still much work to be done," he said.

"Like extinguishing fires?" said Hayato venomously, suddenly rising from his stupor to look at Munisai.

"My lord?" asked Munisai, surprised that the young lord had spoken. He looked to Shinmen, but it was Lord Nakata who spoke.

"Forgive my son, Munisai Shinmen. Being young, it is unknown by him how men should properly comport themselves," he said, and turned to his son, who had returned to lighting incense sullenly.

"Look upon this man, Hayato—here is one named the Nation's Finest! Do you not understand what that means?"

"You flatter me, noble Lord Nakata," said Munisai, bowing. "But that title refers solely to swordsmanship and nothing more. There are much finer men than I within our land. Even so, if something has been done that is unsatisfactory to either yourself or your heir, it would be shameful if it could not be spoken of and rectified."

"It has been a fine day's work, Munisai, indeed. We live on in a world that is less one enemy. But . . . there is the issue of the castle," said Lord Shinmen.

"My lord?"

"The castle of the late Lord Kanno, which was promised by Lord Shinmen to our clan as a most wonderful and splendid gift and a sign of our enduring alliance," said Lord Nakata.

"The ruins of *my* castle, now which are still ablaze outside," said Hayato. The young lord was all petulant fury as he looked at Munisai.

This was the first he had heard of any plans for the castle as a gift, but Munisai nevertheless bowed once more to the lords and said, "What happened with the castle was regrettable, my lords. But in the context of the situation an entirely necessary regret."

"Are you certain of that, Munisai?" asked Shinmen.

"Yes, my lord," said Munisai. "If you would allow me to explain?"

"Please do." Nakata nodded.

"Very well," he said. "My Lord Shinmen led the main body of men up through the valley, while I led a covert force around the rear to try to take the Lord Kanno and the castle itself. Unfortunately our ruse was spotted earlier than I had hoped, and Ueno was more cautious also. We had managed to pass the gate of the stronghold, but a fight ensued with a hundred men or thereabouts to my threescore. Furthermore, Ueno had a chance to barricade himself and the Lord Kanno within the armory of the clan. My men could not hold indefinitely, and neither did I want to prolong an uphill battle for my Lord Shinmen, so time was of the essence—we needed to extricate the lord from the armory as soon as possible.

"I believe there is no faster way to encourage men to leave a building than the prospect of burning, and so we set a fire that in our zealousness unfortunately grew out of control. But it worked, and once the boy lord was in my custody, the Kanno samurai could not fight on with a sword to their lord's throat. They surrendered, in the castle at least, and that is how the day was won, my lords." Munisai finished speaking, and then bowed low once more.

"A stirring account, my honorable Munisai, and I salute your daring," said Lord Nakata, nodding his head once. "But I have to raise a question with you—surely there must have been another entrance to the armory you could have sought, rather than resorting to arson?"

"There were none that were visible, Lord," said Munisai.

"That does not mean an absence of exits, however. Indeed, in our many castles there is always an abundance of passages into each and every room. So it follows that there must be in Kanno's also, no?" said Lord Nakata.

"So it may be, Lord," said Munisai.

He wanted to point out that if there had been a secret entrance, Ueno and Kanno might have used it to escape, but he held his tongue. It would be a futile argument. He could see now what the intention here was—Lord Shinmen had made a mistake, and now Munisai was expected to take the blame for it. This was duty.

"It holds, therefore, that you owe our esteemed guests a formal apology. Do you not agree, Munisai?" asked Shinmen.

"Indeed, my lord." Munisai nodded. "If you should wish it, my immolation by seppuku is humbly offered that my dishonor might be expunged with my blood."

"No, no, Commander. That would be quite unnecessary. It is felt that your simple words would be enough," said Nakata.

"Very well, Lo—"

"Coupled," continued Nakata, "with a tithe from your yearly stipend to help pay for arrears, of course."

Munisai made no outward reaction, but inside he seethed. Money was little more than a concept to him, but to be so publicly indebted to anyone, let alone the Nakata, galled him. Nevertheless, he swallowed that shame and bowed low once more.

"That is the least that could be offered. My estate shall be informed at once. Furthermore, my sincere and humble apologies for my brash and destructive actions are offered to you both, your clan, your ancestors, and to all the descendants you have and may yet sire," he said, and then lowered himself farther so that his forehead was on the ground as he waited for Nakata to speak.

"Very good, Commander Munisai, they are of course accepted," the old lord said eventually.

"Rise, Munisai," said Shinmen, and Munisai obeyed.

"Forgive me further, my lords, but my attention is required else—"

"I wonder why," said Hayato, looking at no one, "I am even surprised at this. It's not as though Munisai Shinmen wreaking destruction with flame is without precedent, is it?"

Something froze behind Munisai's breastbone. Hayato stared only at the cherry of the burning stick of incense in his hand. He did not see his father turn to him and try to wordlessly communicate the danger of speaking slander in front of court. Neither did he see Lord Shinmen, who knew the truth behind such slander, look at the swords at Munisai's side.

"And now he comes offering apologies covered in the filth of a battlefield," continued Hayato, either oblivious to the sudden tenseness or feigning it, smoke coiling around his face. "Does the honorable Munisai not know how to present himself, or does he find contentment in reeking of dung?"

The numb potential for fury passed in Munisai; he realized then that Hayato was a brat and nothing more, picking around at whatever insult he could think of without knowing which was the true one. A great weariness and exasperation came in its place, to such an extent that Munisai committed a fundamental sin and let some of his true self show. He could not stop himself from fixing his gaze on the young lord until Hayato had no choice but to return it hesitantly.

"Apologies are offered, Lord Nakata," said Munisai, "if the very idea of war discomforts you so. Sometimes I forget the delicate spirit of city dwellers differs from that of warriors."

He might have gotten away with it had the koto player not sniggered. But the music's rhythm broke for a jarring second; the woman raised a delicate hand to her face, composed herself, and then continued playing. Hayato turned bright red, and looked at the ground. His father squinted his piggy little eyes harder at Munisai. Shinmen's face had grown cold and still. Munisai turned to look at him.

"With your permission, my lord?" he asked.

"You may go, Munisai," Shinmen said, voice somber.

Munisai bowed once more, rose, and strode off. There was silence as he left, though in some of the downturned faces he thought he could see amusement. There was little doubt the story would be passed around the camp before long. What that would reap, he didn't know, but at that moment he didn't care.

Outside night had fully fallen, but the cooler air did not refresh him. He was exhausted and angry and he could not deny that he felt betrayed, and over much more than what had just happened. That he felt such shameful selfishness only angered him further, and he stalked off toward what was left of Hayato's castle.

They had won, and so the drinking had begun.

Around the glowing embers of the castle bands of men had formed, growing larger as time wore on and final duties were seen to, shouting and laughing with friends old and new. The stores of the fortress had been raided before they could burn, and so now great cauldrons of rice and soup and vegetables were cooking and barrels were being smashed open with mallets the length of bodies.

Kazuteru held his arms out wide as he sang a bawdy old song of victory his father had taught him in his childhood, weaving his way through the groups of men half looking for someone he knew. Though he clutched a bottle of sake in his hand, he was not drunk. Truth be told the drink was bitter and he could stomach no more than a few mouthfuls of it; he carried it merely because he did not want to look out of place among the others. His body thrummed solely with the intoxication of being alive and having survived.

He thought of his father as he sang—the man had died in a war of his own some ten years ago, and the song was one of the few things he had left his son. The little wealth bequeathed to him and his mother had quickly vanished and his mother had been too proud to seek aid from anyone, and so the pair of them had endured with shrunken stomachs in a house that was pawned piece by piece.

But now Kazuteru was a man, and more than that a warrior who had lived through his first battle. Soon his stipend would increase as he rose through the ranks, and so finally he would be able to provide for his mother and ensure that she lived in comfort in her aging years. Fine silk, fine food, a maid or two maybe . . . Why not? It was a night for dreams and glory.

Lingering sensations danced around the inside of his head though, terrible memories of the day—the sound of the man with the twisted leg, the sight of Kanno's cavalry charge tearing down the hill in one fearsome arrowhead, the warmth of his piss streaming down his legs as he stood frozen in terror before those horsemen—but the young samurai curled his lips into a smile and banished them, singing louder and spinning as he walked.

They had all earned it, this one night, to forget the rules and decorum and etiquette that governed their lives. Men clapped him on as he sang and strode, older men who would have snarled at him and called him a fool at any other time. He passed men in fine kimonos bent double vomiting through mouths warped into numb grins, others stripped almost naked pouring buckets of hot water down themselves, long since clean and dousing themselves for no other reason than that it felt good and because they still could.

But time went on and the song had many, many verses. Kazuteru did not know much beyond the first three. He paused, took a wincing slug of sake—most of which he let dribble down his chin—to try to induce memory or inspiration, and as he opened his mouth to sing again, a hand pushed him in the chest hard enough to cause him to stagger backward.

It was Munisai, still in his armor, face pinched into a dull fury and looking at Kazuteru with mirthless eyes.

"You," he said. "Come."

The samurai jerked his chin at the darkness beyond the burning castle and marched off toward it. Kazuteru hesitated for a few heartbeats, shocked both at his commander's sudden appearance and that he had been singled out. He wondered what he had done wrong.

"Do not keep me waiting, boy," said Munisai, neither stopping nor turning.

No one around Kazuteru had noticed, no one leapt to his defense. He felt suddenly alone among those he had thought his comrades. He knew there was nothing to do but obey, and so he skittered after the man and fell into a nervous pace a respectful distance behind him.

It came to him as they walked—the dagger. Lord Shinmen must have said nothing at the time for fear of spoiling the ceremony any further than Kazuteru already had, but he had not forgotten. Munisai must be here to enact some form of punishment upon him. The commander's swords were at his side still. Kazuteru looked at them fearfully. Surely he would be spared for so small an error?

Though was it a small offense? Kanno had been a lord, after all, Ueno a general too . . . He could not tell, and it was impossible to glean any hint from Munisai. The man did not acknowledge him further, merely led Kazuteru toward the edges of the camp until they came to a burning brazier. A pair of guards stood by it and they moved to challenge Munisai, but when they recognized who approached them they bowed low.

"Nothing to report, my lord. All is calm, sir," said one, his eyes cast low.

"Very well. You are relieved. I'll take your post," said Munisai. The two guards looked from him to Kazuteru, guessed whatever it was they guessed, and then scurried off, bowing.

When they were entirely alone, Munisai turned to face the young man and looked him up and down. He flexed his shoulders, rolled his head, and nodded.

"Let's get this over with," he said.

The commander was bracing himself for something. Kazuteru bowed his head, kept his eyes upon the ground, and with a voice that seemed fragile and weak tried to save himself.

"I apologize wholeheartedly, my lord, and beg your forgiveness," he said, his stomach churning. "I did drop the dagger, but I cleaned it as best I could, and I thought that that would be sufficient for what . . . But obviously . . . I apologize, and await your punishment."

Munisai said nothing. Kazuteru swallowed drily, and carried on guessing.

"Perhaps it was the song. Perhaps I was too loud and boorish, and brought disgrace upon you by acting the savage. I apologize for this a hundred times and beg your—"

"What song? What dagger? What are you going on about?" interrupted Munisai, irritated.

Kazuteru allowed himself to look up. Munisai had turned away from him and was slowly unbuckling his armor with some difficulty. The samurai favored his right hand, his left arm sluggish and stiff. A great weariness seemed to come into Munisai the more he struggled. When he finally managed to remove the cuirass, it slipped from his grip and dropped heavily to the ground. There was a ragged tear through the layers of Munisai's underclothes, darkened by blood.

The commander slowly rolled the kimonos off his shoulder, and exposed his flesh to the night. A vicious-looking gash stretched from just under his left armpit to the base of his rib cage near the spine.

"A desperate fool jumped me from behind in the battle for the castle," said Munisai in explanation, and as he spoke Kazuteru watched the split flesh flap and distort painfully. "Got his blade under my armor while I had my sword up parrying. If he had kept his head he would have thrust it straight into my heart, but he was an idiot and he failed and now he is dead for it. Nevertheless, the wound has closed poorly. It doesn't feel right. You'll need to reopen it and clean it."

"Lord?" the young man asked, dumbfounded.

Munisai produced a small bag and threw it to Kazuteru. The young samurai opened it and found a folded paper sachet of salve and a clean roll of bandages inside.

"Lord, I have no experience with medicine. You should visit a healer."

"Who do you think I got that from?"

"But . . . why didn't they treat it?"

"There are others far worse than me for them to tend to. I can bear this, so I did. That is duty," said Munisai simply. "Now, you need to open the wound once more, remove the dirt, apply the salve, and bandage it. Do you understand?"

Kazuteru said nothing, and Munisai lowered himself to kneel with his back to the fire. The young samurai reluctantly sat down behind

him and examined the wound closely. He could see the lopsided way
the flesh had bunched together, probably where the tightness of the
armor had pressed against it, and along it there were angry red eyes
that were still open and weeping. It looked to him like someone had
poorly sewn an overflowing sack of meat together and it was slowly
coming undone.

"Get started, boy," said Munisai.

Kazuteru hesitated, more nervous now than when he had thought
punishment was coming. He thought of trying to conjure an excuse,
but he knew there was no escaping an order from his commander,
however bizarre it was. The young samurai ran his fingers along the
wound. The surrounding flesh tensed in pain, but Munisai made no
sound. The man was perfectly still and silent, staring into the night.

Not knowing what else to do, Kazuteru reluctantly drew his
shortsword and placed it to the worst of the wound.

"Forgive me the pain, Lord," he said, and pushed the blade down.

Again, Munisai tensed, but he remained silent. The elder man
began breathing in long, slow breaths that rose and fell, and after
a spell Kazuteru found himself breathing in unison. It was calming. Kazuteru worked quickly, his sword, still battle-sharp, cutting
through the clotted mess of flesh with ease. He was relieved to see
the wound fall back to a far cleaner and straighter-looking line, but
through this the white bones of rib winked back.

When he had cut all he dared to, he wiped the sword clean of
blood and returned it to its scabbard. Munisai didn't move or speak.
The guards had had a flagon of water with them, and from this
Kazuteru filled a jug to rinse the wound before applying the poultice. The powder was greenish and foul smelling, but as he filled the
wound with it the bleeding stopped almost instantly. That was promising. Then he began to wrap the bandages around Munisai's torso.

At the touch of the cloth, Munisai took a deep breath and seemed
to rouse himself as if from a deep slumber.

"Is it over?" he asked quietly.

"Almost, Lord," said Kazuteru.

It was but a few more moments of binding, and then Kazuteru
knelt backward onto his haunches. Munisai flexed his shoulder exper-
imentally. A slight grimace played across the corner of his mouth, but

the man grunted approval. He gestured for the water that was left in the jug, and drank slowly from it, staring into the glowing coals of the brazier. Kazuteru waited silently for a long while, but eventually he found the nerve to speak.

"Why me, my lord?" he asked.

"You were the first man I found by himself," said Munisai simply, "and you have my thanks." He turned then and looked at Kazuteru, really looking at him for the first time. "How old are you?"

"Seventeen, Lord. Eighteen in the autumn."

"That's old enough," said Munisai, and looked back to the fire once more, his voice wistful. "And how old do you suppose that young Lord Kanno was, earlier today?"

"Nine, I think, Lord."

"Nine years old. That's old enough too. Do you know what his death poem was?"

"No, Lord," said Kazuteru.

"'Sayonara.' Just 'sayonara' in a child's handwriting. It was perfect," said Munisai. There was no hardness in his voice. It was the same tone that he had used when he had spoken to Kanno at the seppuku earlier: sadness and longing. "We should cherish such perfection, because it is fleeting. This is a marred world we live in. Soon you will come to be defined by imperfections. Soon you will come to be defined by your shames. Do not think that the gods or fate has marked you any differently. I did once, and . . ."

There was nothing more. Kazuteru looked on uncomfortably. Munisai seemed vulnerable, and to have seen that was an intimacy he did not know how to deal with. Perhaps the commander realized that too, for he slowly leaned forward and put his good hand on the back of his neck. His knuckles whitened and the man rocked ever so slightly. He took a breath, and then raised his head once more. Gone was any hint of softness; his face was set in determination, his lips tight and his eyes stone.

"I believe that the time has come for me to go and see my son," he said, and then he was up, the kimono rolled back over his body, his cuirass in his hand. He did not look once at Kazuteru as he left into the night.

"Should I inform Lord Shinmen, Lord?" the young samurai

called after him, rising to his feet but not daring to follow. "What should I tell him? Should I . . ."

The call died on his lips. He was alone. Not knowing what else to do, Kazuteru settled himself by the brazier, taking guard duty unbidden. Behind him, the sound of celebrations went on. Before him, down in the valley where the fighting had been, there came only the mewling moans of those left behind and lingering still on the cusp of death. They were bleak and strange company, but duty was duty.

CHAPTER TWO

"Amaterasu," said the monk Dorinbo, and he gestured to the morning sun behind him. "She who illuminates the heavens. The source of all goodness in this world. Receive her blessing."

The pilgrims looked to the sun as best they could, squinting, letting light squeeze through the narrow gaps between their fingers. They had waited since long before dawn in one huddled congregation on top of this high ridge looking east across the ocean, men and women standing and the children sitting cross-legged between their feet.

The monk had appeared just before sunrise, and had ignored them. He had stood and watched the sun as it rose until its roundness was perfect, his hands held upward in praise and the hanging sleeves of his robes shaping his silhouette as though he were a manta ray leaping from the waves in chase of it.

Suddenly he had turned to them and spoken, telling the long story of the coming of the world, of the timeless seas of chaos, and then the isles of Japan falling from the blade of a celestial spear. An untrained man's voice would have grown hoarse, but Dorinbo's did not falter as he told of the first gods and their agonies, of the thundering turmoil that threatened all life and spirits until Amaterasu, golden Amaterasu, had come to be as a tear that fell from her father's eye, a daughter so pure that she made order and peace and love in the hearts of all things.

All the while the sun had risen ever higher behind him, Amaterasu in her celestial form bathing them in light. When the tale at last wound its way to the ascension of the goddess to the higher planes of the heavens to reign as she did now, Dorinbo clasped a balled fist into the other hand and raised them high in salutation to her. The pilgrims mimicked the gesture of prayer, some falling to their knees and pressing their heads to the earth in their earnestness.

"But that is not the end of the story of Amaterasu, not why some of you have traveled the length of the country to come to this small village," Dorinbo said as they lifted their eyes to him once more. "For when she left this world, the time of men came. She watched us from the heavens as we grew, and slowly she came to love us most of all the things she had bequeathed upon this plane.

"She saw that we were weak and scared sometimes, and so she decided to give us one last gift: her own grandson, Ninigi of heaven. It was he who planted the first rice fields that we might eat, and he who taught us how to fight and made us strong that we might fear no evil. Ninigi was too magnanimous ever to claim a throne for himself, but in time his bloodline was rightly praised. His great-grandson became the first emperor, and unbroken for centuries his line has continued to rule as emperor from then until today.

"All that, though," said Dorinbo, raising a cautionary finger to stem another outbreak of rapture before it began, "all that stems from here. It was here, right here in this village called Miyamoto, that Amaterasu carried Ninigi to earth. This was where the god child took his first steps, and where the last footfalls of she who illuminates the heavens ever graced mortal soil."

The monk gestured to the land around them. "This is the bridge between the end of the time of the gods and the beginning of the time of man. No other place on earth can claim such a thing. This little temple is special, and we too are special for we stand in the light that bounces off it. Though her blood does not flow in us, we are all of us the children of Amaterasu, and we stand here in her grace. Let us worship."

They did, offering silent prayers to the sun, imagining a face within whose beauty they could not possibly comprehend.

From down in the darkened alcove of Dorinbo's hovel, the boy Bennosuke watched the cluster of their silhouettes on the high ridge. Gradually the sky above them turned from the peach of dawn to the blue of day. The pilgrims had not noticed his arrival, and nor had he wanted them to; his ugly, scabbed rash brought disgusted reactions, especially from those who thought they basked in the holy and pure.

The boy had cleaned his father's armor before he had come, and that confrontation with his shame was more than enough for one day.

He hovered hidden, waiting patiently. At some wordless sense of completion, the congregation broke. The pilgrims began to scatter, some to pray further at the small shrine of the temple proper, some to see the great waves of the ocean break white against the distant cliffs, and some to start the long journey home.

Dorinbo walked among them as they went, smiling and speaking with them as an equal now in the even light of day. Asceticism had made the monk slight of build, and the ball of his shaven head seemed too large for his thin shoulders, but he was still young and his eyes were warm and trustworthy. He knew where Bennosuke would wait, and slowly he made his way through the crowd to him.

"Nephew." He nodded to the boy.

"Uncle," said Bennosuke, but though he smiled the boy did not emerge from where he lingered. The monk said nothing of it, and together they stood looking out across the pilgrims as they dispersed.

"Busy today," said the boy, "busier than a fortnight ago."

"The high summer is coming. Fair roads to travel and the solstice approaches," said Dorinbo.

"Sermon is the same, though."

"You could hear it from here?"

"I don't need to hear it, Uncle. I can tell from the gestures you use alone," said Bennosuke, and he lowered his voice to a somber parody with his hands out before him. "'We too are special for we stand in the light that bounces off it!' I remember you said that the first time I heard it. I was sitting right before you at your feet, and you said those exact words. Don't you ever change it?"

"That, I fear," said the monk, "could be taken as something of a sacrilege."

"Not the story, Uncle. You know what I mean: the words."

"Have I need to change them?" said Dorinbo. "It must have been some eight or nine years ago now when you first heard it, correct?"

"It had to have been—my mother was there, I remember," said Bennosuke.

"And yet, through all these years still you remember it. The children here today will do the same."

"Don't you just get bored, though, of saying the same thing over and over?"

"Consider that some men believe this to be a way in which things become holy, Bennosuke," said the monk. "I say these words in this place as dozens of men have done before me, and dozens of men will continue to say after I am dead. In this we share an experience exactly, and thus our souls are as one, split only by the shadow of time. I am a vessel for both history and future; my body may change, but my essence is constant. This is one way to the infinite."

He gave a solemn pause and let the boy ponder that before he continued. "That, and a little theatrics and poetry twice a month, never harmed anyone. So—indulge me."

MONKS WERE KEEPERS of words—not just holy scrolls, but old stories and poems, tracts on philosophy, science, and medicine— and Dorinbo adhered to this, tending a library as devoutly as he did to the temple. But where most temples had a body of work of the great minds, at Miyamoto they kept the words of every pilgrim who visited it.

As they prayed, whether peasant or merchant or samurai or lord, the devout were encouraged to write down their wishes and prayers upon a sliver of paper or silk. It was no issue if they could not write, for as long as they whispered it in their soul Amaterasu would understand it, and so the markings of the illiterate were as welcomed as the neatest calligraphy. All fell into a slot before the carved image of the goddess, and then without being read they were taken to be placed in heavy caskets in a dark room carved in rock beneath the earth.

There they would linger for twenty years away from the eyes of the world, kept dry as bones, for every twenty years they became fuel for a pyre. The caskets were emptied and the prayers woven into boughs of twigs that on a dark and holy night would be placed around the temple and ignited. The fire would burn hard, the temple and the prayers would become naught but ash carried upward into the realm of Amaterasu, and then her dawn would come brilliant and bright.

The people would know that the goddess had heard their worries, and that she loved them still.

This was the way it was, and this was the way it had been since before history was written down. All things were impermanent in the end, the tangible flesh and trivial concerns of the mortal world most of all; to deny this was futile, to acknowledge it a step toward serenity.

Twenty winters and twenty springs had passed since they had last taken this step, and so now in the depths of the nineteenth summer Dorinbo and Bennosuke prepared for a night of holy arson.

When from among the pilgrims only a few zealots remained, Bennosuke emerged furtively, and then he and the monk set about working as they had been since the drizzle of spring had ended. Twenty years of prayers was no small amount, and to weave even a single bough correctly took time. There was a precise and holy way of entwining twig with silk and paper, incense that had to be burned while holy phrases were uttered and small bronze chimes struck.

The monk and his nephew gathered the prayers in their endless caskets, wood from where it was left in daily piles by the pious local woodsmen, and then they set to work in front of the temple weaving until Amaterasu was at her zenith high above and the sweat was dripping off them.

The temple itself was a small pavilion perhaps ten paces square. Though it was set at the highest point of the village, the carvings and reliefs set upon it, which in other shrines would be delicately worked dioramas painted in gold leaf and expensive purples, were here simple effigies in faded base colors. An image of Amaterasu in her earthly form was highest, of course. She sat above the tarnished brass gong and the worn old knotted rope that was used to strike it, her face a plain oval in peeled white, the beams of light emerging from behind her devoid of any paint entirely.

She watched over them, steady and serene, as the strain built in every joint of Dorinbo's and Bennosuke's bodies, working hunched over like beggars. The goddess offered no sympathy or divine respite when the boy rose, and he thought he heard the bones of his spine unlock one by one.

"This can't be good for my back." He grunted, stretching and swiveling his hips with his fists.

"I've seen peasants who labored under heavy bushels for decades still stand upright," said Dorinbo. "Come on, just grit your teeth and bear it—two more and we're done for the day."

"You ought to get an apprentice," said the boy.

"A young man who helps me with the running of the temple, you mean?" said Dorinbo, and he gave a small laugh. "I think I may already have one."

"Me?" said the boy, surprised.

"Have you considered it?" said Dorinbo, rising to his feet himself.

"Well, no," said Bennosuke. He struggled for something to say. "It's just . . ."

"What?" said Dorinbo, and the monk waited for an answer that he knew would not come. He was earnest; surprisingly so. The boy realized that his uncle must have wanted to say this for some time, and so he suddenly found himself shy of Dorinbo's gaze.

"You're young," continued the monk when he realized the boy would speak no further. "I know life at a temple must seem boring to you, and I suppose that's true. There's little excitement or glory in the divine or in healing, but that does not mean that there is not pride and worthiness."

"It's not that, Uncle. You do good things for people," said Bennosuke, the words faltering. "I know that."

"But?" the monk probed. The boy stood pinned with his eyes looking around the sandaled feet of his uncle.

"It's just my father . . ." he managed. Dorinbo let out a sympathetic sigh, and his voice softened.

"It's been eight years since he left, Bennosuke. You've worked with me every morning since," he said. "My brother is where he is, and that is not here. He cannot teach you, nor hold any expectations of you. Your mind is too sharp to waste on swords in any case."

"Yes, but . . ." the boy said lamely. He looked at Dorinbo's toenails as though he were counting rings on a felled tree, and felt the empty blackness of that helmet looking into him once more.

"Well, I'll not force you," said Dorinbo eventually. "But you're getting older, Bennosuke. You'll have to choose the path of your life soon. Warriors are not all in the world. You'd make a fine healer, or a priest, or a scholar. At least promise me you'll think about it."

The boy murmured a sound, neither yes nor no. He dropped into a squat and got back to work, and for a few long moments he could still feel his uncle's gaze upon his back, until he too returned to weaving.

Leagues away from Miyamoto, the young lord Hayato Nakata could not stop the curl forming on his lip. What was left of Kanno's castle stood around and above him, a skeletal carcass of charcoal beams interlocking in scorched remnants, framed bleakly against the sky. He stalked about glaring critically upward, hands growing black with soot as he touched what remained.

"Years, my lord," said the master builder, hovering to the side with his eyes only on the ground.

A week had passed since the battle. Hayato had stayed, waiting to see if the castle was salvageable, while his father and Lord Shinmen had already departed. It had been a stubborn hope, he knew, and it had withered day by day as the master builder and his team had swarmed over the remaining structure like beetles picking a corpse clean. Wall by wall and floor by floor they had found irrevocable damage, nibbling away until only what was splayed before them now was left.

"What does that mean?" Hayato sighed, the final glimmer dying within him.

"If you will us to proceed, my lord," the master builder said, sucking air through his teeth as he made predictions he was unsure he could keep, "by the first frost of next winter we could have a roof patched on it. It's too late to do anything this year. Wood needs to be shaped and dried. But even by then, it'd be no thing of beauty. Habitable, at best. To be what it was . . ."

"I meant, what does that mean for me?" said Hayato.

The master builder hesitated. The question was oblique and Hayato's displeasure evident. Nervously he began to wring the handle of his hammer where it hung at his side, but he was spared answering when Hayato's bodyguard stepped forward.

"If you would permit me to speak, my lord?" the samurai said as he bowed, and the young lord nodded. "Our most noble Lord Nakata instructed me that were you to judge the situation irredeemable we were to accompany you back to his side. Do you judge it to be so?"

"Weren't you listening? How could I possibly stay here?" snapped Hayato.

"Then we shall return to your father's castle, my lord," said the man. He bowed once more, and then gave a gesture at the other samurai to prepare for travel.

As they busied themselves readying his palanquin, Hayato stalked away. He did not want them to see his anger; they were all sworn to his father above him, and if they saw it then the old lord would see it too. He kicked a stone, listening to it skitter and drop into the cavern of a cellar that had been exposed to the day. It echoed and died, like everything else here had.

This was supposed to be his escape, his way out from under the watchful yoke of his father, a castle and a frontier entrusted to his management. What did he have now but a monument of ashes and the condescending dotage of a dribbling old fool?

It felt as though he had been gelded. The young lord spat and sidled back to the palanquin, glowering, giving no more than a perfunctory nod at the men waiting on their knees to bear him aloft. The head samurai held the burgundy drapes open for him, smiling as he passed.

"That's it, my lord," he said, and his voice was cooing. "Let's go back to dwell in a nice, comfortable city."

Hayato stopped in the doorway and looked at the man. The smile was held honestly on his face. Beyond him the palanquin bearers were entirely still. They were not permitted eye contact, their faces looking toward the dirt, and the lord got the sense that they were suddenly grateful for this.

They were tense, but it was not with fear.

The young lord looked at them all for a long moment, not sure what he was searching for. Eventually he went inside without saying anything further. There came a sound that might have just been the swishing of the curtains and bamboo blinds behind him, but as he was borne back toward his father, Hayato became more and more convinced that it had been a snigger.

*R*uins stood before Bennosuke also.

He gazed down into the landward valley of the village—the abandoned valley. At the bottom, amid the wild growth of eight years, a cluster of burned stumps and foundations were huddled. A vague outline of what had once been a village could be made out, charred angles and order within the mass of green. It was a view well known to the boy.

This was where his mother had died.

Yoshiko.

Bennosuke barely remembered her. She was a soothing voice in the night, a warm hand that enveloped his and nothing more, no face or tangible memory he could recall. What he knew of her was mostly what Dorinbo had told him: that though she had been born a samurai and was married to one in Munisai, she had a kind heart that drew her to healing. Dorinbo had taught her, and in turn she had tended to the peasants of the village. She set their bones, rubbed salve upon their sores, and sometimes delivered babies.

She had been called to do such a thing one night down in the valley before him, back when it had life there.

An earthquake had come.

A roof had fallen in.

A lantern had tipped over.

And that was it—after that she was gone. Bennosuke had been staying with Dorinbo that night, and he had been sleeping so deeply that he had not even felt the shaking of the earth. What had woken him was distant screaming, and bleary-eyed he had wandered out into the night. Dorinbo was up and out in the grounds already, tying a sack of his medical tools around himself, the sky above him tangerine.

"Go back to bed, Bennosuke," he had said, his voice unusually hard. "It's dangerous."

The boy had obeyed, and while he had lain in a dark room his mother had burned to death. He wished he could have known her. She must have been a wonderful woman—this he knew, for his father so loved her that when he learned of her fate in the morning he was overcome with grief and had left the village, so haunting was it to remember the places they had been together.

The child Bennosuke had not dared to even look at the ruins for years afterward, but eventually he had summoned the courage. Now he found himself returning more and more often. It was a quiet place, away from the disgusted glares of the peasants. He could escape the shame here, and think. He never once went down, only looked, as he did now, clenching and unclenching his fists.

He somehow wanted the ghost of his mother to appear, as stupid as he knew that was, and to tell him what to say to Dorinbo. Bennosuke had gone to the temple every morning for as long as he could remember, whether to help with healing or with worship or for Dorinbo to teach him to read or to count or any number of things. But he had never once considered that this was what his future might hold. He had gone to the temple simply because he knew nothing else.

His uncle had obviously been thinking otherwise. How could Bennosuke deny the monk without hurting him? He knew his uncle was good enough and kind enough that he would surely take a renouncement of the offer as a renouncement of himself. What were the words, the shining explanation? The boy needed to know.

But the ruins were just ruins, the mortal and the spirit world separate as always. There was no answer here, no matter how long he stared.

He left eventually, still torn, still alone. It was time for training.

THE TIME IN the dojo, at least, Bennosuke relished. Every afternoon he came to train in the hall, grueling though it was, for here he could ignore the worries that nagged at him. There was nothing that could not be solved by the strike of a sword, and that was pleasing in the baseness of it.

Hours passed like moments, his concentration perfect as he took in martial form and pattern. Again and again he would repeat the same maneuvers, seeking to make the strange balance and unnatural movements fluid, preparing muscles that would not develop properly until adulthood. When he sparred, the boy would lose himself to the fight, putting the full body of his voice behind the victory cry shouted the moment his wooden sword had exploited the gap and struck gauntlet or helmet or cuirass.

Then, for a few vital seconds, he would feel a rush of accomplishment he felt nowhere else. Those moments were when he could allow himself to believe that he could one day be a samurai.

Not all took it as seriously as he did, however. Boys from the surrounding villages came to be taught, some days only a handful, some days over a dozen. Today was busy, and two boys thought this bought them anonymity. They had started giggling and slapping at each other's calves, one with a wooden sword and one with a pole that served as a mock spear, any pretense of discipline forgotten. The hall's master, Tasumi, had given a wordless bellow of rage and stormed over.

"You think you can come here and fool around?" the samurai snarled, the two boys cowed before him now. His face was slick with sweat, having just spent an hour drilling set patterns of parry and riposte. The other students had fallen silent, looking on.

"No, sir," the one with the pole muttered eventually.

"So why are you acting like an idiot, then?"

"I'm not," said the boy, and then Tasumi cuffed him around the head. The boy looked surprised for a moment.

"What was—"

Tasumi cuffed him again. "Not too clever, are you?" said the samurai.

"You can't do that!" said the boy with the sword, and then Tasumi lashed out with both hands and brought their heads together.

"If you paid attention, maybe you would know how to stop me," said Tasumi.

"Why should I pay attention?" said the boy with the pole, and he looked up defiantly for a moment.

"Oh?" said Tasumi.

"My father works the clan's finances—I'll take his role someday, and then what good is a spear to me?" said the boy, his voice cracking in anger as he tossed the pole on the floor. It clattered in the silence. Tasumi grinned.

"A bead pusher, eh?" the samurai said.

"Yes."

"Counting is important for you, then?"

"Yes," said the boy, but his voice was faltering. He had suddenly become aware of how alone he was in the face of that grin.

"Then let's give you some practice," said Tasumi, and put his hands on the boy's shoulders.

Twenty-five times Tasumi dunked the boy's head into a trough of water, the boy spluttering every count of his punishment, fifty times the boy had to drop into a squat while holding a rock the size of his head, then two hundred times he had to run barefoot around the outside of the dojo shouting an old battle cry at the top of his lungs.

"You shouldn't be so hard on them, Uncle," said Bennosuke when they were finished. He and Tasumi were standing beneath the eaves of the dojo, watching the other boys troop home. The son of the accountant was limping and glowering, his hair hanging around him in a loose and matted mess.

"You can't harden clay without fire," grunted the man.

"You'll drive them away," said Bennosuke.

"They'll be back," said Tasumi, and jerked his chin toward the back of the accountant's son. "That one especially. You think his father would let good coin go to waste? He's paid his dues for the next few seasons, and he won't want to have fattened my purse without something in return. Why are you defending them anyway? They're the same age as you."

The samurai was built like a wrestler. His arms were long and the thick hair upon them was parted by the light ridges of scars. He had entered into an arranged marriage with Bennosuke's aunt when they had been little older than the boy was now. Bennosuke had never met the woman, and Tasumi saw her only a few times a year, for she served her duty as a handmaiden to the wife and mistresses of Lord Shinmen in his stronghold.

But perhaps because there was no bond of blood between them, things were easier than they were with Dorinbo, or perhaps it was simply because Tasumi was a far blunter man. Now that swords were finished with, what Bennosuke had tried to banish earlier in the day seeped back into him. Tasumi noticed the change, saw the wan look that came onto the boy's face.

"You were bloody awful today too, I was watching you," the samurai said, his way of polite inquiry into the boy's well-being. "What's the matter with you?"

"Nothing," said Bennosuke, but the man grabbed his hand and pulled it close to him, yanking the gauntlet off to examine critically what lay beneath.

"Hands like a thatcher, no wonder you can't swing a sword," he tutted, his small eyes focused like an artisan's. "That monk has got you working too hard, prancing about weaving like some woman. Is this because of that great burning you're planning?"

"Yes," said Bennosuke, pulling his hand free.

"Has he told you about why we do that, the festival and the pomp and the ceremony?" asked the samurai.

"The twenty years symbolize the length of time Amaterasu spent in the cave after her brother slaughtered her handmaidens. Her light was gone from the world, and all things came close to death until they eventually convinced her to emerge once more. The world was born anew then," said the boy, using words remembered from sermons. "And so it is when we burn the temple. A new start for all of us."

"Well, isn't that pretty?" said Tasumi. "Want to know the real reason? It's good practice, is what. Every twenty years a new batch of apprentice builders gets to remake the temple—it's small and it's simple and they learn the basics of construction from it, and they get to feel all holy and special while they do it. The monks get a new temple out of it too, so everyone is happy."

Tasumi turned away for a moment, waving one hand dismissively. He looked back into the dojo until he was certain he had registered his distaste at effete, passive things, and then when his honor as a samurai was safe he allowed himself to look at the boy again, this time as a man and as an uncle.

"Look," he said softly, "Dorinbo is a good man. There is worth in what he does, there really is. Just . . . try to remember to think whenever someone tries to sell you on a cause. There is very rarely any divine crusade or something like that. Look for the real meaning of things, not what they are said to be—you understand?"

"Yes, Uncle," said Bennosuke.

"Now—what's wrong?" said Tasumi.

"I . . ." the boy began, and then stopped.

No further words came, because there were none of his own. Visiting the ruins had left a mark upon him as it always did, and what the boy relived within himself was the morning after the earthquake and the terrible fire. He remembered the last words of his father before he had left the village, those final moments before both parents were stripped from him.

"Bennosuke," the man had said, his eyes red with what were maybe tears, thick black smoke curling into the air behind him, "try to be samurai."

His hand tightened on the boy's small shoulder for one moment, and then he had risen and walked away. The samurai had not looked back, growing smaller and smaller until he was over the ridge and gone to the unknown horizons beyond, and that was that.

Bennosuke often wondered if those words had formed the very core of him, or if they had merely kindled what was already there. The simple truth was that deep down he knew that he was meant to be a samurai. It was why he forced himself to face the shame of the armor and to hold his rash-plagued face high as he walked among those who recoiled in disgust. He could not deny that desire was there even if he questioned his ability to fulfill it.

That alone was why he could not become Dorinbo's apprentice: simple gut instinct. To explain it that way would be embarrassing and insulting to Dorinbo, to fabricate a reason and lie to him even more so.

Tasumi would offer no advice—the boy knew that the samurai would simply march up to the temple and shout at Dorinbo for even making such an offer. He would have to bear this sickly sense of shame and burden alone, and he knew the right thing to do would be to address it now before it festered any further.

But he was just a boy. It was easier to distance the world, to close your eyes and pretend nothing existed outside that, and so he took the coward's route, shook his head and let it go. Dorinbo was talking of lives, he told himself, and a night or a week would make no difference to that. Bennosuke could see the relief in Tasumi's eyes at the vanishing of a troubling conversation.

INSTEAD OF BEING honest, they went and speared fish in the river together. They stripped down to their loincloths and waded in, trying to learn the angle of the water's warping. It was a hard knack to find, and Bennosuke lost himself to the challenge until the light began to fade and the cicadas were humming and the swallows began to return to their nests.

He had caught a single, fat fish to Tasumi's three, and they made a sack of their kimonos and put the silver bodies inside. This they hung over the end of their spears and marched home, letting the cooling air dry their bodies. They laughed and talked, alone now that the peasants had retired from the fields for the day. The paddy waters had settled into shimmering orange mirrors for the dying sun, glowing where the rest of the valley had faded into shadow.

As they headed down to the dojo, they became aware of a gathering of the peasants. They were still muddy from their work, and they stood in small huddles looking at the hall apprehensively from a distance. They muttered to one another, and suddenly fell silent when they became aware of Tasumi and Bennosuke coming from behind them.

A pale horse had been tethered by the hall. It was a samurai mount, a tall, strong beast bred for wearing armor and kicking savagely. Livery hung from the saddle, the light blue of Lord Shinmen. Tasumi's eyes hardened in curiosity, but the peasants melted away in obsequious bobs when he looked to them for answers. This was not their realm.

Tasumi hesitated for a moment on the steps of the dojo, Bennosuke hovering with him. The samurai had not been expecting anyone. Greeting whoever it was in his underclothes did not appeal, and his kimono was sodden and stank of fish. But then, if whoever it was was expecting hospitality, they would have sent word ahead. The man shrugged, and then slid open the heavy door as though he were unconcerned.

A man sat cross-legged before the ancestral shrine. He turned, one arm bound tight to his chest.

"Oh," said Tasumi, "it's been some time."

Bennosuke peered into the hall beyond the bulk of his uncle. There he saw the face that belonged beneath the brow of the helmet the boy had cleaned fastidiously since his childhood, the face that he had dreaded and longed to see more than anything else. Of course it had to be him; the specter was finally summoned. There for the first time in eight years, Bennosuke saw the face of his father.

CHAPTER THREE

Night had fallen. Munisai stood in the gloom of his house in front of his suit of armor, looking at it in silence. It had been kept immaculately, as had all the treasures of his youth, and all he wanted to do was laugh in disgust.

The shade of blue was gaudy and effeminate, the perfect lacquer chest plate spoke of time diverted from training to polishing, and the helmet . . . Where to begin? The needless embossing weakened the structure, there was no protection of the face at all, and the crest above the brow was practically begging enemies to grab and twist the thing from his head.

But above all there was the name threaded in brilliant white with such galling arrogance upon the armor.

Munisai Hirata.

The name that he had tried so hard to forget woke things that ached in his heart. He began to feel his chest well as though it might burst with sickness.

Hirata.

The name that he was born to, the name that he had damned, and the name that he had cast aside in favor of his lord's.

"Hello, Munisai," said Dorinbo.

Startled, Munisai turned to see his brother standing in the light of the doorway. A paper lantern glowed behind the monk. He had appeared as if from nothing.

"Dorinbo?" Munisai blurted in surprise, and then bowed apologetically. "Forgive me, I hadn't expected to see you tonight."

"I thought you might have had the courtesy to seek me out, after so long," said the monk, slowly returning the bow.

"I would have . . ." Munisai began, but then he faltered under Dorinbo's gaze. He knew his brother was not talking solely about some mere slight of a greeting. There was much to explain, much of it shameful, and Munisai could find no words.

The monk looked exactly like Munisai remembered him; slender frame, bald head, and most of all a disapproving expression on his face. The silence stretched on and the samurai felt himself start to blush, a mix of guilt and disgrace that he had not felt—or at least not confronted—in some time. Of all men his brother alone had the ability to draw it out of him. He squirmed, until Dorinbo took pity on him and spoke again with warmth in his voice:

"I came because Tasumi told me about your arm. How does it feel?"

"It aches," said Munisai, grateful for the clemency. "Sometimes I lose feeling in my hand. Other times it itches and tingles."

"Would you like me to look at it?"

"If you would—I trust your skill, brother."

Dorinbo gestured to the well-lit drawing room, and wordlessly Munisai followed. There was a creeping silence in the house, and although they walked shoeless upon soft bamboo mats, their footfalls seemed heavy as stone.

The samurai stripped himself to the waist and sat with his back to the lantern. Dorinbo undid the grubby sling—Munisai wincing as the arm dropped dead—and there was a sticky ripping as he peeled the bandage away from the flesh. The monk examined the wound for a moment, and then drew air through his teeth slowly.

"Who tended to this?" he asked.

"One of my men."

"Was he a healer?"

"No. Is it poorly done?"

"I can't even tell . . ." said the monk, and he ran a finger along the edges of the wound, causing his brother to wince ever so slightly. "Did he cut this farther?"

"Yes, upon my orders."

"Oh," Dorinbo said, and it was a somber sound. "Oh, you fool. Cutting of the flesh just mangles it. You can only make timber with an ax, you can't build a house with one."

"I thought that—"

"You thought wrong, brother. Why didn't you go to a proper healer?"

"They were busy," said Munisai. He could feel Dorinbo behind him. Before his brother could draw another blush from him, he continued. "Also, it would not be good for men to see their commander wounded."

"Spare me, Munisai," sighed Dorinbo. "You mean it's not good for *you* for them to see you wounded. Eight years and you haven't changed in the slightest."

Munisai said nothing. Dorinbo began a thorough examination of his brother's body, his fingers probing and prodding, eyes gauging the color of the samurai's flesh and tongue. Then the monk took the arm gently in his and began checking for the many telltale pulses across the length of it, darting across to the healthy arm now and then for comparison.

"Mmm," the monk muttered, his fingers barely felt by Munisai as they pressed between the knuckles of his lamed hand. "Your heart and your organs are strong, your spirit quick. But the wound has stanched the flow of the healing ether to this side of your body. This, we can try to remedy."

The monk busied himself with his art. Sweet herbs were ignited in a brazier to mask the smell of decay. A kettle was boiled and a tonic mixed from powders and pastes, which Munisai was told to drink. The taste was bitter, and it tingled on his gums as his brother began to clean the inside of the wound with a damp cloth. The stench of pus and the aroma of the herbs fought an even battle in the air around them.

Dorinbo settled himself, facing his brother's back once more. Carefully he drew a map in his mind. Around the ugly ridges of the gash, the monk began to see the patterns of the stars in the sky, which the ancient healers of the Chinese had realized coincided with the median points of the body's natural flow of energy. From a bundle of needles of many different sizes, he chose a specific one to act as the anchor, and then he began to impale Munisai's flesh again and again, damming and diverting the vitality of his body toward the wound.

"I suppose," said the monk as he worked, "I should ask where you have been all this time?"

"In the service of Lord Shinmen," said Munisai.

"We are not entirely isolated, here—news carries, you know," said Dorinbo. "You entered his service five years ago, after that tournament you won. I was wondering about the three before that."

"That time is unimportant," said Munisai curtly, for again the monk was prying at something he could not yet face. "Concentrate upon the wound."

"As you wish," said the monk.

The sensation of the needles being worked into him made his skin crawl. Perhaps it was only the tingle of the healing energy, he hoped. His mind wandered, seeking a distraction, and though he tried not to it settled on the boy.

"Bennosuke stays with you now?" Munisai forced himself to ask.

"No, he stays here—is he not here now?" said Dorinbo.

"No," said Munisai, and then took a breath. "But, wherever he is, it seems Yoshiko was not lying about him."

Dorinbo's hands froze, a needle as thin as a spider's thread twisted halfway into muscle. After a moment, the monk spoke.

"Time dispels all delusions. Are you surprised?"

"No. But I was hoping . . ." said Munisai, and the words hung in the air as heavy as the scent of herbs and rot.

"Bennosuke is a fine young man, Munisai," said Dorinbo, resuming his work and pushing the needle down. "He is clever, and keen to learn. Tasumi tells me he is talented and growing strong with weaponry."

"What do you mean?"

"That he would be a fine son to any man, regardless."

"Regardless," said Munisai.

The brothers sat in silence once more, the needles remaining in Munisai's back for the long minutes they needed to have their effect. They waited until the herbs had burned themselves out, and then the monk removed the pins one by one, applied a poultice to the wound, and bound it once more in fresh bandages.

"We shall have to do this many times. Healing will be slow—if it heals at all," he said as he began to replace his instruments in the bundle he had brought.

"Is there anything I can do to help it along?" asked Munisai.

49

"Pray, perhaps."

"Maybe I'll do that."

"We both know you won't," said Dorinbo. Munisai nodded and smiled wryly. Slowly the smile withered, and then he turned his head to look his brother in the eye.

"Did they rebuild the far side of the village?" he asked.

"No. It's still in ruins. Nobody dares interfere with them. Some of the peasants say they are haunted," said the monk.

"Then tomorrow I will go there."

"That might be good," said Dorinbo. He finished packing, rose, and walked to the door. There he paused with his back to his brother, and then spoke again.

"It's not the boy's fault, Munisai. Remember that before anything," he said, and gently slid the paper door closed.

Munisai listened to his quiet footsteps retreat into the night. When he was sure he was alone, he blew the candle within the lantern out, and then went to stand before the armor again.

In the dark, only the brilliant white characters of his old name could be seen in pale blue.

The night was darkest deep in the valley of Miyamoto, where the dojo lay. The hardwood floor made a poor bed. Bennosuke lay uneasily upon it, though the texture of the wood was the least of the reasons sleep would not come to him.

His father had returned.

That afternoon Munisai had exchanged courteous words with Tasumi, and the boy had stood there in his loincloth with river water dripping off his back like a tongueless half-wit. He had almost quailed in shame when his father had eventually turned his eyes upon him; all but naked before him, skinny and gangly and marked with welts. Munisai—the samurai, handsome, strong—had measured him up and down, and although the man had nodded eventually it was impossible to tell what he was thinking.

He had clapped his son on the shoulder with his one good arm, and had said, quite simply: "We will talk further later. For now, I shall retire to my house."

Bennosuke had nodded like an idiot, not having the courage to tell him that he still lived there too. He had watched dumbly his father go, and then had lingered, cursing himself for his timidity. Not knowing where else to go, too ashamed to go to Dorinbo or Tasumi and admit his cowardice, when night fell he had eventually resorted to sneaking into the dojo.

Now he lay, their meeting playing over in his head. He had imagined it before, many times. There had been childish fantasies of Munisai presenting him with the longsword of adulthood and the two of them growing strong together, all his problems magically righted, and there had also been bleaker ones of disgrace and exile. Neither had been true. There had been no drama or resolution. It had just happened, and now he was alone and in the dark, both in body and in spirit. He felt the entire night was the cuirass of his father's armor, reflecting his failure back at him.

"We will talk further."

He heard those words again, short and blunt. The same cruel voices he heard when he cleaned the armor whispered to him, telling him that this was all Munisai could bear to say to him, all he could stomach of looking at what had become of his heir.

The boy tried not to listen. He chided himself for expecting anything more than curtness. He knew that his father was samurai and samurai did not give themselves over to blind emotion. He remembered his father smiling only at the very edges of his memory, when he had been small enough for Munisai to hold him in his arms.

Since his departure there had been only brief missives delivered sporadically from Lord Shinmen's stronghold; instructions for the managing of his estate, the change in their family name, nothing more. Never once had he asked about Bennosuke, because he knew the boy was being raised by others, and he had other things to attend to.

Seeing to your own duty, and having faith in others to do theirs. This was being samurai, and samurai like his father kept their word—in time they *would* talk, and the boy would learn to become samurai too.

This, Bennosuke told himself, had to be.

If that is so, then why do you cower here in the dark? Why don't you act like the samurai you say you are, and try to make the man respect you as you know you should? said his doubt, leering and victorious.

Bennosuke knew that logic would not help him this night. He ached with self-pity, and he hated himself for it. All he could do was wrap his arms around himself, try to find a comfortable position, and long for sleep to steal thought from him.

Insects chirruped, lulling him into a doze. The constant noise created a cloud in his half-asleep mind, and when he heard human voices it was like a lantern coming through fog; though he heard them, it took long moments for the boy to recognize them as real. There were two men walking quickly, arguing with each other.

"That devil," slurred one, "comes back, and expects what?"

"Will you be quiet?" hissed the second.

"Tell me what he expects!"

"I don't know. I don't want to find out either."

They were peasants; that much was clear from their accents. Their voices were hoarse, as though they had been arguing for some time.

"We have to do it. He's up there on that hill, alone," said the first man again. Bennosuke rose and moved as silently as he could to peek out into the night through the bamboo slats of the dojo's doors. It was too dark to see anything but the vaguest sense of movement. "We got tools. Don't need a sword, a sickle'll do just fine. We'll just do it and go. We have to."

"He's not alone. His son's up there with him."

"Good. We'll do him too, clean the village up."

"Look at you—you can barely walk. Turn around, let's go home."

"We have to do it—he has to answer for it!"

"And suppose you fail? You want him to lose his head again and do for the rest of the village? It's too dangerous."

"I can do it," said the first man, and then there was a snort that might have been a sob. "I have to do it."

"No, you don't. Let's go home," said the second voice.

"My sister . . ." said the first.

"I know," said the second man.

"In the fire . . ." the first barely managed, and then he broke down crying. They were drunken tears, loud and sloppy. He bawled for a few moments, until his friend started muttering soothing things to him.

"Let's go home," the second man said eventually, after the heaviest of the tears had passed. The first man assented with a sniffing grunt, and then slowly the sound of the pair faded into the night, leaving Bennosuke to wonder what it was he had just witnessed.

In the morning sun, Munisai walked where he had walked as a child, and it all seemed so alien. He barely even registered the way the peasants melted away from him, bowing low and anxiously, or the way mothers would place their children behind themselves.

Miyamoto was a village like so many hundreds of others in Japan, a great network of paddy fields carved into the slope of a valley so that it seemed to rise like some eccentric curved stairwell. Munisai's estate was on high, the temple of Amaterasu highest of all on the opposite face, and then down on the valley floor the squat, dark shape of the dojo hall dwarfed the humble wood-and-thatch shacks the peasants lived in.

This was all spread before him, but though his eyes took it in he barely saw it. The samurai walked along the ridgeline, glancing around. There, a tree he had climbed; there, the stream he had drunk from; there, a tiny shrine for a rock spirit where he had left offerings. All that was part of what he was, and yet it seemed so distant. Had he really grown up here?

He headed for the landward valley and the ruins that must be there. They were not ruins in his memory, though. The samurai remembered them alive, and then the samurai remembered them ablaze. He hesitated just before he came to the ridge, took a breath to steel himself, and then walked over and downward.

It was quiet. Once it had been a mirror of the other valley, a hub of life and labor, but now all was left to waste. The path beneath his feet was thick with moss and grass and free of any mark of human footfall. He passed a discarded barrel that had been claimed by bees, the dull hum of the insects like some funeral choir. The wind rustled long, ragged grass that burst forth from what remained of the dry and crumbled paddy fields.

None of this concerned him. He was no farmer nor architect nor keeper of bees. What he looked at were the blackened stumps clustered in sad communion in the base of the valley, each as dark as the night had been when he had walked this very path eight years ago.

The remains passed him by, the thickest of foundation pillars and the gnarled ends of tree stumps. All were charcoal. He noticed that on one or two of the larger ones someone had carved ancient prayers for the dead, asking that the souls find peace in the afterlife and that they not return to earth to menace the living.

Munisai reached out and touched one of the stumps softly. It felt cold and dead. He didn't know what else he was expecting.

The samurai walked into what would have been the courtyard of a house. The paving stones, now cracked and mossy, still marked a path around a tree that was long dead. He remembered it in bloom, the pleasant smell of the cherry blossom, and the vivid pink of the petals against the soft blue skies. He remembered the tree catching alight, the blossom igniting and falling from the branches like a shower of fiery rain, taken upon the wind as they turned to ash.

Eight years ago, here.

Perhaps if he confronted this he would find the words to say to the boy. The boy, with his body and face so unlike Munisai's, but Yoshiko's dark eyes looking out at him as if she had never left this world. That he remembered most of all—the last time he looked into his wife's eyes, her on her knees before him.

Munisai sighed, the tightness in his chest growing with every beat of his heart. He bowed reverently to the ruin of the cherry tree, and settled into a meditative pose. Then he went within himself, and began to think.

Bennosuke watched from the ridgeline as his father became perfectly still, his blue kimono the one blot of vivid color among the ruins. It was jarring to the view he knew so well.

Munisai had not noticed he was being followed. The strain of forcing himself here must have been too great. When Bennosuke had woken, he had meant to go tell the man what he had overheard in the dojo last night. He had walked swiftly, but as he had approached the house his legs had slowly frozen as something dawned upon him.

He realized his father would ask why Bennosuke had not confronted the men as a samurai should, and to that Bennosuke had no answer.

Fearing that shameful interrogation, he had begun to skulk away when Munisai had emerged. When the boy realized where Munisai was headed he had followed at a distance, intrigued. The man had not stopped, heading down into the valley seemingly without the fear of trespassing on such a solemn stretch of ground.

The charred stumps around Munisai seemed to grow larger. Bennosuke found himself thinking of the peasants last night. Drunk though they had been—Bennosuke had only a vague idea of what that meant—they had revealed a kind of honesty that was seldom shown. They had spoken the words from their hearts, and they had been hateful and vehement and directed at Munisai.

Why?

He knew he should join his father, to ask this question. But though he sat for some time he could not bring himself to move.

Tomorrow, he eventually promised himself. The man needed time, and so did he; the dead today, the living tomorrow. Tomorrow they would say and do the things that they needed to, though he did not know what they were.

Tomorrow.

Hayato Nakata stalked the hallways with purposeless resentment, looking bitterly at the exquisite art around him. The paper walls were painted in black ink, a motif of reeds around ponds and cranes taking flight. Above them carved into the wood were curling, symmetrical designs of leaves and flowers.

None of it mattered, because none of it was his.

There was no purpose to art, other than to enshrine. It was testament to a man's wealth and nothing more, to say that he could afford to pay someone to do something that had no meaning. To admire another man's painting, then, was to acquiesce to the statement the owner was making: "This exists at my behest, and your wonder at it proves me greater."

This was his father's castle, his father's art, and he would not grant the old man that.

He thought of putting his fist through the paper, smashing one of the cranes in two, but that would be pointless. It would be remarked upon, and then his father would summon him and he would be made to confess he did it like a child. That was all he was seen as now: a child.

A child who dwelled in a nice, comfortable city. He heard the voices and the sniggers of those palanquin bearers once more. He heard them often now.

The old lord entrusted Hayato with nothing that had any real meaning. Hayato knew he was expected just to be, to endure the long days as an insurance that had no purpose in life until his father should happen to die. All he did was drink. He had a bottle of sake in his hand now, and he swigged from it with indolent rage.

He turned to look out upon the world, across the manicured vistas of his father's gardens. He looked at everything and nothing, losing track of time, anger building in him as it always seemed to.

A door slid open behind him. Two young handmaidens were there, pretty like dolls. They were talking to each other quietly, but the sight of the lord checked them into silence. They smiled and bowed, keeping their eyes low. Hayato looked at them with a dispassionate eye, trying to remember if he had taken either of them before.

The hallway was narrow, and they had to file one after the other to pass him. They did so demurely, and he turned so that they had to brush almost face-to-face with him. The first one he did not know, but the second he suddenly recognized. It was the koto player from the palanquin after Shinmen's battle. He remembered a lull in the music and a hot burn across his cheeks.

"What are you laughing at?" he said, stepping forward to force her against the wall.

"My lord?" she said, her face blank and her eyes not meeting his, as was proper etiquette.

"'What are you laughing at?' I said," he snarled, and tried to take her wrist.

Instead she wriggled free and dropped onto her knees, placing her hands and her brow flat on the ground as she blabbered apologies. Her companion stood shocked, but she knew she could not interfere. She clasped her hands together and turned to one side, trying to keep her face still but with worry in her eyes and in the quivering of her bottom lip.

Hayato watched the girl grovel, the black circle of her bound hair bobbing. For a moment he considered bringing the bottle down upon the back of her head, but he stopped himself. He knew she was a particular favorite of his father, and if she turned up to serve him with shards of pottery stuck in her skull, the old letch would ask questions.

She was just another painted crane. The young lord dismissed her with a disgusted grunt, and together she and the other scurried off down the hall backward, bowing and apologizing until they were gone.

It was not her he was truly angry at, Hayato knew, nor the sniggering of some dullwits whose purpose in life was to bear him aloft. You could not punish crows for eating carrion, after all. She—all of them—had merely laughed. It was not they who had insulted and belittled him in front of his father. It was not they who had robbed him of a domain and condemned him to linger here.

No, that was someone else entirely.

That was someone worthy of anger.

He basked in his ability for level magnanimity for a moment, and then the young Lord Nakata went to plan. He had found purpose.

A week of tomorrows passed, but still Bennosuke could not find the courage to speak to Munisai. Instead, he and his father existed in some awkward, unspoken standoff. It was impossible to avoid each other entirely in a village so small, and sometimes the boy would feel the man's gaze upon him from a distance. Their eyes would meet for a second, then Bennosuke would blush, bow, and walk away. Munisai never followed.

The boy followed him, though—he was drawn to the landward ridge whenever he had a free moment in the day, to see whether Munisai was down among the ruins. And more often than not, he was. He imagined sitting beside the man in silent contemplation, that this would somehow make things better. It was a stupid fantasy with a beginning and an end, but no middle. The middle was what he needed to know, and the lack of it eluded and taunted him whenever he put his mind to it.

BENNOSUKE WAS IN the dojo one afternoon with his arm around Tasumi's throat. He was clinging to the samurai's back with his legs locked around his waist, trying to wrench him to the ground. It was futile, for Tasumi was a heavy man and bore the boy easily, but Bennosuke struggled and hauled like a monkey. The absurdity of it got to Tasumi first. The samurai started laughing between his breaths, and it spread to Bennosuke until the pair of them were giggling as they struggled.

Neither one relented, however. What stopped them was a voice, cold and balanced.

"You should never take both feet off the ground in combat," it said, and there was Munisai.

He was on the outside looking in through the wide doors that were cast open in the day. Were it not for the arm in the sling he would have been the very image of samurai too; his face hard beneath a shaven scalp, his shoulders narrow and leading down to a solid, heavy abdomen, a perfect center of balance from which his two swords jutted imperiously. Bennosuke sheepishly dropped from his uncle's back before he and Tasumi bowed in greeting.

"Your uncle is being kind to you," continued Munisai, returning the gesture with a snap of his chin. "Were it a real fight, he would have dropped his weight back down on top of your rib cage, and what could you have done to have stopped it? Nothing."

"It is only sparring, brother," said Tasumi guardedly, for though marriage obliged him to call the man "brother," Munisai was higher in rank than he was. "No need to go for the jugular every time."

"Indeed," said Munisai, but he was looking only at Bennosuke. "Might you leave me with your student?"

"As you wish," said Tasumi, and he bowed twice more before he left. Bennosuke had never seen his uncle so demure.

Then it was just the boy standing before his father. The man merely looked at him. Bennosuke knew he was being evaluated far more closely than at their first meeting. The samurai's eyes were tracing every line of his face. He felt more naked than when he had been wearing solely the loincloth.

Bennosuke fought the blush and forced his eyes up to the man's gaze. Time hung between heartbeats, welling toward something. It became nothing more defined than that, though; Munisai turned away before whatever it was could come to be. There was a look in his eyes, but it was not disgust. That surprised Bennosuke. He felt his confidence grow slightly.

"You study hard under Tasumi?" said Munisai, his back to the boy as he looked out across the village.

"I do," said Bennosuke.

"Good," said Munisai. "You bear a noble name. You must uphold it."

It was an oblique statement, and the boy wondered if he was being tested. Bennosuke thought for what the samurai response would be. After a moment, he asked: "Is our Lord Shinmen well?"

"Our lord is in fine health," said Munisai, surprised at the maturity of the question.

He had received a missive just this morning from Shinmen. When he had twisted open the lacquer tube, he had expected at best scorn for abandoning his post and at worst a command to return and face some form of justice, but the sliver of paper had simply read:

Continue with your duty of the stewardship of Miyamoto. All in order here.

The samurai's face darkened for a moment as he thought of what might be happening in his absence, the color burgundy coming to his mind, but he forced it from himself. A civil conversation with the boy, with what he represented written stark across his face, was hard enough. He struggled for something to say, and could find nothing narrower than: "If you train hard, is it because you wish to be a samurai?"

"Yes," said Bennosuke.

"Tell me, then—what does it mean to you?"

"To win battles and duels, and earn glory and honor," said Bennosuke, this time with no deliberation. He tried to make his voice forceful, as though he might prove his conviction, but all it provoked from Munisai was a momentary turn of the head and a cruel whisper of a laugh.

"My," said the samurai, "you have been isolated out here, haven't you?"

"Well then—what does it mean?" said the boy, hotter than he would have liked. The tone did not seem to rile Munisai, however.

"A man who wonders whether he should eat or not should not. A man who is concerned with whether he should live or die should die," said Munisai. "I have heard it expressed no more succinctly than this."

"I don't understand," said Bennosuke.

"A child cannot," said Munisai.

There was no cruelty in his voice. Bennosuke looked at the floor nonetheless, unsure if he was being castigated. *Teach me,* he wanted to say, but he knew that would appear pathetic. Instead he simply stood, waiting for his father to speak. Munisai said nothing, and so they lingered in silence.

"Come, then," Munisai eventually said, retreating to the safety of what he knew and walking over to the racks of mock swords that hung upon the walls. "Show me what you have learned of combat."

Bennosuke hesitated, seeing that only one hand ran over the weapons. "Your arm, Father, isn't it—"

"Do not call me 'Father,'" said Munisai sharply, and he seemed as surprised as the boy at the harshness in his tone. He took a moment to compose himself, before he spoke once more. "You are much too old to be speaking like that. And my arm is of no concern to you— single-handed shortsword is not my preferred style, but I am adept at it."

That, at least, was honest. With a mock sword half the size of Bennosuke's firm in his good hand, he effortlessly bested both hands of the boy. Munisai's blows were quick and precise at first, stunting the boy's attacks before lunging at him. Then the samurai invited the boy forward, testing him, gauging him, and when Bennosuke thought he saw a glimpse of victory it proved only to be an illusion.

He was turned and repelled again and again, and eventually Munisai brought the blunt edge of the wood down on the boy's wrists a final time. The sword rattled away across the floor.

"Don't bother to pick it up," said Munisai as the boy went after it. Bennosuke obeyed, and stood to receive the verdict of the man: "There are inklings of promise in you. But you use your shoulders too much. The strength of the sword comes from the wrist and forearms. Scything grass and cutting a man are two different things. Think on this."

It was not praise, but it did not shame him either. Bennosuke had started to get angry and humiliated after his first few attempts were parried, but slowly he had begun to realize the ability of the man and found fascination in it.

"Are you really the Nation's Finest?" he asked.

"I won a tournament that granted me that title, but it is a nominal title and nothing more," said Munisai. "I did not fight every swordsman in the country—just those who deigned to attend the old Lord Ashikaga."

"But you must have fought some of the elite?" probed the boy.

The samurai nodded. "Some. Five years ago now, though. Some of them are probably dead."

"What does that matter? You still beat them then."

"It means that younger men will come to fill their void, and they will look to beat me or others like me. And, well," said Munisai, as he looked ruefully at his arm tucked up in the sling, "time is not kind to those who deal in cutting. The best . . . whatever you call it . . . the *epitome* is ever fleeting. But this does not concern me. This is the way of the world, and that title was just a ridiculous prize, a thing of pure vanity."

"Well, if you think that," Bennosuke said, "why did you enter the tournament in the first place?"

It was an honest question that brought another color to Munisai's mind: the gaudy light blue of his old armor. Memories passed through him and disgust followed, dispelling whatever might have allowed him to talk further. His face darkened once more, and he stalked off to replace the mock sword from where he had taken it.

Bennosuke saw the change come into his father. He did not understand it, but he did not want to let this chance escape. Instead of quailing at some imagined fault as he might have done, the sparring had given him a strange confidence. The boy straightened himself up and spoke to the man's back.

"I've seen you, these past days. You go to the ruins. I go there too, sometimes. Might we go together one day so that we can pay respects to my moth—" he said, and then remembered the rebuke of earlier. "To Lady Yoshiko together?"

"Why would I pay respect to Yoshiko down there?" said Munisai, and though his face was almost entirely hidden the boy saw the man's brow furrow momentarily.

"She died there, in the fire," said the boy.

"Of course," said Munisai, and he turned to reveal a carefully neutral face once more. "Of course. It has been some time. I . . . pray to her at shrines and so forth instead. Habits."

"Yes," said Bennosuke. "So we can go?"

"One day," said Munisai. "Perhaps."

The gate of his estate rattled on its hinges behind Munisai, banging open again with the force. Munisai didn't care. He didn't even need a gate; no one in the village would rob him. It was there only for the sake of completeness, for presenting a solid wall framed against the skyline like some fortress. A perfect steward's house, taking all beneath it in its vigil but hiding what lay within.

His mind was occupied, in any case. Night had fallen, and the samurai walked down into the dark valley and its maze of pathways between the still paddy fields. The peasants were long retired to their hovels, the distant murmur of their voices carrying out of the basin. Insects hummed in clouds around the lanterns that burned at arbitrary intersections, and below them frogs gathered in glistening clusters at the edges of the waters to lash with their tongues at any winged thing that strayed too close.

Perhaps they were not the only hunters that night. Munisai felt his skin prickle—more than his wounded arm, this time—and halted. He looked into the darkness, searching. After a moment he walked on.

Down then up, through a holy gate, and then into the grounds of the temple of Amaterasu. The shrine proper was hidden against the blackness of the sky, but the lowly shack Dorinbo lived in glowed from within. The gaps between the cheap planking that formed the wall were painted in dancing orange lines on the dirt. It was an ascetic's abode, and Munisai felt as though he might break the thin door as he rapped upon it.

He did not wait for an answer, sliding it open and then, with more care than he had treated his own gate, closing it silently. Dorinbo emerged from one of the handful of rooms, surprised at the intrusion. He was still wearing his black robe of duty, his eyes not dulled by sleep.

"What is it?" the monk said. "Your wound?"

"One of them," said Munisai, and he could not stop the bitter smirk crossing his own face. "May I enter?"

Dorinbo, confused though he was, nodded and led his brother into what passed for his living room. A half-finished letter to some distant scholar lay upon the floor, the ink still wet. He moved it and his set of brushes and pots to one side, and then gestured for Munisai to sit. The samurai did so, cross-legged and stiff, and Dorinbo joined him in expectant silence.

"The boy," said Munisai eventually.

"You finally spoke to him?"

"I tried," said Munisai, "but it seems that you have not."

"What do you mean?"

"It seems that he is confused about his mother."

"Indeed," said Dorinbo. His body straightened.

"It seems he believes she died in the fire," continued Munisai.

Neither spoke for a long moment. In the corner of the room a small stone image of a Buddha sat in the shade of a carefully pruned bonsai tree. It was weathered with age to little more than a vague, rounded effigy, and within the malformed indentation that was his lap lay the shears for tending the tree. The steel was blackened save for the sliver of the edge that caught the candlelight.

"Do you remember our father?" said the monk eventually. "Do you remember his little games to harden us up, make little samurai of us?"

"I do," said Munisai.

"Do you remember the feel of the edges of rocks when he made us walk barefoot through the mountains? Do you remember the ache in your stomach when he refused us food for days? Do you? Or how about the blows he watched us give each other after those long days when he made us fight for a single ball of rice or a sliver of fish?"

"You make it sound as if he tortured us. Everything he did had a purpose," said Munisai.

"Do you remember the chill of the sea that morning?" said Dorinbo.

"Ah," said Munisai flatly, "your 'malaise.'"

"We were out there in the water for hours. I was hacking up blood with every cough that entire winter. If it hadn't been for the skill of the monks Father sent me to, I probably would have died," said Dorinbo.

"You died anyway, in a way," said Munisai, eyes cold. "The manly part of you. They put their weakness in you, and now what do you have? No swords and a shaved head. No will."

"Oh, I still had will, Munisai," said Dorinbo. "Do you think Father took one of his sons becoming a monk well? Renouncing the glorious path of the warrior our ancestors have trodden from the dawn of time? He had a scourge and a bamboo sword, and a month free to devote to me. You're not the only one who has scars.

"But I persisted. I had seen the path that was meant for me, and he could not break me. What he did, though, with every blow and every drop of blood drawn, was put a terrible hatred into me. I hated him for what he did to me, and I hated him for the way he hated me. And I still do hate him. He's long dead, but when I think of his face I feel something twinge deep in my guts, like a fist clenching.

"This is my shame. Amaterasu teaches us that the world is not perfect—she alone is—but it is the duty of every right man not to sully it further with petty grievance. This is the path to serenity. I want to forgive him, I know I should. But I cannot. I see his face, imagine him standing on the other side of the Sanzu River as a ghost even, and I just want to spit. This is a terrible burden. A damning burden."

"And why tell me this?" said Munisai. "It's not as though I can give you absolution."

"Because, my brother, I will not be the one to pass the same burden on to Bennosuke. Even if he has to face it someday, it will not be because of me. And what you did, Munisai, was more than any scourge could do."

Dorinbo stared at his brother in the silence that followed. Munisai turned his head to face the wall before the blush could start. Through the cracks he could just about sense movement in the adjacent room. He squinted, focused, saw black moving on black. Someone taking care not to be heard. His face hardened, and he turned back to Dorinbo.

"You scorn it, but you don't realize that hatred is useful," the samurai said. "A world built on hatred would achieve far more than one built on love. Hatred focuses men, gives them the will to push themselves beyond what they thought they could endure or achieve."

"It maddens them, is what you mean," said Dorinbo. "A dog will eventually gnaw its own trapped paw off when the pain becomes too great. How is that any different?"

"The dog lives—it's useful."

"A samurai condoning dismemberment," said Dorinbo. "How shocking. A poor example, then, but you cannot—"

"So you have not told the boy?" said Munisai, interrupting.

"No."

"And he has not worked it out himself? Is he stupid?"

"No."

"Someone surely must have told him. The peasants who tend to him or . . . ?"

"Do you think any peasant in this village wants to get involved and risk your wrath after what you did the last time one of them interfered with your family?" said Dorinbo. "I have to plead with them to tend your gardens, for the love of heaven. They're scared of him, because they're scared of you. And what is really cruel about this is that the poor boy thinks this is because of a few scabs on his face."

"You could have told him, spared him that. You had eight years."

"So did you, and where have you been?" said the monk bitterly. "Killing. All I did was try to fill the hole you left, and that hole was there entirely because of what *you* did."

Munisai bowed his head like a penitent man would. The monk was right, he knew. He could not hide in his pride forever. The samurai remembered the silence of the ruins, the wind whipping through the grass.

"Say it," he said quietly.

"What?" said his brother.

"Stop alluding. Give me your full condemnation."

"Can you not bring yourself to?" asked Dorinbo. "Does it shame you to even acknowledge what you did? Does it shame you to remember butchering a village, and then burning it?"

Munisai kept his head low, but his heart was pounding, his pulse throbbing through his body. He was exposed finally, someone else confronting what he alone had confronted since that night. It was as exhilarating as it was sickening, his senses heightened, and he thought he could hear his brother's lips peel back as the monk struck the final delightful blow:

"Does it shame you to remember killing your wife?"

In the moment of silence that followed, the thin wall of the hovel creaked as weight pressed against it. Munisai looked at it from the corner of his eye, took a breath, brought his gaze back to his brother, and then spoke his ache of years.

CHAPTER FOUR

Drunk.

Too much sake, too far from home, too cold. Munisai stumbled along, the stink of cheap sex on him. It was a long walk back to Miyamoto from the nearest town, an hour at least, and on the journey the lust he thought he had already satisfied that night came back to him. The boy was staying with Dorinbo, so perhaps when he got home he would take Yoshiko in bed. That would be good.

He fell up the stairs when he got there and threw open the door to his house. There he saw the inside of his wife's thighs, and the tanned, naked back of a peasant.

Suddenly he felt very sober.

"What is this?!" he bellowed.

On his knees, the peasant dropped Yoshiko's legs and turned to face Munisai, shocked. He was a tall man, far taller than Munisai, and his body was lean with muscle. Yoshiko opened her eyes slowly from her lustful reverie and looked at Munisai, her hair unbound and touched with sweat. She wasn't alarmed in the slightest. Her eyes were spiteful, proud.

"What is this?!" Munisai shouted again, storming in from the doorway.

The peasant rose to his feet and backed away slowly. He looked Munisai in the eye as he spoke.

"Please, sir, don't . . ." he began.

"Don't what?"

"Don't harm Lady Yoshiko, she had nothing in this," he said, and lowered his head in an attempt at deference.

Something happened then . . . a frenzy. He used his sword but he was not a samurai in those moments. Munisai battered and hacked and then there was blood on his face and on his hands. His chest was heaving, and what was left of the peas-

ant was scattered around him. He turned to Yoshiko. The woman had watched impassively from the bed, not even bothering to cover herself.

"A peasant?" he said to her. "What . . . A peasant?"

"A tool," she said.

"How long has this been going on?" he hissed at her. She said nothing. He lowered the point of the sword at her. "Tell me!"

There was no fear in her. Her eyes twinkled and her mouth twisted into a grin and then she started laughing.

"Have you any idea how many times you've come back and lain where he had been? Licked his sweat from me?" she said. "You really are a fool, Munisai Hirata!"

The sound of her laughter cut through him. The immediate reaction of blind shock and outrage was goaded into a focused fury as he realized what she had done, what she was doing. He slapped her, dragged her from the house by her hair, and threw her down the steps onto the earth, sword still in his hand and the breath hissing between his teeth. Still she laughed.

"Shut up!" he snarled, and he wanted to say something more but the construction of words eluded him. In the darkness outside the courtyard, he became vaguely aware of shapes moving. The peasant had howled and howled and now a curious crowd was approaching.

"All of you!" Yoshiko called to them from her hands and knees, and her laughter had become a maniacal, frothing cackle now. "All of you come and see what kind of a man Munisai is! See him for what he really is!"

Munisai struck her backhanded across the face, but it did not silence her. Her fine kimono was twisted around her naked body like a serpent, her breasts and her sex exposed, filthy from the dirt like she was some half-wit kept drooling in rags on a leash. From the darkness there was a dull muttering.

"Whore," Munisai said. "How long has this been going on?"

"How old is Bennosuke?" she asked, spitting blood into the dirt.

"What does that have to do with it?" he said, and then a cold logic crept into him. Yoshiko looked up, and in her eyes Munisai found clarity.

"If he is five, then I would say that this has been going on for about five—" she began, and never finished. Munisai's sword slashed down and took her head.

"Liar!" he screamed in vain at her corpse, and watched as her lifeblood pumped out of her neck.

When it was spent he realized there was silence; the crowd had vanished as soon as he had killed her. They were gone, but they had seen. The peasants had *seen Yoshiko beat him. That could not be. The idea of someone knowing that he was fallible . . .*

Five years? Had they known of this for five years? They must have. Had they been laughing all the while behind his back? It drove the sense from his mind. Only then did he go truly berserk, and go to visit their enclave on the far side of the village.

Then there was light, and fire, and murder . . .

MUNISAI SAT DEFIANTLY before Dorinbo. He had spat the memories in bitter proof at his brother, his voice cracking and spit all but flecking from his lips. Years he had waited to speak of this, and now it was all out; there was almost a manic joy in finally being able to release it.

Dorinbo was shocked. He looked at his brother and tried to think of something to say. But all he could come up with, in a quiet voice, was: "You speak so candidly."

"There is nothing to hide from. Not from you," said Munisai, and then slowly he turned to the wall. He looked between the cracks to the eye he could not see but knew was looking back: "And neither from our audience. Please join us, Bennosuke."

In the darkness of the adjoining room, Bennosuke did not jump or start. The boy slowly took his hand from his mouth, his teeth leaving a line of indentations in his flesh. He had been biting the meat between his thumb and forefinger to try to keep silent as the men had spoken.

That instant of genuine confusion on Munisai's face when they had discussed his mother in the dojo had stayed with the boy. Something was wrong, something a man who hid his emotions as part of his daily life could not disguise. The turn of his head, the furrowed brow . . . It had gnawed at Bennosuke until he had to know more.

In the evening Bennosuke had snuck up to his father's estate and waited. Darkness fell, but his hunch proved true—whatever it was, it gnawed at Munisai also, and eventually the man had emerged with purpose on his face. It had been simple to follow him, to sneak in through the rear of Dorinbo's house, and then to start eavesdropping through the cracks in the wall.

Bennosuke had been excited at first to hear the men speaking unaware of him, but he had grown ever colder the more he had heard. Now he was caught. No thoughts of fleeing entered his head, however, no urge to yelp and scatter; there was a silent, dread inevitability to it. Of course Munisai had known he was there—he had been some implacable phantom that had haunted the boy's life from a distance for years, and now here he was in the flesh to crush him utterly.

Wordlessly he slid open the door and entered the room.

Munisai sat, his arm in the sling and his face grim and triumphant. Dorinbo gaped, aghast at the boy's sudden appearance. The silence held for long moments.

"Is what you said true?" said the boy. It was all he could think to say.

"Yes," said Munisai.

"You killed my mother?"

"Yes."

"And you are not my father?"

"I very much doubt it," said Munisai. "Look at you."

Bennosuke looked to Dorinbo, as though the monk might tell him that Munisai was out of his mind. But his uncle could offer nothing; he was ashamed and angry and shocked and his wits had escaped him. The boy turned back to the samurai.

"And what happens now?" said Munisai. His eyes were narrow, twinkling in the candlelight. "We know how this should end. Are you samurai, boy? Like your mother? Because her killer sits before you, and you have your little dirk at your side. Do you have the courage to do what's right? Attack me."

Bennosuke's hand went to the shortsword at his waist instinctively. The room seemed to grow smaller, the swelling of his throat larger. But numb disbelief began to fade, replaced with the first inklings of hatred and anger.

Munisai was the reason why he had been cursed to solitude, exiled, and humiliated for all these years, not some affliction of the skin. The boy began to *realize* that—he had heard it, but now he *understood* it—and now the man sat here with loathing on his face as though he were not guilty. His knuckles tightened around the grip of his sword, and at that Munisai grinned the grin of a snake.

"No," said Dorinbo, gaining some semblance of sense back—but only some, for he stammered the first words that passed through his head. "You mu-mustn't. This is holy ground."

"You're right," said Munisai, and suddenly he was up with his swords in his belt before Dorinbo could lay a hand on him. "Come on, boy."

The samurai's good hand clasped Bennosuke around the throat and pushed him out of the hovel. He led the boy at arm's length out into the night and down the slope toward the gate that marked the boundary between Amaterasu's realm and the mortal world, where hatred and human fallacy were permitted and ever present.

Dorinbo came with them, his black robe flapping as he tried to pull Munisai's arm away, yelling at his brother to stop. The samurai ignored him, stronger than either of them, and where he chose to go the monk and the boy were condemned to go too. Bennosuke staggered and backpedaled, eyes never leaving those of Munisai, legs never thinking to resist.

"Is your heart weak, mongrel?" snarled the samurai. "Does it falter with the gutterblood of your peasant father? The man I slaughtered like the animal he was? Draw your sword and attack."

Bennosuke longed to. He wanted to take the blade and swing wildly at the samurai, every slash cathartic and honest, years of misery and anger welling up in him. There was a sea of blind emotion before him, and to cast himself into it was so tempting, to become no more than vengeance and primal bloodlust. But something held him back.

They passed underneath the gates, and now on earthly ground Munisai pushed the boy away from him, releasing his throat. The samurai stood with his good arm wide and away from his swords and his chest pushed forward presenting his heart to the boy, his useless left hand almost a five-fingered target where the sling clasped it tight to his breast.

"Attack me!" said Munisai.

"Munisai, stop this madness. Bennosuke—go home now," said Dorinbo, trying to put himself between them.

"Strike me! Cut me!" continued Munisai, ignoring his brother. "Kill me!"

Behind Dorinbo, Munisai's hand grew in size. Bennosuke could all but see it pulsing with the beat of the heart. It was there and open. But he could not attack it. He knew he should, that it was proper to, but . . . His mind was working now, beneath the surface of outrage.

What he saw was the two swords at the man's waist, so very close to his good, right hand.

Bennosuke knew little of pride himself, but he had read enough stories to know how it drove some men. Munisai's armor, that magnificent suit he had cleaned all these years, was the armor of such a man. What would a peasant's bastard, a symbol of his cuckolding written in flesh, mean to such a man? He thought of how easily Munisai had bested him in the dojo, and then it became clear:

Munisai was goading him into attacking so that he had an excuse to kill him, to rid himself of the shame.

"Do you not want to avenge your mother?" said Munisai. "Kill me!"

There was the spur, and Bennosuke felt his body tense. The shortsword seemed to sing from his side. His mother, whom he had never had a chance to say good-bye to, whose very death had been hidden from him. He remembered the few memories he had of her, the echoes of her voice as she hummed songs to him, or how she laughed and smiled at him just for his simple virtue of being.

"Attack me!" barked Munisai, and it would be right and proper to do so. "Strike me! Cut me! Kill me!"

But he hesitated. Still those two long, slender weapons right there. The boy imagined the edge of the sword flashing toward him, imagined the cut that would follow as a cold line drawn across him from which his life would seep, and he quailed. He knew that he was afraid to die, and that was not the way of samurai. Shame coursed through him. His head dropped.

"Kill me!" said Munisai a final desperate time as the boy broke from his eyes, his voice hollowing. "Kill me!"

"Enough, Munisai," said Dorinbo.

The monk's voice had hardened from pleading into somber command. But it was unnecessary. Whatever terrible thing might have come to be, the moment for it had passed when Bennosuke had lowered his gaze. There would be no bloodshed today, and they all sensed it. The monk straightened and looked from one to the other. Bennosuke kept his eyes to the floor. Munisai let his arm drop, his body wilted.

"What is wrong with you?" said Munisai to Bennosuke.

"There is nothing wrong with him," said Dorinbo. "He has a chance to be something higher."

Munisai laughed in disgust. But something was different now, something in his eyes and his voice had changed; a wall had been put back up.

"This is not what you came back for, Munisai," said Dorinbo levelly. "Do not punish the boy for our mistakes."

Munisai glared at his brother, seeking a new challenge, but the monk held his eyes with a coldness. It surprised Bennosuke to see such harshness in his uncle, but even more so to see Munisai relent to it.

"Very well," Munisai could only manage. "Very well."

He looked Dorinbo in the eye one last time and then stalked off into the night, right hand clenched around his swords and his wounded left strapped tightly to his body. The darkness swallowed him, and he was gone.

Then it was just the boy and the monk. They stood for a long time.

"He was right," said Bennosuke. "I should have killed him."

"It was a lure, Bennosuke. He would have killed you," said Dorinbo. "He was goading you. His honor—"

"I know!" snapped Bennosuke. "I know—but I shouldn't care about that! I should have tried! That's what's right! That's what a samurai would do!"

"But you'd be dead."

"It doesn't matter—what kind of a person couldn't attack the man who killed his mother? What's wrong with me?" said the boy, and at that moment he truly loathed himself. Tears of shame pricked at his eyes.

"Do you even know your mother?" asked the monk after a moment. "What is she to you? What do you remember?"

"I . . ." said the boy, and he thought back. Images, flashes of voices and smells, a vague sense of love.

"Now," continued Dorinbo, "knowing what you learned about her tonight, about what she did—does that sound like the same woman to you?"

It did not. He was her instrument of revenge. A tool, not a son. Had she ever loved him, or loved what he would eventually do to Munisai? He did not know, and he would never know. The boy reeled.

"So tell me, why is dying for someone you never truly knew right?" said Dorinbo, his voice soft and kind as he saw the realization creep across the boy's face. "There is nothing wrong with a person who chooses to avoid murder—you did the right thing."

"But a samurai—" said Bennosuke, stubborn beyond reason.

"Perhaps you are something else," said Dorinbo.

"But I should be samurai," said Bennosuke.

Dorinbo looked at his nephew, wanting to remind the boy of his offer of an apprenticeship. But what he saw was an adult's pain on a face still more child than man, and he could not bring himself to place another burden there.

The night was cold and long and always would be, and so with no more words he placed a hand upon Bennosuke's shoulder and led him up to his hovel, to holy ground, where at least they could wait for morning together.

Munisai stalked home still shuddering with rage. He breathed through his nose and tried to calm himself, but it would not come. Around him the still paddy fields reflected the stars like sheets of obsidian, and the urge was to take his sword from its scabbard and slash at them. Cut the stars and cut the sky and cut the universe, just because he could.

But he didn't.

When he reached his estate he flung the door open and then slammed it shut so hard that the twisting of his body tugged on his wound and made him cry out. As his body throbbed with pain, his numb fingers fumbled with a lantern, and then by that dim and frail light he began to prowl the silent halls restlessly.

Soon enough, without even thinking about it, he came to stand before the armor once more.

It taunted him; the extravagance of it reminded him of how obscene a man he had once been, and of course that name that he had damned always there, stitched in white. It was too much to bear. He kicked it, and sent the suit clattering across the floor. He watched as the helmet rolled around and around until it finally came to rest, and in the silence afterward he let a single, low curse escape his lips.

Why would the boy not kill him?

Maybe if he had told the fullness of the story, Bennosuke might have. Maybe if he had told of the crucial moment. But that moment . . . That, Munisai knew he could never admit before another. Here, though, here in the solitude of the house where it all happened—here, he could remember.

There was once a girl who was beautiful, and more than that had a beautiful heart. Her name was Yoshiko.

It meant child of glee, child of joy, and this was the perfect name for her, for every man she crossed paths with fell in love with her. It was said that she had a grace that she must have inherited from a past life, and from the very moment she started to grow into her womanhood she was fawned over. Many an evening she spent dining with men of wealth and renown, hearing boastful stories of bravery, intelligence, wit, and war, and so generous was she that she pretended to believe them.

The offers of marriage duly came, and yet so little differentiated them—the size of estates, the number of maids she would have, the titles her children would inherit . . . Her father listened to each carefully, biding his time for the most prudent choice, but to her it meant nothing.

Sixteen and still she wore the long-sleeved, gaily patterned kimono of the maiden. She lived in a dream and she dreamed of love, and because the gods and spirits were mostly men and Yoshiko was Yoshiko, they allowed her to find it.

Munisai Hirata was introduced to her first at an afternoon of poetry. Two dozen of them, samurai men and women all, sat by a stream on soft grass, with the women beneath paper parasols and the men squinting in the light. A servant would release a floating cup of sake from upstream, and by the time it reached them one by one they had to compose a few lines on a given theme—the flight of birds or the warmness of the wind, say.

It was fun, and they laughed, and even though their words were mediocre no one cared, because the sake was so delightful. Then it came time for Munisai to compete. Though he was a few years older than Yoshiko he was the youngest man there, but he did not act it; he gave a dismissive gesture and then he said with a sly grin:

"I'll write a poem only on the day I die."

It was boorish and arrogant and rude, but as the others feigned polite amusement, at the base of her throat Yoshiko felt something hot and wonderful pulse as she saw him sit there gleaming in the sun.

His name was mentioned a lot in the months that followed, and how Yoshiko listened. Men spoke of a brashness matched only by his precociousness with a sword (and the women added his looks to this, but only away from their husbands), and soon it came to be that Munisai won a victory in a wooden-sword duel against one of the Lord Shinmen's higher-ranking bodyguards. It was no small feat for a man of his age, and he could not hide the pride as he stood before her in the court-yard of her house recounting the tale. He had arrived unannounced and her mother was looking on, bemused, and then before Yoshiko could ask him why he had come he answered:

"I wanted you to know," he said, and then he smiled, bowed, and left.

It changed then; he visited with increasing regularity until it seemed that every other day they were walking the city streets together. They were careful that their eyes never met and they talked loudly of nothing so as not to cause scandal, and yet all the while the backs of her fingers brushing against his knuckles where they lay ever clasped over the scabbard of his sword stole the sense from her.

Knuckles became the softness of palms as streets became secret hideaways; and then came the day when she told him how she felt. They were in a bamboo grove and what she remembered was the vivid greenness of it, all emerald and quiet there among the trunks, their fingers entwined and their breasts so tight against each other that she could feel his heart beating.

As she leaned in toward his ear she hesitated a moment, smelling his hair as he lowered his head to hers. Then she whispered the sweetest thing she could:

"If I can't have you, Munisai, I'll slit my throat."

A naked moment, when she was certain he would reject her, but then a sort of shudder went through him and she felt the longest hairs of his mustache upon her ear.

"I'll do it for us both," he said.

She wanted to cry; he could not have said anything more perfect. As a joint suicide they would leave the world together for their spirits to be reborn as twins— a part of each in the other for all eternity. She did cry, in fact, and Munisai held her until she stopped, and the world was a beautiful place.

Suicide was not necessary, it turned out. For all his gall, to look at Munisai was to see his star ascendant, and so Yoshiko's father consented to a marriage. He marched behind them in their bridal procession to the shrine, and then six months later in the first winter after she left his house in the city to live in Miyamoto he died. A sickness stole him from the world in a matter of weeks, and her mother did not linger long after. She stopped eating, withered, and then she too was gone.

Their names were carved on the family tombstone together, and though Yoshiko grieved she was not distraught, because she was not alone. She knew that Munisai was hers and that was enough.

But what did Munisai have? He was surprised the first time he found himself mulling over the question dispassionately, examining love like a raven at a corpse. He had loved her, he was certain, in that bamboo grove, loved her for what she was with a simple, pure love that she returned.

Time crept in, though, and now that they were married and her affections were secured, what did he feel? He looked at her when she slept, at the whiteness of her hand upon the pillow by her face, and found that his heart no longer lurched. He realized that perhaps he had not wanted her for her, but for the fact that he had something that other men wanted.

That, he was also surprised to find, pleased him.

A callous freedom grew within him. He knew the gods loved him. He was handsome and young, immensely talented with the sword, and he had the wealth of both his family and that which Yoshiko's parents had left them. All this was his and he was not yet twenty-five years of age—so why not take more? A suit of armor with his name shining upon it. More sake. More food. More dice.

More women, just for the sheer hell of being young and virile.

The first night he had come back smelling of a whore's embrace, he had staggered into his bedroom to find Yoshiko kneeling there waiting for him. He felt a rare pang of remorse, such was the look in her eyes.

"Why?" she asked simply.

"Because I can," he said, then shrugged and went to bed.

He felt the bedding move softly with her sobbing body during the night as she lay behind him weeping silently. He was too drunk to care.

In the morning Yoshiko forgave him, but this she never told him. She reasoned it a unique moment of weakness, and if it never happened again then it never happened at all. Desperately she clung to this hope, but it was as futile as it was inevitable; he went and did as he pleased. Again and again and again, and never once did she plead with him to stop—she couldn't understand why she would have to.

Instead it was her tears that stopped eventually, replaced by a numbness that robbed her days alone of any sense of time. Over these unfelt months the emptiness twisted into loathing, most of all at the fact that Munisai was not doing this out of malice. He didn't taunt her, boast of his exploits to try to force cathartic hysterics out of her; he simply did it and expected her to care as little as he did, as a good wife should.

In her memory the perfect emerald of the bamboo grove decayed into putrid shades of rot.

It all seemed hopeless. She knew that she could sue for divorce, but with no family to take her in where would she go? A life of indulgence had left her with no real skill, which meant that she could shave her head and join a nunnery or become a whore herself. She was trapped here, her loneliness abject and total and forever, until one night as she slept she heard the voice of her father.

There was no sympathy in his voice—he reminded her of what he had taught her in her childhood, and then, and in all the subsequent nights he came to her, he asked of whom she was a daughter, of whom she was a great-great-great-granddaughter?

The answer was samurai, and self-pity was not their way. No. A slur on clan or family or name was unforgiveable, and led to one thing alone:

Vengeance.

What else were men and women put upon this earth to do other than to give their lives over to something entirely? And how similar vengeance and love were, for both were born of devotion and obsession—but where love was a shapeless haze with no clear end, vengeance took those same emotions and focused them, drove them toward a wonderful climactic moment.

The promise of that ending, that vanishing point, that one instant of triumph and vindication—that made living for vengeance better than living for love. This, Yoshiko told herself.

On a bitter night she donned a crown of candles and set out barefoot in the dead time after midnight at the hour of the ox. She walked to a shrine in the next *town over, murmuring invocations and carrying a straw phallus that she intended to nail to a tree within the grounds as a declaration to the spirits and her ancestors of her intentions.*

But with the hammer and nail in her hands she hesitated. Still Munisai gleamed in her memory. Perhaps . . . She hardened herself, drove the nail through the fetish, and then extinguished the candles against the wood with them still atop her head.

The next three nights, Yoshiko sat beside Munisai's sleeping body with the dagger her mother had bequeathed her in her hand, staring at him, thinking of how many other women had been where she alone should have been. It could not make her bring the blade from the sheath. For his flesh merely to die was not enough. He needed to see, to understand—to feel as harrowed as she was. How could she do this?

She wandered the hallways, and there she came across his armor with his name in white.

Denkichi was a thresher, a gangly man with cold and callused hands. He was the tallest peasant in Miyamoto, and perhaps it was his height that made him stand out to Yoshiko. Or perhaps not. It did not matter—any one of them would have done. She had to coax him stage by stage into her bed, for he was rightfully timid, but she could still pretend to be the girl she had been in her youth and she won him over eventually.

When they were together the peasant would try to whisper sweet things to her, attempt in vain to speak like an educated man, all the while with the stink of the fields on him and a body that was hard and angular. Yoshiko ignored his words and the sensations and thought of Munisai.

Munisai went on as he was. He had no idea what was happening and was mildly surprised to learn of her pregnancy—their times together hazy and drunken and often unfinished—and as her belly grew there was no change in him. He took on a wet nurse and a midwife to help her along, and then cared as little as he did before.

Yet when Bennosuke came, small and pink and wailing, he became Munisai's pride. He held the boy, spoke to him softly, paraded him in front of friends. Yoshiko smiled at him demurely and properly as he did so, but inside what little was left of her was being eaten away. It taunted her with what they should have had, that joy in his eyes and that babe in his arms. That, they could have created together, but . . .

For five years Bennosuke grew, and there were moments when regret stabbed through her, when she thought about never telling Munisai. But always the love he showed the boy was never shown to her. They shared the name Hirata, the three of them, but Yoshiko realized she had it only in the same way his armor did. Not like Bennosuke had, and it was this that Munisai truly loved—all he loved—and it was this that always hardened her once more.

Denkichi had stayed away during her pregnancy and Bennosuke's infancy, but Yoshiko lured him back. She let him even hold his son sometimes, and while he did so she would hide things of his to leave as clues for Munisai to find later—his sandals or the band he wrapped around his head as he worked.

Munisai never noticed. He would kick whatever it was to one side, or mutter about the servants being more mindful of their things.

Yoshiko wanted to laugh until she cried. She was so little to him that the idea that she could harbor deceit or spite or any human emotion at all simply did not occur to him.

The bamboo grove had lost the color even of rot. It was nothing now. She found herself asking if the entirety of this life was any different. And so it came to that night.

Yoshiko prepared herself for the role she would have to play, a character of exaggerated ice and steel to break him utterly. The moment she had planned for these long years approached, and while Denkichi was inside her she felt a detachment to the world that was somewhere between euphoria and resignation.

They finished early as they always did, but when Denkichi made to leave she pulled him back with her arms around his neck.

"Stay," she said.

"But . . ." said Denkichi, worry on his ugly face.

"He won't be back," lied Yoshiko. "He's away for a week. Stay. I get lonely."

He obeyed because he was simple and thought this was real. They coupled again, and as they did so she heard the footsteps coming up the path. She took a breath, prepared herself, and just as the door was flung open she uttered a silent apology to Denkichi. His karma would be good. Perhaps he would come back samurai.

Then Denkichi's soul was gone and his body was in pieces and she was naked in the courtyard and her nose was bleeding and people were watching and she was laughing in the dirt. Munisai was furious, seething: he felt!

"Whore," Munisai hissed. "How long has this been going on?"

"How old is Bennosuke?" she asked.

"What does that have to do with it?" he said.

She looked up at him then. This was it, she realized, the moment she had lived for—there was only one thing left to say, the final wound that would make her vengeance complete. Yoshiko knew that her ancestors would be watching, willing her on to prove herself samurai, and she longed for the great instant of ecstasy and satisfaction that would rush into her.

But in Munisai's eyes she saw something human there again finally, hurt and angry and vulnerable, and it cut through time. The greenness of the bamboo grove was eternal and they should have been in it together there forever, and what had she made of this life these past years? What had he made of this life?

It shattered the armor of her charade and tears rolled from her eyes as one gasping sob shook her body.

Oh, it was futile, all of it. Shame coursed through her and she tried to suck the tears back up before she hardened her face once more and fixed it into a bitter grin—a face fit to leave this pitiless world with. She was samurai, after all.

"If he is five, then I would say that this has been going on for about five—" *she began, and that was the end of Yoshiko.*

The armor was still scattered before Munisai on the floor. The lantern in his hand had begun to splutter and falter. He barely noticed.

Those tears. That racking sob that escaped her. The instant before she hardened and spoke the words that broke him . . . That was what defined him, and yet his pride as a samurai would never let him tell anyone but himself of this. Not even her son. Not even when he wanted to die.

It had taken him years to even acknowledge it himself. At first he had fixated on that final smile Yoshiko had forced onto her face. He had thought about it every night while he waited for sleep to come and saw it in the edge of every sharp sword that flashed toward him. It filled him with anger and hatred, and those were easy to deal with.

They were false and constructed enemies, though, and he always knew it. Even then, part of him admired her; the samurai in him saw her resolve and dedication in pursuit of a correct and proper vengeance. The rest of him could not hold out forever. Slowly, slowly over the years wandering in the wilderness and then those in Shinmen's service, he gradually allowed himself to admit the presence of the tears, to admit the truth of what he had done.

He remembered the rustling of the sheets and the gentle rocking of the bed as Yoshiko lay weeping behind him that first night he had betrayed her. He thought of that innocent, rare joy he had blithely trampled and tarnished. It tugged at his soul relentlessly, and his anger had turned to shame. He came to realize he had brought what Yoshiko had done to him onto himself with his arrogance, and for that he had murdered her.

Today, after eight years, he had thought at last that he could atone. It had come to him suddenly, when he had become aware of Bennosuke following him as he walked to the temple. What could be more perfect than her son killing him? Tell the story, in vivid, stark detail, steal the wits and the restraint from the boy, and then let him do what he would do; clean and quick and justice done.

But the boy . . .

After he had finished with killing, Munisai had watched the fire burn down within the village for some time, and then had returned to his estate. He did not enter, but instead slumped against the wall on the outside looking down across the valley. Cries of terror, pain, and grief echoed as dawn came, but none approached the house. Munisai sat in his filthy kimono alone, until he looked up and saw Dorinbo there in the daylight.

The monk said nothing. He must have walked through the carnage to reach the house. Dorinbo looked at Munisai, and the samurai knew the monk expected some kind of apology or an explanation, but there was nothing left in him. All he could do was look back.

That silence brought rage into Dorinbo. The monk started lashing at him with his fists and his feet, and Munisai did not stop him. It was the first time he had seen his brother lose control, but he understood why. He accepted the blows, and that if anything made Dorinbo angrier. The monk grabbed him by the scruff of his kimono and spun him around in a flurry, both pushing and dragging Munisai away from the house.

"*Leave!*" *the monk said, letting Munisai go. The samurai stood up and looked his brother in the eye. There were tears of shame and anger there. He could not argue, so he nodded.*

He had gone five paces before Dorinbo stopped him once more.

"*Munisai—Bennosuke is waiting down the road. Change your kimono," he said.*

Munisai looked down. Dried blood was spattered across him. Of the peasant who had cuckolded him, of the peasants whom he had slaughtered, but most of all of Yoshiko. Wordlessly he entered his estate and slipped into fresh clothing, forcing himself not to look at the two corpses within the courtyard and his bedchamber.

When he emerged once more he walked past his brother, neither of them meeting the other's eyes. Down the path Munisai found Bennosuke as Dorinbo had said, sitting on a boulder looking at the smoke in the sky curiously. The five-year-old scrabbled to his feet when he saw the samurai coming. The Hirata crest rode high upon the breast of Bennosuke's small kimono, mocking Munisai.

"*Father? Where's Mother?" he said, looking up at the man. His eyes were sparkling and keen, and his face much too young to tell if Yoshiko had been lying or not. Munisai had sucked the air into his chest and fought the spasm of anger and sadness.*

"*Bennosuke. Try to be samurai," he said, placing a hand on the child's shoulder. The boy's brow furrowed, and then it earnestly formed itself into an expression of determination.*

Munisai left then, not looking behind him once, and that had been that. That was the start of his exile.

The inability to live up to a child's wordless pledge to do something he had no real understanding of could be held as no true failure, but regardless, over the intervening years Bennosuke had not become samurai. Oh, he showed potential with a sword and wore his hair correctly, but they were superficial things only. The boy still lacked something within, a fundamental desire, a base pride that would have compelled Bennosuke to slaughter his father as a matter of instinct.

What could have been a finer justice than that? Vengeance, after all, was holy, and a son avenging a murdered mother was as natural and pure as the sky above. But Yoshiko was Yoshiko. For all her tears she was samurai like he was, and her vengeance had been observed perfectly thus far—why should it get any easier for him now?

Munisai sighed. He would have to find some other way to earn her forgiveness.

He spent a few minutes replacing the scattered armor perfectly on the stand. Later he woke as he often did, forgetting all the years that had passed, and rolled over expecting to find her there, warm and delicate. But as always in the darkness, there were only his blankets and his swords by the side of the bed.

As always, neither of those would accept his apologies.

CHAPTER FIVE

Amaterasu came, and with her the light of morning.

She lit up another faith; a Buddhist mandala hung upon Dorinbo's wall. Bennosuke looked at it from where he lay on his side in the corner where he had slept. Though he had dedicated his life to the Shinto sun goddess, Dorinbo saw nothing wrong with studying other faiths and beliefs, and had a quiet fascination and admiration for the story of the Buddha, a man who valued learning and compassion.

It was a copy of an ancient painting, done in bright colors and bold black lines upon thick cloth and as wide as a man's outstretched arms. Beneath the world sat the devil Enma at his table of judgement, demons holding men before him. Then came a crush of bodies twisted and mangled, a stratum of the lost and the weak who lived upon the earth. Above all were the symmetrical, perfect slopes of Mount Fuji reaching up to the enlightened lands, crude white stick figures of pilgrims climbing upward on hands and knees.

Though it was simplistic it was beautiful in a way, the color vivid and the weird, malformed detail of each little figure captivating. Bennosuke had first seen it when he was a child, and when Dorinbo had explained it to him, he had pointed to the little white figures ascending and said:

"But where are their swords?"

A happy memory, it twisted in his heart now.

Bennosuke lay there until he became aware of voices outside. There was no sermon today; it should have been quiet. Curious, he rose and opened the door to the outside world. He was surprised to find Dorinbo and Munisai there. Neither man looked happy, but their voices were level and measured. Both turned to look at him, and he stopped uneasily in the doorway.

"Good morning," said Munisai, but his words were courtesy only. His stance was immaculately neutral, the traditional, considered poise that samurai affected at rest; chest out, hand sweeping the jacket of his kimono back at his waist so that his swords were unhindered.

"Why are you here?" the boy said eventually.

"Your training begins today," Munisai said.

"Training?" said Bennosuke.

"Yes." Munisai nodded. "As I said yesterday at the dojo, there are inklings of skill in you. Tasumi has laid the foundation, and now I shall hone you."

Bennosuke looked to Dorinbo. The monk made a gesture that he was relenting to Munisai, though it was clear from his expression that he disapproved. The boy turned back to the samurai suspiciously, but said nothing.

"You overcame emotion yesterday," said Munisai at his silence. "You did not attack me, though I provoked you. To resist negating yourself with sentiment in such a way is part of being samurai. If that is in you, then perhaps I can teach you the rest."

The man did not seem to be joking. He held the boy's gaze levelly, and that serenity began to infuriate the boy. There was not a single trace of apology or shame in the samurai, and at that absence Bennosuke felt the hatred and anger of yesterday come into him.

"No," he said, "I don't want that. I don't need it. You think you can still pretend to be my father?"

"I said nothing of being your father," Munisai snorted, amused by the absurdity of it. "You shall call me Lord, as your position dictates."

Bennosuke felt a hot flush of anger at the dismissal, and made as if to move toward the man. But as he had yesterday, he checked himself, and at that Munisai's face turned into a full, mocking smile.

"I hate you," said Bennosuke, and instantly regretted speaking. It sounded futile and childish, and it seemed only to deepen the mirth in Munisai—or perhaps darken it, for though his lips still smiled his eyes lost their gleam and became serious.

"If that is the case," he said, "then accept my training, grow stronger, and then try to kill me."

There was the challenge, and as Bennosuke considered it he saw more clearly the strange look in Munisai's eyes. There had been glimpses of it yesterday as he had barked and raved, but now, held steady before him, he could examine it. A bitter longing, empty and dark.

But whatever it was it was hidden within the disgust. The sight of that made Bennosuke's blood run hot, was his entire and encompassing focus at that moment.

He nodded once, assenting.

"Good, boy," said Munisai. "Come. We run."

The rains of late summer were light that year, the rivers not even coming close to bursting their banks. The green world sucked the last of the waters up voraciously and then began to dry. The paddy fields were drained and the harvest begun, the peasants who hacked at the stalks with crooked back and heavy sickle grateful for the heat relenting from an oppressive humidity to simple, pleasing warmth.

Bennosuke was too. The boy had thought Tasumi a harsh master, but Munisai far outdid him. The samurai had enforced a ruthless regimen of fitness upon him. He introduced strange new ways of stretching, of using the body's own weight against itself, and would constantly poke and twist the boy's joints at awkward points.

Most of all, though, he made the boy run. Sometimes for two hours, sometimes for ten minutes carrying buckets of water, sometimes uphill, and sometimes in the surf of the bay. Wherever it was, however it was done, the man was obsessed. One time, floundering on the floor and retching from his guts, Bennosuke had angrily asked the point of such exercise.

"You cannot fight if you cannot breathe, boy," said Munisai, looking down at him. "You cannot fight if your legs are dead. You must learn to go beyond the threshold of your muscles and your lungs. If you can fight for five minutes, you will win any fight. If you can fight for five minutes after fighting for five minutes, you will never fall on the battlefield."

"I can fight for five minutes," said Bennosuke.

"Prove it," said Munisai simply.

Bennosuke tried to rise to his feet, but it was no challenge for Munisai to kick his legs out from under him. The boy attempted it twice more before he accepted defeat. Munisai looked down at him, eyes challenging, but all he could muster was a glare.

The man had been running alongside him the whole time.

Weeks turned into months and autumn came, but it was not a time of remorse. People waited for the turning of the leaves in the same manner as they did for the cherry blossom of spring; to see a vista of reds and golds and purples was a calming affirmation of the natural progress of life. Men and women of all stations would travel distances simply to view famous panoramas of forests, poets and artists finding new inspiration within the auburn boughs while beneath them young lovers coupled among hidden beds of fallen leaves.

But such things, love and art and serenity, were alien to Bennosuke now. Asleep one night with the door of his room cast open to the world and an orange half-moon hanging huge and fat in the sky, the boy was awoken by the stamp of a foot. His eyes opened to find Munisai standing astride his chest, looking down at him.

"Defend yourself," he said, grinning so wide that Bennosuke could see the moonlight upon his teeth.

The boy twisted, tried to leap to his feet, but it was hopeless. In an instant Munisai pushed him down with his one hand and then forced a knee down upon his throat. Bennosuke began to choke, flailing his legs feebly in an attempt to wriggle free.

"I did not mask my footfalls, fool, and yet I snuck up on you," hissed Munisai. "How can you protect your lord from assassins if you sleep like the dead?"

Bennosuke gurgled, his fingers grasping at the man's leg trying to steal a breath, but the samurai did not relent. He lowered his head closer to the boy's, watching the agony and panic written upon it.

"Just a babe in a cradle," Munisai said, "a lazy child with a head full of stone and no awareness of the world around you."

The samurai waited until the boy's eyes began rolling up into his skull and his tongue was protruding from his mouth before he released the pressure. Though he was free Bennosuke did not try to rise. All he could do was roll upon the floor, sputtering and clutching at his throat while Munisai watched him. After a few moments the man gave a disappointed sigh and left the boy alone with the moon once more.

Bennosuke did not sleep in Munisai's estate again. He sought a bed inside and out where he could not be found, suspicious of every sound.

$\mathcal{A}$ longsword in his hand finally, Bennosuke felt a rush come into him. The weapon was only wood, but it was something to strike and to beat with. It was the most power he had been afforded in some time.

Munisai stood before him in the dojo hall. He had shown the boy new patterns, and now he was inviting the boy to spar and demonstrate that he understood them. The samurai's arm was still in a sling, a mock shortsword in his good hand. He made no move, waiting for the boy to attack, and though he felt exhilarated Bennosuke advanced cautiously—he could not allow himself to expose any flaw.

They traded feint and riposte, dancing around each other until eventually Munisai seemed to stagger and overextend himself, his sword high and away from his body and the length of him left vulnerable.

Bennosuke's first instinct was to go for the opening, to drive the hard wood home on soft flesh, but then something stronger and wiser in him sensed a trap and instead of lunging he skittered backward. Munisai all but spat in rage, breath hissing through his teeth.

"No!" the man snapped. "Why do you hesitate?"

"You'd have struck me," said Bennosuke.

"So? You had a chance to take my throat."

"But I'd be dead, if this were real."

"You do not know that—perhaps I would have missed. All you can be certain of is yourself. Could you have struck me there, a clean kill?"

"Perhaps," said Bennosuke.

"I left a gap in my defense wider than an ocean—of course you could have," said Munisai, anger turning to disgust. "But you shied away from achieving your objective—your sole purpose in a fight, your sole purpose of *being* as a samurai—afraid of getting hurt like some queer Kyoto dancer."

Bennosuke said nothing, knowing that argument was futile. He looked away sullenly, and at that defiance Munisai rapped him around the head with the sword hard enough that the boy staggered backward. The samurai made a dismissive gesture with his hand, tossed the weapon to the floor, and walked away.

The pain of the blow stole Bennosuke's restraint from him, and he could not stop himself from picking the man's sword from where it had fallen to accompany his own. He snarled in fury and began to charge at Munisai's back, longsword in his right hand and the short in his left, wanting to swing both without thought and simply annihilate.

At the clattering of his feet, Munisai turned and half drew his real shortsword from the scabbard. The sight of the metal blade checked Bennosuke and stopped the charge before it truly began. After a few moments of stillness, Munisai gave a curt nod.

"Good," he said. "Not quite entirely the wild boar, blindly charging. A sword in either hand? No strength. No precision. I'd have flayed you alive. There was no chance for you to prevail, and so in this instance stopping yourself was the right decision."

It was not, however, a compliment. Dark amusement crept across his face before he continued. "But I have to wonder if you heeded the lesson, or was it simply cowardice?"

He let his sword slide back into the scabbard with a clack, and then stalked out of the dojo still grinning mirthlessly to himself. Bennosuke watched him go, and when he was alone he dropped into a squat and ground his teeth together and groaned a low and bestial sound of rage and shame and frustration.

It was not the first time he had done so. The blows hurt and the belittlement cut into his pride, but what really infuriated him was that he could not tell whom this terrible anger was directed at.

Was it at Munisai, for what he had done? It should have been, but the truth was that the longer he was around the man, the more he found himself coming to admire him. Crippled though he was, the samurai had a seemingly casual degree of excellence at everything he turned his hand to. The boy found himself wanting to learn from him, and even to earn the man's praise as much as he thought he wanted one day to confront him.

Perhaps the anger was at himself for feeling that. This was the killer of both his parents, a ghoulish impostor of a father. What kind of a person would want to impress such a man? Always too the stinging shame that through all the years he had not been aware enough to real-ize that truth himself. A blind, idiot child he had been, and still was.

But then, was he blind, or blinded? Dorinbo and Tasumi had lied to him for so long, kept him naive. Was it them he hated? They were not even his family, not now. Or maybe it was the peasants for their disgust and their coddling of him through fear of his father alone, or perhaps the sun for shining and the grass for growing? The anger was so big, and he could not explain it, could not understand it, and that only maddened him further.

He could not give in to it. He thought himself a samurai, and samurai were governed by patience and reason and selflessness. The boy forced deep breaths into his lungs, until eventually he could make himself rise and, with a still face, set the wooden swords back upon the racks that lined the walls of the hall.

One afternoon Bennosuke was sitting upon the dojo steps with the skirts of his kimono hiked up. He had run all morning, and now Dorinbo was before him kneading the bared flesh of the boy's knee, prodding and probing and trying to reduce the swelling of the joint with salves and balms as he had done on a dozen different afternoons before.

"You shouldn't push yourself so hard," the monk tutted, thumb digging in to try to force smooth motion from the joint.

"I have to," said Bennosuke. "He wants me to surrender."

"And what would be so wrong about that?"

"Samurai don't surrender."

"You're neglecting your studies—and the binding at the temple," said the monk. "Did you forget what I asked of you?"

"No," said Bennosuke. "I . . ."

"And what do you intend to do with this training? Are you going to kill Munisai one day?"

"I'll try," said Bennosuke, forcing bravado into his voice. "You wouldn't understand."

"I understand so much effort for such a savage thing is a terrible waste of the little time we are given," said the monk sadly. "You could be so much more."

Dorinbo kept his eyes low on his work. Bennosuke felt a twinge of shame, but sad rather than angry this time. He wished he were older and wiser, and had the words to explain how he felt as much to himself as to the monk. At the very least he wished he could force himself to try.

Just then, Munisai appeared. The samurai strode up to them without nodding a greeting, and jerked his chin at the boy.

"I need time with Dorinbo. Busy yourself," he said. Bennosuke did not move. He held Munisai's gaze challengingly, until the samurai smiled, spread his arm wide, and sneered. "Well—that's a manly face. Is today the day you try for me, boy? Found your courage? I await your vengeance at any moment."

But it was not some great moment of destiny; it was just a hot afternoon. Wordlessly Bennosuke rose to his feet, bowed pointedly to the monk but not to the samurai, and then went inside the dojo to leave the brothers alone.

Munisai watched him go, facing the boy always until he was out of sight. When he was definitely gone, the contempt vanished from him. His face became blank, and he commanded Dorinbo with a curt gesture of his hand:

"See to my wound."

"As you wish, Lord," said the monk.

There was the slightest sarcasm in his voice, but Munisai said nothing as he sat down and slid the kimono off his shoulder. Dorinbo removed the bandage, and began to examine what lay beneath.

The arm was not healing well. The wound had finally closed and was starting to form a great lumpy ridge of scar, but that did not mean it was improving. The limb remained feeble and from time to time the samurai still lost feeling in his hand, on which green and blue bruises inexplicably formed.

As he heard Dorinbo sigh and cluck his tongue in bewilderment, Munisai felt his spirit sink. Of course he had known beforehand that no miracle had taken place, but there was always a sliver of blind hope that something had improved even the slightest. If that was stripped from him, despair would take root and begin to rot his will as badly as his flesh.

"How is work at the temple going?" the samurai said, trying to distract himself. "You are still preparing for that burning, yes?"

"Indeed. There is much to do. Progress has been slower as of late," said Dorinbo. His examination over, he let Munisai's arm go and began to rummage through the collection of salves and ointments he had brought to tend to Bennosuke.

"Binding, binding, binding," Munisai said. "It seems rather unnecessary if it is all going to be burned in the end."

"Would you want your corpse thrown onto some bonfire without ceremony?" said Dorinbo.

"It wouldn't matter," said Munisai. "The manner of death is all that defines what is proper or not, not what happens to what remains."

"No, but I am asking you, Munisai," said Dorinbo, and he spoke casually while he unscrewed the lid of the hollowed bamboo pot he had chosen. "Do you personally care for the notion, say, of somebody dragging your body by the feet like a sack of turf through the dirt and then slowly tipping you onto a pile of burning driftwood for you to cook slowly, your flesh roasting and your skin peeling away unevenly so you become a mangled, half-charred thing, and then for the fire to be left untended, go out eventually, and for the animals to come and fight over what is left?"

Munisai considered it.

"No," he said.

"Exactly," said Dorinbo, as patient as he was with children. "And that is why we must do the binding, long and strenuous though it is."

"Well, if the work is that much, you ought to take an apprentice," said Munisai, and he gave a one-armed shrug.

Dorinbo suddenly found the horizon very interesting for a moment. He bit the inside of his lip, and forced himself to work on. Using two fingers he began to scoop dollops of greasy, gray salve from the pot onto Munisai's wound. The ridges began to glisten, and Dorinbo saw the healthy muscles on his brother's back tense. The salve had a sting to it.

"Tell me, then, of the boy," said Munisai as Dorinbo worked. "He seems feeble. What were you doing to him when I arrived?"

"Bennosuke," said Dorinbo pointedly, "Bennosuke. You gave him that name."

"How is Bennosuke?" Munisai conceded.

"Exhausted. His legs are falling to pieces."

"I ask nothing of him that I would not ask of myself," said Munisai, hearing the reproach in the monk's voice.

"He's still a child."

"He's a head taller than most men already," said Munisai. "With a shaven scalp and a longsword he'd pass muster in any army in the land."

"His bones will warp," said Dorinbo.

"Yes—warp and become stronger." Munisai nodded, certainty in his voice.

"Samurai," muttered Dorinbo under his breath. After a moment, Munisai turned to look at his brother for the first time that day.

"I am samurai, Dorinbo—that is true," he said. "But there are times when I wish I wasn't, so that I had the luxury as you do of saying what I felt."

"Indulge yourself," said the monk, meeting his eye. "Pretend you aren't as you are, for just one moment."

"There is no need to—I have nothing I'd wish to say to you on this matter," said Munisai, and turned away once more.

"Well, why break a habit of eight years?" said Dorinbo. "Just break the boy, keep your stoicism and your proud front, and leave me to mind him and pick up the pieces, as you always have."

"What do you mean?"

"You know what I mean," said Dorinbo, his voice low. He forced some of the ointment deep into the wound then, and it stung wickedly. Munisai gritted his teeth and had to wait for the brunt of that to pass before he felt confident that he could speak without betraying evidence of the pain.

"Do you resent raising Bennosuke, then?" he said.

"No, of course not!" snapped Dorinbo. "What I resent, brother, is you returning and stealing him away as though nothing happened. He's as much my son as he is yours. More so, probably. But neither you—nor he—seems to realize it."

Munisai considered Dorinbo's words. His brother was acting like a woman, but there was truth in what he said, certainly. It was evident the monk had cared for Bennosuke rigorously, and Munisai had never once asked the monk to do so. He had just presumed that this would be the case, and indeed, entirely unbidden, Dorinbo had taken Munisai's place. It seemed that apologies were due.

But he was samurai, and samurai did not show the slightest deference to monks, and so he said nothing.

Before Dorinbo spoke again, they were interrupted by the sound of a horn. It was a low, cyclical undulation like a beast singing a prayer, and it carried across the valley before it stopped for a breath and then repeated itself in a higher tone. The pair of them looked up to find a horseman on the ridgeline of the village, a conch to his lips. The man sat beneath a burgundy banner.

"I beg a further favor, brother," the samurai said to the monk, eyes not leaving the horseman as he blew on. "Conceal this wound."

CHAPTER SIX

On the other side of the hall, Bennosuke had busied himself polishing a bundle of war staves after Munisai had
dismissed him, trying to force the anger from his mind
again. His hands had had to fight the urge to take his shortsword
and start shaving the wood of the poles away, slicing again and again
deeper and deeper until what remained was honed into a savage point;
a crude spear with which to do a crude act.

His knuckles grew white and the tendons on his wrist writhed
back and forth, and it was so tempting to be consumed by the mind-
lessness of it that he was almost glad when the sound of the horn gave
him something else to focus on.

Up on the ridge, other horsemen appeared alongside the one
blowing the horn. There were five more of them, each upon a tall
warhorse, and after they had stood in imperious silhouette for a few
moments they began to wind their way down the paths between the
fields in slow single file. The rich color of the burgundy they all wore
almost blended their bodies into the autumn landscape.

The peasants pressed their faces into the ground as the procession passed, and then rose to follow nervously in their wake. They
formed a parade of sorts, the regimented gentry ahead and the lesser
in a mob behind. Now that the lead man had stopped blowing on the
conch their advance seemed funereal. Not one of the mounted men
spoke or even looked at those they passed.

Their eyes were all fixed on the dojo.

Bennosuke rose, the staff in his hands. A single samurai rider was
odd; a band of them coming with such grim pomp was something he
had never seen. The six of them fanned out as they left the narrow

pathways of the slopes, hoof after heavy hoof. At some signal the man with the conch galloped ahead and dropped from the saddle twenty paces from Bennosuke. He took the banner from his back.

"A great honor is yours today!" he called, sinking to one knee and planting the banner in the ground. "A great lord visits your hamlet!"

The herald was young, and his high voice did not carry well. Bennosuke said nothing, unsure of what he was supposed to do. He watched guardedly as the other horsemen came and dismounted. Two of them strode forward, predatory. One was a thin man with a long face, perhaps as young as the herald. Beneath the dust of travel, his riding clothes were more extravagantly and richly patterned than anything Bennosuke had seen. The other was older, heavier, plainer, and he held himself still, with his hand on his sword.

The pair of them looked at Bennosuke for a long moment. The thin man's eyes became disgusted as they took him in—his simple clothes, the sole shortsword at his side and his unshaven crown that marked him a child, and the gangly frame of his body and the red welts of his rash that marked him unclean and inelegant: an undesirable.

"Are you samurai?" the man asked eventually.

"Yes—are you?" said Bennosuke hotly. The contempt in the man's eyes had drawn it from him.

There was a cry of outrage from the other men, and they made as if to run forward and draw their swords. They were blowfish puffing up, no more; not one of them actually let the blade leave their scabbard, and they halted instantly the moment the thin man raised his hand.

"He is more than a samurai," said the herald indignantly. "He is the most noble Hayato Nakata!"

Bennosuke thought about what that meant, and then he knelt, pressing his forehead to the wood of the dojo floor. It was the first lord he had met, but he knew what was expected—especially when five men seethed like leashed dogs by his side.

"At least you know some manners," clucked Hayato under his breath, shaking his head. "Rise."

Bennosuke obeyed, and then, not knowing what else to say, he spoke as he thought a samurai would: "How may I serve you, my lord?"

"This is the village of Miyamoto, is it not?" said Hayato.

"It is, my lord."

"The steward of this village is Munisai Shinmen, then. Do you know him?"

"I am his son, my lord," he said.

"His son?" said Hayato, and then he laughed. "This ugly whelp is Munisai's son! Perhaps his skill is overrated if this is the best he can sire!"

The other men sniggered obligingly, and Bennosuke felt his rash throb in embarrassment. It was as much from his own mistake as Hayato's words—he did not know why he had identified himself as Munisai's son.

"My Lord Nakata," came Munisai's voice from within the dojo, and then slowly he walked out from the hall. "I rejoice at the honor of your presence here, but if you are here for your reimbursements regarding Kanno's castle, you will be disappointed. My wealth resides with my Lord Shinmen in Takeyama."

Though his words were polite his voice was deep and cold. There was no sign of the sling on Munisai, his arms free and crossed and his stance wide. He took in the burgundy samurai one by one, perfectly still, perfectly strong. The eyes of the man alongside Nakata glinted with sudden interest.

"We are here to show you what my 'city-dweller spirit' is made of, you arrogant dog," said Nakata. "We are here to show you that war does not disgust me, do you understand?"

"Indeed," said Munisai, and a small smile played across his lips. The lord had spoken aggressively, and so now he was free to abandon the civility that etiquette demanded. "And who is the 'we' that will prove your mettle, my lord?"

His eyes settled on the samurai by Hayato's side, but Dorinbo chose that moment to make himself known. Hurriedly he scuttled down the stairs and placed himself between the burgundy samurai and Munisai.

"Please, please, please," the monk said, his hands raised in placation. "There is no call for violence this day, my lords. My name is Dorinbo and I serve Amaterasu. My brother Munisai and I would be glad to receive—"

"A brother, a son? Is your mother in there too, Shinmen?" interrupted Nakata, speaking to Munisai and leaving Dorinbo unable to do anything but look back and forth to either side. "The spirits have mercy—why couldn't you have stayed by your master's side in civilization? Why have you forced me come out here to the ass end of Japan to be wailed at by priests and the pox-ridden?"

"I apologize wholeheartedly for the inconvenience," said Munisai, and once more he turned back to Nakata's samurai. "Now—you. Who are you?"

The man did not stride forward. He came with his thumbs tucked into his belt, glancing around casually—showmanlike—until he sighted a length of bamboo across which paddies of rice had been hung to dry before their threshing. He shook the bundles of stalks free and then held the bamboo upright before him, inspecting it as a craftsman would. It was twice the height of a man, the trunk green and ridged and thicker than a human thigh. The samurai nodded, satisfied, and then gestured for a peasant to come hold it.

The peasant he had chosen was a young man, and he did so hesitantly, his eyes upon the ground. Nakata's man smiled at him, and when the peasant held the bamboo upright before him, the samurai put his hands back into his belt once more and turned to Munisai.

"You must know of bamboo-cutting tournaments, my honorable Munisai?" he said amicably.

"I do. That does not answer my question," said Munisai.

"Have you participated in them?"

"Yes."

"What was your record?" said the man. "How long after you cut through did it take for the split trunk to fall?"

"Two heartbeats," said Munisai.

"Two heartbeats?" said the samurai, and he nodded as if impressed. It was a minor feat—not the best, but a substantial show of skill.

Casually Nakata's samurai rolled his head on his shoulders, and then settled himself and locked his suddenly cold eyes on Munisai. Then, his sword was up in the air as though it had skipped any form of motion—it was just in the scabbard and then it was free and high in the sunlight.

What it had done was slice through the bamboo trunk. There were three heartbeats before the cut appeared, a sliver of beige emerging in the green, and it began to topple. What it had also done was slice through the left wrist of the peasant, the speed of the blow batting the severed hand into the air, and on the fourth heartbeat it and the top of the bamboo trunk met the earth.

The peasant shrieked and tumbled backward clutching at his wrist, his feet scrabbling in the dirt in some spastic attempt to flee. Dorinbo gave a cry of horror, and he went to the man's side to do what he could, other peasants coming to try to hold him still as he bucked and thrashed.

To look at Nakata's man was to know that it was no accident. The samurai ignored the desperate flurry of suffering, his eyes locked solely upon Munisai. With perfect stillness and control he lowered his sword to point at him.

"My name is Kihei Arima," he said, and he grinned a vicious grin. "I am known as the Lightning Hand, and men the length of this country call me sword-saint. Munisai Shinmen, I have come to take the title of Nation's Finest from you. Duel me. I have killed six men in single combat—you will be my seventh."

In a fluid motion he sheathed his sword and held his arms wide, waiting for formal acceptance of the challenge. He and Munisai were in a world apart from what was happening just paces from them, and Bennosuke found his gaze flickering from the pair of them to where Dorinbo was trying to force a piece of torn cloth over the stump of the peasant's wrist, his hands slick with blood.

It was an awful calmness, and it grew stranger still when, after a pause that was too long to be considered natural, Munisai began to laugh long and slow and deep.

"You think to impress me with butchery, Arima?" he said. "I'll tell you who dismembers peasants—the degenerate corpsehandlers."

"Watch your mouth, Shinmen," growled Arima, and to his side the peasant whimpered for his children to be taken away so they would not have to see.

"I will watch my tongue in the presence of those I deem worthy," said Munisai, and he was not snarling but speaking as though he were stating amusing facts. "You are a pissant torturer, and you belong in a filthy exiled hamlet along with those subhumans. This is my hall, and this is a place for warriors only."

"I am a warrior, Shinmen—and I am here to fight!" said Arima.

"Then fight Bennosuke here. He's more than a match for you," said Munisai casually, and nodded toward the boy.

It took a heartbeat for Bennosuke to comprehend just what Munisai had said. Stunned, he tore his eyes from the peasant to look at the man. He was amused still, but there was no sign of jest in his eyes. The boy felt any strength and warmth he had within himself being sucked away down some secret hole behind his stomach.

Dorinbo too had heard, and turned from where the peasant was being borne away by his friends to stare aghast at Munisai. "What are you thinking, brother?!" the monk blurted before Bennosuke could stutter a refusal. "Are you serious?"

"The boy needs more practice than sparring and empty recitals of pattern. This isn't *much* more," Munisai said, waving a dismissive hand at Arima, "but it's a start."

"You arrogant swine!" hissed Arima furiously, hand on his sword. "Fine! I accept! I'll kill your son, and then you must fight me! Agreed?"

"There's nothing to agree to—you won't get past the boy. But so be it. Agreed," he said.

Bennosuke's head was darting around, unsure of whom to look to or quite what was going on. Dorinbo was horrified, Arima was furious, Hayato was interested, but Munisai . . . The man still had the tight grin on his lips, but he was watching Bennosuke with curious, piercing eyes. Was it a challenge? If it was, Bennosuke was happy to concede defeat and back out of fighting Arima.

For the slightest of moments, Munisai's face hardened. It was almost unnoticeable, but his eyes went quickly to his own left arm, and then back to Bennosuke. The boy looked closely, and there he saw the sling. It had been concealed well, wrapped around the samurai's wrist and neck to bind the arm into a façade of strength—but it was façade alone.

The man's eyes asked if he understood. The boy did, but it did not make him feel any stronger. There was a coldness creeping through him.

"Just do it, boy. He is nothing to you," said Munisai, loud enough for everyone to hear, and then gestured with his head for the boy to get to it. Bennosuke took an uneasy step down toward the earth.

"What is he to you?" said Munisai again, his voice loud and harsh but now directed at Arima. "This piece of horseshit? This vermin who comes here and calls himself a sword-saint? This tiny-assholed, gurgling vessel of frailty and sodomy, not fit to lick the piss of dogs from the dirt beneath them? Kihei Arima, who—"

"Stop this madness!" cried Dorinbo at Munisai, and then he threw himself into Arima's path. The samurai had risen to Munisai's insults and was making toward him with his sword half out of its scabbard, wanting simply to kill rather than duel. Dorinbo tried to force the blade back in with one hand, the other vainly attempting to push him back, painting dark handprints of the peasant's blood upon the samurai's chest.

"Please, Sir Kihei—I beg you to reconsider. Bennosuke is but a boy! What purpose is there in slaying him? I beg you to stop!" pleaded the monk, but Arima had only murder on his mind. Seeing that, Dorinbo desperately thrust the samurai backward with all his weight, and did the one thing that would distract Arima—he made for the samurai's lord.

"Please, Lord Nakata," said Dorinbo, his bared arms imploring, "I understand you have grievance with Munisai, but Bennosuke is not part of it! What kind of duel is it when a man fights a boy?"

"The best kind," said Hayato with relish, and he tried to wave Dorinbo away. The monk instead fell to his knees and buried his head in the dirt at Hayato's feet. He grabbed ahold of the lord's foot and continued to plead.

"Please! I beg you! I beg you! I'll do anything you ask of me. I'll kill myself! Take my life, not his!" Dorinbo blabbered furiously. Hayato tried to step back from the monk, but Dorinbo clung on.

"Arima," the lord said disgustedly.

The samurai, eager to get back to Munisai, strode up and kicked Dorinbo hard in the ribs. The monk fell on his side wheezing, and

Arima kicked him again just to make sure. Dorinbo curled up into a ball. The Lightning Hand hovered over him, seeking any sign of defiance, then finally he spat on him.

istory is changed by the smallest of things; a single drop of rain, say, is blown by a freak gust of wind into the eyes of a ship's captain, so that in the blink that follows he misses the sign of the reef ahead, and thus a shipload of men are doomed to the depths of the sea. What left Arima's mouth was no more than a pale green gob of phlegm, but within it was the catalyst that put fire in Bennosuke's soul.

When it struck the prone monk on the side of the head, the boy felt a crazed surge of . . . he didn't know what shudder through him. His body felt warm again. The anger of months seemed clear to him then; it had no direction, and it needed none. It just was, and so he used it. It was how he wanted to feel when he had learned the fate of his mother. His heart pumped beautifully. He was no longer afraid.

With a cry of rage so vicious that it hurt his lungs, Bennosuke sprang forward and struck a blow that was more worthy of the title Lightning Hand than anything Arima could ever muster. The staff whipped around and struck the man on the side of the head with a dull crack, just as he turned back to Munisai. The man blinked, and then his jaw came loose, the bone jutting awkwardly into the flesh of his cheek.

But Arima was good; his first instinct was not to scream in pain, but to reach for his longsword and strike. Bennosuke anticipated that, and by the time the man had the weapon but a finger's breadth out of the scabbard the boy had already rapped the staff down quickly. It struck either flesh or steel, Bennosuke didn't care which, and then the sword was loose and skittering on the floor.

Arima grabbed for it desperately, but he was dizzy from the first blow and so again Bennosuke was quicker and flicked it away with the end of the wooden pole. It flashed along the ground toward the dojo, where it came to rest at the foot of the steps. One of the burgundy samurai made a move for it, but Munisai stepped over it. They glared at each other, but their focus quickly turned back to the fight.

Arima leapt back to afford himself the time to draw his short-sword. There was no legendary drawing strike this time, just a man desperately trying to defend himself. The sword slid into his hand and he raised it as a shield while he circled, all the while his jaw spasming uncontrollably.

The boy attacked warily, jabbing low at the man and keeping his distance. Arima dodged and parried, and then tried an attack of his own. Were it a longsword, it might have had some hope of striking Bennosuke, but the short blade was woefully lacking in range. It hissed by a hand's length in front of him, and it may as well have been an ocean's width for all it mattered.

Spurred on by the man's weakness and desperate for the kill, Bennosuke attacked once more, ringing in blows from a distance. He soon became aware of the irony of the situation—if Arima's weapon was too short, his was too long. The man was regaining his wits and his balance, and read every distant incoming blow well. He needed to get closer. He considered going for his own shortsword, but he had no doubt the gap he would leave as he changed weapons would be exploited lethally by Arima. They circled, and then an answer came to Bennosuke.

The boy arched the pole around once, deliberately slowly to draw Arima's guard up, and then after he had parried he made as if to barge Arima in the chest with the pole held in two hands like an oar. The man's eyes leapt with joy, and his sword arced down to strike the staff directly on its proffered center. The metal dug in deep, Bennosuke pushed with all his strength up against it, and then with a harsh snap the wood fractured and the staff was suddenly in two pieces. Arima let loose a small grunt of triumph, and Bennosuke let him savor it. It would be the last joy he felt in this life.

Casting one half of the staff aside, Bennosuke closed in and let the man slash at him. The arc of the blade seemed so slow and so clumsy, and to snatch the man's wrist as it lingered before him so very easy. He jerked Arima's arm toward him and then smashed the remaining half of the staff savagely into the sword-saint's forearm.

Though a sword might cut through a war staff with ease, a human arm is not hardened, folded steel. Arima screamed as his wrist shattered and his hand went limp. The sword slipped from his powerless fingers and Bennosuke kicked it away disgustedly.

The joyous, terrible ecstasy of his first victory came upon the boy then, and he smashed the man on the bridge of the nose with the butt of the staff. That too shattered and erupted in blood, and suddenly Arima, with his jaw hanging off and his nose flattened, looked unrecognizable.

His eyes were spinning in wild panic, and widened further as Bennosuke grabbed him by the collar in an iron grip with his left hand. He drew back the staff and struck him three times in the head, each blow horrendous. The man's skull reverberated like a pot, and then his eye socket shattered on the second blow, and then he was on his knees at the third. But Bennosuke would not let him fall. He held on to the collar, blood dripping onto his fist, keeping the man from cowering into a ball.

"Please . . . Don't kill me . . ." Arima managed through a mangled face, eye flapping on its stem, his voice pathetic in the silence.

Bennosuke struck him remorselessly again and again until he was more than dead, the man's skull caved in and the pink of his brains glistening in the midday sun. Only then did he drop the corpse. It hit the ground with a sad, dull thump, and then the blood soaked into the dust and turned it dark. The Lightning Hand, who had killed six men, was no more.

Moments passed. Bennosuke looked at his shaking hands. They were covered in gore. A fragment of skull winked at him from his knuckle that was wrapped around the bloody remnants of the staff. He flicked the chip away with his free hand as though in a dream, his lungs bellowing from somewhere distant, and then he slowly became aware of the onlookers once more.

Munisai on the steps, his face unreadable. The rest of the burgundy samurai, eyes wide in shock, banner flapping in the breeze and swords undrawn. The crowd of peasants gathered around, once again witnessing the terrible results of a Shinmen's anger. Dorinbo, on his knees, staring riveted in horror at the mangled corpse of Arima.

"You are Munisai's son," the monk breathed quietly.

He thought of going to his uncle, of picking him up and tending his wounds, but then he saw Hayato standing behind the monk, and the fury within him was suddenly renewed. With the bloodied half-staff in one hand he drew his shortsword with the other, and stalked toward the lord. He held the weapons to either side of him, exposing his body and inviting—daring—the lord to strike.

"Are you samurai?" the boy hissed, looking down into the shorter man's face. Hayato's rigid expression of terror and outrage seemed . . . right. The lord made no attempt to answer, nor to go for his swords.

"Are you samurai?!" Bennosuke asked again, and then he spat in Hayato's face as his champion had to Dorinbo. That seemed to wake him from his shock. The lord rubbed the gob away, and his eyes started to dart between Bennosuke and what was left of Arima as he backed slowly away.

"You . . ." he began.

"Yes," whispered Bennosuke, and then Hayato's courage gave in. He turned and fled, mounting his horse at a scrambling canter and barreling through the crowd. Wordlessly his retinue of samurai followed after him in disarray, the herald casting the banner aside to fall in the dirt. They kicked their horses as fast as they dared go through the narrow paths, and Bennosuke guessed faster still once they were over the ridge and gone.

He didn't care at that moment, for suddenly a great weariness came into him. He turned to look at Munisai. The man nodded once. Bennosuke nodded back, and then slowly staggered off. His legs had grown weak without him noticing. The crowd of peasants, as always, parted and bowed before him like a gust of wind blowing through a field of long grass. Blood-splattered and bruised, a man's brains on his fists, for the first time he could understand why they did it.

THE PEASANT HAD his stump cauterized and bound, and as he lay upon a hard mat passing in and out of fevered consciousness, his fellow villagers helped Dorinbo take Arima's body and burn it on a small pyre. It was a proper and decent ceremony, and though it was begrudging they did it because they knew they were not gods but men, and so it was not their place to pass judgment.

That evening, a band of ravens clustered around the patch of earth where Arima had died. They had come for the tiny scraps of meat that had been left upon the ground, but though they were long devoured the birds remained, cawing and circling.

Munisai sat watching them, his arm unbound once more. The cool evening air felt good upon it. His mind was occupied, mulling over the day's events. Thus at first he didn't notice Dorinbo walking slowly toward him, but when his brother was close enough Munisai could smell the charnel smoke upon him. Deliberately, slowly, Munisai let his eyes meet the monk's.

"Are you happy?" said Dorinbo angrily.

"Yes," he said. "Now I know the boy is good. Now I know that Yoshiko's bastard is worthy of my name."

"Your *name*," said Dorinbo, and a grim, disbelieving smile appeared on his face. "I don't suppose you considered Bennosuke could have died?"

"I did. But, as I said, now we know that he is good."

"He's thirteen years old, Munisai."

"My point exactly."

"There is something wrong with you," said Dorinbo, accusingly. "Even for a samurai, there's only death and murder in your mind."

Munisai merely looked at his brother, seeing the hostility on his face. A voice within him urged him to tell the monk that he was wrong—to speak of the parts of his mind that were not filled with slaughter, but rather with the dreams he had of Yoshiko, of how she haunted him, of how he longed to set things right. But, as he always was, he was samurai, and so he kept quiet. Dorinbo waited for a response, and upon receiving none sighed and turned away.

"Fine. So be it. Gain a son, lose a brother. Do not look to me anymore," he said, and walked away into the darkening night. Munisai watched him go. Dorinbo would see sense, eventually. Hopefully.

It had been the monk who had opened Munisai's eyes, after all. The samurai knew that he could not have faced Arima's drawing strike wounded as he was, and so he had tried to goad him into senseless anger, to draw his sword out of the scabbard before Munisai was anywhere near it. Putting Bennosuke forward to fight had been a calculated insult, nothing more. Had it gone wrong and come to Arima attacking the boy, Munisai would have leapt in from the side, honor be damned, and taken his throat out with the shortsword—but it hadn't. Arima had been about to lose himself to his fury, to charge Munisai, and then Dorinbo had intervened.

And so it turned out that it had been Bennosuke who had charged blindly, and seeing what came after that had put something deep and warm within Munisai. When he had started to train the boy, he had hoped merely to raise him right so that he might earn Yoshiko's forgiveness, but now . . . Oh, the boy was strong. The boy was fast. That would make him good, certainly. What was better was that he was clever. That might make him great. His future was bright, and the thought of being able to be part of that dazzled Munisai.

Yet one thing kept flashing in his mind. Bennosuke had spat in Nakata's face. He had spat in the face of the son of a great lord. It was the crudest, strongest of insults. Given how Nakata had reacted over one little barb after the battle with the Kanno, Munisai found himself wondering how the lord would react to this. What would it sow?

That was a problem for tomorrow. Tonight, there was just a profound sense of satisfaction he had not felt in years—not since he had held the infant Bennosuke in his arms, or marveled as the boy unsteadily took his first steps, or excitedly made the boy repeat his first word.

Perhaps Dorinbo was right. Perhaps there was something wrong inside him. Today he had seen the death of a man, and the truth was it had made him feel like a father again.

Over the far side of the valley's ridge, down around the burned ruins of the village, the fireflies danced in the darkness.

Part Two

BLOODFLOWER

犧牲

CHAPTER SEVEN

Bennosuke sat rolling a stalk of grass between his fingers emptily. The sun above him was there in appearance only and a chill had worked its way into him. That was good. Two days had passed since the duel with Arima, and ever since he had felt a desire for solace, a desire for numbness.

Memories were hazy; Arima's corpse he could recall with perfect clarity, but since then it was as though his head were dulled with some form of poison. Focus came and went, came and went.

Surprisingly, Tasumi had been the first to be with him in the evening after the fight; the samurai had been away in the afternoon collecting fees from neighboring villages. Bennosuke was sitting in the garden of Munisai's estate, not knowing where else to go, his clothes still streaked in gore. Wordlessly Tasumi entered and began to check the boy over for wounds.

"What are you playing at, you little maniac? Leaping into battle . . . You could have been killed," he muttered. His hands were warm. Bennosuke said nothing.

"A staff, your father tells me. A staff. Says you cracked his jaw with your first strike," Tasumi continued, and then a smile came to his lips. "Wish I could have seen it. You should be dead, a boy of your age fighting a man—but I suppose you're our Musashi, eh?"

Musashi Benkei was an ancient warrior of legend, a huge man who wielded a staff like no other. The tale went that he held a bridge single-handedly in order to buy time for his lord and his family to perform dignified seppuku, slaying dozens of the enemy as they came to him. He died on his feet with his staff still in his hands, run through a score of times and riddled with arrows. Not one man had passed him, and both his and his lord's honor were ensured. It was held as a paragon of a good death.

Bennosuke wondered whether Musashi had ever hit a man until his skull burst open. But then, the slaughter was always so very clean in the old tales: evil men came to the hero, and then they were dead. As Tasumi's hands traced his flesh, Bennosuke looked upon the blood spattered across his kimono, and saw it had dried a dirty, muddy brown.

The night passed, and most of the morning too, and then he found himself at the temple alongside Dorinbo once more. Instead of binding, though, he was doing something taboo: looking at one of the prayers. The characters upon the yellowed paper seemed alien to him, perhaps because they were civilized and he was not sure if he had the right to read them any longer.

He looked up to find his uncle watching him. It took a moment for the boy to remember he was doing something forbidden.

"Sorry," he said.

"It matters little in the end," Dorinbo said casually. "How are you feeling?"

"I don't know . . . The same, I think," said Bennosuke. "Is that good?"

"I wouldn't know," he said.

"It wasn't like I expected . . . Was it cruel?" asked Bennosuke.

"All death is cruel, Bennosuke."

"But he was beating you," said the boy. "I saved you."

"And that makes it righteous, does it?"

"Yes."

"The strong protecting the weak?" said Dorinbo.

"I'm not calling you weak, I—" began Bennosuke, but the monk interrupted him.

"That's not what I meant at all," Dorinbo said. "What of the man Arima cut the hand from? His name is Akatani. Did you know that? Or was he just a peasant to you? He has three children. He's a thatcher—or he was. Where was your righteous slaughter in his defense?"

Bennosuke could not answer, and at that a grim light of vindication came into Dorinbo's eyes.

"Thus you see the insidious form of samurai chivalry. I'm surprised Munisai has managed to drill it into you so soon," said the monk. "Where men think themselves brave for saving another—but only save those who happen to bear the same name. Let the others burn, for out of the million million things upon this earth, the only ones worth concern are the ones bound to you by such an incidental thing as blood."

"But you don't share my blood, do you?" said Bennosuke coldly.

He immediately regretted it. The bitterness that had crept onto Dorinbo's face as he had spoken vanished instantly, replaced by a moment of genuine hurt. The monk turned away and returned to his work.

Bennosuke watched him. He was angry and ashamed and he felt tears form behind his eyes. Though he wanted to he knew that he could not bring himself to explain that he had not charged out of conscious choice but out of furious instinct, that he had been too scared to fight Arima before his uncle's humiliation removed any thought higher than *kill* from his mind. It was better to be thought of as wicked or callous than as a coward or a mindless beast.

"I'm sorry," said the boy eventually. It was all he could allow himself.

"You don't need to say that, Bennosuke," said the monk, and he looked up for a moment with a sad empty smile. "I thought I might guide you toward the path of the scholar. That you might seek to better the world rather than batter it, but . . . Blood really is incidental, isn't it? You really are the son of Munisai—you were born to be samurai."

I have failed were the words he neglected to speak, but Bennosuke could see them written all over the monk, in the deadness of his eyes and the hollowness of his voice. The boy could not bear to see that disappointment, and so he put his head down and returned to weaving. When he thought his eyes dry and he could breathe without tightness in his chest, words came back to him.

"Why can't I be both?" he asked.

"Both of what?" asked Dorinbo.

"A samurai, and a scholar."

"One defeats the other. Why do you think the samurai consider it a punishment to shave your head and take a monk's vows?"

"I don't know, but . . . why can't a samurai use his strength to seek enlightenment?"

"Because it's like trying to examine darkness with a flaming torch—one destroys the other. To think on things needs a great calmness. To fight, something else entirely."

"I disagree. There's a moment between day and night that is equal, isn't there? Right before the dawn. Why can't a man be that?"

"Because that's not the way men are, Bennosuke. It's sad but true," said Dorinbo, sighing once more.

"No, you're wrong. That is the kind of man I will become."

"Indeed," said his uncle, but his voice was empty.

There was another jump in his memory, another night lost, and now here he was playing with grass like he was a child again. Munisai had summoned him at last, and he could put it off no longer. Bennosuke tossed the stalk to one side as he stood, and as he walked through the village he could feel the nervous eyes of the peasants on his back. He paid them no heed.

"I SUPPOSE," MUNISAI began, "you are aware that Arima was not actually a sword-saint?"

"Yes, Lord," said Bennosuke.

Munisai was kneeling on a cushion, a pan of water boiling before him. Though he was arrayed in a formal posture, the weight of his body upon his calves beneath him, he had exposed his wound to the afternoon air; it looked ugly naked, the slight stench of rot in the air. The samurai clenched and unclenched his left fist as he spoke, and though Bennosuke was sitting a polite and formal distance away, he could not help but notice the feebleness of it.

"What were the clues?" Munisai asked.

"When I countered his strongest attack, his technique afterward was unbelievably weak."

"And what does that teach you?"

"That a true master knows more than to focus on only one kind of weapon or attack, Lord."

"Very astute," said Munisai, and leaned forward to pour the boiling water into a small pewter dish where a small mound of green tea powder awaited. "There's a foolish mentality that pervades Japan: men focus on a single school of swordsmanship, one style, one weapon, one attack until they are perfect at it. That's a beautiful thing, until someone learns how to counter it. Then what good is it? The key to being a good swordsman is to be a good spearman, a good archer, and a good horseman as well. To that end, tell me what your martial training has been this week."

"Seven hours with the longsword, three with the short. Five hours unarmed combat, and two with the spear. Four hours archery, and two of weapon throwing. With the staff—"

"We all saw your staff training. Short, messy, but practical. Show me . . ." Munisai said, and swirled the tea around the dish as he deliberated. "Show me your shortsword technique."

Bennosuke bowed, rose to his feet, drew his weapon from its scabbard, and began running through the rhythmic patterns he'd practiced. *Left slash, downward slash, parry, riposte, right slash, rotate the blade, thrust, pa—*

Munisai suddenly lashed out with his good arm, throwing the dish like a discus. Bennosuke saw the motion out of the corner of his eye, too late to stop it crashing into the side of his head. The dish shattered, the water not scalding but hot enough. Bennosuke clutched his face.

"Be mindful of your peripherals, boy, at all times. That is where the attack that claims you will come from," said Munisai.

"Is that where your wound came from?" said Bennosuke acidly. Munisai bristled.

"Clean that up, and fetch me a new dish!" he barked, and Bennosuke grudgingly obeyed. When he had finished he returned to kneeling. Munisai was silent for a spell, drinking from his fresh saucer, and slowly Bennosuke felt the rancor drain out of the room.

"Did you notice how I goaded Arima?" said Munisai eventually. "How I made him do what I wanted simply with my voice, made him so angry he became reckless? Now he is dead because of it, and I suppose there is a lesson there for both of us. We should try to be calm with each other."

Bennosuke was surprised at that. It was the first civil thing he could recall Munisai saying to him in months. In the silence that followed, the boy allowed his gaze to rise to find the man looking at him differently also; eyes evaluating him meticulously. When Munisai spoke next his words were slow and considered, his voice somber:

"You must be berated," he said. "What you fought with Arima was not a duel proper. You gave no warning—you struck as you shouted your intention to attack and hit him first as he turned. There must always be a warning, even if only a matter of instants. The other must prepare himself. This is what civilizes the act of killing, raises it above common murder. As samurai, we must observe this. What you fought was an ambush, nothing more."

Bennosuke began to protest, but Munisai raised a finger that silenced him. "I say this only as a matter of protocol, however, for what matters most is—you *won*. At thirteen, you won. I must admit, boy, there is great potential in you."

To his surprise, Bennosuke found himself embarrassed by the compliment. "How old were you when you first killed a man?" he asked, trying to divert attention.

"Fifteen. A battlefield. My first lethal duel was at seventeen," said Munisai.

"How did you feel?"

"What do you mean?"

"Did you feel proud, or happy, or . . . ?" the boy asked, and then hesitated at the look of incomprehension on Munisai's face.

"I never felt much of anything. I was young and stupid and thought the world was mine, so I never doubted my victory," he said, and then his brow creased further and he carried on as though the words were alien to him. "What a strange question. Why do you ask? How do *you* feel?"

"I . . . don't know. It felt good when I knew I had won. I felt powerful, I suppose," said Bennosuke, uncomfortably. "But I've been thinking. There was this strange look in his eyes—"

"Eye," said Munisai blackly.

"Whatever it was, it was strange in a way I can't describe. It was . . ."

"Honest," finished Munisai.

"Yes," agreed Bennosuke slowly. Munisai let a small smile cross his mouth.

"One thing you will learn is that although men will laugh and cry, shout and beat their chests, it is more often than not a masquerade. But of course there are some times in our life when we cannot pretend to be anything other than what we are, and right before we die is one of them."

"Arima begged and cried," said Bennosuke, seeing the man's face once more.

"Yes. He was not a strong man, and so he is dead."

"So, what I did was . . . justified? Dorinbo said that all death is cruel."

"My brother is wise in his arts, but his realm is that of life. You and I, we are samurai, and our realm is death. My knowledge of such things supersedes his—ignore his advice on this."

"Yes, Lord," said Bennosuke, though he still felt indecision. He turned his eyes to the floor once more and pondered. Munisai watched the boy for a few minutes, slowly sipping his tea. When the dish was empty, he grunted and then spoke.

"Very well," he said, and with his good hand he slowly reached for his longsword where it lay to his side and slid it between the pair of them. The curve of the weapon was perfect and elegant, the lacquer scabbard glimmering.

"This is the sword awarded to me when I was named the Nation's Finest," said Munisai. "It was forged one hundred years ago by the master swordsmith Sengo Muramasa in Ise province. Its steel was tempered in the great fires, folded fourteen times so that it might prove true, and then cooled with water from the holiest of our shrines. Its weight is faultless, its sharpness beyond compare. Legend states that were I to dip this sword into a river, leaves caught in the current would split themselves against the blade, then reform whole after they passed, so clean would be its cuts. Four warriors wielded it before I have: Ichiro Murasaki, who wandered the length of Japan; Yosuke Ishimura, who defeated all but his brother; Takuya Fukushige, who was loved by all he met; and Toshiro Aibagawa, who was hated by all but his master. Hold it."

Hesitantly, Bennosuke reached forward and placed his hands on the sword. He lifted it slowly, awestruck, and felt a sudden exhilaration rush through him. Here was the meaning of samurai—what he held was to him an instrument of God.

"How does it feel?" asked Munisai.

"Incredible, Lord. It's like the ghosts of those men are with me now. The weapon is beautiful, and it—"

"It's a tool, boy, nothing more. I made that history up. It is not done for a samurai to lose himself to mystique—you should be able to do your duty equally as well with the cheapest blade forged by the most hopeless of apprentices," said Munisai. Castigated, Bennosuke cast his eyes down and made to replace the weapon, but Munisai raised his hand in a halting gesture. "No, keep it. It's yours now."

"Lord?" asked Bennosuke.

"A boy cannot kill a man. Thus you must become a man."

Bennosuke was silent. He considered the weapon in his hands for a moment, and then slowly placed it beside himself. Then he bowed low, placing his forehead on the ground and holding the pose. Munisai was surprised at the boy's restraint, the mature observation of protocol in place of gushing. He remembered how his senses had been dazzled and his chest had swollen what felt like threefold when he had been granted the longsword many years ago.

"Rise, Bennosuke Shinmen," said Munisai slowly, and the boy did as he was bidden. When he had returned to a kneeling position, Munisai nodded to him.

"A sword may just be a tool, but a name is not. You carry my name, and you are a man now. You must act accordingly. Do you understand?" he said. Munisai then produced a folded sheaf of paper sealed with his personal crest and held it out to the boy. "This is formal acknowledgment of you as my son, of your ascension to adulthood, and of your eligibility for service and duty."

Bennosuke hesitated. The sword he would accept without question, for that had been his dream as long as he could remember. But if he took the document it meant that he also formally acknowledged

Munisai as his father. He thought of the blinding rage of the past months, of the fantasies of one day killing the man.

Perhaps Munisai knew this. He did not force the paper on Bennosuke; he held his hand out steady, waiting to see if he would take it. It was another challenge, but within his eyes Bennosuke saw something different. Rather than amusement at his weakness and failure, there seemed a desire for him to overcome. For the first time, Munisai was looking at him as though he were human.

Thoughts of Yoshiko and his peasant father whose name he would never know came to him. But as he looked into their murderer's eyes, he could not deny that the acknowledgment there gave him pride. The sessions with the armor, the long doubt of his youth—finally some of that could be dispelled.

There was the opportunity to make some grand, dramatic gesture by smashing the paper away and spitting and raging, but he knew he would not do it, for it would be a charade only. In the months since he had learned the truth, what had taken hold was what Dorinbo had asked him immediately afterward—did he ever truly know his mother? To whom did he owe loyalty but an imagined specter?

Guilt lingered, though, and Munisai saw the indecision in him. After a long moment the samurai spoke in a voice quiet enough that even if others had been present would be heard by the pair of them alone.

"Do you think this world is perfect, boy?" he said. "Do you think this is the way I would have wanted it? Life is what it is. Surrender your immaculate hopes and bear what you can. That is all we can do."

Though he could not explain why just then, Bennosuke reached for the letter, and as he took it from Munisai's hands he bowed his head low. In later years he would think back and acknowledge that maybe Munisai was right. They were not perfect but fundamentally hollow, and each filled some of the absence within the other as a phantom approximation of necessity for son or father. It was too bleak to be alone, and so they could do nothing but cling to each other as broken beings, as human beings.

"Good." Munisai nodded, and a rare, small smile crept across his face for a moment. "Good. Now—you cannot stay in Miyamoto weaving prayers any longer. The sky is blue, water is wet, and samurai serve; it is time for you to learn to do so. Go to the town of Aramaki and report to Captain Tomodzuna there. He is a man I trained myself, a good man, and I trust him and all those beneath him. You will serve him alongside those men."

"Doing what?" asked Bennosuke.

"Whatever he asks of you. Listen to him. Learn from him. Report to him and no one else—and remember that he knows me, and he will know that you are my son. Do not disgrace yourself. Do not disgrace me."

"What of you, Lord?"

"I will join you in a matter of weeks. There is business I have to attend to. Secret orders from our Lord Shinmen," said Munisai, and at the sudden interest in the boy's face he added, "Secret enough that I cannot tell even you."

"I understand, Lord," said Bennosuke.

"You will leave tomorrow—prepare yourself," said Munisai.

"I understand, Lord," the boy repeated, and this time he bowed once more, rose, and left.

Munisai watched Bennosuke go, determination in the boy's eyes. He smiled to himself. How easy the young were to fool—"secret orders" indeed. He had had no word from Lord Shinmen. These "orders" were given by himself to himself and they were but one word: heal.

His enfeeblement had dragged on too long; he needed to be strong again. He reasoned that training Bennosuke every day, with the exertions tearing constantly at the wound, must have been hindering any progress, and his hope was that given a few weeks to rest and tend to it gently in solitude, the flesh might start to mend.

The alternative, that perhaps it was mangled beyond repair already . . .

The other worry—that of the Nakata—was also taken care of by sending Bennosuke to Aramaki. Once he joined Captain Tomodzuna, the samurai's cadre of men would become a shield for the boy. An attack on one of them would be an attack on all of them, and though the captain kept his men well drilled and Munisai did not doubt their courage or ability to physically protect the boy, the real strength of their shelter was that they were Shinmen's men in Shinmen's town.

Hayato would not be able to get at Bennosuke without starting a bloodbath with allies of his father, and that was a political affront the brat would not be afforded. Going for Munisai as an individual as he had done was an entirely different thing, for it was expected that one who held the title of Nation's Finest would receive challenges from time to time—why not Arima, on behalf of his master?

Neither would he be able to seek Bennosuke out as he had done with Munisai, for the notion of a lord calling a thirteen-year-old without rank or prestige to duel was so absurd it would invite ridicule. Though Bennosuke had spat in his face and that might draw some long enmity, that was a lingering trouble for the future. This was now, and for now the boy was safe under Tomodzuna.

In any case, Munisai expected that the young lord was back at his father's side safe in his court, refusing to admit to anyone what had happened and how badly he had lost his gamble. Reputation was everything to a vain coward like Hayato, he well knew.

Everything to men who carry swords, the sneering ache of his wound reminded him. Munisai set his face and concentrated on squeezing his fist tight enough that he might hold a blade, and he found that he could not feel his fingertips upon his palm.

The owning of the sword put Bennosuke into another daze; trying its weight and searching for the balance of it, obsessing over its every inch like a blind man reading lines upon a face. He allowed himself the conceit of swaggering through the village with it at his side several times, but was disappointed when the reactions of the peasants were much the same—to them he was still one who controlled their life and death at a whim, only now he had a slightly longer reach.

Bennosuke slept, and then he found himself standing on the landward ridge of the village the next morning, a traveling pack strapped across his back and the swords at his side. The sun was still rising, the sky peach and yellow, and the warmth felt strange upon his newly exposed scalp. For the first time he wore his hair in the adult style, his crown shaved and the remaining hair oiled, bound, and folded upward to lie atop his head in a thin dark line.

Tasumi, Dorinbo, and Munisai were there with him. Though they had stopped ostensibly to have a final look across Miyamoto, instead he found himself looking at them.

Here were the three men who had shaped his life: the samurai, who had put muscle to bone, sword to hand. The monk, who had taught him of goodness and the wonder of the world. The father, who . . . The father.

Munisai became aware of the boy's gaze, turned, and spoke flatly: "You shouldn't linger."

None of them really knew how best to begin, and so Tasumi took the initiative as well as he could, awkwardly stepping forward and bowing to Bennosuke while he murmured platitudes of health and good fortune. They were vague and uncertain, and after Bennosuke returned them equally tentatively there was an uncomfortable pause between them, until the samurai suddenly exclaimed, "Ah, I should give you a gift, shouldn't I?"

He patted around himself, flustered, searching for something appropriate, and soon he reached up one of his billowing sleeves. He emerged eventually with a small throwing dagger held in a sheath that could be bound to the arm.

"Here, you can never have too many," he said, handing it to Bennosuke. "Do us proud, eh?"

"I'm your Musashi, remember?" said Bennosuke, and his uncle smiled. The dour samurai clapped the boy on the shoulder once, bowed, and then stepped back.

Dorinbo came next. His face was hard and his eyes grave. They bowed to each other, and then Bennosuke handed the monk a folded sheet of paper.

"It's a prayer, Uncle. Please don't read it. Burn it with the others," said the boy. Dorinbo nodded. He bowed and then made to step back without saying anything, but he stopped himself.

"What you told me you wanted to be . . . perhaps you can. All you can do is try," he said. "And remember . . . do not follow a creed or others blindly. You have a choice in everything."

"I understand, Uncle. Thank you," said Bennosuke, and though he smiled Dorinbo remained tense.

"Remember that the only choice you have is to do as Captain Tomodzuna bids," Munisai said as Bennosuke turned to him, and there seemed to be rare mirth in his eyes. They flickered toward Dorinbo, but the monk acted as though no one had spoken. The amusement withered and for a moment the boy became aware of a coldness between the two men, but he ignored it. He bowed to Munisai and said:

"I shall serve him faithfully, Lord."

"I've given you everything you need already," said Munisai, and nodded at the sword at the boy's side. "Keep your head down in labor, keep it up if others question your honor—try to be samurai, Bennosuke."

"I will, Lord," said Bennosuke, who bowed once more and then said in a low voice, "I hope that your mission does not hinder you too long, also."

"It shall be accomplished," said Munisai, face entirely straight. "But it is no concern of yours any longer. Nothing here is. Focus on what is ahead of you, boy."

"I understand and obey, Lord," said Bennosuke, and then they looked each other in the eye. For the first time, Bennosuke realized he was taller than Munisai.

After a moment the samurai jerked his chin toward the path leading away from Miyamoto, and the country beyond it. Bennosuke turned and took a few hesitant steps toward it. It was not the first time he had left the village, but it would be the last time that he would call it home. The boy looked back.

"Too scared?" asked Munisai, before anyone else could speak.

Bennosuke clenched his jaw. He bowed low one final time and forced himself to walk.

"Good," said Munisai at the boy's back, and turned back toward the village. Tasumi soon followed.

Before Miyamoto vanished entirely from his sight, Bennosuke stopped one last time. He turned for a final look, unsure of when he would see the village again—if he would see it again—and he found that Dorinbo was still watching him, small as he was in the distance. The boy waved a hand to the monk, who clasped his hands together into the prayer position and raised them high to the sun in farewell.

Bennosuke swallowed and carried on walking. Perhaps Amaterasu would be watching over him.

CHAPTER EIGHT

The first pang of true loneliness hit Bennosuke that night. He had used some of the modest amount of coin Munisai had given him to pay for a bed in a small country inn. Other men slept alongside him, snoring contentedly, but Bennosuke felt his guts twist and thought he might vomit.

He had thought himself alone in the village, but the fact was he had simply been ignored. Dorinbo and Tasumi had been there each day for him. That night he had eaten dinner in a crowded room and he had never felt more isolated. Everyone seemed to belong to a group but him, and he was certain people were glancing at him, whispering about this strange, rash-marked supposed samurai.

It did not help that he did not feel like himself. It was more than just the new styling of his hair; for the first time he was dressed like a man. In addition to the sword, Munisai had given him some of his clothes as well, so that now instead of a practical, rough dark kimono, frayed around the edges, he wore garments of fine silk—the underclothes beige and patterned subtly with interlocking zigzags, the overjacket that left his arms free and hung down beneath his waist a deep dragonfly green. Gone from his feet were the comfortable straw sandals of youth, and in their place were square wooden ones that raised his soles a finger's length above the earth to keep his stockings free of any dirt and keep his posture dignified.

He was out of place in body and mind, and it would get worse, he knew. These were simple strangers, most of them traveling merchants or artisans, barely a sword among them. When he got to Captain Tomodzuna and his barracks, he could scarcely imagine how other samurai who knew his father would treat him.

This, he realized, was the price of the longsword. He had thought earning the weapon would be liberating, but instead it was exactly the opposite. Freedom had been afforded to him as a child—the freedom to vanish when he felt shy and to work as hard or as little as he liked. His only masters had been himself and his family until now, but now the sword anchored him to the world and bound him to serve.

Munisai served Shinmen—more than that, trusted him. This was being a man, and this he would have to endure. He had entered the realm of death when he had killed Arima, and now he would have to adjust himself to resigning any individual claim to his body. His soul was his own, and with his body Shinmen or Tomodzuna or whoever above him could do as they pleased, command what they liked of it. Bennosuke would prove himself samurai, and worthy of Munisai's legacy.

His father's legacy, he meant. He would have to get used to saying that. The summer had passed so quickly, and his world of this autumn was not the same as the one of spring. Everything still felt strange, and he hoped that time away from the man would allow him to gather his thoughts and for a new mind-set to calcify.

The legacy of his actual father bore down on him also. Every samurai could trace his bloodline back through a dozen generations; surely that meant that ancestry mattered. Bennosuke knew he could fight, but so could a mad dog. Would the peasant blood in him reveal some innate cowardliness or ignobility?

A shiver passed through him. It felt as though cold and heavy shackles were around his arms and legs and neck, and these he knew were the ones of adulthood. In response to this he, the supposed man, pulled the blanket over himself like a child hiding from imagined monsters, and waited for morning.

THE TOWN OF Aramaki was the closest settlement of any size to Miyamoto, and though it paled in scope to a city proper, it had grown prosperous enough to banish any trace of the rural. Its great fortune was that it was sited upon the major road that led from the western tip of the isle of Honshu to Kyoto, golden Kyoto, and so the wealth of a quarter of a nation's worth of merchants and traders passed through it.

So audacious had this made the town that they had paved the streets in stone, wide and flat to ease the use of carts—actual carts with great wheels and pulled by oxen or horse, not litters hoisted aloft on the shoulders of men, as was the norm—and these teams of man and beast lined up at clogged intersections.

Throngs of people flowed around and between them, a thousand different missions for the day; there an apprentice seeking raw material for his master, there a messenger skittering on his heels bearing a sealed lacquer tube as fast as he could, there a courtesan worrying that the waxpaper parasol above her brow was held at the perfect alluring and feminine angle. To see and be among them all was bewildering for Bennosuke.

He had been to the town a few times before, but he had been young and had simply sat on Tasumi's horse while the samurai had gone about his business. The place had seemed a lot less smothering sitting above the thrust and press of the crowd, and now he struggled to tell the difference between one street and the next. To him it seemed there was only one building after another; another inn, another blacksmith, another merchant loudly hawking his goods to all passing by.

Eventually he stumbled upon the guardhouse, though it would have been easy to miss it. It was a squat, ugly thing, the dark tiled roof of it emerging above eaved stone walls blackened by the years, humbled by the surrounding merchant warehouses and inns that displayed their wealth in lurid paint and elaborate carvings.

The moat surrounding it had once been five paces across, but the widening of the roads for ease of commerce had not taken the economics of sieges into consideration, and so what was left was essentially a gutter the depth of which was twice the height of a man. The original bridge remained, though, arcing out into the street and providing a small amount of shade for laborers to sit in and doze.

Atop the gateway were two severed samurai heads upon spikes, their hair immaculate and their faces as clean as men just bathed. Beneath them carved on slabs of wood were their names. The pair must have been executed in the morning and they would be gone by the evening most likely, for to let any sign of rotting or corruption show would be an obscene disgrace to even the gravest of enemies.

Indeed, a man waited diligently with a long pole to swat at any bird that might try to peck at them, as the two were not displayed to be humiliated; they were there to show from the cleanness of the cuts to their necks that they had died a dignified seppuku and all shame was therefore expunged. It was no hanging threat of law, but an example of fine men who believed in it and the moral order of all things, and who had demonstrated that belief in the purest fashion.

Redeemed though the pair might have been, their dead gaze did nothing for Bennosuke's nerves. He stood before them for a few moments summoning the courage to enter. First impressions counted a lot, and he knew that his rash already counted against him. These were the men who would hold his life as theirs, and he needed to convince them that he was worthy of that trust. He clutched his hand around the longsword at his side, and pushed on over the hump of the bridge.

The courtyard within was practical in design, square and hard and bereft of tree or sand or art, but also, mercifully, of the crowd of the street. A handful of Shinmen's samurai were there, engaged in labor or drills or hearing the complaints and disputes of storeowners and travelers who felt themselves wronged. Lining one wall was a low, wooden cage in which miserable men sat in filthy sawdust awaiting judgment.

Bennosuke had no eyes for any of them. He had set his face in what he thought was confidence, somewhere between earnestness and a scowl, and he marched directly to the guardhouse proper. An aging samurai sat cross-legged in a room open to the day, a small forecourt in which people could stand without removing their sandals before him.

The man was leafing slowly through a ledger of yellowed paper, and did not look up as Bennosuke approached. The boy swallowed as he strode, his stomach squirming. In his head, he practiced the lines he had been muttering under his breath all morning and ran through the motions of his hands as he would present Munisai's missive. When he came before the man he snapped out a bow he hoped was appropriately military.

"Sir," he said, "I seek Captain Tomodzuna."

"You're out of luck, then, I'm afraid," said the samurai, eyes not leaving the ledger. "The earthquake last week caused a landslide up in the hills. He's away assessing damage to the roads."

"Oh," said Bennosuke. Suddenly his preparation was for naught; Munisai had told him to report to the captain alone, so what now? He found his throat growing tight and he barely managed to croak, "Ahh, when will he back?"

"Tomorrow, most likely," said the man. "I'm the lieutenant here, though—can I help you with anything?"

"Ah, no," said Bennosuke, and as his face began to warm he put all his concentration into keeping a stammer from his voice, hoping not to betray any hint of indecision. "I'll, ah, I'll come back tomorrow, then."

The lieutenant looked up at him for the first time, putting the document down. "Are you all right, lad?" he asked, seeing the unease of the boy. "Are you in trouble?"

"No, no, I'm fine, really," said Bennosuke, his mind whispering to him that he was a fool and it was going wrong and he had to leave, he had to flee. "I'll be going, ah, thank you."

The boy bowed twice like a lowly courtier opening a door for a noble would, and then scuttled back across the courtyard and out of the gate as fast as he dared, feeling the back of his neck burning.

The lieutenant rose to his feet stiffly, slid his feet into a pair of sandals, and slowly walked out into the courtyard trying to work the crick from his back. He watched the strange boy until he was gone, and though he was merely bemused by the encounter, he became aware that someone had taken a far more vivid interest in the lad—in the cage, one of the prisoners was pressed up against the bars.

"Friend of yours?" the lieutenant asked, strolling to stand before him.

"You have to let me out now," said the prisoner, eyes locked on the space where the boy had been.

"It seems you have a fundamental misunderstanding of the way jails function," said the lieutenant.

"I've sobered up. You can't keep me here—I've committed no crime."

"Is that so?"

"A few tables overturned," muttered the prisoner.

"You struck that girl, and don't even try to deny it. Face was all swollen up, the poor thing."

"It was a backhand, I didn't punch her . . ." said the captive, and when that simply hardened the lieutenant's face, he sighed and waved a resigned hand. "Then I'll give her a handful of coins, or a bucketful—do you know who my master is?"

"Yes," grunted the lieutenant ruefully. "There's a reason you're better off than some of your friends in there."

Within the cage the handful of other captives glowered through bruises and scabbed blood. The prisoner, an empty stomach the worst of his maladies, ignored them.

"If you know who he is, then you know to let me out now," he said to the lieutenant, and for all he wanted to deny it, the lieutenant knew this was so.

After a few moments he reluctantly produced a bundle of iron keys from his waist and began to search through them.

"Think that could be you up there?" he asked, nodding at the backs of the two heads over the gateway as he flicked the keys around the ring one by one. "That kind of dignity? There's a place, you know, where they send the savages—the thieves and the arsonists and the ravagers of women—and you don't get that kind of respect. There's scourges and nails and red-hot iron and all kinds of things, and if you're not careful, lad, no matter who your friends are—"

"Will you shut up and find that damned key, you old fool?" snapped the prisoner. "I need to get out now!"

The keys froze in the lieutenant's hands. He looked at the prisoner for one dark moment, and then he casually tossed the bunch of them to one side. "Oh, would you look at that? I seem to have misplaced the keys," he said, and then, scratching his head in pantomime, he ambled over to scoop a cup of water from a cistern. "Perhaps a cool drink of water might clear my head and help me remember where I put them, hmm?"

He took a pointedly small sip, his eyes not leaving those of the prisoner. The man in the cage's hands tightened on the bars, his lips becoming thin. The lieutenant counted twenty heartbeats before he took another tiny mouthful from the wooden cup.

The prisoner understood, held his tongue, and sat back. He was not an idiot or a lowborn—he was samurai, and beneath the filth and the flecks of sawdust that stuck to him, he wore a rich burgundy kimono.

ALMOST AS SOON as he left the guardhouse, Bennosuke was cursing his stupidity and his timidity. It was some great warrior who got flustered by nerves and a conversation that did not follow the minutiae he expected. Mighty was the soldier who was sickened with shyness, indeed. He would have to wait until tomorrow to return. Sidling back sheepish and asking for lodgings would just make him appear weaker yet, and so now he would have to find somewhere to stay on his own.

He wandered around, as lost as he was before. Inns were easy to find, but here in the center of the town and upon the merchant's road, they were all too rich for his meager purse. Men stood outside offering him fine shellfish and beds warmed by beautiful girls and songs played by master musicians and all manner of things, but not one could give him simply a mat and a roof and a bowl of rice.

Bennosuke walked and walked with no success, growing ever more despondent. His feet began to ache, the thongs of the sandals between his toes grating raw the soft flesh there, and eventually he admitted defeat. He stopped and sighed, casting his eyes round dejectedly as the people pushing past him muttered about his obstruction of their passage.

The boy found himself next to a potter's shop, a small place open to the street with vases and bowls displayed upon chests and tables. In the center of the room the potter himself sat upon woven straw mats, painting a plate. He was an old man, a small length of rope bound around his skull keeping his gray hair out of his eyes, his tongue running the length of his lips as he worked.

Bennosuke broadened his shoulders and stuck his chest out, for though he was miserable he knew that he should still try to appear like a man as he moved to stand in the doorway. He coughed pointedly and then spoke in a voice striving for depth: "A moment if you will, good craftsman."

"Eh? What're you wanting?" said the potter irritably, blinking his focus away from the detail he was painting. The pair of swords silhouetted at Bennosuke's side checked his tongue. "Oh. Ahah, a thousand apologies both honest and eternal and so on, young sir. You would care to become a patron of my humble establishment?"

"No, I am samurai," Bennosuke said, enjoying the man's reaction. "What do I need a plate for?"

"To eat from, sir?" the old man said. Bennosuke flushed slightly, and his shoulders fell to somewhere more natural. His masquerade of grandeur had failed twice now; perhaps humility was worth a try. He licked his lips, and spoke in a less pompous tone.

"That may be, but I am searching for cheap lodgings. Could you help me?" the boy said.

"Which way are you going, sir?" the man said, thinking. "Westward or Kyoto bound?"

"I . . ." said Bennosuke, beginning to construct a lie, but then he remembered honesty was part of humility. "Actually, I'm staying here. I'm to serve under Captain Tomodzuna."

"Oh—you're Lord Shinmen's man?"

"Yes."

"Ah, I used to serve the old lord, the current Lord Shinmen's father, sir, years ago," the potter said, nodding as though he were a sage. "Carried a spear for him through two battles, one up in the hills and the other over to the east somewhere, sir. Killed three men, sir."

"What do you mean?" said Bennosuke, confused. "Artisans are forbidden weapons."

"We weren't always, master samurai. Whole armies of artisans and peasants used to be drafted to serve the lords, until one day they decided we no longer had the right blood to wield spears," said the man. "Wish they had done it before I dangled my ass out over the edge of hell for them. Or they hadn't done it at all."

"Who are 'they'?"

"Who else? The government, samurai, you know—your folk," said the man. "Hierarchy is everything, isn't it, sir? Above all sits the emperor, out of the sight of us, and then there's what . . . ? My lot is to serve you samurai. You serve our Lord Shinmen. Lord Shinmen has some power, but not so much. He serves the great lords, and above them still sit a handful of men who have no formal name for their kind of power. Call them greater lords, if anything, and the closest one to us is the Lord Ukita. And whom does he serve?"

"The Regent Hideyoshi Toyotomi," said Bennosuke.

"Indeed, and when he came to power he was the one who decreed that none but samurai could have swords or spears," said the man, and then a malicious glint came into his eyes and he leaned in closer. "And therein lies the interesting thing."

"What?"

"Toyotomi was born a rice picker. Why do you think he never took the noble title of Shogun—he's forbidden it! Fought his way up through the Oda clan, took power bit by bit. Forgot where he came from along the way, prevented anyone else from following him, and sure enough kept his swords and his country," said the man, and then smiled as he realized the tone he had taken. "I'm not bitter or anything."

"You shouldn't be," said Bennosuke. "You let them take your weapons from you, after all."

"Hard to say no, what with your wife and your mother and father all at home under the yoke of samurai, none of them with a spear or an ax between them. Still, one door closes, sir. Afterward I got started here, and well . . . I suppose I have your kind to thank for this," the old man said, and gestured around his shop with the same smile as before upon his face.

"Well, that was the choice you made," said Bennosuke. "I'd die before I surrendered my swords."

"Would you, sir? Really?" said the man, slyly enough that Bennosuke could not respond, and the potter's smile unfurled completely at Bennosuke's silence. Sardonic as the grin was, the boy felt himself smiling in return. It was as though the two of them were sharing a dirty secret.

"It's a dangerous game you're playing," said Bennosuke. "If another samurai heard you slandering them or the regent so, he could lawfully kill you. Why do you say such things?"

"I don't quite know, sir," said the potter. "Maybe it's because I'm old enough that I'm no longer bothered about dying. Or maybe it's because you're young enough that you might listen, sir."

Bennosuke made to reply, but a scream of challenge came from behind him. The boy turned, caught a glimpse of burgundy motion rushing toward him, and then something flashing at his head. Impulsive instinct made Bennosuke's body take a step to the side, and whatever it was it slashed past him close enough that he felt air upon his face.

It was a sword, he realized.

There was a young samurai in a burgundy kimono before him, murder in his eyes. The blade in his hands swung around for a second try, but he was slow and Bennosuke found his own body lunging forward to grab at the man's wrists. The boy's ankle hooked behind his, the full brunt of his weight barreled onward, and then the burgundy samurai was sprawling on his back.

A cry went up as the man tumbled, and then a scattering as the passing crowd, which had been stupefied by the sudden commotion, saw the naked blade and understood. Bodies started pushing outward, away from Bennosuke and his attacker. But one body came inward—another burgundy samurai pushed through the current of the crowd, cried his challenge, and then threw himself at Bennosuke with his sword high above him. His belly became a target and, quicker than he thought he could, Bennosuke dropped to one knee, drew his shortsword, and stabbed. The hilt of his weapon met flesh, a twist of the blade as Tasumi had taught, and then he withdrew.

Blood came with the sword, warm where it spattered across him. The man shrieked, staggered, and collapsed with his hands clawing at the wound. The first samurai was scrambling back onto his feet, hands pawing at his sword in the dirt. The boy's eyes flicked up into the great, panicked circle the crowd was forming behind the samurai. He saw him then: striding forward, face contorted in fury, three more burgundy men at his side.

Hayato Nakata.

"Get him! Get him! Get him!" the man screamed, finger jabbing at Bennosuke. Any pretense of lordly decorum was forgotten; he was driven solely by the base lust to avenge the insult of the boy spitting on him.

His remaining samurai drew their swords and charged. Four men coming for him now, Bennosuke knew he was hopelessly outmatched.

There was a moment of horrible indecision as his eyes darted between the weapons coming to claim his life, and then some deep part of his brain ignited once more and stirred him into desperate action.

He could not fight; he had to flee. Hurdling the man he had stabbed as he writhed upon the floor dying, Bennosuke bundled the old potter to one side and made for the small doorway at the rear of the store. There had to be an escape through the back of the building somewhere—a way to get to anywhere but here.

Throwing himself through it and then under the low beams of the house, behind him he heard cries of rage and the shattering of pottery as Hayato's samurai pushed after him. He flung another door open, and he found himself in a room with a great kiln that shimmered with heat, the potter's tools spread around. An old lady looked up from a bowl of food, surprise written across her old, round face.

"Where's the way out of here?" snapped Bennosuke, and she pointed mutely toward a small door.

The first of his attackers entered the room behind him as he twisted past the kiln. A large wooden handle protruded from the oven mouth. Bennosuke pulled it out, whatever it was, and hurled it at the man. The red-hot coals that had been on the end of the shovel soared through the air and caught the samurai full in the face. The man stepped back, screaming horribly and flailing at his head, his stumbling body filling the doorway.

Grateful for the seconds, Bennosuke hurtled through the tiny door and found himself in a narrow back alley. There was barely enough room to walk straight, so the boy skittered along, half turned sideways. The alley was riddled with byways, and he picked one at random on the right, then one on the left, then came to a halt and pushed himself flat against a wall, listening. He was panting, he realized, and he did his best to silence himself.

Clattering, shouting, and the rapid *clack-clack* of wooden sandals on the rough stone paving echoed around him.

"Where is he?!" shouted one voice.

"He can't be far!" shouted another.

"Tear his eyes out, ugly bastard dog!" came a third, thick with a pain and fury born of scorched flesh.

The samurai wasted no time deliberating, and split up to search.

Bennosuke listened as the echoes of their harsh footsteps fanned out around him. The alleys were more of a maze than the town itself was. Cursing under his breath, he tried to control the panic welling up inside him.

He had no clue how they had found him, but there was no time to think of that. An instant alone had saved him; the instant the first samurai had been honor-bound to offer between the cry of his challenge and the sweep of his sword from behind. He was living on such instants now, whereas Nakata's men had all the time they needed to slowly squeeze him into their trap.

Bennosuke would give them no further advantage; he slipped out of his own wooden sandals. The stone of the alley was shade-cool on his feet as he started sidling along like a ghost. He listened for the clattering of the samurai footfalls, turning when he felt them too close, reversing along his trail if he needed to, waiting for a glimpse of an escape. His stockings grew sodden with slime, his head whipping around like a hunted sparrow's, seeking attack from wherever it would come.

Braced for action, he did not expect to round a corner and find a man with a woman pressed up against the wall, taking her from behind. The pair of them had their eyes closed in passion, the man running his hands through the length of her hair and the woman with the skirts of her simple clothes hiked up and held in her mouth.

For a moment they did not notice him, but perhaps Bennosuke gasped in shock, or perhaps some primal sense of awareness kicked in, for the woman opened her eyes and saw him there, and then the skirts fell from her mouth and she was shrieking.

She stumbled backward down the alley trying to cover herself, and the man moved himself between her and Bennosuke. But he was a peasant or a merchant or an artisan, and so instead of protesting or threatening the man started bowing and apologizing to the swords and the shaven scalp he saw upon the boy, and all the while still the woman howled in embarrassment.

"Shut up! Shut up! Shut up!" Bennosuke hissed to them both, but it was hopeless.

He scrambled past them, his heart pounding so hard now he was having trouble distinguishing between it and the samurai's footfalls.

The boy heard them shouting to the lovers, demanding to know which way he had gone. As he turned another corner he offered a prayer for himself to become invisible, but the gods were not listening.

One set of footsteps had not headed for the commotion of the lovers. Bennosuke lurched along, listening to them, and suddenly as he came to an intersection they became much too clear—the samurai was around the corner. The boy's stomach leapt up into his torso, certain for a moment that the man could see him somehow and was swooping in for the kill.

But no—his footsteps were unhurried. The samurai was not charging, but searching still, unaware he was so close to his prey.

There was no nook or avenue he could dart down this time, no choice but to fight. Swallowing, Bennosuke withdrew his longsword as silently as he could, the faint scrape of metal on wood sounding so horrendously and revealingly loud to him.

He raised the weapon above his head and began to count downward. After three he would jump out and strike—a downward slash, no room for any other attack in the narrow space—and hope that the man was within distance.

Three.

The sandals were slowing, becoming more and more cautious. Had Bennosuke been wrong? Did the samurai know he was there?

Two.

One slow step after another—he had to know. Had to. Bennosuke steeled himself for the wound that would almost certainly come.

One.

Bennosuke dashed out and the man was so close that he almost collided with him. The samurai let out a shocked yelp, and began to move to raise his sword, but Bennosuke was already poised. His sword sliced down and buried itself in the man's head so far that it split one of his eyebrows in two. It was a crude, horrific blow, and the man let out a ghastly scream. He collapsed awkwardly, and the sword was so deeply wedged into his skull that his weight tore it from Bennosuke's grip.

The distant footsteps stopped for a moment as the scream bounced its way to them, and then the *clack-clack-clack* returned faster as they came for him like wolves.

The sword had bridged itself between the two walls as the man had fallen. The samurai's lips still murmured mindless sounds, his dead eyes open and rolling upward as though they were trying to see the blade. Bennosuke tried not to look at his face as he went to prise his sword free. The footsteps converged on him like a noose, and so he abandoned any hope of cleanliness and simply placed his foot on the man's neck and pulled with all his strength. The sword came free with a sucking, cracking sound, sticky strings of hair and gore sticking to the blade.

"He's here! Here! Here!" a voice yelled behind him.

Bennosuke turned to find Hayato pointing at him from farther down the alley. Instead of fury there was now childlike excitement on his face. But he made no move toward Bennosuke, nor did he make any attempt to draw his own sword. Of course he would take part only in the hunt, leaving the danger of the kill to others.

"Are you samurai, runt?" he called, amused.

What could Bennosuke do but run? Hayato followed after him, his voice breaking with laughter as he called out to his men.

To his right Bennosuke glimpsed a crowd, a blessed, heaven-sent crowd that filled him with a moment of elation. Cutting down that alleyway, he burst onto the street. It was another road, busy with people as the one before had been. As indistinguishable as the one before had been too, and that was no good, for Hayato and his men would surely know the town. Bloody sword still in one hand, Bennosuke grabbed a passing man roughly by the shoulder and spun him around.

"Where's the road out of town?" he bellowed at the man. The man cowered in shock for a few moments, and then his wits came back to him and he waved vaguely up the street.

"Get him! Kill him! Now! Now!" came Hayato's shrieking, suddenly close. Bennosuke turned, anticipating the arrival of the samurai, but instead he saw only the lord's arm appear out of the alley's mouth, still pointing. Hayato must have been turning and gesturing to his men to follow him, unaware that he was still so close.

Suddenly, all he could see was that arm.

He should have continued to run, completed his escape, but that arm called to him. What he remembered was the sight of the peasant's hand spiraling in the air as Arima had cut it from him, and Dorinbo's voice castigating him, and now suddenly here was a chance for revenge, to prove that he truly was righteous. What he felt was the sudden animal thrill of turning the hunt—of the joyous knowledge that he had been weak but now he was strong and majestic and imperious.

Bennosuke lunged toward Hayato and whipped his sword down in a silver arc. It connected just above the lord's biceps, the boy was sure of it, but for a brief moment the arm remained the same and he thought somehow he might have missed. Then a great tear appeared along the kimono's sleeve, and the arm flopped to the ground.

It lay there, twitching like a dying fish out of water, and the scream that came out of Hayato was horrible to hear. It was a high-pitched wail of utmost agony, both the noise of a simple animal experiencing a tremendous, unendurable pain, and that of a conscious, intelligent being realizing that it was mutilated and lessened.

So piercing and pitiful was it that it broke the spell Bennosuke had been under. Revulsion cut through him as he realized what he had done. The carp had torn the swan's throat out; lords were untouchable and golden, but now there was part of one upon the paving slabs.

Hayato stumbled out into a street that was suddenly empty around them. He almost tripped over his own limb and collapsed to his knees, the stump of his arm whirling spasmodically. The lord looked up into Bennosuke's eyes—genuine terror there, far worse than anything Arima had shown—and then he fell farther and began pathetically scrabbling away along the ground on his rear.

Behind him a burgundy samurai emerged from the alley's mouth. He took in the scene in one shocked instant, but then he roared in anger and raised his sword to attack Bennosuke.

"No! Nononono! Leave him! Help me!" begged Hayato.

The samurai halted unwillingly. Bennosuke leveled his sword at him, his pulse rushing through his ears. The weapon shook in his hands, drops of blood falling from the blade as it juddered. He could see the fury in the samurai's eyes, could see the coiled power in his shoulders and his desire to kill. The samurai was burned; skin scarred red, a large, fresh blister weeping under his right eye, a ragged constellation of black scorches across his kimono.

The man wanted to attack, definitely, but Hayato was his lord, and a lord's command was paramount. Whatever revenge the samurai wanted was secondary, and so he broke and bent to tend to Hayato, tearing cloth from his sleeve and starting to stanch the flow of blood.

Bennosuke did not wait for the other samurai to arrive. He took his chance and bolted, shoving his way through the crowd. The town of Aramaki melted away at some point, but he did not stop running. He ran for Miyamoto, ran until he collapsed to his knees, his sword falling from tired and numb fingers as he gasped for air. Birds sang in the trees above him, brown leaves falling as the wind rustled the branches. So peaceful, but no rest to be had here now—no rest until he was safe in Miyamoto once more.

CHAPTER NINE

"Death," said Lord Shinmen, a sticky glob of seasoned rice held in his chopsticks before him. "The Nakata hunger for no other recompense."

Munisai watched his lord pop the rice into his mouth and chew, the sound of the mastication alone breaking the silence. They were taking a private meal in the foreroom of Munisai's household, candles burning behind paper shades. Munisai was feigning coldness to keep his wound hidden deep within his kimono, and he had remained mute for a long time.

A tense week had passed since Bennosuke had arrived back in Miyamoto. They had elected to wait for whatever would come to them. When Lord Shinmen had been spotted approaching that afternoon, Munisai had felt both vindication and relief. He could sharpen his swords no further.

Haste had been on Shinmen's mind; he and his light complement of guards had all been on horseback and carried no standard or banner identifying themselves. Should an enemy have come across them, they could have slaughtered Shinmen and claimed innocence, thinking them no more than roving bandits.

Munisai had a mind to reprimand his lord for such negligence, but the truth was that Shinmen's thinking a private concern of his worthy of such risk both flattered and honored him. Indeed, when Shinmen had dismounted from his horse and allowed Munisai to raise his head from the dirt where he had pressed it, the lord had had such a look of concern about him that something deep within Munisai had stirred.

Perhaps, in the months since he had last seen his lord, he had come to his senses and realized the poison of the Nakata.

But no, their taint was not quite shed; Lord Shinmen had come as a neutral emissary, and slowly he had spoken of his liaisons with the Nakata clan. What he spoke of was not good, but neither was it unexpected.

"Death," said Shinmen again, if only to banish the absence of sound.

"How is Nakata weaving his tale?" Munisai asked.

"The young Lord Nakata says Bennosuke was victorious in a duel with his champion Kihei Arima," said Shinmen. "He said the duel was well fought and fair, and that much I can just about believe. Were it any other thirteen-year-old, perhaps not. But your lad? Perhaps. He must be skilled, or lucky."

"Both," said Munisai.

"Either way, after he left the village Nakata went to Aramaki, and stayed there," said Shinmen.

"Too ashamed to go home defeated," said Munisai, and he ruefully conceded within himself that this was a possibility he should have considered.

"That could be it." Shinmen nodded. "But he claims he was inspecting the town and the garrison for me. Captain Tomodzuna was away during the incident, but according to his men the only thing Hayato was inspecting was the interior of taverns, drinking and working himself up into a fury. There were disturbances nightly.

"Then the day comes. Nakata says your son ambushed them on a thoroughfare. He killed one man straight off, and then cut off the lord's arm. Another man fell, and then, realizing he was outnumbered and the element of surprise had gone, your son fled the scene."

"Do you believe that?" said Munisai.

"I cannot be sure," said Shinmen. "The witnesses are conflicted at best. Some claim they saw a scuffle between Nakata's men and a samurai matching your son's description some streets away, others say they saw Bennosuke charging Nakata while the lord was unarm . . . while the lord was weaponless."

"I trust you've considered the sway Nakata's riches might hold over people's memories, my lord?"

"It makes no difference. Not a samurai among them. Peasants, merchants, artisans; I wouldn't trust their word any more than I would a fox's. All I know is Hayato Nakata is now missing an arm," said the lord, and sighed before he continued. "Tell me—do you think your boy would do all that?"

"He fled back here barefoot," said Munisai, remembering the bloody state of the boy's soles. "If he'd planned this, I am sure wearing sandals might have occurred to him."

"Indeed," said Shinmen.

"Bennosuke claims that Nakata was the aggressor, and I believe him. The boy is hotheaded but he is not a murderous fool. I trust him," said Munisai, and he needed the slightest of pauses before he could say the next words: "He is my son."

Shinmen did not notice the lull—why would he have? To him that was merely a fact, not an avowal. The lord continued: "Nevertheless, Nakata is a great lord. His word carries a great deal of weight."

"I shall cede to whatever decision you deign to make, my lord," said Munisai. "As always, my will is as yours."

"Munisai, you do not have to feign," said Shinmen, surprised at the lack of protest. "You can reveal to me your true feelings."

"I have none that you do not keep within your own heart, my lord," said Munisai.

"You weren't always like this," said Shinmen, amused by the obsequiousness now.

"Thankfully, I remembered who I ought to be, my lord," said Munisai, his face still as ever. Shinmen gave up.

"Very well," the lord said. "This situation is troubling, but you should not worry. I am sure this quarrel can be sorted out before it festers. We shall go to Lord Ukita; Nakata is sworn to him as much as I am. There we shall find resolution. There should be no conflict within our alliance."

"As you wish, my lord," said Munisai.

"You can trust me, Munisai," said Shinmen, seeing the doubt in the samurai. "I know Nakata. We shall come through this, and your boy too. Have faith in me, my friend."

Munisai bowed to his lord, and could not help but flush inwardly at the extravagant compliment his lord had paid him: *friend*. But he could not share Shinmen's confidence.

No other recompense but death.

Munisai kept his silence, and wondered if Yoshiko's spirit was watching, so close to where she had died.

Lord Shinmen was staying at Munisai's household and his samurai were barracked down in the dojo, so Bennosuke had come to the one place where there was space left for him—the temple of Amaterasu. The boy sat and looked down across the lights of the village at night, listening to the hum of cicadas. As it always did at times of stress, the rash upon his face was throbbing and he had to fight the urge to scratch at it.

He had been at the temple most of the week. His feet were in ruins, caked in bloody scabs and ugly, pus-filled blisters caused by the panicked flight away from Aramaki. Dorinbo changed the bandages daily, but the wounds were slow to heal. Bennosuke could just about walk now, but nothing more than that. Hobbled, he had had nothing else to do but sit down alongside his uncle and busy himself with the binding of the prayers.

The time of the great pyre drew near. They were down to the last few chests. Dorinbo had worked with a furious devotion, and Bennosuke had tried to keep pace. The binding had helped take his mind away from imagining the beating of war drums and burgundy banners appearing on the horizon.

He tried to tell himself he wasn't afraid. Men had tried to kill him—twice now—and he'd come out the other side of each encounter. But inexorable dread overwhelmed him. A lethal fight was frightening, but it was an immediate terror overcome by both the fact that he could rely on his own skill and the thrill of victory. What Bennosuke faced now was the opposite. He felt powerless and small, and he hated it.

The boy wished that he could see it as Tasumi and Munisai did. Both the samurai seemed impervious to doubt or worry. Indeed, Tasumi had laughed when Bennosuke had told him, his face creasing up and the peals booming around the empty dojo.

"You threw hot coals at one of them?" he said when he could find a breath. "Mercy, boy—you're a sadist, you."

"It was the only thing to hand," Bennosuke said sheepishly.

"What of my little present?" said his uncle.

"Oh," said Bennosuke, remembering the throwing blade. It was still attached to his left biceps. He had forgotten all about it.

"You see, you need to think, Bennosuke. All the coals did was anger your enemy and buy you a few seconds. Had you used the dagger, you'd have taken his throat out and bought yourself even longer."

"I see, Uncle."

"All's well in hindsight, I suppose. It's not like it made a great difference. Remember for next time, eh?" Tasumi said, and then chuckled again. "Coal to the face! Hah, it's unique if it's anything."

"What do you think will happen?" asked Bennosuke when his uncle's mirth had subsided.

"Let them come," the man said with a shrug.

Munisai had not even reacted when the boy had been brought before him, Dorinbo and Tasumi carrying him between them with his mangled feet off the ground. The samurai's face was as stone as he listened impassively to Bennosuke tell of Nakata's ambush.

"You should have killed all of them," he had said simply when it was done. "If they were all dead, no one would have known it was you. There are plenty of masterless warriors wandering the country. Why not one of them who did it?"

Munisai had nodded in dismissal then, and that was that. He had barely seen his father for the rest of the week.

Bennosuke knew that to both samurai this situation was like holding on to driftwood in a deep, raging river. If you panicked and thrashed, you would tire yourself and drown struggling. But if you trusted the current, and simply relaxed and focused on holding on, eventually you might be carried to land once more.

It was easier to understand the philosophy than to feel it. Bennosuke found his eyes drawn, like a tongue probing the absence of a tooth, to the distant specks of lantern light twinkling around his home. There he knew his fate was being decided, and . . .

He forced himself to look away, behind and into the small building where Dorinbo was sitting. The monk was reading poetry by candlelight, legs crossed, completely still. After the initial shock of his return and examination of his feet, like the samurai the monk had seemed little changed. Yet on them it seemed fitting; on Dorinbo it seemed odd.

The monk became aware of the boy's gaze, and slowly looked up.

"Are you all right?" he said. "Do your wounds need tending?"

"No," said Bennosuke. The monk tried to go back to reading, but found the boy's eyes too distracting. He looked up wordlessly, expectantly.

"Are you angry with me?" asked Bennosuke eventually.

"No, Bennosuke," he said. "Why would I be?"

"I killed again," said the boy.

"You're samurai; this is what happens," said Dorinbo.

"What do you mean?"

"Death snaps back and forth because of stupid, stubborn pride. Nakata insults your father—your father insults him back. Nakata tries to kill your father—you kill Nakata's champion. Nakata tries to kill you—you cut off his arm and kill his men. Now what do you think will happen?"

"Nakata will try to kill me again."

"Exactly. And for what, in the end?" asked Dorinbo. Bennosuke had no answer.

"What should I do?" he asked.

"Do? I . . ." said Dorinbo, and he shook his head and sucked air through his teeth. "Try to survive, Bennosuke."

"I can do that." The boy nodded. "I can fight the Nakata."

"No—do you see? I say survive, and you interpret that as fight. That's the samurai way of thinking you chose when you killed Arima, and that's what I mean."

"What?"

"Can you fight the entire world?" said the monk. "For this is the way it works, the way it is if everyone behaves as you are. Everyone blindly assenting to the paths trodden a million times before, until they are eventually crushed by them."

"Then what should I do?"

"Run. Live."

"No. I can't do that."

"For what reason, other than a foolish ideal? The fear of shame, the fear that Munisai or Tasumi or the hells know who else will think less of you?"

"I won't run."

"Then you are complicit in your own annihilation, if not now then certainly at some point in the future," said Dorinbo.

"Stop talking like this," said Bennosuke.

"You'd prefer I lied and coddled you like a child? I won't. You're old beyond your years, Bennosuke, and that is what torments me the most—that your life has barely had the chance to reach its potential," said Dorinbo. Bennosuke saw tears glistening in the man's eyes, and that took from him any retort he might have made.

"I'm sorry," he said softly.

"You do not need to apologize, Bennosuke," said the monk. "It's a cruel world to demand such of one so young. That, I think, is why we are allowed to come back."

"Perhaps," said Bennosuke.

He looked back across the valley, to spare them both embarrassment. The lights of lanterns still twinkled. Bennosuke found himself reminded now of the lanterns of the Obon Festival of the Dead; orbs set to float upon the lakes and rivers of Japan to represent the souls of the deceased, drifting away and slowly flickering their flame out in the darkness.

In the darkest hours of the night Lord Shinmen slept soundly, a belly full of alcohol. Four samurai stood guard in the gardens outside, while Munisai prowled the black hallways of his house. An assassin would have to be prescient to think of attacking Shinmen here, but protocol demanded a watch, and so it was done.

The shadows being empty, inevitably he came once again to where his old suit of armor hung. Shinmen had laughed in disbelief when he had seen it.

"You honestly wore this once?" he had said.

"Munisai Hirata did, my lord," Munisai replied.

"Ah; sincerest apologies, my dearest name-sworn," said the lord in slurred, mock seriousness.

He was acting like he had previously, before the rot of Nakata had set in. He was open, a warmth in his eyes that was rare in the nobility. Munisai had never met another lord prepared to joke as Shinmen did, nor another who seemingly trusted as he did. Lords were supposed to have a healthy streak of fox's blood in them, a thousand different faces for a thousand different allies and a thousand different plans for a thousand different sacrifices.

But Shinmen—Shinmen made you believe.

His mind wandered back to his last night as Munisai Hirata, the eve of the final of the Grand Tournament. He had been in a cheap tavern, drinking bad sake by the bottle, not caring that tomorrow he had to fight one of the finest swordsmen in the country. That was a dawn away, and that was more than he needed. But then men in fine blue had come for him.

It had been a little over three years since he had killed Yoshiko and left Miyamoto; his kimono was a shade of grime, his hair and beard wild. Long, matted strands that had long grown out of the samurai style fell from his head, while his beard straggled off his chin in curly wisps. He had not bathed in weeks, and he could see disgust at the stench written across the faces of the men as they bundled him out into the street.

Good. Let the miserable pricks suffer.

The rage and hurt that had been so fierce in the weeks and months immediately after killing Yoshiko had by then settled into a dull, seething resentment of everything. He eyed everyone suspiciously, kept his jaw permanently clenched and his sword loose in its scabbard. He just wanted to kill and it took restraint not to fight the blue men, but he had no wish to spend the next day getting tortured to death for breaching the peace.

The streets of Osaka were always busy, but now they were packed because of the tournament. The samurai had to push their way through the crowd, and they were not helped as some stopped and stared at Munisai, whispering to one another. He had become infamous; it was a wooden-sword tournament, a test of skill and not a display of gore, and the competing samurai were expected to show some level of restraint. Munisai—a masterless, bedraggled warrior in the midst of immaculate soldiers—had managed to crack two ribs, fracture an arm, and finally strike a man so hard on the side of his skull that his eye had filled with blood and then gone blind.

Though many protested none could stop him, and he learned the level of his notoriety from the morbid eyes of the onlookers. The angry part of him took a certain antagonistic pride, but the hidden, honest part hurt. It reminded him of his youth, when he had walked proudly while men looked at him with admiration and women with lust.

There was no ease to be found in his guards either; Munisai recognized the shade of blue his escorts wore. His family, the Hirata, had been sworn to the clan Shinmen for generations, and he had shirked that duty when he had fled to wander the wilderness. The lord was not famed for forgiveness.

The samurai led him to the castle at the heart of the city; it was newly built, its walls still pristine white and unmarked by battle. It was labyrinthine and well designed, a series of concentric battlements layered upon a man-made hill, and their little group passed through many bottleneck checkpoints until they reached the noble guest quarters. There they stopped outside the doors of a residence—not the biggest and yet not the smallest—where more samurai in blue stood guard.

An old samurai, his hair cloud white, awaited. The richness of his kimono told Munisai that he was important. He looked at Munisai disdainfully, eyes running up and down him until they met Munisai's challenging glare.

"I want you to know that if you make one move toward our lord, you'll be killed," the man said curtly. "I don't care how good you are, I've enough men to drown you in bodies if need be."

"While you would be, I should imagine, running very quickly in the other direction," growled Munisai, and the samurai's face tightened in disgust.

"You will keep a civil tongue in your head, and I am warning you if you so much as look at my Lord Shinmen in the wrong way . . ." the man said.

"I won't attack your lord if he doesn't attack me first. Let's get this done with," said Munisai.

He surrendered his longsword, but custom permitted him to keep the short one at his side. The elder samurai looked at that warily as he made a coded knock upon the door, waited for the several locks to be undone, and then gestured for Munisai to follow him in.

It was a small, plain hall, a cursory potted tree in one corner and the walls bare wood, but there were at least twenty samurai crammed into it. They sat in tight rank, glaring at Munisai as he entered. The lord upon the dais took his attention, for it was not the Shinmen he was expecting.

The old lord had been—well—old, and so he must have died while Munisai had been gone. This new, younger one watched Munisai with interest as he made his way through the narrow space and sat himself down in the center of the room. The gathered samurai made a pantomime of disgust at Munisai's appearance, but Lord Shinmen's face was inquisitive, and he rubbed his chin as he looked Munisai over.

"They say after decades of practice some great masters of ki can summon their energies from within and strike a man a deathblow using only their will before he has even had a chance to draw his sword. But you, Munisai Hirata," said the lord, in a tone so grave it was practically subterranean, "you, I suspect, strike a deathblow to the nose before the man has even had a chance to see you."

"What do you want?" asked Munisai gruffly, angered by the playful twinkle that had jumped into Shinmen's eyes.

"Show respect!" snapped the white-haired samurai, who had settled cross-legged on Lord Shinmen's right. He slapped his hand down on the floor for emphasis, and it echoed around the room.

"I want to know why you have shirked your duty to me, Hirata," said the lord smoothly, holding Munisai's gaze. "I want to know why the first I hear of you in years is when you materialize at this tournament. You are sworn to me, are you not?"

"I am no man's vassal," said Munisai.

"But Miyamoto falls within my lands, does it not?"

"I am no man's vassal," repeated Munisai, flatly. His tone seemed to goad Shinmen into probing further.

"Your family has been sworn to govern Miyamoto village for decades now, a village within my domain, and so it holds that you by your very blood serve the Shinmen clan, does it not?" the lord asked. Munisai glared at the floor, unsettled and irritated.

"That may have been true once. But now things are different. The Hirata serve no one any longer. I am the last of them, and if this is all you had to say, I am going to go now," he said slowly and definitely, and made to rise.

"You will leave when you are dismissed!" snapped the man by Shinmen's side, and once more he struck the floor.

"Have you any idea how annoying that is?" growled Munisai, lips still loosened by alcohol and unable to keep it from slipping out. There was a threat in his voice, and so the samurai behind him leapt to their feet and made to draw their swords with cries of outrage. Munisai had barely gotten off the floor—he had grossly misjudged how drunk he was and found his legs sluggish and unsteady—when Lord Shinmen's voice rose above the others.

"Hold!" he barked. "All of you, hold!"

The samurai obeyed, barely. Munisai faced them warily. He saw just how badly outnumbered he was, and his mind raced for any kind of solution, any form of escape.

"Lord Shinmen, why order us to hold? Let us put an end to this farce," said the elder samurai. "The other lords will thank us. We'll save them the embarrassment of this savage wretch even having a chance of winning the tournament."

"That, or we could raise the wretch higher," said Shinmen calmly.

"What do you mean?" asked Munisai, his back to the lord. His eyes were darting from samurai to samurai, trying to guess which one would strike first, which one had the strongest bloodlust in his eyes.

"Would you walk with me, Hirata? I promise there will be no tricks, no poison blade waiting for you," said Shinmen.

"Lord!" hissed the commander, "I have endured your scheme thus far, but surely even you can see the folly of it now? How could you hope to reason with this animal?"

"Hold your tongue, and stay back," said Shinmen with a dismissive gesture.

Munisai risked a quick glance backward. Shinmen merely nodded and beckoned a hand toward the paper screen door at the back of the room. It was a strange, bold move for a lord to invite anyone to be alone with him, let alone a potential enemy, and the curiosity this aroused in Munisai moved him to raise himself slowly out of his fighting crouch.

The gathered samurai watched him cautiously as he slowly took one reverse step after another into the room beyond the hall, refusing them the chance to strike him from behind. Shinmen slid the door closed, and then they were gone from his sight. The lord nodded to an even smaller door leading outside, and together they walked.

They passed from the orange of lanterns into the blue of the night, up onto the battlements of the castle that overlooked the city, lights glimmering before them and the murmur of a hundred thousand voices on the breeze. Shinmen leaned his elbows upon the parapet and took it all in. Guardedly, Munisai moved to stand beside him. The air was cool and refreshing, and he found his mind began to function on more than base, hostile thoughts. He waited in silence for Shinmen to speak.

"I apologize for my commander," said Shinmen after a moment, eyes not leaving the nightscape. "He is diligent, but there is diligence and then there is zealousness, I suppose. But it doesn't matter: he doesn't trust me. He thinks me 'unpredictable.' So he'll be gone soon. It's being seen to. We must stand as one in this clan, or we shall not stand at all.

"In any case, I will soon be in need of another in his role," he said, and he turned to look at Munisai then, eyes giving a wordless proposal. Munisai looked away, more out of shock than anything.

"I am not a commander," he said.

"Your father was," said Shinmen, returning his gaze to Osaka. His voice became warm and wistful with memory. "Shogen Hirata. Now *there* was a samurai. Did you know he was the only man my father permitted to touch me when I was growing up? He certainly loved to prove the point. He knocked two of my milk teeth out once; cracked me across the face with a spear butt because I'd been in the paddocks startling the horses. He scared me, but I grew to respect him. I'd see the way he protected my father, or the way he'd organize things, and I'd just . . . *know* that things were safe, that they were under control. Do you understand? It's hard to explain.

"I was there the day he died. I wasn't sad, but I wasn't happy . . . I don't know if melancholy is the right word. I . . . It was a good death. If I had a choice I would hope to die like it one day, not lingering and sick and just waiting in bed for my soul to flutter out like my father did. No, your father . . . Do you know how he died?"

"Why are you telling me this?" said Munisai uncomfortably. Of course he had heard the story, but like most of his past life he had tried to numb its memory and consign it to oblivion. Yet he said nothing as Shinmen carried on speaking.

"It was a battlefield like any other, I suppose. It wasn't my first battle, but it must have been early, because I remember my face was burning with spots. I was excited, though. I had a new horse, a man's horse, and I wanted to see how fast it could run. Of course, then the killing began and I started feeling sick and scared. Bodies everywhere, men screaming, the stink of blood and fear, you know . . . It's funny how we get used to it, isn't it? How we lose that common sense.

"Anyway, your father sees me going green, and he rides over and slaps me around the head, and tells me to pull myself together. Yelling at me about composure of a lord in public, to pull my armor tighter, not to jerk the reins of my horse so hard . . . It's all good advice, but it's going in one ear and out the other, and then the arrows came.

"Archers on the battlefield loose their arrows high and arcing into one great cloud, and people say you can hear them whipping and cracking through the air as they come, but that's not true. You catch a glimpse of movement in the sky, and your first instinct is that it's just a flock of birds. But then your eye can't ignore this flock of birds that is getting larger and larger, and then you realize it's heading right for you. And then they drop down among you—*into* you.

"Your father leapt on top of me, pushed me from my saddle, and shielded me with his body until the last had fallen. He made no sound, but when he let me up I could see them sticking out of him. That was the first time I realized how big war arrows really are, the length of your arm with that big heavy blade to punch through armor—they seem a lot smaller notched on a bowstring. But your father's got two in his back straight through his plate, and the one that killed him, I'm sure, that had snuck under the lip of his chest piece and down into him. Into his lungs, maybe, or lower. The shaft is barely visible; it's deep down into him wherever it went. He doesn't make a sound, just looks me up and down as we get to our feet. He sees I'm fine, and then he hops back on his horse and signals the attack on the archers who fired on us.

"We win the battle, and hours later he's still in the saddle. He's bound the sword into his hand so it wouldn't fall. He's gone gray and cold, but his eyes are still open, still fierce. The arrows are still sticking out of him, but no one wants to touch him because it's *perfect*. Soundless, loyal, on the battlefield. The immaculate death for a samurai. People kneel to him. Kneel to his memory. Shogen Hirata . . .

"He was samurai, yes. And to think, thanks to yourself, all the name Hirata is now known for is murder and savagery and arson. I wonder what your father would make of that? I wonder if his spirit moans in shame, wherever it is?" said Shinmen, voice suddenly cold. He looked at Munisai then, gauging his reaction.

His eyes pierced him, and Munisai knew the lord had his measure entirely. Only one man had been able to do that before, and that was Dorinbo. There were no words he could say, for his mind was blank with shock and shame. All he could do was glare, and slowly a smile spread across Shinmen's features.

"He was samurai, and though you claim not to be, as much as you bark 'I am no man's vassal!' . . . I think you are too, Munisai. Why else would you have entered the tournament? Why not have just vanished into nothing, swum out to sea, and not come back? I know that you forced your entry into this tournament with your noble Fujiwara blood. Would a man determined on nothingness so loudly proclaim that? No, you want your name to be known, you want to be recognized. You want purpose.

"Well, I can give it to you. You are strong—fight for me. Become a samurai once more. Together we can take Japan by the throat. We are young and brave and daring, and more than that we *are* unpredictable! This stagnant country of old fools in silver towers is there to be taken, and we can do it! Bodies and souls, down on the battlefield;

you and I, Munisai. We can do that—and restore pride to the name Hirata."

Fire and warmth were dancing in the lord now, and he stood face-to-face with Munisai. For his part, Munisai felt something igniting within him that he had not felt for a long time. But it was quenched by a familiar aching sense of damnation that before had driven him into great rages, but now anchored him with a terrible shame.

"That name is too far gone to redeem," said Munisai quietly.

"Then take mine," said Shinmen, and his eyes were honest.

THE NEXT DAY, washed, shaven, and wearing a fine kimono in Shinmen's shade of blue, Munisai had walked into the arena with a wooden sword in his hand and for the first time in years a sense of belonging and duty in his soul. The duel was over quickly; his foe overextended himself, Munisai batted his sword to one side, and then his opponent winced as he anticipated the savage blow he had seen Munisai strike in the bouts before.

Munisai's sword whipped around, and stopped to rest gently on the man's neck. The man breathed out, surprised, and then the applause slowly began.

He was samurai.

It was all a great gamble, Munisai later learned. A neutral lord had been present at the tournament, and Shinmen hoped a victory in his name would persuade this lord of his strength and to side with him in a war he was planning. Munisai had felt a momentary sense of betrayal, a childish pique that there was no sense of destiny moving his lord's hand, but then he considered that everything the lord said had come true. They had fought as honest samurai, and Munisai had earned the respect of men once more. Just as a perfect seppuku eradicated whatever deceit or treachery came before, what mattered was not motives but the perfect unwavering execution of an ideal.

Even if his soul was damned, Shinmen had enabled him at least to try to atone, had given him the sense of worth he needed to be able to face Miyamoto and Bennosuke once more. If the man who had spoken to him then on the eve of that tournament was truly back, then perhaps there would be a chance.

Now, in the household where that lord was sleeping, Munisai

began to think of the future rather than the past. He stalked away to chase shadows once more until the dawn, daring to hope.

THEY RODE EARLY next morning. Munisai insisted they fly Shinmen's standard this time. The banner was unfurled, and then they were up the slopes of the valley and gone from Miyamoto below them. Bennosuke turned slightly in his sleep, the clattering of the hooves too distant to wake him. The boy could not help them, for what followed was politics.

The quick pace of the ride was difficult on Munisai's arm. Every time the beast bucked or reared it tugged the dead limb and wrenched the wound. Eventually he had to wrap a cloth around his face to hide his grimace of pain. He was sure to mutter loudly about dust getting into his mouth as he did so.

One samurai, however, continued to look curiously at him. He was young, and turned his eyes away embarrassed every time he was caught, but still he persisted. During a short break, the two found themselves together, atop their horses as the beasts drank from the shallow stream they stood in.

"Your arm, my lord?" he whispered.

"What of it?" said Munisai, aggressively.

"It . . . heals?" said the young man, checking over his shoulder as he asked.

"It was never wounded. You imply that I am feeble?"

"No, Lord, of course not," said the samurai, flustered. "I— forgive me."

The samurai bowed, and kicked his horse away as slowly and politely as he could. Munisai let him cower for a few moments before he pulled the mask down and called to his back.

"Kazuteru," he said, and the boy turned. "You did a fine job. My thanks."

Pride crossed his young face for a moment, before Kazuteru remembered that a samurai should be humble. He composed himself in an instant and nodded, and then rode back to the body of the men as though he had received an order, nothing more.

Munisai pulled his mask back into place and beneath it he smiled grimly. No need to tell the lad his work had been futile.

Onward still, the narrow rural pathways soon changing to flat roads fifteen paces wide, as well monitored as they were traveled. They passed caravans of merchants and other bands of samurai as they headed for the city of Okayama, the site of the castle of Lord Hideie Ukita. Ukita's domains were in the southwest of Japan, as were those of Shinmen and Nakata, and so they were sworn to him. Ukita wielded a level of power perhaps only eight other men could rival in the whole country.

He and his clan were truly blessed, for his power was as much the result of simple good fortune as it was due to any innate scheming. From ancient times their territories had been famed for rich deposits of high-quality iron, and thus swordsmiths and forgers of armor flocked to the region. Soon, the reputation of swords made from Okayama steel soared to high renown, and with that came the samurai.

So many warriors had come over the centuries that nobody— save for the clan's highest-ranking and most incredibly diligent accountants—was sure of the full extent of the present might of the Ukita clan. What was known was that at a whim, Ukita could summon five thousand men to die for him. With a few days' notice, easily ten thousand. Give him a week, and double, perhaps three times that would follow him. It was a personal force that any other lord in Japan would be hard-pressed to equal.

Indeed, it was so strong that even at twenty-four years of age, the current Lord Ukita had been judged sufficiently wizened to join the Council of the Five Elders.

The Council was a recent but prestigious creation. The Regent Toyotomi, over sixty years old and bedridden, had long been aware of his mortality. His heir was a boy of five—being confined to a bed made certain activities easier to arrange—and Toyotomi knew that he would not see him come of age. Thus, he chose five of the most powerful men in the country to swear to raise his son to manhood, and ensure his dynasty.

The reasoning was that the Council safeguarded the future of Japan, but the truth was they were essentially five men standing in a ring with knives at their neighbors' throats. Toyotomi was no fool, and so he cannily chose five lords who above all hated one another.

Their many enmities and grudges would prevent factions from forming, and thus one man or side from rising to steal the country from
his son.

That one man, everyone feared, was the warlord Ieyasu Tokugawa.
Men called him the Patient Tiger, and he was unofficially the successor
of both Toyotomi and Toyotomi's master, the long-dead Nobunaga
Oda. The three of them had fought the long and bloody campaign
that had given them control of the country, and with Toyotomi fading
it was the military might and cunning of Tokugawa that now shone
brightest. Though he lacked the sheer numbers Ukita had, such was
his tactical genius that if the Patient Tiger was inclined to make a grab
for power, the outcome of the conflict would be hard to predict.

That was entirely what the Council was there to prevent, however, and while the regent still lived it worked. Enfeebled as he was,
Toyotomi still had the power to order the seppuku of any of them,
even Tokugawa. All wishing to keep their guts in their rightful
place, he and the elders presented an amicable front of unity, revering
Toyotomi's son. But when Toyotomi finally died and that threat was
removed . . .

Munisai felt the fingers of the world enclosing him once more in
every hostile, suspicious checkpoint of their ally they passed through.
Miyamoto had lulled him into peaceful concentration, isolated and
thinking only of the boy. Now here he was, back in the realm of politics and intrigue. He tried to focus; what mattered was Ukita alone.
Let the lord have any scheme of nation or armies of thousands—all
Munisai wanted was his ruling on a single youth.

But the lord's designs were overwhelming; the city of Okayama
swarmed with samurai. Munisai lost count of the number of shaven
pates and top knots he saw among the crowd, and he found himself
marveling at the sheer frantic number of them all. The sounds of
anvils being struck seemed to ring constantly from every corner—
constructing, sharpening, preparing. Before them on the streets,
bodies wormed among one another. Their escort, a captain who had
been assigned them a checkpoint back, was unimpressed.

"I apologize for all this delay," he said to Munisai, eyes glittering
with anger as they waited for a merchant to move his cart to one side.

"Is it always this bad?" Munisai asked.

"Only recently. It's turning into a human swamp," said the man. "My Lord Ukita provided ten thousand samurai for the invasion. Apparently, we didn't get very far."

More politics, more distractions. That Toyotomi could not become the shogun because of his low birth haunted him, and so now the old man sat in his bed, thirsting over maps of Korea and China, seeing himself as the heavenly emperor of both. Even the lowest Japanese was more worthy of a throne than those the mainlanders called divine, after all.

The first invasion five years ago failed ignobly, unable to overcome the millions of Chinese and Korean warriors who opposed them. A second had been launched earlier this year, and already it had faltered. Should it fail too, it might break Toyotomi's spirit, and some already saw carrion birds circling the regent.

"It's a nightmare to catalog them," continued the captain. "Coming back by the boatload, their papers lost or burned. We have to write up new ones on the docks. Most of them need to send riders off to their homes, asking for identification by their families, waiting cramped on their ships. A clean-shaven man is fully bearded by the time the gates open for him.

"That's just the half of it too. Once they get in, ten thousand shamed warriors here, all looking to prove their honor again? That's trouble. Fights every night, crucifixions the next day, but no matter how many they nail up as an example they still keep getting into it. I don't understand it. It's like they got infected with barbarity from the chinks. I'll be glad when the War starts, to be honest." He sighed.

The War. When had they started calling it that, differentiating it from the kind of war that had existed in Japan for centuries, the kind that Shinmen and Munisai had waged upon the Kanno earlier that year? The War they all knew was coming. A straight fight for all or nothing in the void Toyotomi would leave.

"Won't be long now," grunted Munisai from behind his mask.

"It'll be good to get it out of the way," said the captain. "I'm sick of the waiting. I don't even care if we win or not."

"We won't lose," said Munisai.

" 'We'?" said the captain with a wry smile. "There's no guarantee we'll be on the same side by then, though, is there?"

There was no malice in his voice. Knives at each other's throats impassively. The world of samurai. Ukita's castle appeared, still under construction but beautiful and imposing nonetheless. Someone was hastily stringing up Shinmen's blue standard upon the walls, but Munisai barely noticed.

His eyes were locked solely on the ten feet of burgundy silk alongside it.

MUNISAI FOUND HIMSELF looking at Ukita's wife during their audience. She sat behind and to the side of the lord, silent and demure, her long hair parted in the middle pooling on the floor behind her. Her real eyebrows had been shaven off; in their place the two smudges of charcoal up near her hairline painted her eternally serene. Once or twice, her eyes caught Munisai's, and they reminded him of Yoshiko. The two women looked nothing alike, but the memory of his wife seemed to dance around him constantly now.

Did a similar hatred or misery lurk behind those eyes? Did Ukita's wife despise Ukita and scheme for his downfall? Or was she his confidante, the classical, traditional rock of a wife who tempered the male fire with reason and compassion? The woman's face was unreadable, perfectly noble and samurai. She could be Yoshiko or she could be an angel—but Munisai could see only the former. That was good, in a way. This was her son's fate; Yoshiko should be here.

He wanted her to be here.

For her part, Ukita's wife was here solely as part of a masquerade. Normally women would not be permitted to witness the affairs of men. Yet Ukita had no wish to air such a bitter quarrel within his faction before the gossips and visiting emissaries of his court—they all already spoke of the attack, of course, but lacked the proof that a public hearing would give them—and so the lord and his guests had come to a private, minor hall hidden within the bowels of the castle to ostensibly share a private evening as friends and allies.

It was not surprising that the Nakata had also come to entreat Ukita. Munisai was not overly concerned, either. A confrontation was inevitable, and today was as good a day as any other. They had arrived a day or two before, but Ukita had been too busy to receive them until now; they had not had a chance to spread their poison yet, and that was good.

There were no guards present—they had been ordered outside and told to keep their ears closed to anything but cries of alarm. Each of the three groups were sitting a precisely measured, polite, safe distance away from one another; Shinmen and Munisai on one side, Nakata and Hayato opposite, and between them on a raised dais Ukita and his wife.

Though the Lord Ukita was a young man, there was a coldness in him that added years. His face was hard, and his eyes were unsettling in their relentless calculation. They scanned and tabulated, as though the world were an abacus that could be read and understood with the simplest of logic, before a few beads were shifted to best benefit Ukita.

"The understanding that is to be gleaned," said the lord, using the elaborate courtly tongue in a voice like a river slowly freezing in winter, "is that the son of the most honorable Munisai Shinmen has mutilated the body of the son of the most noble Lord Nakata. If such a comprehension proves to have an element of veracity to it, then this is a most troubling and unwelcome development within the ranks of the allies of the clan Ukita."

"Such a comprehension is truthful, Lord," said Lord Nakata, taking the initiative. "Were any eyes to gaze upon the ruination of the son of Nakata, they should surely weep."

Slowly Ukita turned to look at Hayato. The young lord seemed barely there, in truth. A pall of sickness hung over him; he was gaunt and sweat sheened, his sunken eyes distant save for the occasional spark of lucidity. The stump of his right arm was hidden, though it was clear to see it pained him still.

"The eyes of the clan Ukita remain dry as of this moment," pronounced the lord. He turned his head away, resumed a neutral gaze favoring neither party.

"It is begged that the most noble clan Ukita considers the suffering the son of the Lord Nakata is enduring," pressed Nakata, as delicately as he could.

"The son suffers physical pain now," said Ukita. "But with time it shall pass and the fact remains that many men before the son of the most noble Lord Nakata have lived full lives with missing limbs."

"Life is not the sole concern—an incomplete body is marred in the eyes of that which passes judgment in the worlds beyond. Whenever death finds the son of Nakata, may it be decades away, the son is damned because of this mutilation," said Nakata.

"Glory be to the fate, then, that decreed that the son of Nakata was born into a position of prestige that allows the son to have either grievous sin or righteous virtue rendered by his hand even if he lacks one," said Ukita. "Eternal souls and karma are not the concern of the clan Ukita; the restoration of amicability upon this mortal plane is."

The walls of the hall behind the lord were painted with a great mural of a natural landscape. The land and the sky were painted in two tones of gold leaf, while the twisting branches and vines of trees were done in black, rendering them an odd void in the shimmering background. Ukita's kimono was the exact same shade of black as the trees, and he seemed absorbed and magnified by the mural. Munisai wondered if it was coincidence, or a subtle trick to unsettle visitors.

Nakata removed a fan and opened it with a definite snap. He began to shake it back and forth in a vague impression of fanning himself, and tried to look Shinmen pointedly in the eye. Lord Shinmen was rigid with unease, his spine locked straight, but he did not meet Nakata's squinting gaze.

Munisai felt the hope within his chest grow slightly.

"It is begged that the clan Ukita considers not the consequences of the incident, then," said Nakata, giving up on Shinmen, "but the very act itself. A lowborn samurai—with no disrespect to the most honorable Munisai Shinmen—attacked a lord. This is a treason against the simple laws of nature. To deny this is to deny the walls of the castle in which this esteemed audience sits, the walls that enshrine and enthrone."

"If an interjection may be permitted, the blood of Munisai Shinmen runs with nobility," said Munisai, keeping his head low and humble as he spoke. "It must be noted that although such a one has no castle or standing army and is honored to serve another, the family line flows unbroken to the most noble Fujiwara clan. Thus the boy is no mere lowly samurai."

Munisai was speaking truthfully. He had documented proof of his family tree that traced back centuries to one of the three noble clans of antiquity. Naturally all the lords and great lords could do so, but anyone else who could prove their lineage was considered high-born. Day to day it affected little other than a slight sense of prestige, but now it was an important bargaining point.

That Bennosuke happened to be more peasant than he was Fuji-wara was a fact known only to Munisai.

"If the blood of the most honorable Munisai Shinmen runs with that of Fujiwara, then the most honorable Munisai Shinmen is as noble as this clan Ukita," said Ukita simply. "What intrigues the clan Ukita, what therefore becomes pertinent, is why such an incident should occur. To the party of the most honorable Lord Shinmen and Munisai Shinmen, it should be asked pertinently whether the charge of the assault being unprovoked is agreed upon?"

"Such a charge is vehemently contested, Lord," said Munisai.

"As this clan Ukita thought it would be. Indeed, the preceding reputation of the most honorable Munisai Shinmen—awarded the title Nation's Finest before the eyes of this lord—seems to preclude such a notion of berserk savagery being inherent in the soul of his heir," said Ukita.

Munisai was surprised to hear a trace of admiration in the lord's voice. The hope became a dull throbbing. The only objective law in the world was that which the world gave to men when it sent earth-quakes or tsunamis or plagues or famine. Men unto themselves were prostrated before the altar of the whim and fancy of their superior, and if that superior happened to smile in your direction for whatever reason, then that was that.

Nakata knew this too.

"Might the clan Ukita be reminded," the lord said, the first hints of open irritation in his voice, "of the time when the most honorable Munisai Shinmen was named Munisai Hirata, of even the first rounds of the tournament the clan Ukita witnessed when the most honorable Hirata appeared as a vagabond bone-snapper? Or," he continued, and the flapping of the fan grew a bit stronger, "perhaps if that is insufficiently savage enough for the most noble clan Ukita, then perhaps the arson and eradication of a village and the murder of Yoshiko Hirata are?"

"Might the Lord Nakata be reminded not to deal in accusations and rumor," said Ukita sharply.

The lord turned to look at Munisai, seeking a denial, but Munisai remained silent. He was shocked that Nakata had brought that up. It was a definite gamble, as no formal charges had ever been laid against Munisai, and such a slandering of character was a bold move to make in the extreme politeness of the setting. Men had been put to death for lesser insults.

Lord Ukita waited, but Munisai could not bring himself to offer any rebuttal. He felt the eyes of Ukita's wife upon him, and another pair of eyes that watched from within his haunted soul.

"Indeed." Ukita nodded eventually, and Munisai thought he could sense disappointment. "In this case, then, the clan Ukita shall rely upon the testimony of the law. It is to be asked of the most noble Lord Shinmen what conclusion his brave men reached as to the origin of the incident?"

"Inconclusive, my lord," said Shinmen.

"Inconclusive," echoed Ukita. He pondered that for a moment, his body rocking ever so slightly. Nakata raised the fan to his face, trying to draw Shinmen's attention. Munisai's lord kept his eyes on the floor.

"Disquiet," sighed Ukita. "Disquiet in the soul of the clan Ukita. Long have the clans Shinmen and Nakata been as one with this clan. Men who were the clan Ukita before this current clan have trusted the strength and canniness in war of the most honorable Shinmen, and relied upon the generosity and consideration of the most honorable Nakata. Times darken. Unity is needed.

"As a matter of honor, it is to be taken that the clan Nakata will accept no other form of compensation other than death?" asked Ukita, and Nakata nodded vehemently.

"The most honorable Munisai Shinmen is already in debt to this clan monetarily. There is little point in merely accruing more," said the lord. "Nothing else could be offered that could replace one drop of the blood of Nakata."

"Very well. It is understood that the most honorable Munisai Shinmen opposes the request for death. But the opinion of Lord Shinmen, who should happen to call Munisai Shinmen vassal, has yet to be heard," said Ukita, and turned to the lord. Munisai noticed Nakata was staring intently—expectantly—at the man.

"Impartiality is impossible for this clan," said Shinmen. "Thus it secedes from the deliberation. Bloodless amicability is wished for, but this clan shall abide by whatever decision the most noble clan Ukita should deign to give."

"So be it," said Lord Ukita.

Munisai had not expected his lord to plead for him, and neither would he want it. As he had five years ago, Shinmen had given him a chance alone by using his rank to bring this before Ukita, and that was more than enough. Lord Nakata beseeched Shinmen with his eyes. Perhaps they had brokered some deal that only now Shinmen was reneging upon.

Yet whatever further hope had leapt in his heart at that instantly faltered when he looked at Ukita. The subjective whim of earlier had faded into impassive calculation, weighing a skilled sword against the value of gold. The man had countless samurai already, and what fed them? What armed them?

"Bennosuke Shinmen is just a boy," Munisai said, speaking before he realized it. "It is begged that the clan Ukita consider the mistakes of childhood as it passes judgment."

"Boys do not wield longswords," said Nakata, and Ukita nodded again in agreement. Munisai clenched his jaw.

"He's just a boy," he said, throat tight.

"Nevertheless," said Ukita, and he said it in such a way that Munisai knew Bennosuke was doomed before the words had left the lord's mouth. "Regrettable as it is, for the crime of the mutilation of the son of the most noble Lord Nakata, Bennosuke Shinmen is ordered to commit seppuku at the earliest convenience."

For the first time, Hayato's face changed from the expression of listless fatigue it had been wearing. A grim happiness spread across him. Lord Nakata had a glint in his small, squinting eyes. Lord Shinmen merely looked down, and Ukita at the gold on the walls once more.

But Ukita's wife and her brown eyes gazed straight at Munisai, and it was as though he was no longer in the castle of Okayama far from home; he was back in his bed in Miyamoto on that first drunken night of betrayal and the sheets were tugging on his soul as Yoshiko sobbed.

He sighed sadly. So be it. He had known deep down it was always going to have to come to this, no matter how much he had deluded himself on the journey that Ukita might pardon the boy. He thought back to Dorinbo's words on the night after Bennosuke killed Arima, the monk telling him that he had a mind filled only with death. His brother was right. That was all he knew. There would have to be more death; the last resort he knew had been his only true option since the boy had returned to the village barefoot and covered in blood.

"Why?" Yoshiko asked simply, tears in her eyes.

"Because I can," said Munisai, standing over her.

He bowed his head in resignation, and then Munisai slowly reached for the shortsword that was always by his side and drew it from the scabbard in his good right hand. The blade twinkled like the gold leaf on the walls as he held it out horizontally before him. His hand was strong and steady. Lord Nakata and Hayato tensed, and he could feel Shinmen do likewise. There was a frightened pause as they weighed up Munisai's intentions. His actions were slow, deliberately measured, but everyone knew Munisai's skill. If they tried calling the guards, or fleeing, he could easily dash their lives away before aid could arrive. His gaze was locked on the Nakata.

"Munisai," said Ukita slowly, "I would advise you to reconsider this. Sheathe your sword, or you will surely die."

Munisai could have laughed. The great lord didn't know how right he was. He summoned his strength and his courage, and then he committed himself entirely to his fate. He struck a devastating blow to which Hayato and his father had no riposte.

But for the first time in his life, Munisai did it without using a sword.

CHAPTER TEN

A week later, the grass of Miyamoto rippled around Munisai's feet. It was long, dry, and ragged, the color of straw, but Munisai didn't care. It was home, and it was a sensation. Over the past seven days the idea of both had become indescribably exquisite.

He crouched, his heart still pounding from the exertion. That too was wonderful, his blood warm and vital, and he thought that he could feel it flowing even through the skin of his fingertips. Breath came from him, in out, in out, tickling the smallest hairs of his beard.

From the ridgetop he looked down upon Miyamoto. The fields were dry now, the harvest gathered and the husks left in stacks to be burned later. Across the valley, a peasant child hiked her skirts up and leapt into the last remaining water in the irrigation ditch as her friends looked on and cheered. Her furious mother fished her out, scolding her to no avail.

In the sky above, a flock of swallows headed for the ocean, fleeing the coming winter for somewhere warmer. They hung in the air for an instant as they turned, a hundred little bodies swerving as one, as though they had felt Munisai's eyes upon them.

To his side stood Bennosuke, alive.

They had come up here to spar, the dark wood of the dojo suddenly constraining to Munisai. The boy had stored a fortnight's worth of energy as he waited for his feet to heal, and now that he could walk once more he had quickly tired Munisai.

"I've been thinking, Lord," Bennosuke said now, barely out of breath.

"Upon what?" said Munisai.

"Of what we will do when the Nakata come for us."

"Oh," said Munisai.

He had returned from Okayama only last night. There were a lot of consequences for what he had done. A lot of ends that had had to be tied. He had not had a chance to explain to the boy. Bennosuke's vigor had trapped the words in his throat.

"What we could do is go to that ridge over there," said the boy, and waved at a distant outcrop of rock with the wooden sword he had been using. "Do you see how it funnels into one high point? They wouldn't be able to surround us, nor sneak around the back, so they'd have to come at us a few at a time. That'll make it a little fairer for us."

"No," said Munisai.

"I know you think your wound has crippled you, Lord. But even with one hand you are better than any man Nakata could send against you. I'll stand on your left and shield your bad arm. That way we can stand together. That way we can do it."

"No, Bennosuke," said Munisai. He knew well the thrilling rush of determination that coursed through a man when he had dedicated himself to action, and could see it in his son now. The poor boy, excited for naught. "Nakata won't be coming for a fight."

"What do you mean?"

"Arrangements have been made."

"What arrangements?" said the boy.

Munisai let out a long sigh. He rose to his feet, and reached out with his good hand to clap the boy on the shoulder. Bennosuke tensed, and Munisai realized then that the only times he had ever touched the boy since his return in the summer were to strike, grapple with, or throw him.

He remembered holding him aloft, the softness of him when he was little more than a baby. It was a good memory, a good feeling, and that he could feel it again while looking at the boy now despite what he knew . . . That was something he had never expected.

"You have surprised me," Munisai said. "Your talent. Your strength. I have only had a few months with you, but there is little else I can teach you of weaponry."

"You're still better than me," said Bennosuke.

"Of course—but I have taught you the ways for you to become stronger than me already. It remains for you to practice them on your own, until you surpass me."

"You won't teach me it?"

"I have only one thing left to teach you. An important thing."

"What do you mean?" said Bennosuke. Munisai's grip grew tight on his shoulder.

"How to die the best of deaths," the samurai said.

The words had bounced off the gold leaf of Ukita's chamber:

"The seppuku of Munisai Shinmen is hereby humbly offered in place of that of Bennosuke Shinmen."

Munisai held the shortsword before him steady and straight. He bowed low and proffered it toward the Nakatas. Father and son could not take their eyes away from the blade. Ukita knew, however, that danger came from the man, not the weapon, and he looked beyond the steel to Munisai.

"Are you sincere in that proposition, Munisai?" he asked, the courtly tongue abandoned but his voice still cool.

"Entirely, my Lord Ukita," Munisai said. The great lord nodded slowly.

Shinmen had his eyes downcast, resigned. He and Munisai had discussed this as a last resort, but the lord had been hopeful of a better outcome. He was reluctant to lose his best soldier, but he knew that seppuku was well within Munisai's rights—and more than that, ultimately a correct and proper resolution.

Ukita's wife looked on silently. She could have screamed and cried like some women were prone to, but her face remained still. Munisai was glad. Having her here, having what her eyes reminded him of steadied him. Lord Ukita checked on her from the very corner of his eye for but a moment, and then turned his head to the men in burgundy.

"Do you accept such a brave offer, Lord Nakata?" the great lord said.

"I . . ." stammered Lord Nakata, and finally he took his eyes away from the sword to meet Ukita's. "No, we do not. It was not Munisai who committed the crime. We want Bennosuke punished. Whatever Munisai could offer is irrelevant."

You want me alive so you can keep bleeding me of coin, thought Munisai, trying to keep the hatred out of his eyes.

"It does not appear that way to me, Lord Nakata. The life of a swordsman named Nation's Finest? Might I remind you of the implications of that title?" said Ukita.

There was clear admiration in his voice now. Many lords had been present when Munisai had won that tournament. This Ukita, if he had been there, would have been eighteen or nineteen. An impressionable age. Munisai counted his blessings. Nakata, however, was not so moved.

"Honor dictates that we are allowed to choose whom our retribution is visited upon," the old man said, forbidding Hayato to speak with an abrupt raising of the hand. "Munisai has done little to offend us. Bennosuke has attacked our blood. Thus it is he we want dead."

"Does not honor also dictate acquiescence to your superiors?" asked Ukita. "Who, in this matter, state that Munisai's offer is a fair one."

"I wonder if the regular tribute this clan offers upward within this hierarchy is considered fair as well?" said Nakata bluntly.

Ukita moved his head back as though he had been slapped. A lord should never be reminded of his dependencies. His eyes glistened with anger, but they quickly returned to their objective calculation. He knew he needed Nakata's gold.

"Very well," he said thinly. "On account of your clan's long and continual support, I will offer you a compromise. First, I may forget the insult you have just uttered in the presence of my wife. More than that, so very much do I appreciate you, I condone the following—Munisai Shinmen commits seppuku, and his son Bennosuke must shave his head, renounce his samurai status, and become a monk. Thus the boy is punished. Do you accept?"

Lord Nakata shook his head, the first signs of open anger on his face. But before he could speak, Hayato preempted him.

"That is a most benevolent and proper ruling, my Lord Ukita," said the young lord smoothly. "Of course the clan Nakata gratefully cedes to your will. More than that, we would like to make known our admiration of the gallantry of Munisai Shinmen. Surely tales will be told of his sacrifice in a hundred years."

The compliment was so hollow it seemed a threat in Hayato's mouth. Munisai looked suspiciously at him. Hayato was a good actor—his face appeared genuine. But Ukita too saw a mantis beneath butterfly wings, and as the great lord spoke he looked solely at Hayato.

"Then it is settled. I hereby decree that Munisai Shinmen shall commit seppuku to atone for the crime of his son Bennosuke, who shall in turn devote his life to the holy ways. I would like it to be known that should anything cause this decree to go awry in even the minutest of fashions, I should take it as a personal, unforgivable insult, and the perpetrator should undoubtedly become my enemy.

"To this end, I am appointing Lord Shinmen, who has declared his impartiality and allegiance to both parties in this quarrel, to adjudicate and ensure that my wishes are carried out with due accordance. Do you accept this position, Lord Shinmen?"

"Of course, my Lord Ukita," said Shinmen, and bowed formally.

Munisai smiled inside as he watched Lord Nakata fail to catch Shinmen's eyes once more. Now there would be no further revenge after Munisai was dead. Now the ritual would be performed by honest hands, hands that he had trained himself. There was nothing the Nakata could do.

He had beaten them, and beaten them honestly.

"Good," said Ukita. "Then so be it. Let us drink together, and let this bad blood pass beneath the bridge so that our three clans now reunite to become stronger than ever. Let us drink to the memory of Munisai Shinmen, and the paragon of a life he led."

Not a paragon of a life, Munisai thought, for Yoshiko was ever there to remind him, *but a paragon of a death—yes.*

Four men raised pewter dishes of sake—Munisai one of water—lifted them in salutation to one another, and then drank. Life was suddenly beautiful. Munisai was going to die, and it was good.

$\mathcal{B}$ennosuke's eyes were wide enough that Munisai could see himself in them. He tried to keep his face still, in contrast to the boy, who wore everything he felt openly—his lips moved, his eyes jumped through confusion, anger, and sadness, and then he shook his head and pushed Munisai's hand off his shoulder.

"No," he uttered.

"It is the only way," said Munisai.

Bennosuke could not accept that. He began to conjure escapes and excuses, growing ever more frantic and vehement as Munisai refuted them calmly one by one. They could not fight; they would fall eventually and then their names would be disgraced and stricken from history. Nakata would not turn on Bennosuke after the ritual; Shinmen would ensure against any further bloodshed. It was not Bennosuke's fault; it was not he who had insulted Nakata first, nor he who had brought Arima to Miyamoto.

"No," said Bennosuke again.

It was all he could manage eventually, any other rationale spent. Munisai watched the boy as he dropped into a squat and folded his head into his chest. He did not come out of it, rocking back and forth, young knuckles white across the back of his neck.

"This is being samurai, Bennosuke," said Munisai. "I told you before, our realm is death. You know only the easier half—killing. But now it is time for you to learn the harder half. The better half. The half that truly defines us."

"No," said the boy, face still hidden, voice barely above a whisper.

"Death is nothing, Bennosuke—does a snake fret when it sheds its skin? My soul will leave this body and then"—*come back higher,* he wanted to say, but the words caught in his throat—"go where it goes, and the world will continue."

"When?" the boy managed.

"This afternoon," said Munisai.

Bennosuke was crushed anew. He gave another cry, part anger and part anguish, and walked a short distance away. The boy fell to the ground and sat, looking through unseeing eyes toward the sea. Munisai let him.

Time passed, until the sound of drums from behind them broke their contemplation. They turned to see the first riders arrive, men on horseback carrying burgundy banners above them. They were the forerunners of a procession that wound behind them in staggered, honorific groups for almost a mile. Nakata and Shinmen had arrived in Miyamoto.

The boy rose and came to stand by Munisai. They watched silently as the horsemen began to wind their way down into the valley toward the dojo, the peasants gathering into worried clusters. The drums grew louder.

Munisai was despondent for a moment. He had hoped to have more time with the boy. But then, he had already wasted eight years, hadn't he? He could have no regrets now. There was one last thing he had to explain. He forced the words out, before he could brood upon them.

"I need my sword back," he said.

"Why?" asked Bennosuke.

"You must sacrifice something also—you are to become a monk," he said, still watching the distant valley. "That is what was agreed with Ukita."

"But . . . no. I'm samurai," said Bennosuke.

"The sword, Bennosuke," said Munisai.

"I'm samurai," the boy repeated.

Munisai turned to face him, to try to explain. He knew that the boy would be angry—this would seem a castration to him, so soon after he had gained his manhood. He had prepared the arguments, as he had with the revelation of the seppuku, and he opened his eyes, ready to weather the anger, expecting to see defiance, fury, and resentment.

Instead, silent tears streamed down the boy's face.

Why does he cry for you, murderer?

Bennosuke was still, no racking sobs escaping him. The tears simply had nowhere else to go. Munisai's face hardened. He wanted the boy to be angry, because anger was easier, but Bennosuke simply started cuffing at his eyes ashamedly. Munisai pushed him to no response. "Look at you—I give you a golden chance to prove yourself and you weep.

"Let me tell you of vengeance. Gods are vain and fickle, but vengeance is an honest thing born of man alone. It is as natural as breathing and as old as time, and it overrides all—even duty to your lord. It does so because it is itself a duty, a holy moral duty, and anything can be forgiven in its name—so long as you are prepared to give everything for it. This is being samurai. Do you understand?

"Your mother did—Yoshiko knew what being samurai meant. I wronged her and became her enemy, and instead of crying and wailing, because she was samurai she committed herself to revenge. She debased herself and humiliated herself, bore all manner of shame, all to ruin me utterly. And she succeeded. Even I . . . Regardless of what I did, even I, the one she wronged, can respect the purity of that. She was a good woman, and you ought to be proud to be her son.

"Now tell me, does her blood run in you? You are a child born of vengeance—will you live up to what made you?"

Bennosuke said nothing. He had dried his eyes, but his face remained red as he looked at the floor. Munisai snarled wordlessly, pushed him again, grabbed his chin, and forced his face up. Again he saw himself in Bennosuke's eyes, his own little more than furious narrow slits.

"Do you intend to recite sniveling prayers for the rest of your life? Or are you, as you say, a samurai?"

"Samurai."

"Then you must uphold the sanctity of vengeance," said Munisai. "It is that simple. You have an enemy in the Nakata and they must die. Take the sword from my dead hands. Live like a dog. Do what you must, endure whatever shame and humiliation will be thrown at you, commit your life to it—just make sure Hayato Nakata dies. Do you understand?"

"Yes," said the boy.

"This is no small promise, boy," said Munisai. "This is what will define you. This is what will define the fate of your soul. So tell me— what are you?"

"Samurai."

"What will you uphold?"

"The sanctity of vengeance."

"Good," said Munisai, and let the boy go.

"But why . . . why do you have to die?" said Bennosuke after a few moments. "Why can't you come with me, and together we can get revenge?"

"I'm teaching you," said Munisai, and a grim smile came across his face. "You are not a weakling or an idiot, boy. I know you can succeed. And when I said commit your life to this I meant it, for death will be the only thing that proves your vindication and removes all shame—death by your hand or theirs."

He held his hand out for the longsword, still smiling. He was surprised how much effort it took to hold it steady. Bennosuke looked uncertainly at the weapon, and then handed it over. Munisai slid it into the sash around his waist.

"Quite a burden it must seem," said Munisai. "But now you are coming to see the way the world is—peasants tend the fields, and they live. Artisans entertain, and they live. Merchants handle money, and they live. Samurai serve, and fight, and then they die. But only the names of samurai live on afterward, and we have the great gift to choose the stories that will be told about us."

"I . . ." said Bennosuke. Confusion was written upon him.

"Watch this afternoon. You will see that seppuku carves a finer testament to a man than anything that could be set in stone. You will see the way men speak of me when it is done, and you will understand," said Munisai.

"But . . ."

"You must not interfere, Bennosuke," said Munisai, seeing a change behind the boy's eyes. "Promise me that you will only watch, and that you will learn."

"Yes, Lord."

"Good."

Across the valley, a large palanquin breached the ridge. It was burgundy, and shimmered like a peacock. It was far too wide to be carried down the winding paddy field paths, and so the two dozen men carrying it began the ritual of setting it down.

His time with Bennosuke was ended. Munisai had to go present himself, and then prepare for death. It was so fleeting—this afternoon, thirteen years, forever. Then what difference did these last seconds make? A lot, he knew. He looked at the boy.

"Bennosuke," he said, and the boy looked up. "You are a fine son. Regardless."

It was not enough, but it was all he had.

LORD SHINMEN MET Munisai halfway up the slopes of the valley. Behind him the many men the Nakata had invited along with them were being marshaled to their proper places. Munisai was not surprised at the number of them. The Nakata thrived on ostentation, and what better pomp than the end of an enemy?

In truth he was pleased. Many eyes watching meant that many mouths would bear testimony of his immaculate death.

They talked for a short while of nothing. Before Munisai excused himself, Shinmen presented him with a small cask. It was wet and smelled of seawater. Inside were four large oysters still alive in their shells, a favorite of Munisai's, a rare delicacy. He had told no one of this, but Shinmen had known nonetheless.

He bowed to his smiling lord, speechless at the gift.

Back within his house, he stoked coals under a cast-iron grill, prised the oysters open with a knife, and then placed them over the heat to cook in their half shells. The gray flesh slowly began to sizzle. He watched them, savoring the smell, listening to the pop and hiss of seawater as though hearing it for the first and not the last time.

They were soon ready. Normally, even as he enjoyed them, at the back of his mind he would worry about them turning his stomach. But what fear had he of that today? Perhaps because of that absence, the four oysters tasted perfect.

His last meal done, he bathed with scented oils and soaps, shaved the pate of his head and his face, and bound his long hair up into the top knot. Then came time to dress.

The ceremonial kimono he would wear was a beautiful, perfect white. Donning it was a ritual and a challenge; the garment was designed to stop his body thrashing and spasming obscenely once his head left his shoulders, and so it contained many hidden constricting belts and binds. He found that tying them with his enfeebled left hand was nearly impossible. Munisai resorted to trying to use his mouth, but found that he simply ended up contorting himself into progressively stranger poses.

Sighing in resignation, he spat a cord out of his mouth and let the kimono slump around his feet. He realized how ridiculous he must look, half naked and half trussed for death. Suddenly he felt like laughing.

"Autumn, they say, is the best season to die," said a voice behind him. He turned to find that Dorinbo had entered the house quietly and was standing in the doorway. "You see neither the death of the world in winter, and neither are you robbed of the promise of life that spring offers. The perfect cusp.

"Of course, these are the same men who describe what you are to perform this afternoon as the bloodflower. Quite how much faith I put in the words of men who see petals blooming instead of red blood being soaked up by a white kimono, I don't know."

"You've come," said Munisai, "brother."

"I've come, brother," said Dorinbo, and he gestured at the garment on the floor. "Would you like some help?"

There was no enmity in the monk's eyes. Munisai nodded assent silently, and his brother entered the room, picked the kimono from around his feet, and began to arrange it. Dorinbo's binding of the prayer boughs had been good practice. He worked quickly, tying the knots with a surprising strength.

"I came to say thank you," said Dorinbo as he worked. "It is brave of you to do this for Bennosuke."

After a moment Munisai forced himself to say, "It's not just for him."

"What do you mean?" asked Dorinbo. Munisai could feel his brother's expression, even though the monk was behind him. He looked at the floor as the words slowly and awkwardly crept out.

"Today, I cross the Sanzu River. Yoshiko will be waiting for me there, upon the far banks of the dead. I wronged her. She did not deserve to die. But what I will do today: dying for Bennosuke—dying for *her* son. She'll forgive me, won't she?"

"I'm not in the habit of giving blind absolution, Munisai," said Dorinbo quietly.

"But she has to," said Munisai. "A death for a death—the karma balanced."

"This is no simple mathematics, brother," said Dorinbo, and he let out a slight sigh that was half irritated and half pitying. "Let me ask you—are you really sacrificing yourself in atonement? Or are you merely saying that, and killing yourself because deep down within your soul it pleases your pride?"

"What are you talking about?" said Munisai. "That is not it at all."

"Your soul is yours alone, and only you know the depths of it. But I've seen you wandering around last night and today with this wistful smile on your face, like a great poem is ending itself around you. Like things are so very . . . *proper*. And I can't tell which this is—sacrifice or vainglory."

"I am certain of myself," said Munisai.

"Well then, tell me, if so certain are you that this *is* sacrifice," said Dorinbo. "In all the years since that night, have you ever once felt shame or a need to atone for all the peasants you murdered alongside Yoshiko?"

"I . . ." began Munisai, and faltered.

He hadn't. It left him reeling for a moment. The monk had spoken so casually, never breaking pace in his work. Part of Munisai wondered if this was what it felt like in the final moments of all the men he had killed—a helpless gaping at a masterful, fateful blow that appeared to have been struck with the utmost ease.

"Yoshiko will forgive me," said Munisai, shaking his head. He could not be distracted, and so he forced the monk's thoughts from his mind. "She has to."

"I truly hope so," said Dorinbo. "It is not my role to pass that kind of judgment—I leave that to higher things than us, and those you must face this day. They will be far harsher than I, so do so honestly, brother."

He finished tying the final binding. The monk stepped around from behind Munisai, and took a few paces backward to cast a critical eye over the finished appearance. He nodded approvingly, and then picked up the large overkimono.

"Regardless—thank you, Munisai," he said. "Bennosuke will be raised well."

"He already has," said Munisai. "Thank you for that—for everything."

Dorinbo held the overkimono open, and Munisai slid into it. It was pure white too, with large, bamboo-wired shoulders that arched out and hid his true shape. Dorinbo tied the thick white sash around his waist, and then came the swords upon the left hip as always. It was finished. There was nothing left to do but die.

They both knew this. They looked at each other in silence for a moment, and then Dorinbo bowed. He went to the door and slid it open. The afternoon sun poured in, and the monk took a deep breath as he let it wash over him, motes of dust caught in the light dancing around him.

"Would my arm ever have healed?" asked Munisai, if only for something to say in the silence. The monk turned to look at him through the corner of his eye.

"No," he said, "not without a blessing from the gods."

It was not funny, but they laughed anyway, for it was better to remember each other like that than the coldness between them. Munisai felt sudden regret wash through him for that, and all the years of separation before it. But it was forlorn and fleeting. When the smiles had died on their lips, Dorinbo lifted one hand in a gesture to the high sun.

"Amaterasu is watching," he said. "Die well, Munisai."

"I shall," said Munisai.

They bowed to each other, and then the monk left. Dorinbo would not be attending the seppuku. The next time he saw Munisai, his body would be cold and his soul gone to face whatever judgment that he could not give.

Kazuteru approached Munisai's house with trepidation. A great burden had been placed upon him. He stopped, checked his kimono, checked his hands for dirt, checked even if his breath smelled the slightest bit rotten. Nothing had deteriorated since the last time he had stopped thirty paces before.

The gate of the wall that surrounded the estate was open. He saw no need to knock; Munisai would be expecting someone, if not him. Silently he entered the courtyard, and found his commander standing with his back to him, staring at the minutest details of a tree.

"My Lord Munisai," he said, dropping to one knee and bowing his head. Munisai turned to him, the white shoulders of his kimono wide like two turtle shells, a dry purple leaf in his hand.

"Kazuteru?" he said after a moment.

"Yes, my lord," Kazuteru said, whatever small amount of pride he felt at being remembered dwarfed by worry. He licked his lips. "Our Lord Shinmen has nominated me to be your second."

It would be he who struck Munisai's head from his shoulders once Munisai had forced the dagger up into his stomach. It was a duty that was an honor in name only. At best you performed the role flawlessly, and no one remembered you. If you made a mistake—failing to cut the head from the body in one swift stroke, or swung too hard so that you overbalanced and staggered like a drunkard—you would be cursed as one who soiled another's ultimate moment.

Those were worries for the ritual itself, however. The first possible dishonor was being refused by the one who would perform seppuku. Kazuteru kept his head down, awaited Munisai's judgment. He honestly didn't know which answer he would prefer.

"You are rather young for this," said Munisai.

"I am, my lord."

"But Lord Shinmen selected you?" the samurai said.

"He did, my lord," said Kazuteru, and strange though it was, it was true. An older samurai from the lord's personal bodyguard would be expected; one who Munisai knew well. But it was Kazuteru whom Shinmen had summoned, and the young samurai's protests of age and inexperience that he had ignored.

"You are young, but you are loyal to me, Kazuteru," the lord had said warmly. "Your loyalty is unquestioned. You will wait for my command to strike. Other samurai, who are closer to Munisai, might take pity upon him and take his head too soon. It is difficult not to. But you—I know you are loyal to me above all others, and will wait for my command to strike so that the ritual can be finished properly. You can do that, can't you?"

"Of course, my lord," Kazuteru had said, and bowed.

"Do you believe yourself capable?" asked Munisai now.

"Yes, my lord," lied Kazuteru.

"Very well, Kazuteru," said Munisai. "You displayed your skill with the shortsword to me once before. I trust your longsword is equal in ability."

"I shall not fail you, my lord," said Kazuteru. He pressed his head as close to the ground as he could go without dirtying his forehead, and offered up a prayer for this to come to be.

"Is all prepared at the dojo?" asked Munisai, once Kazuteru had risen.

"Yes, my lord." He nodded.

"Then let us go," said Munisai, and he let the leaf fall from his hand to rest upon the carefully raked sand. The samurai's wooden sandals left footprints beside it that the servants who tended the gardens would hesitate to erase the next morning.

They walked down side by side toward the dojo. Munisai did not look back. The village was utterly silent, the peasants having been ordered to stay in their hovels for the afternoon. Guards wearing both Shinmen's blue and Nakata's burgundy bowed as they passed.

A palisade of white cloth had been erected around the dojo, preventing anyone unworthy from seeing inside. Priests of both Shinto and Buddhism circled the building, chanting low and tossing purifying salt before them. Munisai stopped fifty paces short.

"Give me a moment," he said.

"Very well, Lord," said Kazuteru, not knowing if this was to be expected but not wanting to question it. "We shall await you. The north entrance is on our left. I shall enter from the south."

"Of course," said Munisai. Kazuteru bowed to him, and then left him alone.

Munisai had never before realized how massive the sky was. He looked up at it, a perfect blue streaked with high white lines of clouds. The sun shone golden on him, so small. Even through his sandals the gravel beneath his feet had texture he would never have imagined. There was the scent of burning herbs upon the breeze, escaping from within the dojo as they sweetened the air there.

He brought his eyes back down to the earth. He found himself close to a barrel, and then he found himself looking down into it. The water within was deep and dark and still and clear. His face looked back at him clearer than in any copper mirror.

One worry alone remained to be purged. It had grown sharper the closer he had come to the dojo, the closer he drew to the ritual. He had panicked on the ridge when he had seen Bennosuke's tears. The sudden confrontation with honest emotion had shocked and flustered him, and then the samurai within him had spoken in defense. He had not said what he—the very essence of him, his true, secret self—had wanted to say to the boy, which was:

Live, Bennosuke. Your simple survival would be a better revenge upon the Nakata than any amount of limbs you could lop off. Live, Bennosuke. Even though it goes against everything that I believe in, I cannot deny that the very base of me wants you to live.

But he had proved a coward for that moment, and his last words to the boy had been harsh and dogmatic. There was nothing he could do to correct that either—the moment was gone, like every other moment he had known, and the boy was in the dojo now alongside men in front of whom he could never admit such feelings.

He wondered if this was what the true measure of a life was—the number of words unsaid and the deeds undone you left behind. But what of the things you said in error, or the things you did and regretted? He had those as well. Finding balance, reason, or meaning was impossible now. Men had spent decades pondering such things and found no answer, and what time did he have left now? The rest of his life, of course, and that was not enough.

Munisai took deep breaths, and forced the anxiety out. He needed emptiness. He could not face the seppuku as he should if he harbored even the smallest doubt in his heart. He told himself that as Shinmen had given him a chance once before, he now had given the boy a chance and nothing more—and if the boy was worthy, as he knew him to be, nothing more was needed.

A final breath as a man.

Just live, Bennosuke, he prayed. *Hear this, somehow.*

Looking down into the water, Munisai disavowed himself of the notion that what looked back was the entirety of him. He became a vessel for his soul, nothing more. He realized the truth—that he was a wonderful idea constrained and trapped within a prison of tubes and meat and phlegm.

His hand plunged into the water, shattering the image. The ripples calmed, and Munisai was gone.

$\mathcal{B}$ennosuke awaited; they all awaited in perfect silence.

Tasumi was to his left, his face solemn. Around the walls of the dojo hall men knelt in ranks. The Nakata had invited them from Ukita's court in Okayama to come and bear witness, and many had wanted to see the end of a renowned swordsman like Munisai. They were from all across Japan—samurai, courtiers, emissaries, and nobles—all wearing the formal winged overkimonos in many different colors and liveries.

None wore white, though. That color was for the dead alone.

Lord Ukita had not deigned to come, and so Lord Shinmen, Lord Nakata, and Hayato sat upon small stools in the position of honor in the center of the hall, hands upon their knees. They sat with distant eyes and stony faces.

Bennosuke had watched the Nakata suspiciously, but he had seen nothing to suggest that they planned to do anything other than follow the ritual through. There was none of the smug triumph Bennosuke had expected. Hayato had not even looked at Bennosuke, though the boy eyed him warily.

There was little he could do in any case. For the first time since he could remember, he was without his shortsword. Though his head was not yet shaved like a monk, he had been made to cede the weapon, so there was at least some appearance of his punishment. He felt uneasy without it.

Neither did he want to disrupt the ceremony—not because his father had ordered him not to, but because he wanted to understand it. He did not know why Munisai had chosen seppuku instead of fleeing, why he had spoken of it with reverence and the adulation of a lover in his eyes. He could not share the sense of anticipation in the air now; the men neither lewd nor voyeuristic, but sitting rigid as though they were daring to look upon some holy artifact, bracing themselves to bask in its purity.

Why were they this way? These were men in high positions from across the breadth of the country, not some isolated, sick cult of degenerates, yet they had gathered to watch a man spill his guts. The only way to understand it must be to experience it. If seppuku was the true measure of man—as these men all evidently believed—then Bennosuke wanted to see, to feel, to know what that was.

Even if it meant watching his father die.

His "father" . . . It was shameful that he had cried before Munisai, childish and embarrassing, but that he had done so told Bennosuke that perhaps he had accepted the man further within himself than he had thought. At the very least the process had begun, but now whatever may have come to pass and whatever peace they may have found in time was being ripped away before it could flourish.

He hated how his life had become. He wished for the simplicity of childhood once again. But childhood was gone, and now a man's task lay ahead of him. He thought of Munisai's words of what a samurai ought to do. He thought of vengeance and looked at Hayato once more. Still the young lord was unreadable.

Could he fulfill what Munisai had asked of him? Could he give his own life in the pursuit of that? He did not know.

Perhaps, when Munisai had shown him how to die, he would. All he could do now was wait. All he could do was try to be samurai, like those around him.

They became aware of Munisai's arrival by the vague shadows of the men standing watch around the outside of the dojo bowing one by one as he silently passed, gray and spectral upon the white of the palisade. Things assumed a measured pacing now, heartbeats carefully counted and actions slow and deliberate.

The north door of the dojo slid open, and Munisai entered. He waited until it was slid closed behind him once more, and then he bowed low to all present. He silently came before Shinmen and the Nakata, where he lowered himself to his knees and pressed his head to the ground. The lords nodded back to him, and he rose to a rigid kneel.

"The most honorable Munisai Shinmen," intoned a courtier from the side, teeth blackened and his mustache long and drooping, "commander and vassal of the most noble Lord Sokan Shinmen. You are summoned here by the will of the most noble Lord Hideie Ukita to immolate thyself through cutting of the stomach to atone for the crime of the mutilation of the most noble Lord Hayato Nakata committed by your son. Do you question this?"

"No, my lords," said Munisai. "May my actions today expunge all shame."

"As they surely shall," said the courtier. "The ritual proceeds."

After bowing once more, Munisai surrendered his swords, which were placed upon a rest nearby. From behind a folding screen three small buckets were brought before him. One contained hot water, a second cold. Equal measures were ladled into the empty third, so that the temperature was a median. Munisai dunked his hands into it, and washed them. Then he brought a ladleful to his lips and swirled it around his mouth. A small bowl was held before him, and he let the water dribble out into it.

Purified, he let his hair down from the top knot of living samurai that rested on the shaven pate of his head. Hair was worn in that manner to balance the helmet, but Munisai had no further need for armor now. Instead, out of consideration for those he would leave behind, he pulled the hair back, wound it over upon itself, and then tied it at the base of his skull so that it jutted outward like a curved, black baton. This was the style of those about to die, for it would allow the head to be handled easier.

A length of white hemp was brought out and laid upon the floor. Munisai rose to his feet and slipped out of his overkimono, then knelt at the southern end of the hemp, facing north. A bunch of sacred flowers and herbs arranged carefully in a thin vase was placed opposite him.

"Would the honorable Munisai Shinmen care to write a death poem?" asked the courtier.

"It is proper for it to be so," said Munisai.

Water was mixed drop by drop with black powder to produce ink. A brush and a length of paper were placed before him. Into a small cup, a careful four measures of sake were poured. It was offered to

Munisai, and he drank half in two sips. The cup was placed down, the brush taken up.

He began to write. There was no deliberation; he had planned his words beforehand. Bennosuke watched—they all watched—his hand dance across the paper, enchanted.

"Would the honorable Munisai care for the poem to be read aloud?" asked the courtier when the samurai had set the brush down.

"It is proper for it to be so," said Munisai.

The paper was carried to the courtier reverentially. The man held it before him, careful not to let the ink run in ugly rivulets. He read it once silently so that there would be no mistake, thick lips working over his black teeth. Then he took a breath and began to intone somberly:

Eight years hence from there I wandered,
The break of seasons around me squandered.
I am but a leaf, wilting, shrinking, passing on,
Yet the tree beneath me: paragon.

There was a rippling of silent heads as men nodded, thinking they understood the poem. Bennosuke knew otherwise; he knew that these words were meant for him alone. A paragon—one who understood and upheld the sanctity of things.

Munisai finished the sake with another measured two sips. The cup was taken from him along with the writing tools, and placed behind the screen. A man returned. He had a raised wooden platter in his hand, the ceremonial dagger resting on it. It was placed before Munisai, and the blade glinted silver as he took it in his hands and tested the sharpness against the back of his hand. He nodded, satisfied, and handed it back to the man, who began to wrap the center of the blade in white silk a ritualized twenty-eight times.

It took time. As he began to wind, the southern door was opened. Kazuteru entered and bowed to the gathered men.

"My name is Kazuteru Murayama. It is both my honor and privilege to have been accepted by the most honorable Munisai Shinmen as his second," he said.

They bowed back to him, and the young samurai walked silently to stand by Munisai. He was not acknowledged; Munisai's eyes were fixed, distant, as though they were seeing beyond the walls of the dojo.

Kazuteru bound the sleeves of his kimono up around his shoulders, freeing his arms. He slid his longsword silently out of his scabbard and drizzled some of the holy water upon the curved blade. Holding the sword carefully before him, he took his place on the white hemp, placing his stockinged feet behind and to the left of Munisai. He readied himself to strike, holding the sword in the correct position—hilt close to his cheek, elbows high and level with his eyes—and then began to focus on the hairs on the back of Munisai's neck. Kazuteru swallowed, concentrated on those dark lines, prayed to whatever might be listening to let his sword find its way cleanly to them.

When the dagger was correctly wrapped, it was returned to the platter and placed before Munisai. He looked at it for a long while, eyes upon the point. The man to Bennosuke's right bit the inside of his lip.

"The ritual shall be completed in its entirety," said Munisai. Across and back, silently, and some of those watching were moved to nod their approval at his courage and his properness. "May this act earn your pardon, my lords."

Munisai picked the dagger up, right hand upon the tightly wound cloth. He forced his weak left hand under his right, clasping it tightly so it would not slip when it became slick with blood. He placed the point of the blade on the left side of his stomach, the sharpness cutting through the first layer of silk effortlessly . . .

. . . *There was a moment of euphoria, where everything seemed perfect—he could see forever, the sun high and golden, the son low and watching, herbs sweet in the air, all were part of him and he part of them* . . .

The dagger went up. Immediately Bennosuke could see the white silk of the kimono turn red. Save for one tiny exhalation of breath, Munisai made no sound. His eyes were open, the tendons on his neck ridging in agony. Blood began to drip upon the floor, and to that pattering beat Munisai began to wrench the blade across.

Sharp though the dagger was it still required a fierce effort to cut across the belly. Munisai's hands juddered as he slowly drew a ragged red line across himself. His teeth were gritted so tightly that Benno-suke thought they must shatter. Another hiss of breath escaped him, nothing more. A pink mass of entrails began to emerge.

The soles of Kazuteru's stockings began to grow damp with blood as the stain of red spread outward across the hemp like a flood-burst river over a plain. Even from behind he saw the extra effort Munisai needed to turn the blade, felt the savage spasm of Munisai's body as he did so, heard the fresh, thicker spattering of darker blood upon the floor. Still he waited, sword tight in his hand, willing his commander onward, praying that at the rapidly approaching moment he would not fail him.

Bennosuke too urged Munisai through the final terrible inches. He felt his heart beating in admiration, even as the intestines began looping out of Munisai's stomach uncontrollably. This was bravery before him, silent and horrific and noble.

Another two savage jerks, a last surge of horrible strength, and it was done. Munisai had made it, and still no noise had escaped him. Kazuteru saw Munisai's shoulders sag in relief, and then the man leaned forward and stuck his neck out—perhaps subconsciously—inviting the blow. Kazuteru allowed himself a moment to check for the signal he knew Shinmen would give, but to his surprise the lord remained still. He waited, confused.

Guts splattered upon the hemp. Munisai shuddered in silent agony. Bennosuke sensed something amiss. He too looked across to Lord Shinmen. The lord's face was uncertain, worried, and the boy wondered what was troubling him. All it took was the simple wave of a hand to command the final blow, nothing more.

But in looking over at the lord, the boy became aware of someone looking at him—the only other face not looking at Munisai—and it was then that he saw the Hayato Nakata he had expected to see today. The young lord's eyes were malicious and triumphant and leering, and the one hand he had was resting a fan gently upon the wrist of Shinmen.

Betrayal. Lord Shinmen had betrayed them.

In those numb moments Bennosuke saw the plan unfurl itself before him—the Nakata didn't want to merely kill Munisai, they wanted to ruin him utterly. They had persuaded Shinmen to withhold the killing signal until Munisai screamed, and so Munisai would destroy himself in front of a countrywide room of witnesses.

And what could Bennosuke do now? Nothing. He had no weapon, and if he acted he would definitely spoil Munisai's death. He knew that the only chance Munisai had left of keeping his honor as he had planned was if he managed to endure in silence to the end. It was a small chance, for it took a long while to bleed to death, but it was all there was.

Hayato turned backed to Munisai, now that he knew that Bennosuke knew. No one had noticed him look away, engrossed as they were in the spectacle before them. The burgundy lord awaited the damning scream, and Bennosuke could only watch helplessly also, praying for his father to have the strength to deny it to Hayato.

Suddenly Munisai shuddered and the slightest of gasps escaped his lips, and then the man lurched forward. He put a hand out to catch himself, not dead yet. He remained on all fours, his insides spilling out of him, and still he did not make a sound. The dagger remained lodged in him, shaking and glimmering with the jerking of his body.

Kazuteru looked imploringly at Lord Shinmen once more, but still he gave no signal. Kazuteru wanted to strike, imagined himself doing so, no longer worried about failure—but he could not disobey his lord. His hands grew tight on his sword.

On it dragged, seconds marked only by the writhing of tubes and the falling of blood. Munisai's hand bunched the hemp within his fist, white knuckles showing through the red. The blood grew slower, pumping from deep within, gushing out now in spurts to the time of his faltering heart. Each small eruption gave Bennosuke hope that Munisai could endure, that it would be the final one and his father would simply lay himself down and die.

But seppuku was seppuku. Suddenly, inevitably, Munisai jerked as though he might be coughing, and then a moan escaped his lips. There was no intelligent voice in it, an instinctive gurgle, long, low, and guttural like a dead wind. The gathered witnesses recoiled in shock and surprise. As they did so, Lord Shinmen ripped his hand free of Nakata's restraint and pointed to Kazuteru.

Gratefully, the young samurai struck.

He had hoped, hoped against hope, that Dorinbo had been wrong and that maybe the spirit of Yoshiko would be waiting for him. But she was not here.

He had passed beyond sensation, so that although he was aware his body was hurting he no longer cared for it. What was hurt to him but a memory of meat? He thought his eyes saw this world and the next, but he knew that they did not see Yoshiko. He was alone. It made no sense. She had to forgive him. That was the way it was meant to be.

Munisai became aware that he—his body, not his soul, for the two were rapidly splitting—was making a sound, and he could not stop it. There was a vague inkling that this was wrong, that somehow sound was bad, but then he found that he could no longer remember what sound was. That was attached to the living world, and to that he felt no more kinship.

There was another sensation suddenly, a sharp sting on what he used to call his neck, and then the world started to spin. Colors and shapes swirled and bounced around him, but there was no Yoshiko, and then the darkness started to come. It swept over him, and he was so alone and there was no Yoshiko there was no Yoshiko there was no Yoshiko there was no . . .

Dorinbo knelt before the temple. It was night. He was weaving the final bough by the light of a paper lantern. Wordlessly Bennosuke approached and knelt beside his uncle.

The village was empty now, the visiting samurai departed. Bennosuke had been ignored, and as they had left he had heard words recurrent in their conversations—*shame, coward, disgrace, Munisai.* There were varying levels of skepticism, but then men with purses fat with Nakata gold had intervened. They insisted that Munisai had arrogantly arranged beforehand that he would signal his own decapitation and had failed miserably. Thus the Nakata had their victory. Even men not in allegiance with them would carry the news of the shaming far and wide, and Shinmen would not deny it for he had chosen the Nakata, and so the truth of the tale would become undoubted.

Only one person had spoken to him directly. Hayato Nakata had addressed him from the awning of his palanquin, the dozens of men bearing him aloft looking on.

"Are you samurai?" he asked, glee writ across his face. "Are you samurai, monk?"

With those simple words, as Munisai had said he would, Bennosuke understood. He had watched the last of the samurai disappear in silence, and then slowly he had wandered up to the temple, where his father's body had been taken.

It lay inside the small shrine now. Dorinbo had taken the head and the body, cleaned them, and wrapped them in a shroud. Bennosuke could see the vague outline atop the boughs stacked inside. A pyre of prayers, hopes, and dreams for a damned man.

Bennosuke watched his uncle's hands as the monk worked. The bough was almost finished—he was weaving the penultimate prayer into it. It was Munisai's death poem. He saw the characters of *paragon* once more, and then they were gone, swallowed into the mass of the bough. A single prayer remained, a folded piece of paper unworn by time. Dorinbo held it out to Bennosuke.

"Do you remember this?" he said.

"No," said Bennosuke.

"You gave it to me on the morning you left for Takeyama."

"Oh," said Bennosuke. It seemed a long time ago. Dorinbo unfolded the paper.

"I thought we weren't supposed to look at the prayers," said Bennosuke.

"I think this one no longer holds any truth," said the monk, and then he read from the prayer. " *'I, Bennosuke Shinmen, hope to be the finest samurai I could possibly be in the service of Lord Shinmen'* . . . I'm right, am I not?"

"Yes," said Bennosuke, but he knew that his uncle was wrong: Dorinbo was thinking Bennosuke was not to be a samurai. That was not the part of the prayer he disagreed with.

"Amaterasu need not hear it, then," said Dorinbo, and then he folded it up once more and handed it to Bennosuke. The boy slipped it inside his robe.

"In that case, it's finished, then," said Dorinbo. "Twenty years for this. Would you care to place the final bough?"

"Should there not be others here? Pilgrims?" asked the boy.

"I shall keep the fires stoked for a week. They will come then, and then they will pray," said Dorinbo, and in the darkness Bennosuke became aware of the vague outlines of great piles of wood. How busy things must have been here, and in all the months he had spent with Munisai he had not noticed, had not cared.

"It would be an honor," said Bennosuke.

"There's space at Munisai's feet," said Dorinbo. Bennosuke rose, picked the bough up, and approached the temple.

The small shrine was surrounded by boughs now, each crisp and dry and awaiting the flame. The cramped interior of the shrine was lined with boughs too, surrounding Munisai's body. On his knees, he lifted his father's legs and slotted the final bough beneath them. Then he pulled the shroud to one side and looked at the corpse.

The blow to the neck had been swift and clean and had severed Munisai's head neatly. Dorinbo had placed the head as though it had never been harmed, the cleaned wound a dark blue smear around his neck. A fresh kimono masked the terrible wound to his stomach. It appeared that the man was merely sleeping. There was no hint of the agony and humiliation he had suffered.

Bennosuke bowed low and reverently, held it for several seconds, and then he rose and looked over Munisai's body. It felt disrespectful, but he needed to do it. He spotted the shortsword easily, laid as it was beside Munisai's right hand. But what he needed, he could not see.

"It's here, Bennosuke," said Dorinbo calmly.

Bennosuke turned to look at his uncle. The monk was holding Munisai's longsword in both hands before him. Bennosuke slowly clambered down from the temple and then took the sword from Dorinbo's hands. He was surprised, and he looked at his uncle.

"We both know that you are not a monk. You are Munisai's son, not mine," the man said quietly.

"I would have stayed, but . . ." said Bennosuke awkwardly. "Nakata will return and kill me if I do."

"Is it that, or is it that you want to go and kill him?" said Dorinbo. Bennosuke remained silent. He wanted to explain himself to his uncle, but he knew it was futile, just as Dorinbo knew it was futile to try to force him to stay.

The monk rose to his feet, and then removed the paper covering from the lantern exposing the naked candle. He picked a torch from the floor, and held the oil-soaked rag to the flame. It ignited, flaring bright, and the monk slowly walked to the temple pyre. He lowered the torch to the first bough, and then the burning had begun. As flame slowly erupted around the base, Dorinbo clapped twice, bowed, and then lifted his hands high in the gesture of Amaterasu's prayer. Then he turned to look at Bennosuke, silhouetted by the rising flames behind him.

"We are the children of Amaterasu, Bennosuke. We are born to burn to ash and then to rise again. Our bodies burn. Sometimes our cities burn. Someday even our mountains and our rivers may burn. But we always come back, and where we rise to after that is entirely our choice. That is Amaterasu's gift to us," said the monk. He gestured to the fire behind him, the first flames licking around Munisai.

"This is the ash of your childhood. So go now, and raise yourself to where you want to be," he said, and then bowed.

Bennosuke thought of speaking, but realized he had no words. He looked at his uncle for a long time before he bowed back, and then he slid the longsword into the sash at his waist. It felt right. Then he turned and walked into the night, the hopes and prayers of twenty years rising into the sky behind him and the image of his father's body as it withered in the flames burned into his eyes.

Dorinbo watched him go, and then silently he started to pray.

Part Three

THE CHILD'S CRUSADE

CHAPTER ELEVEN

Snow rarely fell in the south of Japan, save for on the peaks of mountains, but the chill of winter was bitter all the same. Men and women bundled themselves in layers of thick cloth, the children barely noticed or cared, and the elderly grumbled that this was a freeze harsher than any before and was thus irrevocable proof of the encroaching doom of the world.

For the time being at least the world went on, and under a clear morning sky a peasant worked chopping wood. The light was bright and sharp enough that he had to squint at the lumber he guided his ax to. He had a pile of firewood tall enough to last the week already beside him, but he did not stop. With the earth hard and unworkable until spring, the man found himself chopping simply for something to do.

"Greetings, friend," came a voice, and the peasant turned to find two men there.

The one who had spoken was standing about ten paces away, smiling, his breath misting in the air, while another watched from the pathway on which the pair of them had evidently been walking. They both wore heavy traveling gowns that hid the shape of their bodies, their hands tucked away from the cold.

"Greetings," the peasant said guardedly, bowing and then resting the ax across his shoulders. The men did not carry swords and both had full heads of close-cropped hair, so fawning subservience was not required.

"This village is Miyamoto, is it not?" said the man, still smiling.

"Aye." The peasant nodded. "If you've come to see the temple, it's not being rebuilt until the spring."

"While that is a shame, I journey instead because of the monk there—I hear he is skilled in healing," said the man.

"He's a clever one, yes," said the peasant. "You don't look sick, though."

"Thankfully I am in good health. It is my son; the boy has developed a rash. Men say the monk's boy had the same affliction, and that he managed to cure it."

"You're wrong there. That boy was flecked like the night sky with scabs and poxmarks for as long as I remember," said the peasant.

"Perhaps it is a recent cure—have you seen the boy lately?" said the man.

The peasant thought for a few moments. "No, now that you mention it. Not since autumn, at least."

"Well, I shall journey to the temple all the same," said the man, but he did not seem truly dispirited. "My thanks for your time."

He bowed, and then the pair of them left. The peasant watched them go, shrugged, and got back to work. The roads often brought strange men in with them, and it was no business of his if they had set out in the opposite direction to the temple.

An hour later the two men were hunched around a wretchedly small fire hidden in a copse of bare trees. They knew very well which village this was and where the temple was located, for they had visited it when they had first arrived four days ago in the guise of pilgrims. But though they had lingered abnormally long at the grounds—they were very pious, they had told the monk—they had not seen the boy who was supposed to be there.

That was unexpected, and so this thicket had become their home while they had watched the roads in and out of Miyamoto and had questioned as many people as they dared.

"It seems the lad truly isn't here," sighed the second man, aimlessly flicking ash from the fire with a stick. "What a miserable business."

"Do not let bleakness take your heart, my brother," said the first, though his tone was hardly a contrast.

"This whole thing is just odd."

"Odd requests bring odd amounts of money."

"Why don't they just march their samurai in and take care of it?"

"This is a matter they have been warned away from. Direct action would attract unwanted attention," said the first. "Regardless, we have accepted the job—"

"*You* accepted the job."

"And the people who gave it are not ones we have the luxury of failing."

"So we're stuck with it, then," muttered the second. "What do we do?"

"Well, there are a few options," said the first. "We could wait here freezing our asses to the ground until the lad comes back from wherever he has gone—if he is coming back. Or we could search every temple and monastery from here until we find him on the off chance that he has, as I was told, become a monk. Or I suppose we could go back and tell them that we couldn't find him, waive our fee, and most likely the majority of the blood in our bodies."

"Isn't that wonderful?" said the second, and tossed his stick away petulantly. "This whole thing is disturbing. Slipping poison into soup is one thing, but this business with the arms? That's just morbid. They want that sort of thing done, they should send a filthy corpsehandler."

The first looked up, sudden inspiration in his eyes.

TWO DAYS LATER, the body of a tall young man was found in a ditch. It appeared as if nothing was wrong with him, his face as calm as a man at meditation, save for the fact that his arms had been cleanly chopped off and spirited away somewhere. That might have caused some consternation, were it not for the fact that the man was a corpsehandler.

They were the builders of coffins, the executioners, the butchers, and the tanners—the ones mired in decay and death and carcasses and the lowest of the low because of that irrevocable contamination. Wise men estimated them to be at best one-seventh of a true human being, so the dismemberment of what was a tainted parody of a man in the first place made little difference in the scheme of things.

No one mourned for the armless body except his mother. His father, when he learned of his son's fate, had tutted and sucked air through his teeth before he nodded and pronounced:

"Well, he must be in a better bloody life than this one."

❄

*W*inter passed, Amaterasu grew in strength once more, and so came the spring and a cherry blossom beautiful. The petals brought delight and then withered as they always did, and it was some weeks after the flowers had fallen that Kazuteru accompanied his lord to the estate of the Nakata.

As he expected, the grounds were opulent beyond anything he had seen. The gardens were one flowing piece of art: still, clear ponds crisscrossed by elegantly carved, arcing wooden bridges that led to immaculately raked beds of sand and gravel. Fat, pale carp swam beneath blooming lotus pads, rising to the surface with their mouths gaping and flapping expectantly as the samurai passed.

The castle hold itself, seeming like an afterthought, was guarded by men wielding long halberds with bands of gold set around the wooden shafts, each weapon inlaid with more than Kazuteru himself owned.

Before they could marvel at that ornamentation fully—or, Kazuteru suspected, perhaps notice any frailty in the fortress itself—they had been quickly led away to the mansion where the lord resided and shown to their resplendent quarters. Beautiful girls tended to each of them, and they were offered rest and relaxation in hot water that Nakata had had channeled from a natural spring almost a half mile away. Then came dinner.

Lord Nakata himself, his son Hayato, and Lord Shinmen sat centrally on a dais, and then ten bodyguards from both clans sat in rank along either side of the hall they were in. Kazuteru was on the farthest end of Shinmen's line. Slivers of fresh, raw ocean fish sped that day to this mountain hold lay before him on a gold-leaf-painted lacquer platter. The chopsticks in his hand were plated in carved silver at the end.

Kazuteru looked at them dumbly. Still he found himself surprised to be in such situations. He knew deep down that he did not belong here surrounded by such splendor. He had not earned it. He was much younger than the other men he sat beside and of no exceptional skill with the sword, yet in the wake of Munisai's seppuku he had been promoted to serve in Shinmen's personal retinue.

He had accrued an accidental and unwanted fame; how he cursed the invention of the woodblock printing press. The damned machine was a recent triumph of Japanese engineering—that is to say, someone had found one in Korea half a dozen years ago in the first war and brought it back with them—and it allowed what would have taken an artist and a team of apprentices an hour to achieve to be done in a matter of moments.

The prints it produced were far from great art, of course, simple black outlines more often than not illustrating well-known tales and stories, but for the first time they were allowing the common man to fancy himself cultured. The presses therefore resided somewhere between a novelty and the foundation of an industry, growing in popularity in Kyoto and Osaka and Edo, and so it followed that, like any trend, of course Nakata had purchased one. His machine had been kept busy these recent months printing by the score a particular scene titled *The Revelation of the Nation's Finest and All That Lay Within Him.*

Kazuteru had first seen it in the barracks where he stayed, a group of samurai passing a copy of it around with stony faces. It had been one of the more expensive copies too, for an artist had gone over it by hand with red ink, lovingly picking out entrails and splashes of gore. What it showed was Munisai's seppuku; a caricature monkey of a man on his knees with a sword in his belly, his eyes pinched shut in childish agony, tears rolling down his cheeks, and his tongue poking out.

The samurai behind him, conversely, was tall and handsome and strong, his sword held steady and proud, disdain in his stoic eyes. The perfect contrast to what squirmed at his feet, and by that immaculate man's face was clearly printed the name Kazuteru Murayama.

"Well, *you* came out of this well, didn't you?" one of the samurai had said, his eyes narrow and venom in his voice.

Kazuteru had tried to protest his innocence, tried to tell them that he found it embarrassing to be singled out so, but they had not listened. They were obliged to condemn Munisai, of course, but there was an unspoken acknowledgment that his death had been suspicious and so the words they spat were protocol only, and to hate Shinmen or the Nakata was to speak against the very thing that made them samurai.

That left Kazuteru, and so he had become their surrogate abomination.

Yet despised though he was by his own comrades, because Lord Shinmen did not protest the contents of the print and allowed for it to be openly disseminated in his own realm, the veracity of it became indisputable to the other thousands of men of all castes who saw the print. Munisai was disgraced, Kazuteru renowned, and so it came to be then that visiting dignitaries and courtiers would ask to meet him.

It had happened so often that Lord Shinmen found it expedient to simply promote him to the bodyguard rather than summon him each time, and each time when he was presented he could see the look of disappointment in their eyes that who knelt before them was not some legendary warrior but a young man barely out of adolescence.

Just another shame to bear; at least his mother was benefiting from his fattened stipend. Unwanted by those beside him, an anticlimax to men of a dozen realms, Kazuteru kept his eyes down as his lord and his ally ate, and plotted, to the sound of a koto harp played by unseen hands.

"Our regent's war in Korea is almost spent," said Lord Nakata once the formalities of etiquette were done with, the polite inquests of health and subtle praise and honor he and Shinmen exchanged with each other exhausted. "'Do not let my soldiers become ghosts haunting foreign lands,' his latest decree."

"So I have heard," said Shinmen. "And though I pray it to not be true, my emissaries in Kyoto tell me our regent is all but spent himself. His health is failing, and then . . ."

"And then," said Nakata, and nodded.

The War. That was what they could not permit themselves to say. Once the Regent Toyotomi vacated this world, the whole of Japan would be thrown to the wolves. The tiny fiefdom struggles that had plagued the country would cease, petty grievances and domain disputes put to one side in favor of the true prize.

"When that happens—may it be ten years, nay, ten lifetimes away, of course—what is our plan, my ally?" asked Lord Nakata.

"We shall side with our Lord Ukita, as always," said Shinmen. "My will is as his—unless?"

"I do not engage in deceit," said Nakata, his ever-squinting eyes hiding any chance to see if he spoke the lie all lords spoke without shame. "I too intend to remain with our Lord Ukita. But therein lies a clarification—remain alongside, not be blindly absorbed into his numbers, as will be his urge in the marshaling of forces."

"Oh?" said Lord Shinmen.

"I intend to remind him of my independence from him. I would ask your help, my closest ally," said Nakata, and then at Shinmen's look of discomfort added, "Do not worry so. I do not plan violence against him. No—new enemies should not be made now. I merely wish to remind him that I—that we are capable."

"How?" said Shinmen.

"A Gathering of the Horse," said Nakata.

"A Swarming Hell?" sputtered Shinmen.

"Let us keep our tongues civil, my ally," said Nakata. "A Gathering."

Nakata wanted to be delicate about it, but Kazuteru had seen such an event in his childhood and he knew his lord had spoken fairly. Other men called it the Crush or the Melee or the Whirlpool, and these were apt names also. He remembered the thunder of the hooves, the overwhelming fury of it, hundreds of men on horseback as fierce as on a battlefield but there for sport and not for conquest. A spectacle as dangerous and costly as it was marvelous.

The samurai would ride in a great circle that grew slowly ever tighter and ever faster. When they were pressed flank to flank and the ground was truly shaking, a wooden ball was lobbed into the center of the mass, and then the chaos began.

The goal was to grab the ball and then escape from the mass of bodies without being unseated. No weapons were allowed, but that did not make it any less dangerous. It became little more than a brawl, frenzied horses kicking and ramming and men clawing and punching at one another. To fall or to be wrenched from the saddle was to be sucked into a sea of stomping hooves, and from there very, very few men escaped unscathed.

To win had as much to do with luck as it had to do with skill, but nevertheless the man who bore the ball free won great honor and respect for both him and his clan. For that reason, rare though they were, a Gathering always attracted men from far and wide seeking glory.

"What think you, my Lord Shinmen?" said Nakata, his eyes gleaming with self-congratulation.

"As impressive as that may be," said Shinmen, recovering from his initial surprise, "might I remind you, my dear ally, that even combined our cavalry number but a fraction of our Lord Ukita's."

"Oh, I don't intend to win the thing, nor try to scare him with simple weight of numbers. The staging of it and the sight of so many lords and warriors heeding my invitation will display to him that, should I wish it, I have options," said Nakata.

"That is not without risk. We do not wish even to put the idea in his head that our loyalty wavers."

"Mmm, true," said Nakata.

"Allow me to suggest something—we enter a time of steel, my lord, not gold," continued Shinmen. "Steel is what you need to display, and fortunately steel can take the form of more than just a sword in the hand."

"What are you suggesting?"

"Go ahead with the Gathering, my lord, but show him another strength. Our cavalry cannot impress him, and gold inspires only avarice in such times. Knives grow longer. Of course I do not suggest our Lord Ukita harbors such malice, but should an accident or ill health befall you—the heavens forbid such a thing, my dear ally—our Lord Ukita might see a chance to"—he had to pause to choose an acceptable wording—"satiate his avariciousness toward your wealth. You must discourage this, remind him that your clan resides in more than just you. You must show him the strength of your line."

"My line?" said Nakata.

"Yes," said Shinmen, and then he turned to Hayato. "And thus the Lord Hayato here enters our consideration."

"What—you expect me to ride?" said Hayato, surprised as much at the sudden attention as the implication. He had been eating in a world unto himself, months of indolent recuperation having returned weight and health to him.

"Yes," said Shinmen.

"Do I need to remind my dear ally of something?" said Hayato, the empty sleeve of his kimono between them.

"What better way to display the strength of heart of the Nakata? A one-armed man riding in a Gathering has never been seen," said Shinmen.

"Never been seen because he's fallen off his horse and gotten trampled before it could even begin," said Hayato. "No, I absolutely refuse."

"Oh, come, my young lord," said Shinmen. "There comes a time when every man from peasant to nobility must play a role for the good of the clan. Men shall speak of your bravery the breadth of the country, and our Lord Ukita will realize that the Nakata possess something more than coin."

"Oh," said Lord Nakata, and his old, jowly face was lighting up now, "oh, my ally, that is a quite wonderful idea. Romantic indeed!"

"Father!" said Hayato, more shrilly then he intended, for he took a moment to compose himself before speaking again. "I cannot do this. Have one of our commanders ride in my name, or . . ."

"That misses the point entirely. What is remarkable in having your men serve you? That is their duty," said Shinmen. "Do it."

Shinmen spoke the last two words quite levelly, but Kazuteru had spent enough time around his lord to recognize the undertone in them. There was something more than just command or plea in them—a subtle anger, a nuanced vindictiveness that neither of the Nakatas noticed.

There had been one evening some months before when Shinmen had, unusually, summoned him to his personal chambers. Kazuteru had found the lord sitting before a meal barely touched and a bottle of sake still full to the brim. A copy of the seppuku print was in his hand. The young samurai bowed and knelt a respectful distance away, waiting for the man to speak.

"Do you think it was cruel?" said Shinmen eventually, eyes not leaving the print. "You were the closest to him, at the end."

"It was seppuku, my lord," said Kazuteru. "It is supposed to be cruel."

"I know that, but . . ." said Shinmen, and he seemed to be struggling for words. "Could you feel anything from him?"

"No more than any other man there, my lord," said Kazuteru, not quite understanding the question. He had waited for something further, but the lord seemed only to grow more agitated. Slowly he held the paper to a candle, and watched it as it ignited in his hand.

"I am not a human being. Do you understand this?" he said as the flame spread across the cheap paper. "I am a clan. A heart of my own does not lie within my chest—a heart of a thousand years does."

He held the paper until the fire reached his hand, and then he dropped it upon the floor and tipped the sake upon it. With his finger, the lord pushed the sad little dregs of resultant ash as though he was reading auguries.

"You must think the will of a lord boundless, but it is nothing to the will of an aeon," he said, a hollow sadness in his voice—the voice very much of a human being. The lord had said nothing more, and had eventually waved him away.

Kazuteru had remembered witnessing that fragment of the man, so at odds with how the lord appeared from day to day. Often he had wondered if it was a singular bout of emotion or whether it always bubbled somewhere behind the mask of his face. And he remembered also that, during that strange delay at Munisai's seppuku before Shinmen gave the signal to strike, it was Hayato who was sitting next to him.

Here, now, plotting the Gathering, the pair of lords were opposite each other. It was impossible to know exactly what Shinmen was thinking, but it seemed to Kazuteru that there was no grand plan here, no hidden machination escaping his eye—Shinmen was moved by a simple, personal dislike. Forcing this on Hayato was a trivial and small thing, so very far from anything that could be considered revenge, but it was all he could do. The clan had chosen the Nakata and not Munisai, and thus the human too was bound to them.

"I agree thoroughly—you shall ride," said the Lord Nakata, and he carried on before Hayato could interrupt. "There need be no danger to you either, my son. You will ride with my bodyguard around you."

"Father . . ." said Hayato.

"Do you doubt their ability to protect you?" said Nakata, and it was a cunning move, for Hayato could not publicly belittle men sworn to the head of his clan. The young lord tried to think of something he could say, but the words eluded him and after a moment he sighed in resignation.

"Fine, fine. I will ride," the young lord said, and looked down sullenly to shove a chunk of fish into his mouth with his one remaining hand.

"Splendid, splendid, splendid!" said Nakata, and he raised the pewter dish he was drinking from in toast to Shinmen. "The country shall resound in awe of the Nakata. Oh, how splendid!"

"Indeed," said Shinmen, and returned the toast.

They finished the many decadent courses of the meal, slept under sheets of Chinese silk, and then in the morning Shinmen, Kazuteru, and the rest of the retinue departed, the same beautiful girls who had served them throwing petals in front of the dirty hooves of their horses. They carried with them the first tidings of and invitations to the clan Nakata's Gathering of the Horse.

It was not the news that the country was waiting for—that was still lingering on a death bed in Kyoto—but it spread quickly all the same.

CHAPTER TWELVE

The empty street seemed to swim in front of Bennosuke. It rippled and pulsed, a dizziness that gnawed at him. It was a familiar sensation born of exhausted delirium that plagued his waking moments. He wished the world would stop moving, that the ground would seem solid beneath him just for an hour, but he knew that he could not rest. He had a mission.

The Gathering. A fortnight away.

No time to waste—the boy shook his head and forced focus into his mind. He scurried out of the alleyway he had been hiding in and though he was exposed in the center of the street for only a moment, it felt like a naked lifetime. He dived in gratefully among the dark shapes of the warhorses opposite, hiding himself and dreading any call of alarm. None came.

His hair was long and wild, matted into thick strands. His clothes were rags tied to him as much as worn, his body filthy and gaunt. The nail of his ring finger on his right hand had fallen out and was only half grown back, tender and ugly. The swords at his side were bound to him with a length of rope.

The night went on around him. The horses were solid things bred and trained for the chaos of a battlefield. A wretch like him would not startle them. They were tethered in front of an inn, from within which the murmurs of dulled, drunken conversation could be heard.

The horses' owners were samurai, and so confident were they of the impossibility of their theft that they had left the horses fully saddled and had not even bothered to tether them beyond a cursory loop. Bennosuke's gnarled fingers untangled the reins of the closest one and then, crouched low in a scuttling mess of elbows and knees, began to try to lead it away.

The beast was reluctant to move. It turned at first, obedience drilled into it, and it took a couple of halting paces away from the others. But something seemed odd to it, and it halted, shaking its muzzle and snorting. The boy tugged at the reins, and the horse whipped its head back with such casual power that it almost tore them from his grasp.

"Come on," hissed Bennosuke, but the pretense of giving a command gave way to desperation. "Please."

Haltingly, the horse came. It did not like leaving the safety and warmth of its companions, but hoof by hesitant hoof it obeyed the insistent hauling. The boy led it toward the darkness, away from the inn, which was illuminated by lantern light, all the while keeping an eye on the door of the building. Once he was enveloped by the night he would risk the noise of riding, but not until then. Time dragged, the shade beckoning him, tantalizing.

He was but paces away when he heard the door being thrown open. Bennosuke froze, and hid himself dumbly behind the horse. Peering through the beast's legs, he saw a samurai stroll out onto the inn's porch. His kimono was thrown open, baring a chest gleaming with musky night sweat. The man leaned against a pillar and stared out at nothing. His dull eyes fell upon the boy and the horse. It took a moment for him to realize what was happening.

"Thief!" he bellowed, and suddenly the night erupted.

Bennosuke hissed a curse and scrambled up onto the horse's back. Other samurai were staggering out of the inn, shouting threats at him and commands to one another. Panicking, he slapped the horse on the hind with a balled fist and kicked his bony heels into its flanks. The beast screamed and bolted into the darkness much too fast, jerking and lurching blindly from side to side, tossing its rider around in the saddle like a sack of straw.

It was impossible to see where they were going—though the boy could not tell if the blackness came from the night or whether his eyes were screwed shut—and so all he could do was bend down and hold on. Abandoning the reins, he wrapped himself around the neck of the horse, his legs behind him being thrown wildly free of the stirrups, each stride of the horse putting a hand's width of air between his ass and the seat.

Undignified though it was, he managed to cling on, but soon the strain of having its rider in such an unusual position slowed the horse. It took a moment for Bennosuke to realize the animal was slowing; he readjusted himself in the seat and tried to spur the horse onward in a controlled manner. Instead the animal lost interest in movement at all and stopped entirely, content to let the boy kick and slap in vain as it caught its breath.

There came the sound of hooves from behind, and then Bennosuke sensed—not saw—something cannoning down the pathway toward them. His body froze, aware of approaching danger but unwilling or unable to move. The galloping sound reached its peak, and a second before the impact a shouted curse broke the air as the other rider realized instinctively that the way was blocked.

Too late. The samurai's horse barreled into the side of Bennosuke's with a hollow smack of rib cages and saddle frames. The impact drove the wind from the boy. It felt as though every bone in his body was vibrating. The world tipped as his horse fell onto its side, and then his back met the hard earth, half his body underneath the horse's flank.

The landing knocked the sense from him, yet sensation remained.

The pressing weight of the horse was there and then not, as the horse scrabbled and righted itself.

Motion, pulled by the feet; his twisted body was still caught in the stirrups, dragged for a moment until he fell limply free.

What might have been his stone felt a face atop of it, or perhaps the other way around?

Something touched him, turned him over.

Warm, blowing breath, the stink of sake upon it.

Cold, hard thing against his neck.

A noise that he understood expressed anger or displeasure.

Then there was light.

Another rider came, a samurai carrying a lantern in his hand, and the restoration of sight slowly brought wits back to Bennosuke. He realized there was a man kneeling on his chest, his face muddied and furious as he held what the boy guessed to be a sword to his throat. He lay as still as he could.

"Idiot! Damn bumpkin half-wit bastard!" the samurai on top of him was snarling. "You steal a horse and you can't even ride?"

"Hold," said the man on the horse. The other samurai were with him on their horses too, curling around them all like eels in a barrel, barely visible at the limit of the light's edge.

"Could've snapped my neck, falling from my horse," growled the kneeling man.

"What do you expect, charging on blindly ahead into the darkness like that?" said the rider. "You should have stayed with the light. In any case you're fine, and you apprehended the thief. Commendable work."

"Thank you," said the kneeling man, mollified slightly. "What do we do now?"

"Crucifixion is the punishment for major theft," said the rider, but the kneeling man uttered an irritated sigh.

"Agh, the execution site is a morning away. Let's just slit his throat and toss him in a ditch," said the man, taking his eyes off his captive for the first time and turning to the man holding the lantern.

"Crucifixion is the letter of the law," said the rider.

"Do you feel like riding that far tomorrow? Do you want to waste more time out here in the middle of nowhere? I don't."

"Hmm," said the lantern samurai, considering.

Though his life hung in the balance, his fate being determined by a simple debate of diligence or convenience, Bennosuke had neither the strength nor the presence of mind to do anything. All he could do was lie and watch the rider as he deliberated. The man's face was cold, a scar running from under his nose breaking across his lips and then stopping at his chin.

"Swords," said one of the other men after a moment, somewhere behind them. That broke the rider's thought, and both he and the man on top of the boy looked to where Bennosuke's weapons had fallen. The kneeling man uttered a single low curse.

"He stole them too, probably," he said. "Look at him—he's just a bloody peasant. Let's just do it now."

"Are you samurai?" asked the scarred rider, ignoring the man.

"Yes," spat Bennosuke, for though he was enfeebled and filthy, the boy would not allow himself to deny that.

The kneeling samurai grunted in disgust, and removed the sword from the boy's throat as he stood up.

"Fantastic," he said, glaring down. "Now we *have* to crucify you."

THEY BOUND BENNOSUKE with heavy rope using a technique that had been perfected and ritualized over centuries. The rope restricted him entirely, crisscrossing his torso and forcing his arms to his sides and his legs together at the knees, and they slung him over the back of one of their horses like a sack of rice and cantered back to the inn. He was hoisted from the eaves of the building, and hung suspended facedown over the street he had been sneaking through not an hour before.

The boy had thought the theft would be easy. The hamlet was small enough that it lacked any sort of watch or guard. The five samurai were here only to collect taxes from the outlying countryside. He had watched them for two days before he had made his move. Though the Gathering was in two weeks, he needed time to reacquaint himself with riding a horse. His feeble attempt at escape was proof of that.

Bennosuke knew that he should have been scared, captured as he was, but the truth was it was the most comfortable night he had spent in a long time. So meticulous and intricate was the binding that he felt not a single point of uncomfortable pressure. It was as though he was floating, rocking gently back and forth like a baby in the crib. Compared to the nights of the last months, where the boy had scrabbled in the dirt and shivered on hard ground for hours, it seemed a hanging luxury.

It was a miserable existence he had eked out. When he had left Miyamoto he headed straight for the Nakata clan's domain, certain that some god would turn favor upon him and deliver Hayato immediately. But though he lingered for a month in the shadows of the city that the Nakata called their capital, living frugally off the last of the coin he had managed to scrounge from within Munisai's house, Hayato for the most part remained behind the fortified walls of his estate. He might as well have been in the heavens for all that Benno-suke could get to him.

Only once had Bennosuke seen the young lord, glimpsed for a heartbeat through the bamboo blinds of a palanquin surrounded by dozens of bodyguards. He was traveling somewhere, a grand parade of course, and the boy had hidden within the kneeling crowd paying homage to their master. Even if he had had a bow and arrow, he was not confident he could have made the shot, and throwing himself into a blind charge was useless. Both would have resulted in his death while Hayato lived on.

His coin faltered and his certainty wavered, and in its place came the fear that eventually, wandering homeless on those streets, he would be recognized by some agent of the Nakata. He fled and headed to the countryside of the neighboring domain—that being of a Lord Shingo he knew nothing about—thinking that he would be able to earn food and lodgings, however meager, while he bided his time waiting for a plan to present itself.

But he had not known just how hated masterless samurai were. People saw the swords at his side and the deteriorating clothes upon his back and practically spat—if a samurai was masterless he had either disgraced himself or failed his lord utterly, and nobody wanted business with a troublemaker or an incompetent. He was shooed from town to town, the kinder hamlets offering him a bowl of rice gruel as pittance to speed him on his way, the harsher ones an escort of disgusted steward samurai.

A few times he had dared to hide his swords in the woods, wrapped his head in a cloth, and tried to pass himself off as a low-born. He would wait with a huddle of the other bedraggled jobless corraled like a herd of goats, awaiting employers seeking men to dig or to carry loads of stone or to turn the wheels of the great thresh-ing mills when the winds or the rivers were low. But his height or his rash or his educated accent or the simple fact that no one knew him singled him out, and while others were chosen by the dozen to shuffle off in teams of the pitifully grateful, Bennosuke was told to find work elsewhere.

How scarce food became. After the autumn harvests anything outside storerooms or the depths of the seas vanished. Bennosuke, stranded between the two, saw the fruits of neither. He considered hunting for boar or deer—the sin of consuming red meat was allowed in times of starvation—but he had no bow and even less of a clue about how to track the animals.

The rivers too were mostly denied him, for he had no net and the choice spots that were shallow enough for him to wade in and stab fat carp or salmon had long since been claimed by nearby settlements and were guarded against poachers. Occasionally he would find some secluded spot and try for the smaller, nimble fish, but the long hours of trying would usually yield no more than one or two skinny things the length of his foot that were in any case mostly bone.

In this they were like him; the flesh upon him withered as he fed upon only what fortune delivered him, sometimes going days without anything resembling a proper meal. He began to suffer from cramps, some so strong that he would rip his kimono away from himself and stare at his belly under the jutting bones of his rib cage, convinced it was tearing itself free of his body. His insides were ruined, his bowels water, and his toilet was whatever hole he scrabbled in the dirt for himself.

The dizziness that came with this starvation was the worst, though. That feeling of complete exhaustion was his constant companion, the world rippling before his eyes. Things seemed a dream sometimes, distant and throbbing. At times lucidity would return and he would find that he was in a completely different place from where he last remembered, or that he was loudly talking to himself. He worried for his mind as well as his body.

But he had endured, and three months ago wooden boards advertising the Gathering had been posted in every town, all boasting of the one-armed man who would ride. Bennosuke knew then that what fate or destiny had withheld before was being granted him now. He could hardly believe that Hayato would consent to surrender himself to such danger, regardless of how many men he would have protecting him.

In a mass of hundreds of men and horses, in a press of bodies that swarmed and thrusted to dozens of different plots and designs, even the most vigilant of men would struggle to spot the six inches of soot-blackened steel of a concealed dagger, for example.

Oh, they would very well spot what happened after, but Bennosuke was unconcerned with that. So long as Hayato died, the boy would be content; he would have proved himself. Whatever would happen to his body after that could not harm his pure, immortal soul.

But first, to ride in a Gathering you needed a horse, and, well . . .

He should be scared, he knew, but every fiber of him was exhausted. The lanterns beside him were so warm, the swaying back and forth so comforting, and any sort of worry seemed so distant.

His eyes closed, and he drifted into a deep sleep.

THAT SENSE OF well-being vanished when the rope suspending him was cut in the morning. There was no warning; he woke when he hit the ground, landing facedown and unprepared. He tasted blood in his mouth as his jolted senses reestablished themselves. He blinked in the sudden light, forgetting for a moment that he was bound and wondering why his limbs were immobile.

"Get up, you little masterless bastard," said the samurai standing above him. "You've a long walk ahead of you."

It was the man who had fallen from his horse the night before. He was still angry, a spattering of raw wounds along one side of his brow testament to the tumble, and he rolled the boy over roughly with his foot. He unbound Bennosuke's legs and then dragged him upright, before reattaching a shorter rope around his ankles so that the boy could move his feet no farther than a forearm's length apart.

As the samurai rose to stand face-to-face with him after securing the rope, Bennosuke realized he was taller than the man. The samurai noticed this too, and it only infuriated him further. He roughly forced Bennosuke's head down as he led the boy to his horse. There was another rope there attached to the saddle, and this was looped around his neck.

Leashed, he looked around. The other four samurai were waiting, their horses already prepared for riding. They watched him dispassionately, their eyes cold. The samurai with the scarred face, evidently the leader, gave a gesture. One of them approached, and Bennosuke recognized his own swords in the man's hands. The weapons had been lashed together and attached to a collar, which the man placed over his head now. On the front of the scabbards a piece of paper was affixed, heavy black ink characters daubed on it. Bennosuke read them upside down:

A SAMURAI THIEF, they said.

"When we arrive at the execution grounds, your swords will be taken and shattered," the scarred samurai said, raising the boy's eyes to his own. "Then they—the filthy, subhuman corpsehandlers, you understand?—they, who are higher than you, will drive the shards through your hands and your feet, and you will die over a number of hours. Thus to all who renounce the privilege of their birth to act like the debased."

Another gesture and another man came forth. He had a large, bell-shaped straw helmet. It was an instrument of shame, designed to encircle the head entirely and hide the guilty and the disgraced from the world. They forced it over him, and save for the tiniest sliver of light where the rim of the helmet met his collarbone, his sight was taken from him. He heard the men as they mounted, and then came the crack of a riding whip and a sudden sting as it connected with his shoulder.

"Walk!" came the command from behind him, so he obeyed.

Blind, hobbled, and bound, Bennosuke started to panic as he realized what was happening. He cursed himself for succumbing to sleep instead of struggling to free himself. His breath echoed around the inside of the helmet like wind through a cave. There was no give in the ropes, no chance to move his arms, which were pinioned tightly behind him. He tripped and stumbled often, over the unseen road or if he misjudged the length of the rope tied around his feet. There was no hope of running.

"Come see the fate of one who steals," one of the samurai behind him would announce occasionally, loudly and irregularly enough that Bennosuke guessed he was addressing onlookers witnessing this spectacle of the law. "Come see the fate of a samurai who has reneged upon his pride."

The rattling of the swords against his chest taunted him with how enfeebled he was, but it was these words that really tore into him. Here he was, branded and paraded as a villain, when he was as ragged and starved as he was precisely because he had chosen not to be one—the horse had been the first thing he had attempted to steal all these long months.

Oh, how tempting it had been to consider with his stomach screaming and his hands shaking. It would have been so easy to wait by some isolated road for a merchant to pass by and to intimidate him into handing over coin or food or the clothes upon his back, or to sneak into some unguarded house and help himself to whatever he found inside. He was big and he was strong—or at least he had been—and he had swords at his side. Who could have stopped him?

Only himself, and he had done so. He was on a pure mission, a saintly mission, and though Munisai had told him his death at the successful end of it would exempt him of all sin and shame wrought to get to that point, that did not seem to Bennosuke an excuse to abandon morality. Any act would be forgiven him, but the act itself would remain; what he would leave in the world would be the shame and hurt he forced upon others. This could not be.

The legendary staff-wielding warrior Musashi Benkei was not renowned for the number of men who had fallen by his hand in his last stand, after all. What the stories told in excruciating and admiring detail, and what the paintings of him focused on with rigorous and adoring brushstrokes, was the torturous number of arrows he had been impaled with before he fell. That was what defined a samurai—no, that was what defined a hero: how much pain and suffering you could endure and triumph in spite of, not how much you could inflict and triumph because of.

So the ravenous hunger then, the nights sleeping outside upon the earth, the blisters upon his feet, and the dizziness—they were all just arrows slowly running him through, he had told himself. *You are Musashi,* the voice in his head had whispered, *and these are the things that you will be judged by when this is all done. Long after you are dead and this flesh is but a memory, people will hear of them and marvel at your virtuous determination.*

But all for naught. The theft of the horse had been a necessity, so he had attempted it and failed, and now here he was being shown before men not as a paragon but as the embodiment of ignominy. For hours they walked, and he could hear the disgusted muttering of those they passed above the crack of the whip and his own labored breathing.

At some point he felt his bowels let go uncontrollably, as much from the neglect of his body as his fear, and hot liquid dribbled down his leg. Not one of the samurai noticed any difference. Tears stung his eyes at the humiliation of the act, of the fact that he had become so low that shitting himself made no difference to how others saw him, but most of all from the realization of his failure. He was going to die in total disgrace while Hayato still lived.

For a while he was grateful for the helmet.

Slowly his captors grew silent, no one left to parade him in front of. They were going far from the civilized parts of the world, down paths that no men wanted to tread but some nonetheless had to out of duty. In the body were organs that produced piss and bile, things that were necessary but corrupted by their very being, and so too in the world: they were headed for the filthy, cursed places that the corpsehandlers called their home.

Dread grew in Bennosuke, the hair on his arms standing on end. The boy did not know exactly the location they were headed, for these outposts and hamlets of the unseen castes were hidden away unmarked on any map. They were condemned to lie on the beds of dried-out rivers where rice would not grow, for were they near bountiful land the contamination of so much death would surely pollute the earth and grow malformed crops bitter to the tongue.

Death defined samurai—taking heads or pulling out their own intestines—but that was a culture of mortality that understood and cherished the inevitability and honesty of it. In these places the undignified practice of dismemberment was carried out upon the lower beings incapable of understanding such things, inflicted on the criminals at the execution grounds or upon animals that were torn and hung and dried and worked by tanners and morbid craftsmen who knew a dozen uses for the secret materials contained within a carcass.

It was, ultimately, the difference between art and industry, and it was, ultimately, the difference between being remembered and being forgotten. No one spoke of these places, no poems or paintings for those nailed to crosses, no one to care for whatever brought the damned there. Those who entered were eradicated utterly from the world.

Hayato lived, and Bennosuke had never been. That was what all these months of suffering had achieved.

Even the birds seemed to grow silent the closer they got. Bennosuke felt his jaw begin to quiver as he became aware of a sound in the distance: the piteous howl of a man, all terror and misery, and it dragged on and on and grew louder and louder, welcoming him to the place of his annihilation.

CHAPTER THIRTEEN

The swords rattled on Bennosuke's chest as the men stopped suddenly, a harsh tug on the leash dragging him backward. There was a moment of silence and contemplation. Perhaps this was as close as the samurai dared to go, as though they feared being irrevocably corrupted. The poor wretch screaming ahead of them, whoever he was, screamed on.

There was a foul stink in the air; the tangible rottenness that hung around these hamlets was not fit for decent men to smell and duly why they were exiled so. It was the greasy smoke of men as carrion, the curling salt plumes of flesh charring as the bodies of the condemned were burned. It was the stench of the huge vats of the tanners, filled with the piss and filth of man and beast that they needed to work their ghastly, essential craft.

After a few moments there came the sound of a gate opening ahead of them, and a voice called out: "Good day to you, sir."

"Oh . . . good day to you also, sir," said the scarred samurai, and he seemed surprised for a moment. Yet his tone was guarded but respectful; whoever had spoken was a samurai of equal standing. "You serve my most noble Lord Shingo also?"

"Yes, that we do," said the man.

"Ah," said the scarred samurai, and his voiced eased slightly. "Please forgive my rudeness. So many horses tethered here, it confused me for a moment."

"No need for apologies. I agree this is quite abnormal," said the man ahead.

"Might I ask why so many samurai are here in so foul a place?"

"A notorious criminal has been caught," said the unseen samurai. There was pride in his voice and the smile he must have worn was easy to imagine: the vanity of the triumphant predator. "A whole gang, in fact. A most troublesome cohort of villains finally brought to justice, and we are simply here to ensure that it is done."

"You ought to just have slaughtered them where they stood," tutted the scarred samurai.

"Oh, that was my urge, I assure you. But my superior personally wishes to see them ended," said the man. "They were very troublesome, for quite some time, and so we wait for him to arrive."

"I understand, and I sympathize with you for having to linger here. But have you room for one more in the jail?"

"I don't see why not," he said, and now they were talking like they were old friends, united in their abhorrence of criminals. "Where else do thieves belong but nailed up?"

"I thank you," said the scarred samurai, and then Bennosuke heard the gentle pat of hooves as he rounded his mount on the boy. "Well then, 'samurai,' it seems we part here. Face your judgment bravely, and perhaps the spirits will not be so cruel on you. I, though, have no such mercy."

Seated on the horse, it was no great effort for him to lash his foot out and kick Bennosuke in the head. It did not hurt much, striking him on the side of his skull and the straw helmet shielding him for the most part, but nevertheless a whimper escaped him.

Bennosuke felt the leash being tossed, and then he was yanked forward. Hands grabbed him, pushing and pulling him into the enclave. He stumbled blindly, seeing only through the sliver of the helmet; a sense of crude buildings and dank mud. He saw the feet of men as he was passed from the skirts of kimonos and fine sandals of samurai to the crude leggings and straw boots of the lower-born guards, and above them all the screams of the tortured were ringing loud like the bleak peals of lamed pack animals losing sight of the herd as it marches ahead in the darkness, hope and warmth and rightness moving onward and away, always away, fading into nothingness before them.

The guards hauled him inside a building and then down a short, steep stairway. They took the helmet and his swords away, but left the ropes around his body, and then he was forced to his knees and shoved inside a low cage of thick wooden bars. His knees gouged tracks in the sawdust upon the floor, and a gate was slammed and locked behind him.

"Won't be needing these again," laughed one of the guards on the outside, waving his swords before him before setting them upon a rack on the opposite wall. "A samurai for you, boys."

Bennosuke wriggled to his knees like a serpent. What light there was hurt his eyes, but he saw that across the cage a group of men were huddled. They were tough looking, about a dozen of them with their bodies lean and filthy and their hair and beards wild and fierce. The bandits. They were looking at him warily, suspicion and hatred in their eyes.

"Hello, samurai," said one of them, his voice cold.

Their nails were dirty, their hands clawed, and the boy realized then that though they were quite still, not one of them was bound as he was.

THE GUARDS LEFT them, up the stairs and then out into the light once more, bolting the door behind them. What happened down there was nothing to them—men did not come here to be monitored. They came here to be slaughtered, and if that happened down in the darkness of some murky cell instead of in the baking sun atop a crucifix, it was of no great concern to them.

The bandits looked at Bennosuke for a long while, a silent court. He tried to meet their gaze fearlessly, but he had little defiance left; he knew that he was trussed and at their mercy.

"Don't look much like a samurai," said one eventually, his accent coarse. "Raggedy little bastard, is he not?"

"Swords is swords," said another.

"Aye," agreed the first.

"What's he here for, then?" said another, and now they all began to talk as though he could not hear them.

"He's made a big bloody mistake somewhere, that's for certain."

"Murder?"

"Samurai don't murder, do they? It's all pretty words for them, though men lie dead all the same."

"Rape?"

"I doubt that, his balls have barely dropped."

"I haven't raped anyone," said Bennosuke, forcing what little bravado he could muster into his voice. "Nor have I murdered. Now, I would ask for you to untie me."

They laughed at his interruption, a cruel snigger that passed through them all. The boy had tried to speak imperiously, as a samurai should speak to peasants, and it must have looked ridiculous in these circumstances. It seemed to kill their interest in him, though—the sport perhaps too easy—and they started to turn back to one another. The boy sensed that his arrival had interrupted something. They were all huddled in a corner, looking inward as though they were plotting something.

Of course they were plotting something—they were bandits. If they had an escape planned . . .

He hesitated. Would the purity of his mission be compromised if he collaborated with the low? His father had said "at any cost," but he was talking in terms of death and self-sacrifice; acceptable, noble terms. But Bennosuke knew he could not escape on his own. It was either die like a criminal and let the Nakata live, or live like a criminal for a moment and let the Nakata die. One had vengeance, one did not, and so the boy shuffled toward the men on his knees.

"Please, untie me," he said again.

"Look to yourself, boy," said one. "We're accounted for."

"Please!" Bennosuke said, and some of the desperation leaked into his voice. "Are you to be killed too? We have to get out of here. I can help you."

"How?"

"I don't know. Anything."

"You know anything about locks?"

"No."

"You have a saw on you for these bars?"

"No."

"Then what use are you to us, eh?" said the man, disgust in his voice. "You aren't anything now. Can't even move your arms. Just flapping around, a fish on land, you are."

"My swords—we can use them," said Bennosuke, jerking his chin to where his weapons lay outside the cage.

"Aye, we can." The bandit nodded. "We don't need you for that, though, do we? Believe it or not, working a sword isn't that hard to figure out."

"Please!" begged the boy.

It was all he had left, but honest as the plea was it withered before the bandits. There were snorts of irritation, disgust, and pity before they turned away to start murmuring among themselves once more. Bennosuke was left alone and ignored on his side of the cage. The boy started to writhe and struggle against his bonds with a final desperation, but they had not loosened simply through his wearing of them.

He flailed in vain until, defeated and exhausted, Bennosuke collapsed onto his side. He felt the coarseness of the sawdust on his burning cheek, the weeks-old stench of it as bitter as the tears in his eyes. There was terror and defeat in his heart. Closing his eyes, he wished himself somewhere else—to a place where the starvation and the long, cold nights had not been all for naught, had been more than a prelude to nothing. The familiar dizziness pressed at his temples like two thumbs gouging his brains.

When the pain passed he found his eyes were open again. Through the mass of the peasants he became aware of a single face looking at him. Older than the others, hard and lined and missing one eye. The remaining eye was upon him; cold, judgmental, condemnatory.

It reminded him of Munisai. He could not bear it for long. Bennosuke turned away, still burning with shame, and awaited oblivion.

THE DIZZINESS CAME and went, and Bennosuke found himself growing faint. Perhaps it was the stench, or perhaps exhaustion or starvation, but he knew that it was most likely fear. He drifted in and out of sleep where he lay, taking in glimpses of consciousness that seemed to swim before him until a fresh pang of disgrace drove him back into senselessness.

Day faded into night, orange into blue, and then back into orange again as weak oil lanterns were lit. At some point he felt hands upon him. It took him a moment to connect the sensations in his head, and a moment longer to realize that they were gentle. He felt a thigh under his side and then the ropes tying him being loosened.

He looked up and found it was the one-eyed man.

"There's enough suffering here," the old man said quietly in explanation.

The binds fell free eventually, the many knots taking time, but then for the first time in a day the boy could move his arms. He rubbed them, seeing the bright red lines molded into what flesh was left atop his bones.

"Thank you," said Bennosuke.

The man nodded, and sat back stiffly. The other bandits lay where they had been, some sleeping and some simply staring up at nothing. From outside, the wailing of the tortured persisted even now, but raw agony had been replaced with a pitiable emptiness. It was a haunting sound, a dying sound, but the stillness of the night was strangely calming.

"What's your name?" the old peasant asked, keeping his voice low.

"Bennosuke," said the boy. "Yours?"

"Shuntaro," he said. The weak flame of the lantern lit up the ridges of his face. His eye had been gone for some time, the remaining lid withered into a vestige, but it was weeping from the beating he must have sustained in his capture. "How'd you end up in here, Bennosuke? You say something out of turn to your master?"

"Theft," said the boy.

"What did you steal?"

"A horse."

"Why's a samurai stealing horses?"

"I needed one," said Bennosuke. It sounded pathetic, but he did not want to reveal much.

"Well, you fouled that right up," said Shuntaro. "I thought samurai were supposed to die rather than let themselves be captured, anyway."

"I didn't have the chance," said the boy hotly.

"I wasn't judging," said the man. "And you'll have plenty of time to die tomorrow, in any case. After us."

"You're all together?" asked the boy, and Shuntaro nodded. "The samurai outside said you were bandits."

"He's right—we're a notorious crew of demons sent from the pits of hell to plunder and kill. Look at us and tremble," said Shuntaro.

Their hostility gone now, in the darkness Bennosuke saw a group of bedraggled men as wretched as he was. He looked back at the old man, and mirth leapt into the one eye he had. "That, or we were hungry."

"You stole to feed yourselves?"

"Perhaps. I was the head of a village. Taxes and tithes were too high, because of war. War, war, war, always a war, whether in the east or the west or the north or the south. 'Don't worry yourself over it,' the tax collectors said to me. 'War's the sole concern of samurai!' I said. 'It's the game of samurai—it's the concern of everyone,'" Shuntaro said, and his face contorted in disgust. "They think they're the only ones who suffer, because they do the fighting. But who pays for it? We do. The peasants—down to the last grain of rice. They'd take it out of the mouths of our children just to give some archer an ounce more strength to fire one more meaningless arrow in the name of some fool I'll never see perched on an ivory saddle."

He realized how vitriolic his voice had become, and he took a few moments to calm himself before he spoke levelly once more. "Anyway, that was all a few years ago. You know what happens to those who don't pay their tithe, and, well . . . Eventually, here we all are. You know, I'll welcome it almost . . . Once it's all done, I fancy I'll come back as an owl. Free and alone in the quiet of the night. Sounds wonderful."

"Aren't you going to escape?" said the boy. The man considered it, shrugged.

"Probably," he said, dabbing at his weeping socket absently. "It's quite the trick, though. You saw the samurai outside, right? They're the problem. The guards here, bloody corpsehandlers, we could maybe take them if it was just them—but the band of samurai took us when we were free and armed. There's no way we can fight our way out now."

"What about my swords?"

"There's a score of them out there," snorted Shuntaro. "No man'll ever take on twenty samurai with a pair of swords and win."

"But—"

"No. Anyway," the man said dismissively, "the cage is the problem. It's only wood, and we could bash our way free if we had time, perhaps. But the noise would attract the samurai, and then they'd run in and stick us with spears. We need the key for that lock on the gate, and then to escape without being seen."

"How are you going to do that?"

"I have a plan for the samurai, at least. The good men of the law who hunted us down will make a visit tomorrow, expecting to see us killed. They'll want to see us here, caged, taunt us probably, and then I'll act."

"Can I help?" Bennosuke said. "I can't die here."

"No, only I can do this," he said. "It's only right for me to do this. When it's done, though, I won't be in any position to stop you escaping too. No one deserves to be crucified . . . Well, not over a horse."

"Thank you," said the boy.

"Now you have to put the ropes back on," said Shuntaro. "If the guards see you free they'll be suspicious. I'll do it loosely, though. You won't really be tied up. That all right?"

"Yes."

"Good." The old man sighed, and it seemed he was speaking to himself as he began to loosely loop the rope around the boy's torso once more. "Life is all a deception, lad, never let anyone know the true state of things around you. Then you'll have the surprise over them."

When the work was done, Shuntaro shuffled back to nestle among his men and closed his eye. Bennosuke watched him as he slept. The man's empty eye socket lingered half open like half the face of death; a skeletal sentinel taking in all in its blackness. The lanterns flickered, and outside the screaming and the night went on.

WITH THE LIGHT of dawn, Bennosuke found that the sense of dread had left him. He was not safe, he knew that, but he had a chance. That was more than he had had yesterday, and the simple hope of having an avenue of escape—more than that, of being able to influence his own fate—was soothing.

Shuntaro and his men continued to sit huddled together as morning came around them. Some were awake and some slept. They gave no greeting to Bennosuke when he rose, as tense as he was. Perhaps the old man had not told them what he planned either. They waited, motes of dust hanging in the light all around them. The screaming had ended, Bennosuke realized, to be replaced by birdsong. Not the braying of carrion birds, but the lilt of gentle summer creatures unable to understand what men were doing to one another so close by.

But there was no need for carrion birds when samurai were here, and when they came they came as crows; a murder of them marching quickly, their feet passing in front of the low window. The door was thrown open, and they stalked down into the jail. A half dozen of them scoured the room for danger, checking that the gate remained locked and that the prisoners were all accounted for. One came across Bennosuke's swords. He poked them with his toe, and then gave a disgusted glance at the boy where he had shuffled apart from the bandits.

"The most honorable Marshal Fushimi approaches," barked one, and then he and his men moved to the sides of the room and stood to rigid attention.

There were more samurai crowding the mouth of the stairway, and they made way to allow Fushimi to come down into the jail, the stairs rattling under his riding greaves. He was a tough-looking man with a cloth clutched across his mouth, his eyes pinched in revulsion and anger. To be among an enclave of the corpsehandlers disgusted him, but he would endure.

His expression did not change as he came to stand before the cage and looked across the bandits. It reminded Bennosuke of the way the peasants used to look at him in Miyamoto. When the marshal caught sight of Shuntaro, however, his eyes lit up.

"Ah," he said, from behind the cloth, "this must be the Yamawaro of the Red Hills."

"Sir Fushimi," said Shuntaro plainly, and ducked his head in a bow. A yamawaro was a mythical, one-eyed mountain ogre, a filthy, rag-clad beast that delighted in evil mischief. The men around him glowered.

"You know manners?" asked Fushimi.

"I know manners, sir," said Shuntaro.

"Then you will come and kneel before me as I pass judgment upon you," said the marshal, and pointed at the ground. Without a word, Shuntaro obeyed. His men parted, and then he knelt in the formal way and kept his eye on the ground.

"I name thee a canker," said Fushimi after a considered pause. "A troublesome disease of which we have at last cured ourselves. Theft and murder and arson . . . All manner of havoc and mayhem you have created. You are responsible for the massacre at Takasago village—"

"I contest that, sir."

"You were identified by the survivors."

"I was there, sir, I do not deny that. I contest that it is named 'massacre.' It was a battle between armed men, and we won."

"It will be recorded in history as a massacre, and remembered as such."

"That I cannot contest, sir," said Shuntaro meekly.

All that separated the two men were the bars of the cage, spaced widely enough for an arm to fit through. Bennosuke watched the old bandit's hands, seeing if he had a blade concealed, or was preparing some form of attack. But they were empty, fists not even clutched in anger. He had the stillness and pose of a man at worship. Fushimi seemed puzzled, or at least surprised by this too. He looked at Shuntaro for a while before he spoke again.

"'The Yamawaro of the Red Hills,'" said the marshal eventually, lingering over the words. "Do you know your infamy? That started as a sobriquet alone, but now some people actually believe you live in the rock of the mountain itself as a spirit and emerge to steal children away at night. For a while I feared that might be true. I chased your shadow for so long, I began to doubt there was a body attached to it. But now here the flesh is before me, finally beaten. Just a man after all."

"That I am, sir," said Shuntaro. "As are we all."

"No. We share a like body, you and I, but our souls our different."

"How, sir? I see the sky and feel the wind the same way as you."

"There are many reasons, but the simplest and most profound is that you are afraid of that which you face today," said Fushimi. "You are afraid of death."

"Are you not, sir?"

"No."

"Have you ever faced it?"

"Every time I have drawn my blade," said the marshal, and banged his fist against the weapons at his side.

"That is mortal risk. That is different," said Shuntaro. "Have you ever held a baby as its body withers to nothing, for the breast it feeds upon has run dry with the starving of the mother? That is death."

"How very vivid," said Fushimi. "But the breasts my children suckle from will run full and ripe and young until the sky falls, while you—you are all to be speared like rabid dogs before the sun is down."

"Might I plead clemency, sir? For my men?" asked Shuntaro.

"Of course you may not."

"I do not know all the ways of the civilized, sir," said the old bandit, and such was the careful poise of his tone that Fushimi allowed him to speak. "But surely in all the history of war there must be some case of a surrendered army being spared by the sacrifice of the general?"

"A civilized surrender is seppuku, from the highest lord to the lowest soldier. Any who choose to remain alive after the shame of defeat excuse themselves from the ranks of the civilized, and are to be treated thusly," said Fushimi, and as Shuntaro began to speak again the marshal cut him off curtly. "I am no wrangler of law, merely a giver of it. You are all to die."

At that Shuntaro's body sagged, his head falling low enough that his brow touched the earth. Fushimi's eyes changed. They did not gleam in vicious, sneering triumph, but there was vindication there, a reaffirmation that behind the clouds the sky was still blue.

"See—your heart quails," he said.

"I am disappointed, not afraid, sir," said Shuntaro.

"The spirit of a man like you does not come back, you know, not even as a beast or a rock. You face the damnation of the myriad hells. Does that not scare you?"

"I am unafraid, sir," said Shuntaro, "because I know that when I get to whichever particular hell I go to, I shall have the pleasure of sinking my hand up to the wrist in your mother's waiting cunt."

Shuntaro looked up then, met the marshal's gaze, and as he held those two narrow, cold eyes with his one, he hooked a finger into his empty eye socket, snapped his wrist in a flick, and then gobs of coagulated blood and pus and whatever other murk lingers on the inside of men spattered across the front of the marshal.

"Spear me like a dog, will you? You think I'm afraid of that? I've already been speared," spat Shuntaro, and he pulled his jerkin open to reveal a twisted patch of scar across the side of his stomach. "I'm afraid of nothing you could possibly do to me. Crucify me. Cut me to pieces. Bring all your men, and I will teach you like the children you are. I will show you how to die, I will show you my body and my soul and whatever else you want to see, and then my ghost will come back to make whores of your daughters."

Fushimi had made only the slightest of flinches as the filth had landed on him, the hand holding the cloth to his face dropping in stunned disbelief. But as Shuntaro had continued the skin upon his face had pulled back into ridges of complete and utter fury, his lips curling into a snarl until his teeth seemed fanged and his face looked like some carved wooden theater mask of a devil.

"Find a cauldron," the marshal barely managed to breathe. "Find oil."

He did not remain with them. Fushimi stalked up the stairs, his whole body taut with rage. The other samurai, shock and anger on their faces, followed their master outside and shut the door behind them.

Alone once more, Shuntaro had a strange look on his face. All in the cage looked at him. The old man breathed out through his nose.

"Well, it's done," he said, and smiled wanly. "My plan."

It broke the spell. The other bandits realized that what had just happened had actually happened, and so they swarmed Shuntaro, surrounded him, bludgeoned him with questions and anger and disbelief. The old man weathered it like stone.

"Why?" said one with tears in his eyes, and it was he who drew a response from Shuntaro, the man looking at him for a moment with what seemed like shame across his face. "That's not a plan—what are you doing?"

"My son, surely you of all people understand . . ." he said to the younger man, but then he stopped, composed himself, and spoke to all of them. "No. Listen to me. You are all of you as my sons.

"For years you have followed me without complaint, even though it was my choice that started all this. You have shown me loyalty, and all the best in men, and in this life I cannot repay you for all that that means to me. This is . . . I've distracted them for you. They'll all be watching me now for however long it takes, which means that you can escape. You'll have to figure out how to get out of the cage, but I know you can. And then just run. Forget about me, just go and run and run until you feel that you are safe. Find a new home. Have sons and daughters and live. Do you understand?"

"No, Shuntaro, we can't leave you," said one, the voice of them all.

"You must," said the old man.

"They're going to butcher you."

"I know that."

"We can't—"

"It is too late to change it now," said Shuntaro. "This is the way of the world. I have nothing more to give to it, and so it is my time to go. Do not fail me. Get out of this cage, and leave me to die."

Though his voice had quavered, he alone had kept dry eyes. But he had reopened a wound when he had dug into his socket earlier, and so now a rivulet of blood was trickling down his cheek. It gave him a strange symmetry with his men, who were all either blinking back tears or openly weeping.

It all seemed so alien upon men so hard. Bennosuke watched them as they severed a bond the boy had never known.

IN A CHARNEL hamlet, where the corpses of animals were rendered down to make leather or glue or plectrums of bone that would someday strum delicate melodies upon silk strings in fine halls, and where the crematory pyres stopped only for the severest of weather, a cauldron and oil were not hard to find. They soon came back for Shuntaro.

It was all done in silence. The door opened, and two samurai came down and opened the gate. Shuntaro was kneeling, waiting, and he crawled out and rose to his feet of his own volition. Not one of his men moved. Their eyes were rimmed red, staring hatred at the two men who tied their leader up and then led him up the stairs. Shuntaro did not look back, and then they were gone.

The boy found himself wondering what Shuntaro had really intended. Had he expected to be able to talk Fushimi into letting his men go? Perhaps he had been counting on a streak of honor from a code he did not really understand to force the constable's hand. That was always going to be a vain hope; a farmer could hope to argue with a samurai as much as the deaf could hope to sing.

But when that failed, Shuntaro had offered his life and in doing so shown at some primal, fundamental level that he did know the way of samurai. The difference, Bennosuke realized, was that he had offered his life for others. Samurai offered theirs more often than not to recover their own pride.

The boy thought on that in the silence. No one spoke in the cage. They all knew that screams would be coming soon, and they listened for them with the dread of imagination. Each of them envisioned blades or whips or brands, and each knew that the samurai up there had an imagination as vivid as theirs but with the means to make it a reality.

Yet the truth was they also longed to hear that horrendous sound, for that would be their signal to start their escape; if Shuntaro was in agony, then the samurai were distracted and he had fulfilled his part of his plan. It was a terrible thing to anticipate, but they could not deny that they did with a mixture of shame and fear and twisting in their guts. They crouched or squatted in tense repose, their eyes unused and staring at the floor, their ears sifting for the minutest whimper.

The heavy door lurched opened, startling them all. The crash of wood was much too close and much too sudden, and the bandits swiveled like panicked sparrows. Two of the corpsehandlers entered. They looked as though they had purpose, and they came down to stand before the cage.

"Right," said one, wasting no time, dropping into a squat so he was at eye level with the prisoners. "You're bandits, and famous ones at that. That means you have something stashed somewhere. We want it, whatever it is—gold or weapons or anything."

Shuntaro's men did not respond. The corpsehandler grinned. He was remarkably clean, his teeth as full as any man's and his eyes quick and clever. From a bag at his waist he produced a thin stoppered vial made from a hollowed young bamboo trunk.

"This is a nice little concoction of viper's spit and poison leaves and mushroom caps," he said, still grinning. "Drink it and you'll be dead within a minute. Tell us where you left your goodies and it's yours. Only enough for one, mind, so first one wins it."

Silence.

"Come on," said the corpsehandler, the grin faltering, "you really ought to take this. I've seen what they're preparing for you out there."

"Ask the samurai," said one of the bandits, jerking his chin at Bennosuke, and the others laughed.

"A nice idea, but we already have his treasures there on the wall," said the crouching man, laughing with them in an attempt to build repartee, and waving a hand to where Bennosuke's swords were hung upon the rack. His partner picked the weapons up and rocked them as he would a baby with a sarcastic leer upon his face.

"Now," said the crouching man, still smiling, "I don't believe for a moment that you have left nothing behind unclaimed. What you have to understand is that you are dead already. No one will remember. No one will care if you 'betrayed' something. This is a simple choice between agony or a quick and private end. Do you understand that?"

"'Viper's spit and mushroom caps,'" said one of the bandits mockingly. "You think we're stupid? No vipers in these woods."

"I cut the fangs myself," said the man, and he leaned in close to the bars. "We breed them. Snake leather fetches a fine—"

He was interrupted by his friend, who had placed the swords between his legs as though he were endowed by the gods, poking him in the cheek as he mimed masturbation. The first one tried to stop the disgusted grin on his face as he slapped them away. "Take this seriously."

"I am taking it seriously," said the second man, and he slung the swords into his leather belt and as he spoke started marching up and down in mockery of a samurai's stride. "I told you they wouldn't spring for it. Just look in their eyes. Pride, there. Stubborn gang of pricks, like a bunch of samurai."

At that an inspiration for further mirth came to him, and he turned to Bennosuke. "You, come here," he said. The corpsehandler stood close before the cage, as imperious and majestic as a man in rags could be. Bennosuke stumbled forward on his knees, making a show of how he was bound.

"What do you think, eh, samurai?" he said, and his hand was running back and forth across the handle of the longsword, a similar gesture to before, though now he was unaware of doing it. "You think they suit me?"

Though he kept his eyes down, the boy saw dull iron keys hanging at the man's waist opposite the weapons.

"You're wearing them wrong," he said.

"What?" said the man.

"You've got them upside down," said the boy. The corpsehandler had thrust them into his belt with the edge downward so that the smooth arch of the swords appeared a shallow dish. "Imagine the swords are bows. You want the string at the bottom toward your feet so that the edge of the blade curves over the top."

"What difference does that make?" said the corpsehandler.

"You can't strike from the draw with the edge downward like you've got now; it's hard to get any real strength going underhanded from low to high. Overhand, though, you can flick it out in one movement, bring it down, and take an arm off or attack the chest," said Bennosuke. "There's another reason too, you know."

"What is it?"

"It makes it very easy for people to disarm you," he said, and shook the ropes off himself.

The look on the corpsehandler's face for one glorious instant was of complete shock. He could do nothing as Bennosuke's hand whipped out through the bars and grabbed the handle of the shortsword, could only watch as the inverse curve of the scabbard all but caressed the blade free, and could only yelp as Bennosuke grabbed the back of his head, hauled his body against the bars of the cage, and leveled the point of the sword at the quivering base of his throat.

"Give me the keys," said Bennosuke, and he knew he was grinning as he said it. "Give me the keys, or I'll skewer you."

A set of hands came from behind and grabbed Bennosuke's, forcing the sword forward. The blade lanced up into the corpsehandler's neck, and the flesh split and blood flowed and then the man was gurgling and sputtering his terror through the hole in his neck as he died on his feet.

"Stop fucking around," hissed a bandit in Bennosuke's ear, driving the sword in farther, his knuckles white over Bennosuke's.

The other corpsehandler stared in complete shock, and before he could move out of his squat the other bandits threw themselves against the cage and grabbed for him. They hauled him against the bars, four or five of them taking his arms and his legs, and then fingers were around his neck and over his mouth, and the man whimpered and struggled and bit down upon any flesh he could find, and blood flowed and men swore in pain or anger, and the corpsehandler thrashed and he thrashed until he weakened and his face turned red, then purple, and then he was dead.

The bamboo vial lay upon the floor, the stopper fallen out. No liquid was inside. The bandits dropped the pair of bodies to fall alongside it. In the silence Bennosuke stared at the blood on his sword for a moment, then at the open eyes of the corpsehandler from whom the blood had come. That was cold murder, he knew, and in his head something whispered:

Would Hayato Nakata look any different with his throat slit?

Though there was no sound he knew that it was Dorinbo's voice. For a moment shame coursed through the boy, but he quickly shook it away. This was a low deed to beget the high, he told himself, no more than that. The sword stopped quivering in his grip. He looked up to find the bandits frozen like the thieves they were, listening to see if they had been heard and if men were storming toward them now. There was neither footfall nor bark of command.

All they heard was a distant, agonized screaming.

"It's now," said one, trying to keep what he knew that sound meant from his mind. "Let's go."

Things happened quickly; they fished the keys from the body, unlocked the gate, and began to pour out. Bennosuke retrieved his longsword from where it lay, and when he brought it up he found the bandits were looking at him, suddenly fearful. He tucked the weapon into the rope around his waist, raised his hands pointedly away from the hilts of both blades, and nodded in attempted solidarity. They did not look convinced, but there was no time for debate.

The bandits slunk up the stairway to ease the heavy door open and peeked out. No one there, they began to scuttle out, bent double, as though being close to the ground might hide them in the light of day.

The screaming was rawer here in the open air. A thin plume of smoke rose into the sky above the shimmering of heat, the source of both hidden from view. The sound tore at each of them, but they turned their backs on it and made for their escape, dashing from one hiding place to the next.

Bennosuke followed them. The bandits must have been brought here with their eyes uncovered, for they knew where they were going. The enclave was not a large place, and it was only a matter of a few dozen thumping heartbeats before they turned a corner and saw a crude wall with a cruder gate of nailed planks hanging wide open.

There, by the gate, horses were tethered. Big, strong warhorses, saddled and loaded with baggage. The boy looked at them like an idiot for a moment, scarcely believing his luck.

Three samurai stood at guard. They stood facing outward, knowing that no threat could possibly come from behind, and with little more noise than the thrashing of a man having a bad dream the bandits took them. Skilled in ambush, they rushed the warriors in silence and leapt on them from behind, wrestling them down three to a man with their hands clamped over the mouths of the samurai and reaching for the swords at their waists. Blades came out and then down, and it was done.

The bandits began to scatter the horses, slapping the beasts on the hinds to send them galloping out into the wilderness. None of them could ride, and now the samurai would have to chase them on foot. Bennosuke took the reins of one before they got to it, and though they stared suspiciously at him they said nothing. The boy simply stared at the beast in a dazed euphoria, patting the muzzle; he was alive and free, he had a horse, and the road was before him. None of those possibilities he would have envisioned the day before.

They were on the threshold then, their freedom right there, and yet they hesitated. Unspoken, something ran between the bandits that forced them to stop and look at one another.

The screaming persisted. The smoke still rose.

"Come on," hissed one. "We've no time."

"We can't leave him," said the rearmost, looking back at the plumes curling in the sky.

"Are your wits gone?" said the first man, walking backward and away as he spoke. "We have to go now!"

"I can't . . ." said the rearmost, and that was all he could formulate. He looked at the rest of them, and with tears in his eyes he shook his head, bowed a good-bye, and then ran back into the village.

"No! Idiot! Come back!" hissed the farthest man. He made to go after him—they all did—but he forced himself to stop after a few faltering steps.

Three other men broke, though, and they charged back into the village toward the flames. Those who remained beseeched them to stop with voices as loud as they dared raise them, but either they were not heard or the men could not bring their legs to be still. Bennosuke watched them vanish into the streets of the hamlet, once again witnessing something he could not comprehend.

The bandits who were left had no choice but to leave. The samurai would be alerted soon enough, and so cursing and crying they began to flee. The boy hopped up into the saddle, and he kicked the horse as fast as he dared go. This time there was light, and though he was far from comfortable atop the animal he did not fall.

The road out of the hamlet quickly became wooded, and the bandits began to vanish into the trees. Bennosuke let them go; the samurai would search for them before him. He followed the cleared path, ignoring the first two trails leading off it before arbitrarily choosing the third, a narrow trail that led up a hillside. It wound along, branches whipping at him from above and his horse whinnying on the uneven ground, but suddenly it opened out and he could see back down the slope across the tops of trees.

The enclave of the corpsehandlers was there before him, small and distant.

In the midst of it, surrounded by a ring of crucifixes held high on pillars, the blackened diagonal crosses of some of them still bearing sad, ragged corpses, was not a cauldron but a huge square copper bath of oil on top of a bonfire. The samurai who had not set out in pursuit of the bandits stood around it, looking on in impassive, ordered ranks as within it five men writhed in silent agony. The boy could not help but look at the little figures as they flailed.

There had been no chance to save Shuntaro. He had been dead the minute the samurai had taken him from the cage. They could not have spared him even a moment of pain. Did they think the simple fact of their presence would bring him comfort, or was it to comfort themselves that they were not cowards? Was it to show that they understood duty and honor in some bleak and agonizing way?

What would that achieve? What did that even matter?

One of the men who had turned back, he remembered, was the one Shuntaro had called his son. Which was he? The bodies were naked, twisting and entwined in senseless agony, so far away.

The hill he was climbing was the tallest for some distance, and the boy saw then the village in the scope of the world; the sole mark of man among tree and slope and rock and river and sky and cloud. The village was so insignificant within all that, stripped of all import by scale, yet for those men who had chosen death for the sake of loyalty, or duty, or love, what happened there was everything.

It was ultimate and pure and meaningless. The mountains would no more tell of the righteousness or perversity of it than vapor could of the shape of water.

Above it all the smoke still rose as it had above Munisai's pyre, and he couldn't understand. The vista swam and bobbed, and Bennosuke realized the dizziness was back. The exhaustion had caught up with him now that the thrill of escape was passed, and he felt only loosely present in his body. The world was big and they were far and he was free was all he knew, and so he turned and spurred the horse away from this place of death to go and find the place of his own.

CHAPTER FOURTEEN

An earthquake woke him. Bennosuke's body rocked very little, but the old beams and pillars of the inn rattled noisily. One of the men he slept beside muttered a hungover curse, his breath musky with sake and bile, and then slept once more. Bennosuke remained awake and watched the man snore, envious of something lost to him forever now. It was the day of the Gathering.

He rose, washed, and ate. The inn was busy, but not with samurai. His berthmates were merchants, musicians, shoers of horses, cookers of food, poets, dancers, idiots who drooled, and wide-eyed fanatics, all the entourage of people who had come to the Gathering for spectacle or profit. They eyed Bennosuke warily.

He ignored them, preparing himself. He checked that the dagger Tasumi had given him a year ago was firmly strapped to his wrist. The thongs of the sheath were tight enough that he could feel the blood swelling his veins on either side of the cord. Then it was invisible under the sleeve of a kimono, and he was gone from the inn.

For the first time in a year he felt some measure of comfort. There had been numerous sacks and pouches hanging from the horse he had taken from the enclave, and within one, to his delight, he had found a small bag of coin. He had slept in real beds and eaten real food, and even had money left over to bathe in a hot spring and buy new clothes for himself.

As he had lain in the waters, he had had a mirror brought before him and saw how he had changed. He had not thought of his appearance in months. His face, golden in the copper expanse, was gaunt. The bright red welts of his rash had mostly faded, though some remained, but he saw and felt with his fingers that those that had gone had left little flecks and scars across him.

His hair was odd—his shaven scalp having grown in a quarter of the length of his longer hair—and it was tangled beyond what any comb could part. There was nothing to do but hack it off. Eventually he was left with a finger's length of hair that fell around his head as it had not done since he was an infant. He tossed the discarded strands into a brazier, and the stink of them as they had been incinerated was foul.

The horse awaited him in the stables. It was comfortable with him now. Bennosuke stood in the straw looking at it for a moment, and then he took it by the muzzle, closed his eyes, and pressed his forehead against the mare's. Of all here, she alone knew who he really was and what this day meant.

The fortnight since his escape from the corpsehandlers had passed quickly, a lot to remember from the riding lessons Tasumi had given him in his childhood. He had been taught the basics of balance and control, but he had never been allowed to ride at a gallop, only cantering around a paddock in circles while his uncle had called advice to him. A horse at full pelt, legs pumping and body writhing, was something else.

Again and again and again Bennosuke tumbled from the saddle, and each time he picked himself up winded or bloody, always he found the horse looking at him. The first time he had uttered an apology to her for his failure he had been surprised, but the urge grew within him. Soon the boy was whispering to her constantly, telling her of his mission, of Munisai and Hayato and why the latter needed to die.

It was good to have a companion after so long alone. It was good to have a witness. He spoke on and on, as much to himself as to her, and he remembered the long, horrendous moan Munisai made just before his death and the triumphant sneer of Hayato. Around him his anger grew and hardened like armor.

Driven toward vindication, slowly they had made progress—the mare had come to understand his smell and weight, and he how best to ride her. He was no master, certainly, and was uncomfortable without the reins in his hands, but then, he did not need to be comfortable. All he needed was a dagger in one hand. All he needed was reasonable balance. All he needed was courage. These three things he was certain were his.

In the stable in the light of his last morning, the mare nuzzled in his grip. He smiled, ecstatic for a moment. The day was here, finally here, and he told her this under his breath and thanked her for being here at the end, at this summit that all his suffering had led to.

Bennosuke allowed himself the smile for only an instant, though; there was still much to do. He composed himself, forced neutrality onto his face, and then he mounted and rode for the tournament grounds.

As the horse wove between the crowds, he wrapped a cloth loosely around his face and donned the helmet of the previous owner that he had found among the other bags and satchels strapped to his mare. It was a cheap thing the color of a pot, but it covered his head well enough. It was not a brilliant disguise, but then, genius subterfuge was not needed. The streets were thronged with enough people that spotting him would be difficult even if Nakata's men were looking for him. What guards there were lounged idly at attention, talking to one another or watching the tournament from their perches. Bennosuke passed untroubled. His stomach squirmed, excited at his infiltration.

An archery contest was under way. A track four hundred paces long had been cleared, and men would gallop down it controlling their horses with their knees as they tried to hit three small targets with a full-length longbow. To hit even two was a feat. A crowd watched, the samurai among them shouting boisterous encouragement while the lessers there clapped and sighed in polite and deferential amazement.

A platform surrounded by a burgundy palisade had been erected for a collection of lords and dignitaries to observe from. Bennosuke allowed himself a few moments to look within as he rode past. Hayato was not there, but the old Lord Nakata was, his eyes squinting more than usual as he strained to see whether the targets were being struck. In between riders he spoke and laughed with the nobles with him, oblivious to the boy's gaze.

The Gathering itself would take place in an enclosed field, heavily guarded at the boundaries. To sneak in unnoticed was impossible, and to try to charge through and batter his way to Hayato would be the ignoble kind of suicide. Bennosuke would have to enter like any other man, by registering to compete. A line of men stretched some distance as they waited to give their names to Nakata's bureaucrats. He hitched his horse, joined the line, and kept his head down.

Large boards were being erected above and around them, with freshly carved wooden plaques being hung upon them showing the names of the entrants and which lords they were riding for. Each name carried a little dedication beneath it:

MAY AUTUMN NEVER FIND THE CLAN NAKATA!

SOUTHERN WINDS BORE ME HERE, AND TO THE NORTH I SHALL RETURN UPON THE GRACE OF THE NAKATA!

NAKATA! NAKATA! A HUNDRED GENERATIONS! NAKATA!

Behind his mask, the boy's lip curled. He wondered if they were genuine or if the burgundy lord was employing some poor man with a chisel to think up a thousand different variations on the same theme.

The line moved quickly; soon it was Bennosuke's turn before a registrar. He was a harried man with ink-blackened fingers, and though he spoke the formal introductions to the boy in the polite courtly tongue, not once did his eyes leave the heap of documents he was rifling through.

"Greetings to thee on this day, brave rider," he intoned in the throes of routine. "The thanks of the most noble Lord Nakata are extended to thee for coming to add to such a marvelous spectacle. It is assured your participation shall be just, and memorable, and glorious. Might the honored rider who stands before this one who thankfully serves the most noble Lord Nakata write his name?"

The man gestured to a brush and ink, and as he continued to sort through his papers the boy wrote the name he had prepared. He had given it some thought, well aware that using his own was impossible. When this was all done he would be unable to speak for himself and there was a chance his body might not be recognized. Therefore the name he gave here might be the one that was carried with the news, and if that was the case then this needed to be a message also; a covert affirmation to those who could guess the truth.

The four characters were quickly written. The registrar took the document and examined it, checking he had the reading of the name right:

"The most honorable Musashi Miyamoto?"

"That is so," said Bennosuke.

The Musashi of the village indeed, as Tasumi had called him after he had fought Arima. He hoped that his uncle would smile when he heard the tale of the death of Hayato Nakata, would know that the boy he had trained had proved himself.

To the registrar the name meant no more than any other, though. He picked up a brush of his own and began scrawling quickly on a separate document.

"And the matter of the fee, most honorable Sir Miyamoto?" he asked as he wrote.

"Fee?" said Bennosuke.

"Yes," said the registrar, "the fee of entry—from which most noble lord shall we ask it? Whom shall you represent in the Gathering of the most noble Lord Nakata?"

Panic took hold of Bennosuke for a moment. The announcement boards had not mentioned any cost. But why would they? That would be rude and presumptuous. Of course Nakata would take any chance to earn money, and of course he would look to weed out any scoundrel. The boy had but a handful of coins left, nowhere near enough.

The registrar looked at him expectantly. Before that could warp into outright suspicion, something clicked in Bennosuke's head.

"It is the honor of this rider to represent Lord Ukita," the boy said.

It was a reasonable gamble—Ukita was a powerful man, and perhaps there would be enough riders already representing him that one more would go unnoticed. It seemed to work; the registrar nodded, and continued writing without a fuss. Bennosuke allowed himself to breathe again as he waited for the document to be finished. But then the man looked up.

"Ahh, Sir Kumagai?" he called beyond Bennosuke. A short, wiry samurai turned. He had been talking jovially with a few other men wearing livery different from his.

"Another one of your men," said the registrar, and he politely gestured toward Bennosuke.

"Eh?" he said, and came to stand before the boy. He looked up at him suspiciously. "Who're you?"

"The most honorable Musashi Miyamoto," the registrar informed him.

"All mine are in, I thought," said Kumagai, and he squinted closely at Bennosuke, eyeing up the size of him. "Take that helmet and mask off, I can't see you properly."

Bennosuke hesitated, but he had no choice. With his face truly bared, Kumagai's suspicion changed to surprise.

"Frost of hells," the man said. "How old are you?"

"Eighteen," lied Bennosuke.

"Ha! Try again, son," said the man.

"Sixteen."

"That's better," he said, satisfied. "What's a lad like you doing here, Musashi?"

"Want to ride in the Gathering, sir," Bennosuke said, and he affected sheepishness.

"Why didn't you come with the rest of us?" asked Kumagai.

"Thought you wouldn't let me," said Bennosuke, improvising wildly. "I just want to bring honor to Lord Ukita is all. Sorry, sir."

"Well," said Kumagai, and he softened slightly, "I suppose I can't fault you for that. Weird-looking bugger, though, aren't you? What happened to your hair?"

"An accident, it's . . ." he stammered lamely, a nervous hand running through his short mess of hair. There was the urge to bolt, certain that some guard of Nakata's must be looking now, recognizing him. Kumagai tilted his head, clucking his tongue behind his bottom lip.

"Ah, why not?" the man said with a shrug eventually, and then he turned to the registrar. "Please add this man's name to our entrant list."

"As you wish," said the registrar, and bowed low. "On behalf of the most noble Lord Nakata, good health and fortune are wished for thee."

Kumagai tapped the boy on the arm and led him away. When the registrar was finished writing, he handed the document to a craftsman who knelt behind him. Quickly the man began to carve into waiting cedar. A short time later, though Bennosuke would not see it, the name Musashi Miyamoto was hung up alongside the hundreds of others. Beneath it was written:

MY LIFE FOR THE NAKATA!

WHEN BENNOSUKE HAD retrieved his horse, Kumagai led him through the checkpoint that separated the samurai preparing for the Gathering from all others. The boy held his breath, again sure that he would be singled out with his face exposed, but the Nakata guards there recognized Kumagai. They passed pleasantries with one another, and then the guards smiled at Bennosuke and wished him good luck. The muscles in Bennosuke's back loosened gradually, the unseen knife he was certain was waiting slowly vanishing from his mind.

Kumagai seemed friendly, speaking freely of nothing with a casual warmth in his voice and an affable glint in his eye. Bennosuke would have guessed his age at somewhere in the early thirties, not yet marked by lines of age or gray hair. His nose had been broken at some point and had healed slightly out of line. Though he was short and thin he did not seem slight, and he carried himself with a solid, considered poise.

He offered no reason why he had allowed the boy to join him, but then, why would he? This was just an afternoon of sport for him, and the decision no more than a harmless kindness to some impetuous young fool.

"Miyamoto, you said your name was?" he said. "Are your family horsemen?"

"Not especially," said the boy.

"I can't say I know your father."

"I don't much know him either," said Bennosuke. "He died in Korea. My uncle too."

"The first one?" said Kumagai, and the boy nodded. "Ah, I see. I was there last summer. That was bad enough. You ever hear of a hwacha?"

"No," said Bennosuke.

"A devil's machine made for cowards," explained the man. "So it follows the Koreans use them. It uses blackpowder like the European muskets do, or more like skyrockets I suppose, but . . . it's not either. Imagine a cart with a box with two hundred holes in it on top, and in each one of these holes is an arrow or a rocket—or both. I don't know. They light it somehow, and then all two hundred arrows fire at once, screeching like falcons and fast as lightning. It's like the rain of hell, focused on one little bit of earth. Took us to bits, it did. Killed near fifty of the men I was marching with, just like that. Tore our formations right up, again and again."

"How many times did you encounter them?" asked Bennosuke.

"Enough," said Kumagai.

"And you just kept marching right at them?" asked Bennosuke.

"What else are we supposed to do?" said the samurai, and he laughed. "What are we, bloody Chinese?"

The other men of Ukita met Bennosuke with indifference. There were nearly thirty of them huddled around a tall banner in Ukita's livery, saddling their horses and tightening their armor as they eyed the clusters of other samurai, gauging their threat. Kumagai explained the boy's circumstances, and the men nodded disinterest and then turned away.

"Now get suited up, and be ready within the hour," said Kumagai. Bennosuke said nothing. "You did bring armor? A banner?"

"No," said Bennosuke, and Kumagai laughed again.

"How are you going to bring honor to our Lord Ukita if you're not wearing his colors, lad?" he said, smiling. "My word. Your heart's golden, but your head's addled."

Kumagai went and fetched a toughened underkimono and an old cuirass, which he dropped casually at Bennosuke's feet, and then placed a banner that carried his lord's livery carefully into the boy's hands. Still smiling, he left the boy with his men and went back to his post at the registrar's desk.

The material of the underkimono was coarse and stank of sweat and grass. The cuirass was worse. It matched his helmet in a way, a ratty old thing that was in essence little more than a heavily padded overjacket. It was too small for him, pinching at his shoulders and pressing down into the top of his stomach. He felt restricted. Another man helped him mount the banner on his back. It stood a full body's length above him, the rectangle of material held open always by the right-angled frame. It was clumsy and awkward, and he worried about his balance atop the horse.

But if it was a hindrance, it was a shared one. All wore banners, even the lordless men, but underneath them men were clad in everything from full suits of armor to little more than strips of cloth protecting modesty, depending on whether they valued protection or agility. Bennosuke was just another shabby and faceless participant among them, and that was perfect.

Kumagai came back some time later. The registry was over, the ride soon to begin. He held his arms out to his sides and the other samurai wordlessly placed his armor upon him as a team, quick and efficient. His armor was fine, his helmet crested, and his face hidden by a red lacquer mask that was carved into a snarling demon's grin. Auburn horsehair had been fashioned to form a drooping mustache and a fierce, bristling beard.

"Swords, boys," he said, and gestured at a crate.

His men began to strip the weapons from their sides and place them inside it one by one. Though etiquette technically permitted them to carry the shortsword anywhere in daily life, this was sport; passions sometimes flared beyond control, and with a sword to hand regrettable actions could be undertaken. It was a mark of common respect for honest competition that any weapon be relinquished.

Bennosuke lingered, suddenly unwilling to part with his blades. It was stupid, he knew. For a year now he had committed himself to what he would soon do, but to place the swords down for the final time would be a severance of sorts; like cutting loose the anchor that bound him to this world. He wondered what would become of them—would they be smashed to pieces by a vengeful Lord Nakata, or would they simply be left to molder in the crate, to be foisted off on some new recruit?

Or would the swords be taken away, stolen by some disciple, and placed in a shrine dedicated to ideals noble and pure? Would young warriors make pilgrimages to see them ensconced above incense-burning braziers, the mournful bells of a shrine pealing as the yet-to-be-born bowed low, their eyes misting with envy and longing as they read the words of an ancient scroll that marked Bennosuke Shinmen as a samurai who knew the righteous order of the world?

He blinked. Perhaps the delirium of exhaustion had not quite left him. But the vision had come to him so suddenly and vividly that he wondered if the breath of Munisai's ghost had stolen into him. Could that be so? If it was, then it was vindication; it must mean that some entity of heaven favored him and his course by allowing his father to communicate with him. Warmth—or at least a glowing determination—filled his heart.

Swords were symbols. Souls had worth. For the poems yet to be written about the latter, he lowered the former into the crate, closed the lid, and then pulled himself up into the saddle.

A GONG WAS being struck slowly, a call to assembly for those riding in the Gathering. Kumagai led his men at a brisk canter toward the field, weaving their way through other bands of samurai either mounting or already on the move. Ukita, as a greater lord, commanded a deal of respect, and Bennosuke could see it in the looks of apprehension his livery caused. It was a strange sense of anonymous and assumed power, mounted on another man's horse in another man's army, his face hidden from the world. It felt good. He leaned from side to side in the saddle, testing the weight of the armor and the encumbrance of the banner.

"Musashi," called Kumagai, and gestured for him to ride alongside him. The man's voice was muffled behind his snarling mask, his eyes barely visible. "Don't do anything stupid, you understand? This is dangerous. Stay with us. You fall and you'll not be walking away. The last thing I want to do is bear a lad with a mashed head home. That's . . . dishonorable."

"I'll be fine, sir," said Bennosuke.

"Stay with us, don't even think of going for the ball," said Kumagai. "I'll look out for you. Don't get any stupid ideas of glory into your head."

"I understand," said Bennosuke.

"Good lad," said Kumagai, and he laughed. Bennosuke thought he could see the glint of an eye in the dark holes of the face guard. "Rare fun, this."

They rode on. A familiar shade of blue lay up ahead; Lord Shinmen's riders stood, finishing their preparations. Bennosuke recognized some of their faces, most of all the young samurai who had struck Munisai's head from his shoulders. None of them seemed enthused, grimly looking back at Ukita's men as they passed. Kumagai snapped his head down in a battlefield bow, which was returned without luster.

"Surprised they've got the nerve to show their faces," said one of Kumagai's men once the blue samurai were behind them. "It'd take more than a wooden ball to get back their honor."

"The pride of Munisai Shinmen," said another, and there was cruel laughter.

"Silence!" barked Kumagai, fiercely whipping around to face them in his saddle. "They are allies of our Lord Ukita, I remind you!"

"More's the cursed pity," someone muttered. Kumagai pretended not to hear it.

BENNOSUKE LET HIS horse fall back into the body of the pack and glanced sideways at the men who had spoken. He was not angry with them. What they had said was proof that what he was doing needed to be done. The boy put his right hand to his left wrist, and he felt the hardness of the knife even through his armor.

They rode into a bottleneck of men and horses that waited to be allowed into the arena. Above them, on a platform that had been erected over the main gateway, a man stripped to the waist continued a steady beat upon the large, burnished gong. Bennosuke felt the hairs on his body stand on end, the reverberation scintillating as it counted onward, counted downward.

THERE WAS NO check for weapons; that would be insulting. Men and horses shuffled flank to flank under the gong and then into the field proper, which was enclosed by a palisade of burgundy and white material. Bennosuke felt a stab of apprehension as he took took it all in, the arena a lot smaller and the number of riders a lot greater than he had anticipated.

Men called greetings to one another as they sat waiting in their clan groups, the bamboo slats of their banner poles cracking in the gentle wind. Around the outside of the palisade, onlookers had gathered, jostling one another for position while the children they held on their shoulders giggled and waved.

A lordly platform overlooked the field, large and tiered. The lords sat highest upon it, and arrayed below them in descending importance were the lesser nobles, consorts and wives, dignitaries, and guests of the court. To Bennosuke they were nothing but distant balls of seated, colored kimonos, but he could guess who sat highest of all even without the hint of his burgundy attire.

Let me meet Hayato before that platform, Bennosuke prayed. *Let him have a good view. Let the old man see blood.*

What seemed to be the last of the competitors rode in. Men waited as their steeds nervously hopped from foot to foot. The horses could sense the anticipation in the air. Samurai twisted in their saddles, clutched their reins tighter, looked to one another, and smiled maniacally. It was war without weapons.

A drum roll began, a dozen men pounding on the heavy taiko skins from somewhere unseen, and the sudden thunder sent a pulse through both man and beast. A cry of salutation went up from men outside, and then into the arena came Hayato and his bodyguard. Their dozen horses were identical purebred stallions large and black and fierce, their banners adorned with streamers of paper and silk that curled and fluttered like the trail of comets behind them.

Bennosuke saw Hayato Nakata as he passed, he and his men riding the circumference of the arena once to bask in adulation. The young lord had his helmet off, and though he did not seem comfortable he made an effort to smile and look heroic, waving to the crowds with the one hand he had. The stump of his other arm was concealed artfully by his armor, and a man rode close enough on either side of him to keep him steady.

The boy's mare whinnied slightly as she felt her rider tense.

The Nakata rode to a halt somewhere toward the center, no doubt awaiting the ball to be thrown to them. Bennosuke did not take his eyes off their banners, gaudy and standing above all others. The drums came to a climax, and then there was emptiness until a single man appeared alongside the still gong. He gave a long and wordless yell, and the sheer strength of his voice was impressive. It carried across the ground as well as the drums had, and he held the note until all were looking at him.

"Hail, our esteemed regent Hideyoshi Toyotomi!" he called once he had their attention, raising one fist theatrically in the air.

"Ten thousand years!" yelled the mounted samurai in return, their voices a unified bark.

"Hail his majesty, the sovereign of heaven, our emperor!" called the man.

"Ten thousand years!" screamed the samurai once more.

"And hail our benevolent and noble Lord Nakata!" bellowed the man finally, his voice breaking with the force he put into it.

"Ten thousand years!" came the uncertain reply. That was a prestigious list Nakata had placed himself at the head of, and the samurai were caught between courteousness to their host and sacrilege.

The herald began to explain the rules of the game circuitously, his language honorific and unwieldy even if he had been merely speaking. Screamed as it was, it took some time simply to say they should get the ball out and through the gate upon which he was standing. As he howled, it occurred to Bennosuke then that as they had no weapons, Hayato's men would not strike him down instantly. They would wrestle him from the horse and bind him, and then images of prolonged torture at the clan's leisure came to him. He remembered the misery and terror he had felt within the straw helmet. That he did not want to know again. He would have to plunge the dagger into his own throat once Hayato was dead.

It was not seppuku, but good enough. Having made that decision, to be the master of his own fate, he suddenly relished what was to come. What had been welling in him peaked—he was terminally alive, and he locked the far bobbing banners of the Nakata in his sight.

Another man clambered up alongside the herald. He was huge

and bared to the waist, a heavy ceremonial rope hung with paper folded into lightning bolts tied around his belly. In one hand he held a sling, and in the other massive palm he held the ball. The orb was polished, dark wood the size of a human head, tied with red streamers, and the object of everyone's sudden attention. The herald dropped to his knees and watched as the giant wrapped the ball in the sling and then let it hang by his shins.

The giant waited for expectant silence, and then he began to rotate the ball with the slightest movement of his wrist, the circular motion almost insignificant. But at that gesture the samurai kicked their horses and began to trot around the arena following the direction of the ball's spinning. Gradually the slinger began to increase the size of the spin and watched as the horsemen spurred their horses faster in time.

"Follow my lead," said Kumagai, not looking back at his men. "We stay on the outskirts until I say otherwise."

When the giant could swing it no wider one-handed, his arm out by his side, he began to pass it around his body from one hand to the other. A grin broke over his face as the horses below him started to canter. Hoof fall began to drown out any other sound, and the world became a myriad of colors for Bennosuke as the banners flicked between one another and the horsemen began to press inward. His mare whinnied and kicked as she was buffeted.

"Ukita!" screamed an unseen rider from beyond them, his voice passing quickly. "Ukita! Eat shit!"

"Knock that bastard from his horse, whoever he is," growled a samurai ahead of Bennosuke, the man taking his eyes away from the ball for but a moment to try to spot who had shouted.

Atop the platform the giant took the sling in both hands and began to spin his body now, around and around. Men stood in their saddles as their horses broke into a run. Tighter they became, Bennosuke's stirrups meeting the flanks of other horses and the feet of other men. Ukita's samurai pressed around him, shielding him. A human yelp came from up ahead, brief and stolen quickly downward, and then their horses stumbled for a moment over something beneath them.

The slinger put the force of his huge back into it, hunching his shoulders. It was an impressive piece of skill for a man of his size to balance on so small a platform as he whirled, the ball almost straight before him. Now the gallop began, and the noise of hooves became that of a pounding, white-foamed river, relentless and overwhelming and driving forward, always forward.

With a yell the slinger committed to the final rotations, ball dipping high to low, and then he released it. It sailed high into the air and flew like some rogue eclipsed sun, a hundred pairs of gauntleted hands reaching up toward it like pagans at prayer. A great roar went with it, from the riders, from the crowd, and from the lordly platforms. It arced and then plunged into the midst of the riders, gone from Bennosuke's sight, but the boy felt as much as heard a sudden frenzy from somewhere within the press of men.

"Keep riding! Not yet!" yelled Kumagai, standing and straining to see. Bennosuke spared every glance he could to see how close they were to the Nakata. The burgundy men must have been near the center of the melee, for they barely seemed to move. The tips of their banners became as the polestar, a firmament around which the boy could gauge his frantic rotations.

"Ukita! Ukita! Die!" came a sudden fierce cry from ahead. A rider appeared as if from nothing against the flow of men, his horse wide-eyed and frothing in terror and the samurai's face much the same in rage.

There was a frantic instant of parting for the wild charger, and then he was among them, his arm out trying to hook someone, anyone wearing Ukita colors, from their saddle. Bennosuke's body froze, and all he could do was watch dumbly as the man struck him across the chest before vanishing into the mass behind them. The boy tumbled backward, the reins knocked from his hands. For a second he hung in a failing, flailing equilibrium, and then he felt his foot come free from the stirrup and his body begin to plunge into the stomping mass of hooves below.

A hand locked around his ankle before it passed entirely over the flank of the horse and he was lost, and then another Ukita samurai leaned down and wrenched the scruff of his armor up. Together the two men managed to right the boy without breaking pace, and gratefully Bennosuke clasped the reins once more and slung his body close to the horse beneath him like a drowning man holding driftwood.

"You all right?" barked one of the men to him, and all the boy could do was nod.

"Anyone see who that was?" screamed another.

"Just bloody watch for him again, we'll get him if he comes back!"

Bennosuke ignored them, focusing on his balance. He was panicking, his equilibrium impossible to find once again, and all the while the banner kept catching in the wind, threatening to whip him from his mount. The hours he had spent practicing in the past two weeks seemed for nothing. Bennosuke hung on grimly, until he saw Kumagai suddenly slash his hand across and point toward the center.

"Now! Let's go! Come on!" he screamed, and wrenched his horse into a turn.

He had spotted an opening through the swirling outer rings of riders to the eye of the whirlpool, and he and his thirty riders plunged into it in a loose arrowhead. The impact that they made as they collided with the central mass of bodies drove the wind from man and beast, a shared exhalation of pain. Kumagai's horse rose and clambered over another in desperate panic, knocking the rider off, and onward they all scrabbled over a floor that writhed.

There was no galloping in the center, barely any motion at all. They pushed on and forced other men around them, moving at the whim of the tide of crowd. Here, trapped in the crush, there were as many riderless horses as there were those still guided by men, and what samurai were left were in the frenzies of violence, wrenching and punching. It seemed to Bennosuke that this must be a glimpse of a hell of some sort; a press of bodies and flesh so tight, and nothing but animal terror and human hate between them.

"There!" barked Kumagai, his voice breaking with laughter as he pointed. "The ball!"

A young samurai had the darkwood ball clasped to his chest, his knuckles white around it as other men clawed at him. His horse was not moving, held tight by those around it. Behind him, Bennosuke saw burgundy advancing. The Nakata were going for it too.

Achingly slow, fighting for every inch, the Ukita turned their horses and began to try for the ball. But their collective will was irrelevant; they were a mere part of a mass that heaved and pulsed with desires and plots. They became entangled, their horses buffeted and spun like leaves on a river, and then suddenly another group of men were intersecting with them, pushing through them.

Someone grabbed at Bennosuke from behind, fingers hooking around his shoulder. A samurai was falling, seeking any purchase to try to save himself. He was not Ukita, and his fingers were gouging and tearing at Bennosuke, clutching at his helmet and then his face, his eyes, his mouth. The man was heavy, Bennosuke was off balance, and then the two began to slowly sink together.

The boy was lying almost straight across the back of his horse before he started hitting the man, lashing out with his elbow and the back of his fist again and again. The man could not see where the blows were coming from, and he swore and cursed in confusion and pain, but he held on. Bennosuke bit down on the fingers in his mouth and tasted blood as he desperately tried to wrench himself up, twisting his body and hauling upon the reins.

There was a snapping sound, and Bennosuke imagined for a moment that it was his mare's legs popping with the strain, but it was too loud and too brittle to be bone. His body shot up suddenly free, and he felt lighter. He turned, and down through the legs of the horse he could just see the vivid color of his banner held in a hand frantically trying to shield itself. The man had clung to whatever he could, and the weight of a body was too much for mere bamboo.

The remnants of the splintered standard stood up behind him like a primitive spear as he twisted in the saddle, disoriented and alone. Somewhere Kumagai was still laughing, but he was gone from Bennosuke's sight. So too for a horrible few moments were Nakata's banners, but they were tall and gaudy and eventually he saw them—and then beneath them Bennosuke saw Hayato Nakata. The lord was not thirty paces away. The dagger throbbed on his wrist.

Knowing that his father was watching, that the forces of the world that believed in righteousness were with him, he forgot about Kumagai and the Ukita. He needed their shielding no longer. He tried to turn, to make for his goal, but he was held in limbo, pressed and pinned by the whirling embrace of the throng. It was a form of torture to see Hayato so close, and he found himself screaming in frustration and anger at his immobility. He dug his fingers into the manes of the horses nearby, as though he might drag himself and his mount across the gap.

Then without warning, the vagary of the crowd suddenly favored him, and he burst forth on a wave of bodies. People seemed to part for him, and he was carried to Hayato so fast that their armor clattered together with a slap. The lord turned quickly, and Bennosuke saw that under his helmet his eyes were wide and terrified, darting around in their sockets.

"Get away from me!" he mewled, his voice high and pathetic. He did not recognize Bennosuke; he just saw another unknown entity in a world the lord did not understand. That was not good enough. Hayato had to know who was killing him. Bennosuke pushed his head so close that the brows of their helmets touched.

"You! Away from him! Away!" growled one of Nakata's bodyguard, but he was too far to intervene. He gestured in vain, as trapped as Bennosuke had been a moment before.

"Are you samurai?" hissed Bennosuke, ignoring the shouting as though it were a world away.

His eyes bored into Hayato's, and he could see confusion come into Nakata for just one moment. The lord pulled his head back to try to examine the face before him, close enough still that the boy could smell his breath. Bennosuke knew that this was his ultimate moment. His right hand went up the sleeve of his left, wrapped around the hardness of the dagger's handle. The boy closed his eyes, and willed the image of Munisai to spur him forward, to vindicate him . . .

Instead, what he saw was five small men in a distant bath of boiling oil, naked and flailing. He saw the sky and the earth and a ring of crucifixes around a dirty little hamlet, and he saw no meaning to any of it. The little figures writhed and writhed forever . . .

"Away! Away!" came the bodyguard's voice.

Hayato's eyes held his, and the lord's throat was there, exposed and soft. The blade was strong, but the hand that tried to grasp it was weak. Bennosuke could not bring the weapon forth. His body was cold, paralyzed by a chill, and though his father's ghost and righteous entities of heaven must be screaming, he knew then that he could not kill Hayato, because he was too afraid to die.

"Away!" said a voice in his ear.

The bodyguard had managed to squirm close enough to the boy to put a rough hand on him, and then he forced his body between the boy and the lord. Still Bennosuke could not move, but he knew his chance was gone. He had failed.

"Who is he?" asked Hayato. "Who is he?"

The lord never found out. Bennosuke forced his horse around before he could be unmasked, and then he pushed and pushed until he was free of the swarm, and then the mare ran, galloped out of the arena with the joy of the unshackled, past wounded men and horses with broken bodies, through the crowds and the vain shouts of guards until they were gone. Gone from the Gathering and gone from the town, and once he was out of sight of other men he fell from the saddle, moaning and sobbing in wracked, wretched shame, put his hands on the back of his head, curled himself into a ball and then forced his brow down into the dirt where he knew it belonged.

The bowl of noodles grew cold before him. Two boiled eggs split in half floated in the frothy, orange soup. Bennosuke watched the soft yolks within them slowly harden with the heat. He had wandered into an inn, still wearing the old cuirass from the Gathering, and had spent the last of his coin on the meal. But he could not eat it.

He was an empty thing pretending to be a human, and he sat blankly. This was not a moment he should be feeling, not a future he had considered. He wondered what he should do.

Well, something thought, *you know what you should do. You know what a coward like you deserves. But then, you're too weak for that, aren't you? That's why you're here. That's why you linger.*

The boy tried to ignore the voice, but he knew it spoke the truth. He lived that moment again and again, saw the gap in Hayato's armor and his jugular pulsing once more, and each time he tried to imagine a reality in which he had had the courage to strike. But always his arms were weak, always he pulled away, always he fled.

Why? Why this sudden outbreak of animal self-preservation? Why this sudden care for flesh when he had neglected his body for the year before in sole pursuit of that moment? He couldn't answer. Was it simple fear and cowardice? If that was so, why had he seen Shuntaro and his men at that crucial moment, and not some primal image of death or decay?

It didn't matter. Whatever the reason, he had failed Munisai utterly, and his sullied soul remained anchored to this world of shame.

The yolks of the eggs coagulated before his dead eyes.

There was a clatter of heavy boots at the door, the curtain that hung across the entrance cast aside. Kumagai was standing there, half stripped out of his own armor, his swords back at his side. He scanned the room quickly, and almost missed Bennosuke tucked cross-legged into the corner of the inn.

"There you are, Musashi, you mad little bastard," the man said, and he stomped across to stand before the boy. Bennosuke met his gaze, but said nothing. It was like looking upon a memory from a dream.

"Been looking for you," said Kumagai, expecting an apology, but the boy offered none. "Where'd you go? Hmm? Why'd you run away? Thought you'd got killed or something. Been searching the wounded tents for you, all of us have."

Still the boy kept silent. Kumagai shrugged and sat down. He shuffled under the small table, picked up a pair of chopsticks, and then helped himself to one of the halved eggs. He sucked it down with relish.

"Didn't win, in any case. Never even touched the ball. Some gang of fools from the south got it out. Found that bastard who was telling us to eat shit, though, afterward. Didn't find out why he was after us, but he won't be . . . besmirching us again," said Kumagai, a dark, satisfied grin on his face. He licked his lips of the sauce, and waited for the boy to share his mirth. When he did not, the man looked at him suspiciously.

"What's wrong with you, eh?" he said. "Horse crush your balls or something? Where is your horse, anyway? We were looking for it hitched somewhere, but it's not outside here."

Bennosuke just looked back. The words meant nothing to him. Kumagai looked at him again for a few moments, and then he cast his eyes down and nodded somberly.

"Ah, I understand," he said. "It fell in the Gathering? It snapped its neck in a fall? I see. Well, it's a hard thing to do, to lose a horse. Love them, don't you? Like a woman, but a horse won't complain if you ride it for hours. Or ride another one, eh? Aye. I understand. It's hard, lad. Hard. I've done it myself. But it's just a horse, Musashi. Not the end of the world. Unless . . . Was that your father's horse? Well, that's . . . I can't say anything there. But memories are more than things, you understand? That was his, but it was not him, right? Just remember him, and you'll learn to live with it. Perhaps. I don't know."

Bennosuke had set the animal free once he had found the strength to stand without feeling the crushing weight of shame. He had ripped the saddle and the reins from it, slapped it on the hind, and watched it gallop off. What right had he to put binds upon another living thing?

That, and she knew.

"Hard though it is," Kumagai said after what he gauged to be a pensive pause, "you can't let it get the better of you. You have to think. You forgot these, didn't you?"

Bennosuke realized the man had been carrying his swords. The samurai slid them along the floor to him. The sight of those, of the longsword that had once been at Munisai's side, drove a fresh spasm of pain into his heart. The boy did not dare touch them. Kumagai took another egg for himself, this time with his fingers.

"You'll need them, lad," the samurai said, sucking his fingers clean. He looked around the inn suspiciously, though there were no other samurai present, and then leaned in conspiratorially. "The Regent Toyotomi is dead."

He sat back as though to let the magnitude of that sink in. Still Bennosuke did not speak. What was that news to him? That was the world of samurai, and he did not belong to it any longer.

"A week ago." Kumagai nodded. "We only just heard after the

Gathering. Our spies from Kyoto are the best. No one else here knows. You know what that means, right?"

War. The War.

"We have to return to Takeyama. Our Lord Ukita no doubt has a plan. We've wasted enough bloody time looking for you—we have to leave now. It's time for us to stop being sportsmen, and to be soldiers."

He jerked his head at the door and sat back as if to rise. Bennosuke considered it. A soldier did not have to think. A soldier just did. That might be good. He was not dead, and nor could he die today, and there was food and a bed and warmth. A moth, primal and banging around the flame of simple sensation. That was what he was.

He nodded, picked up the weapons he was not fit to wield, and rose with Kumagai. The two of them exited the inn into a country that was at war but did not know it. People enjoying a last day of merriment before lines were drawn and chaos came as it had not done for decades.

"Cheer up, you miserable bugger," said Kumagai as they passed through the door, and he pushed him playfully on the back of the head. "It was only a bloody horse."

Part Four

SEKIGAHARA

A Day of Glory and Rebirth; The Sundered Realm Made Anew

The Twenty-First Day of the Tenth Month, Fifth Year of the Era of Keicho

(The Year Four Thousand Two Hundred and Ninety-Six by the Old Chinese Methods, Sixteen Hundred Years Exactly After the Europeans Killed Their God)

CHAPTER FIFTEEN

The hawk skated upon a sea of cloud, so close to the surface Bennosuke thought he could see tendrils of mist whip around its claws. It circled, circled, circled in elegant stillness, the silhouette navy on steel blue in the dawn light.

Fog had rolled in through the night, its thickness and depth such that it obscured the basin of the valley but left the peaks of the ridges where the boy now sat exposed. Bennosuke had not been able to sleep, clad in armor as he was. He had wandered up here in the darkness, as had other men, and together they had huddled, praying or sharpening swords or like him simply waiting and watching the hawk.

Somewhere, down in the mist below, there were two armies, from here invisible and the noise of them muffled. No one knew quite how many men were there; after a hundred and fifty thousand counting seemed pointless. Beyond that was a summoning of warriors the scale of which had not been seen before. It was everyone, ultimate, climactic.

A week ago no one had known the name Sekigahara, but it was here in this valley where the fate of Japan would be decided.

The hawk keened, a piercing sound that made Bennosuke shiver and gave him gooseflesh. Perhaps other men might have called such a cry portentous or auspicious, but to him it just compounded the overwhelming feeling of strangeness. Here he was, present at the end of a war that had meant so little to him but had swallowed the lives of so many other men the country over.

It had been two years since the Gathering. The seasons had passed by, felt as little more than incremental changes in temperature and length of daylight to him. Work and steady diet had rendered him tall and strong, the body of a man his already though he was barely past sixteen. He had changed, and the truth was that sometimes the flesh felt no more his than the gauntlets or the cuirass he wore now.

It was not a new sensation. The War had welled and welled over the long months leading here, but Bennosuke had seen none of it. Kumagai and his men had been sent to hold a mountain pass, vital but well away from the fighting, and there they had stayed until they had received a summoning from Ukita a month ago to join this great host that had marched to Sekigahara.

Back then, before open conflict had erupted across the land, Kumagai had made no real effort to ascertain whether Bennosuke's story was true. Miyamoto was a common-enough name that a search through the clan records would yield dozens of families, and rather than waste time sifting through them all he had simply permitted the boy to fall in with him and his men.

The samurai had had other preoccupations in any case. He was a horseman and a leader of cavalry, but in being sent to guard that pass so far away from grazing pastures they had had to surrender their steeds. Bennosuke was relieved to be spared the search for another horse, one less burden for him. For Kumagai, however, the idea of being holed up, of being stationary, seemed to make him uneasy.

"Our most noble lord is being wise and biding his time, holding what he has. I cannot fault the strategy," the samurai had said again and again, and every time he did so Bennosuke could see the longing for a saddle in his eyes.

They had practically burst forth from the fort when the order had come a month ago; down from the hills into the troughs and the plains, and their eighty men had joined there with another eighty, and then they had met a band of five hundred, and then that too had been absorbed into a force of two thousand, and it grew and grew until the land swarmed. The samurai had marched and on either side of them rows of the lower born had knelt with their faces pressed into the dirt.

Ukita and the other great lords had chosen to meet in this valley simply to rally their individual forces into one colossal host and then plan the great offensive out upon the vast plains to the east. Sekigahara was wooded and they held the high ground, and entrenched within the forested slopes they had believed themselves safe and free to spend however long they liked fawning over maps and proposed strategies.

It had been no small surprise, then, when yesterday the enemy had been sighted marching on them. Fearlessly they had come, heading straight into the cleared bowl of the valley just before night fell, endless blocks of men marching in formation from over the horizon. They had arranged themselves for battle in the darkness, their lanterns slowly engulfed by the coming of the fog, and the sheer number of those lights had been daunting. Bennosuke had heard uneasy conversations around him in the night, the men trying to convince themselves that it was a deception, that each warrior of the enemy was carrying two.

The boy had ignored them mostly. He had watched the lightening of the sky as he watched the hawk circling now—still, peaceful, apart. The bird swooped upward above the fog in a flowing arc, hanging at the peak for a single majestic instant. But it was a part of this imperfect world and had to obey its laws eventually; it turned upon itself and dived downward, vanishing into the mists below.

The Lord Ieyasu Tokugawa was a known falconer. Perhaps the hawk returned to his hand, somewhere hidden down there.

*T*okugawa," said the Lord Ukita, his hands steepled before his face, "Tokugawa, Tokugawa, Tokugawa."

You've played this well, he added ruefully within his head.

The lord's palisade was below the mist line, a ring of thick silk open to the sky. The flickering of lanterns was unable to dispel the fog that painted the world the color of a sword. In this gloom Ukita sat on a stool, a hastily drawn map of the area spread before him on the floor, the heavy slashes of black ink glistening in the feeble light.

The valley was the shape of a stubby dog's leg, and the map showed Ukita and his allies splayed out in a vague horseshoe on the three surrounding slopes of the "paw." In the center of them, in the basin of the valley where the village of Sekigahara was—an insignificant mass of farmers' hovels—the entirety of the enemy was dismissed with a few diminutive characters. Thousands of unknown warriors in unknown formations there summated quite blithely as "Tokugawa."

That lack of knowledge worried him deeply; logic could not be applied to the unknown. He chewed the inside of his lip, the motion very carefully hidden by his hands. Ukita did not want to show any sign of anxiety to the other lords and generals gathered there—from eager adolescents to the pensive ancients, all sitting, standing, pacing. He was the great lord, though, and they all waited for his command in silence. The noise of the thousands outside was smothered and distant.

How had it come to this?

It was a war for a title no one claimed to want: shogun. Each of the former Council of Elders vowed that their sole intention was to continue to humbly protect the child of the late Regent Toyotomi until he was of age to take power. Each of the former Council knew that the others were lying, of course, and of course each knew that they themselves were lying too. To be shogun was everything, all that their ancestors had planned for, and that the fortune was theirs to be born into a time where they had the opportunity to take it . . . Oh, it made the heart sing.

So tantalizingly close. As everyone had expected, it had been Tokugawa who was first ejected from the Council within months of the regent's death for his "dangerous ambition" and "unusual deception." As no one had expected, Tokugawa had flourished afterward. The Patient Tiger proved his name, winning allies to what should have been a hopeless cause, whispering in the right ears, promising land and gold that wasn't his to some while lopping off the heads of others.

And the strategy had worked. Lords from the East and from the North flocked to his banner, pledging allegiance, his forces swelling until they matched the combined might of the four most powerful men in the country. It had been masterfully done, almost unbelievably so, and part of Ukita longed to join the man and share in such genius. But he had made his choices and sworn his oaths, and here they all were.

Tokugawa. Those small characters, black on white. Ukita tasted blood.

❄

ord Shinmen also had a map within his private palisade—and a message. He twisted the lacquer tube open and snatched the rolled paper from within. He read it, and then raised his eyes to his gathered bodyguard and adjutants.

"Our dear ally Lord Kobayakawa all but names our most noble Lord Ukita traitor," he said, "and by extension ourselves also."

"If Kobayakawa has communicated such with the other lords . . ." said one man, momentary concern in his eyes.

"He will have done so," said Shinmen, and he waved at the mound of message tubes upon the floor to his side. "As has Ishida about him to me, and Konishi about Kikkawa . . . I would not be surprised to learn Tokugawa had turned the ground itself to his cause. I expect a quake at any moment."

There was a nervous attempt at laughter from them all. It faltered not solely because it was a bad joke, but because all knew that there was the true worry. Why else would Tokugawa have the courage to march into this valley where he would be surrounded—unless he wasn't surrounded at all? It stank of treachery, and frantic messages and accusations had been flitting back and forth between the lords all night.

If anyone was false Ukita would be the obvious suspect—he or the Lord Kobayakawa. Of all the lords there the two of them had the largest forces, each approaching twenty thousand men. They duly held the most vital positions in the line of battle too, Ukita the center and Kobayakawa the right, with the minor lords like Shinmen sworn to either of them filling in the gaps between.

Shinmen sucked air through his teeth, ran his fingers over the map. If Kobayakawa switched his loyalty, he could simply roll the mass of his men around and envelop the rest of the army within minutes. Shinmen looked at the layout of the forces, and he did not know which name worried him most: Tokugawa or Kobayakawa.

Or Ukita, the honest part of him added. The lord had neither shared nor shown any intention of betrayal in the preceding week—but you didn't advertise conspiracy until the knife was in the back, did you?

He felt a rare powerlessness. Though he could command the life and death of hundreds, he was minor here; this was the fate of millions, of a nation. There was nothing to do but prepare. The lord stood with his legs wide and his arms outstretched and his men came to him with his armor. They bustled around him, cladding him in layers of leather and cloth and wood and iron, working with the speed of strong hands and practiced routine.

The young lad Kazuteru came to him last, bearing his helmet. The samurai placed it upon his head, and then tied the thick, soft cord across the lord's chin. Shinmen looked at him, and suddenly he was reminded of what his own definition of loyalty had wrought. The familiar thought came to him that Kazuteru, who had struck the head, was some sort of vessel, and that part of *him* lingered on within the young man before Shinmen, watching.

"I'm sorry," the lord murmured.

Kazuteru looked confused for an instant, and before he began the instinctive apology etiquette demanded when you did not understand a superior, a messenger clattered into the palisade:

"Orders from our most noble Lord Ukita, my lord!"

Advance!" bellowed the Marshal Fushimi. "The order is given, warriors of the West! The day has come! Glory to you all, your ancestors weep at the chance to partake in such a battle! The order to assembly is given! Make your way to your posts!"

The marshal rode along the ridgetop above the fog, weaving his horse between the clusters of men who for whatever reason had found their way here in the night. In peace he was a giver of law and now in war he was trusted to bring order to this host. What was a marshal to do but marshal?

He saw the men all around him on the slopes, hunched over like gangs of ravens on branches looking down upon the world. The accents that he heard were a strange and awful corruption of the language he spoke—the central, true tongue. These samurai were men from the farthest parts of Japan, from the western tip of Honshu and from the southern isles of Kyushu and Shikoku; he understood but one word in three, and he wondered if they comprehended any more or less of his speech.

All the clans drawn here, a countrywide coalition focused on no more than a mile square of land. Fushimi was disgusted; these men were practically Ryukyuan, Korean, Chinese. Oh, that on this day of days he should be alongside men of this caliber.

He rode on, one hand on the reins, the fingers of the other running over his armor absently. The suit had been worn before him by his father and his grandfather and his grandfather's grandfather, and through scores of battles had proved itself true. Hidden beneath the decorative thread that lay over the cuirass he found a familiar ridge; a long gouge from a sword strike that had been repaired years ago, filled in with molten metal that had hardened across the bowl of the stomach like a tumescent vein.

Fushimi's fingers went back and forth across it, back and forth across the vein, the lifeline, and he wondered which of his ancestors had born this blow, and if the successor had toyed with it as he did now, and whether they were watching, willing him onward through this as a bastion of propriety among the mongrels and the disloyal and the . . .

"We advance!" he yelled again before his thoughts ran too blackly, looking for men he could recognize, the few he trusted. "To your posts, all of you! Advance!"

$\mathcal{B}$ennosuke watched the man on horseback pass him, screaming his commands, repeating his message to all whom he found. He looked vaguely familiar, but the boy could not remember where from. Perhaps it was just the disgust in the man's eyes, evoking old memories of Miyamoto. He didn't care, and neither did he brood for long; he rose and placed his helmet on his head, for he had his orders.

That was where the two years since his failure had gone, Bennosuke knew—orders. That was what made a soldier's life a soldier's, and what had made his life as mindless and numb as he had hoped.

As he followed the other men trooping down, he looked across the clouds wistfully before his descent and envelopment by the fog stole the serene view from him. He remembered the graceful curve of the hawk's flight; curling, curling, upward, equilibrium, and then down and gone.

And then he too was gone, down into the mists and into war.

From somewhere distant there was a fog-stifled roar that unfolded like a peal of thunder. A cannon perhaps, or a rank of muskets firing. At what, Bennosuke could not tell, but as he descended the frantic preparation that had been hidden by the fog engulfed him. He walked through narrow paths that wound their way through the trees, but because they were crowded scores of men had abandoned them entirely. Their spectral silhouettes flitted between the upright obelisks the tree trunks had become, fading from black to gray to invisible within a mere twenty paces.

That consuming fog and the twisting of the paths revealed brief images before stealing them away; men racing past, armor clattering, others shouting fiercely as units came together. Barricades of sharpened bamboo spears laying ready, the ribbed green trunks as long as two men. A fletcher desperately tarring feathers to shafts, any sort of art forgotten in the simple need for arrows, and behind him another man struggling to roll a barrel of gunpowder to waiting arquebusiers. A stony-faced samurai staring into a copper mirror checking that the pate of his head was immaculately shaved, a boy to one side holding his razor. A dog leashed on a chain and black as coal snarling and leaping around and around in maddened circles, drool flecking from its maw.

All here to fight were samurai, and so all carried swords, but they were the secondary weapons today. Men bore further armaments, be it spear or halberd or bow, ready to fall into formation and play the desperate game of counteracting; spears taking cavalry, cavalry taking missile troops, and missile troops taking spears.

There were great warriors present, some dripping with armor so fine it put Munisai's set in Miyamoto to shame, painting them as angular demons, but most men could afford only the basics of protection: a simple cuirass, an iron conical helmet tied under the chin, and then toughened underkimonos of leather and cloth to protect their arms and legs. Some did not even have that, the armories of clans having been entirely depleted.

Though it was overwhelming, Bennosuke wove his way through all of it, having made careful note of his path to the ridgetop the day before. Eventually he came to men he recognized, the first of the eighty whom Kumagai commanded. These samurai gave Bennosuke nothing but curt nods of respect as he passed, and he in turn gave nothing more back.

Even after two years, they were fellow soldiers only.

The fort that Bennosuke, Kumagai, and his men had been stationed to hold was set upon a bleak and barren stretch of land, nestled at the narrowest point between two rocky slopes so steep they were practically cliff faces. Though a garrison had been maintained there for centuries, what buildings and fortifications there were had not been designed to withstand the firepower of modern cannon and musketry. That would need to be remedied, and when they arrived the first tentative steps of cladding the frail wooden walls in stone had been made.

Craftsmen would come to finish the job, they were told, but none did. Every man in the land who knew how to cut or shape stone suddenly found himself diverted to the great cities and set to the task of adding extra ramparts and buttresses to the castles there. They took the best quality stone with them, adding armor upon armor upon armor while those on the outskirts and boundaries were left vulnerable.

A limb could be sacrificed, the heart could not—the logic was sound but hard to swallow for those of them in that limb. Kumagai had clucked his tongue, but rather than wait for Tokugawa to come knocking with a rain of fire, he eventually decided they would persevere and try to learn the ways of architecture themselves. He ordered his men to take from the walls around them, chipping away malformed, fractured lumps of rock and stone, which they would pile around the wooden beams as best they could.

It was tiring work, muscles forming on all of them, but Benno-suke liked it. When he had a pickax in his hands he did not have to think, he could just do. There was a purity in it; nothing more than the next swing, nothing to acknowledge but hard stone. But they could not dig forever, and when work was done for the day there was always the uncomfortable closeness of the others.

When he had first joined them, they had wanted him to be the surrogate little brother. They had joked with him, called him friendly diminutives, roughhoused with him as they tried to coax some form of light or mirth from him, all to no avail.

They had started to realize this only on the night that they had made him drink for the first time. He had coughed and spluttered and forced the sake and the stronger spirits down because they expected him to, and then the next thing he knew he was crying, and he could not stop himself. The world was spinning, and he was blubbering hot, wet tears of shame, and the other samurai were sitting staring stonily, embarrassed for and by him. He knew this and he was ashamed, but still the racking sobs had come because inside he knew he was alive when he should be dead, and he couldn't explain that to them.

They stopped inviting him eventually. He became a pariah again, and though he knew he deserved it—these men were samurai, after all—the sensation of being alone among them made him feel hollow in his bones. When they were not working or sleeping and when the other men had gathered to talk of nothing in the long hours while waiting for an enemy that never came, Bennosuke sidled away to practice the sword.

The men left him to his strange ways, no one interested enough to unravel whatever it was that made him act so. He obeyed them, and that was enough. But time dragged on, and in the way of idle groups of men they began to search for entertainment wherever it could be had.

Early one evening, with the stone around the wall standing as high and as broad as a man and with the heavy sun just beginning to set, the boy had headed off to the corner of the fort he used in place of a dojo. He was not out of sight, for there was nowhere to hide here, but far enough away that people could pretend not to see him—if they wanted to.

He was running through a defensive technique meant to ward away pole arms when he became aware of being watched. Two samurai were standing a short distance away, chewing balls of salted, hot rice.

"A strange form you're using," said one, a narrow-eyed man of minor rank named Goto. "You never told us where you studied, Musashi."

"My father taught me, sir," said Bennosuke. He made as if to continue, but Goto strode forward, pushing the last of the rice ball into his mouth and wiping his hands on his clothes already dirty from labor.

"Looks pretty in and of itself, but is it functional?" he said. It was not a challenge, but genuine curiosity.

"I've never fought a duel, sir," said Bennosuke.

"Looks like you're spoiling for one, the way you're practicing."

"We're at war. Swordsmanship will be useful, sir."

"Indeed. How about some real practice?" Goto said. "You against me, wooden swords, traditional rules?"

"I cannot dig if I am injured," said Bennosuke, feigning modesty, and growing more uncomfortable the closer the man got. "For now, digging is my duty, sir."

"Don't be so pious your whole life—forget all that. Everyone else has certainly forgotten us up here," said Goto, nodding at the ragged wall. "Come on, lad. A wager change your mind?"

"I have no money to gamble, sir."

"Then what do you have?"

"Nothing, sir."

"What about your armor? You're still wearing the old scrap Sir Kumagai gave you, right?"

"Yes. But it is not scrap. It is perfectly serviceable, sir," said Bennosuke.

"So is your hand when you can't find a woman, but you'd rather have one over the other, wouldn't you?" Goto laughed. "So how about my gauntlets against yours? Mine are much finer, nothing for you to lose."

"I'd rather practice alone, sir."

"Come on," said the man, and a small crowd was gathering now.

Bennosuke felt his throat seizing up and thought about simply walking away—running away, his shame taunted him—but then from the crowd came Kumagai. The man was stripped to the waist and caked in dust from the day's work.

"How about I order you to duel?" he said, slurping from a mug of water. There was no malice or command in his voice, but he had that glimmer in his eyes that he had worn in the Gathering.

The man loved his sport, and orders were orders.

His hand forced, Bennosuke nodded silently. Goto took a wooden sword, and as he did Kumagai and the other samurai backed off. They became silent in complete respect for the duel, and in that quiet Bennosuke and the man bowed to each other. They readied their swords, and at the slightest of nods from Kumagai the duel began.

Bennosuke let Goto lead the fight. He had no intention of engaging him properly; if the other men saw nothing out of the ordinary, perhaps they would not bother him again and would leave him alone to his shame. There was nothing original in Goto's attacks, and Bennosuke dodged or parried them easily and then offered predictable counters to them. After he had judged a length of time had passed that would earn him neither humiliation nor praise, he braced himself to let the man strike him. Goto saw his chance and whipped his sword up ready to strike.

Bennosuke found his body snapping toward Goto's in a wickedly quick motion, and then the blunt point of his sword lanced up and connected with the base of the other man's throat. There was a hollow, meaty impact, and for a moment the man looked angry and surprised before his body realized what had happened and he dropped to one knee, wheezing.

It was a moment of shock everyone shared, not least Bennosuke himself, so quick had been the thrust. Something he had thought had perished forever within him had seized control of his body for that instant—pride. It would not let him lose, not even a meaningless thing like this, not even when he wanted to. The boy cursed himself inwardly.

"Throat—valid strike," said Kumagai, and he took another loud gulp of his water. "Looks like you're down a pair of gauntlets, Goto."

Bennosuke tried to keep his face still as the men dispersed.

Kumagai remained, looking at him for a long while. The samurai said nothing, and Bennosuke tried not to look at him, but he could not help but be aware the glimmer in the man's eyes had grown. Eventually the samurai nodded at the boy, his cheek dimpled slightly, and then he too was gone.

❄

It had carried on through the months, bravado and wounded pride and simple boredom driving people to challenge him. Piece by piece he had upgraded his armor until he had cobbled together the suit he wore today—hanging oblongs of shoulder and thigh guards, a proper helmet with a neck and face guard, much finer than those of most men of his age.

The others glowered, of course, stripped of cuirass or greaves, but they could not deny his skill. They resented and admired him. He was their champion stranger, the best among and apart from them.

There in the Sekigahara morning they nodded and he nodded, and that was all the comradeship between them; without a word Bennosuke followed them to where they were starting to congregate around Kumagai. The boy fell in toward the back, letting men sidle past and around him, for he could see well enough over their heads.

Kumagai was oblivious to them for the moment. He was perched on top of a platform, a construction of bamboo and wood that was supposed to function as a guard post, squatting as he held a burning length of match cord to a dark metal tube. A few moments later a single rocket shot upward out of it. It vanished almost instantly, swallowed into the gray void above them, and through the cloud eventually came the sad little pop of the explosion.

"Agh . . . Do you reckon anyone saw it?" Kumagai asked the man he shared the platform with. The samurai could only shrug in response, and Kumagai rubbed the back of his neck pensively. "This is going to be interesting to organize."

He rose, turning, and as he did so he seemingly became aware of the men assembling before him. The samurai grinned at them, spread his arms wide.

"Well," he said, "I trust you've heard?"

"They couldn't have come yesterday, could they?" called someone from the crowd, mirth in his voice. "This bloody fog."

"We are not in command here," said Kumagai, playing along. "We can see to the end of our spears—what more do we need to concern ourselves with?"

"Are we really advancing?" came another voice, a little more somber though far from grim. "We're fortified here—should we not let Tokugawa come to us?"

"That would be sound if we were united, but you know it as well as I—treachery looms," Kumagai said, quite freely. "I believe our most noble Lord Ukita is trying to force the issue, engage battle before any further deceit can worm its way into the hearts of lesser men."

"Which lord is false?"

"Who knows? All of them perhaps." Kumagai shrugged. "In any case, we go forward as an example to others. Even if we are surrounded the light of our courage will shine for generations. Our most noble Lord Ukita has always been a man of logic, has he not?"

The men barked an assent; Bennosuke kept his mouth shut. Something in his stomach was twisting. War, he had thought, was supposed to be as considered as a poem. The general made his commands carefully, knowing the full extent and risk involved. This was how it had been since the days of ancient China. You could not play a game of shogi if you did not know the pieces . . . or the layout of the board, or even the other players.

From behind the lot of them there came a great cry to make way; a band of cavalrymen scores deep cantered by in single file, riders bent forward so that the banners strapped to their backs did not get entangled in the branches of trees. Kumagai looked at the mass of them wistfully for a moment—there had been no time to retrieve their horses—and then his thin face twisted into a bitter grin as he screamed at their backs.

"Enjoy it!" he howled, and his eyes were glimmering as his voice broke into laughter. "Enjoy it, you lucky bags of shit!"

Bennosuke watched the samurai, this leader of men, as he capered above them all and the knot in his stomach grew further. It had been with him since he had seen the scale of things, and it had grown like a tumor as he realized how seemingly chaotic this all was and how inconsequential he was in it. It was a strange and arrogant dread, but he could not deny it.

Overcome, the boy told himself, *ignore it.* That was a human fear, and he had sworn to be a soldier, and soldiers obeyed.

In the wake of the cavalry came another messenger on foot, bereft of any armor and seeming small following the warhorses. He scrambled to a halt before Kumagai's platform. The man bowed, and then kept his hands on his knees as he snatched words between the heaving of his lungs.

"Apologies, Sir Kumagai," he gasped. "Orders . . . No time for written command, no chance for the proper signaling."

"There is nothing to apologize for—I am already all too aware of that," said Kumagai, still grinning, and he tapped the tube the rocket had launched from with his foot.

"Our most noble Lord Ukita comes himself, such is his bravery," said the messenger. "He asks that you lead your men downward and form up in squares at the foot of the slope below the forest. Await further instruction there."

"We go alone?" asked Kumagai.

"No, no," said the messenger, and he grinned in savage anticipation. "We all go. A great day beckons, does it not? Our most noble lord and his closest allies, the Akaza, the Uemura, the Shinmen, and the Nakata, side by side. Tokugawa will drown in his own dead."

Kumagai snarled an affirmative, and then the messenger hurtled off once more to find the next officer. Somewhere drums had started beating, deep blows struck on tanned cow skins splayed as wide as the spread arms of a man, counting out the time to thousands of warriors as the orders filtered through. A host shook itself into life, and the ground itself seemed to shake.

Seemed to shake. Bennosuke could not tell for certain if it was from actual footfalls, or if hearing one name had simply made him feel as though his bones were vibrating.

The Nakata were here.

CHAPTER SIXTEEN

They marched downward three abreast, each clutching a spear before him. Bennosuke was alongside Kumagai, as he had been for over a year—the boy had become the man's foremost bodyguard. Since perhaps even that first duel with Goto in the fort, Kumagai had understood Bennosuke's ability with the sword, and it was a matter of duty and expectation for the superior to be guarded by the best. A mute protector, a dog with its tongue cut out; Bennosuke played the part well.

Onward, downward, all of them trying to keep time to the drums that pounded. The incessant sound came like a distant heartbeat through the fog, but the ground was churned and slick with dew and men stumbled and slipped and rattled the straight-edged blades of their spears against one another. The boughs of the trees above formed a gray tunnel of sorts, and to battle they went like an eel burrowing into the seabed.

At one point the tunnel revealed to them a samurai hanging from the boughs of a tree like a monkey wrapped in metal and lacquer, and he howled at them as they passed, a crazed look in his eyes and a mad grin across his lips.

"U! Ki! Ta!" he shouted, gesticulating in time with his fist.

"Hwa!" spat every samurai in response.

"U! Ki! Ta!"

"Hwa!"

"U! Ki! Ta!"

"Hwa!"

Such was the noise that Bennosuke could feel his helmet vibrating on his head. It hummed into his skull and made his skin tingle, and the sound only grew and grew as more and more men took up the cry all across the slope. Dozens of tunnels, dozens of columns of men and horses grim or terrified or exultant.

One such column appeared to their side for a few moments, samurai trooping forward at an angle to that of Kumagai's men. The color was murky in the foggy gloom, but their livery and their armor were burgundy. Bennosuke's heart leapt, and his hands fumbled to put the mask of his helmet up and across his face, as though at that distance the Nakata might suddenly recognize him out of all the men here.

Beside him Kumagai turned at the boy's sudden motion, and then grinned as he saw the sliver of Bennosuke's face that was left visible between the brow of the helmet and the dull, curved iron of the faceplate.

"Ought to keep your mask off, Musashi," he said. "Air will start to stink during the battle, you should enjoy it while it's fresh."

The boy barely heard him. He watched the Nakata samurai until their pathways diverged and they were gone, obscured by tree and fog once more.

He didn't know why he was so shocked. Of course the Nakata would be here. Every lord was here. But that he would see them had not occurred to him until now. That shade of burgundy, as dulled as it was in the mist, awoke things in him. Shame, of course, was paramount, but something else was beneath that; something hard.

On they marched, and soon the trees began to thin before they vanished entirely, leaving a wide and gentle slope before them. Kumagai held his hand up, and his men followed him, fanning outward to march ten abreast. They happened across a line of archers without a shielding unit in front of them, and so they halted there and stood waiting in a loose square, their spears bristling.

It took time for the thousands of others to emerge from the forest and to find their places, but slowly they did and silence began to fall. The air was still, the banners held in hands or born upon backs motionless. Bennosuke realized that the mist was thinning, or perhaps the light was waxing stronger with the rising of the hidden sun, and that gradually the distance he could see was growing.

Ranks and ranks of warriors behind him, faces as gray as the fog, but he was not interested in them. A conch blew high and undulat-

ing, and then what he sought revealed itself: out of the forest came
the lords.

There was a gaggle of them and their bodyguards, all on horseback. They were beautiful in a way, befitting of sunlight proper
and not the dank vista that awaited them. The armor they wore
were things of master craftsmanship that had been marveled at by
unknown thousands, adorned and covered by overjackets and capes
of finest silk that held patterns within patterns. Above them jostled
the right angles of banners bearing clan insignia and prayers written a
thousand years ago, these prominent above the crests of their helmets
that were shaped like crescent moons or the antlers of stags or hung
with brilliant white horsehair.

Ukita was at the head, resplendent in a saddle like a throne, with
five banners proclaiming his lineage arrayed behind him like a peacock's tail. The others formed themselves around him—Lord Akaza,
whose livery was black; Lord Uemura, whose livery might have been
a dark green but was obscured in the low light; Lord Shinmen, who
wore that familiar shade of blue; and there, at the edges, the Nakata.

Bennosuke could see nothing else, and some part of him that had
long lain dormant was suddenly rapt and trying to see if Hayato rode
among them. But the mass of lords were armored, distant, obscured
by fog and bodyguards, and there was no way to tell where one burgundy man began and another ended, let alone if one lacked an arm.
The boy peered on as Ukita in turn scanned his forces, and then sent
a handful of his adjutants to ride up and down the lines to ensure
things were in order, the formation suitable.

The riders returned shortly, shouting readiness. With a flourish
Ukita produced a large war fan made of iron plates nailed to bamboo spokes that, when unfurled, became as large as his torso. Of
course it too was a beautiful thing, painted intricately with a flight
of cranes dashing between the beams of a rising sun. It was an orna-
ment that commanded thousands, a lovely and tyrannical fetish, and
slowly Ukita raised it above his head and then brought his arm down
to point with it toward where the enemy must lie.

"Well, boys," said Kumagai, "here we go. I trust you all."

He gave them a last grin, and then snapped the faceplate of his
helmet into place, that snarling demon's visage that dripped with

auburn mustaches. His spear in one hand, he drew his longsword with the other and leveled it at the unknown fog ahead.

"U! Ki! Ta!" howled a distant, familiar voice.

"Hwa!" barked thousands for a final time, and then the armies of the West sallied forth.

They went at somewhere between a march and a jogging pace, eager for combat but hesitating because they could not see what exactly was waiting to fight them. Bennosuke scanned the mists, wondering if the minutest darker shade of gray was the first sight of Tokugawa's men or the simple curling of vapor.

The farther they went, the more he felt the knot in his stomach was ready to burst. This great thing that had swallowed him had no head, no mind, no thought. Ukita waved his fan up and down, up and down as he ushered his army onward, as content as a child swatting at a fly. But then, he had bodyguards waiting to throw themselves over him should the slightest danger come his way, didn't he?

Why had he stayed with Kumagai? Bennosuke asked himself. Why had he not left a week after the Gathering, gone home to Miyamoto and Dorinbo? His uncle would have forgiven him any shame. But he knew that Munisai's armor would have still been there, ever ready to taunt him.

Why was he asking these questions now, and not once over the last two years?

Bennosuke knew why, deep down. It was riding behind him at a measured, comfortable pace, and he was torn between looking ahead and looking back. Within that mass of lords and bodyguards and banner and horseflesh, that myriad of colors and pomp, the Nakata burgundy was still there.

"Archers!" came the sudden cry, a frantic flurry of arrows being notched as the line stumbled to a halt.

The Tokugawa were there before them, rows of men dark gray on silver mist, so many that the rear of them could not be seen. They stood waiting silently. Ukita's archers drew their bowstrings back, the arquebusiers sighting their guns, but no order to fire was given.

Before the Tokugawa stood one man, awaiting. A champion.

Of course there would be one. If this was to be a battle for the country, it needed to be blooded in the proper ways. To shoot him or to loose a volley at Tokugawa's army while he stood there would be to admit cowardice. Slowly, unbidden, bows were relaxed, the barrels of arquebuses lowered.

The lone samurai between the armies calmly drew his sword and bowed to them. He was a big man, his armor both magnifying his size and making his bare head seem small in the wide expanse of his shoulder guards. His voice was confident, a deep tone that carried easily across the mist.

"My name is Seibei Matsumoto," he called. "I am of the Yoshioka school. Send me your best."

His challenge was issued, and so the battle could not start until the clash of champions was over. This was etiquette, as proper as seppuku, and so Ukita's army was honor-bound to respond. Even Bennosuke had heard of the Yoshioka school, a renowned sect from Kyoto, and so when Seibei offered his challenge there was a few seconds' pause as men gauged their chances.

A samurai eventually marched forth. Bennosuke could not see the man's face, and when he made his introduction to Seibei he spoke so quietly his name was lost. His attack was fierce, quick slashes that had no doubt claimed enough lives over the years, but Seibei merely stepped around them, never raising his sword from his side, not even to try to parry. He waited for an opening, and when it came his sword lanced out and took Ukita's man's throat in one quick motion.

Seibei bowed to his corpse, bowed to his men as they cheered his name once, and then he gestured to Ukita's army.

"Again," he said.

A man carrying a spear walked forward. He bowed to Seibei, and asked whether he would accept a duel against the weapon. The Yoshioka samurai nodded curtly, bowed back, and then the fight began. The spearman came so close to winning; Bennosuke was certain he had impaled Seibei at one point. A feint and a lunge brought the spear down into Seibei's groin, but the Yoshioka man must have had fine armor, for he merely pushed the blade downward, stepped over it, and then the fight was his.

Once more Seibei bowed, once more his men called his name, and once more he spoke to Ukita's men.

"Again," he said.

There was a protracted pause this time. Seibei was good. Benno-suke had found himself peering over his shoulder in the interim. The lords had pushed forward to get a better view of the duels, and he in turn now had a better chance to look for Hayato. It was still too hard to identify anyone.

"Musashi," said someone close by. "You can take him."

"What?" he said.

"Aye," said someone else. "Aye, you can. Go on."

It took a moment for him to realize they were talking about Sei-bei. Before he could protest, every man near him was speaking. The words they said were those of encouragement, but in the tone of them he could tell that he was being offered up as a sacrifice. He turned to Kumagai, expecting him not to cast his bodyguard aside, but behind that red demon's mask his eyes were glinting his special shade of amusement.

"Do it, Musashi," he said. "Take that Yoshioka bastard to pieces."

Winter in the fort. Bennosuke had been on watch, up in the wooden tower with his breath frosting in the air. The night was still and clear, the stars above the color of ice. Beneath him, away from him as they always were, the other men were clustered around a firepit. The boredom and isolation had truly set in; what had started as a game of Go had degenerated into one man betting the others he could spit the stones into a cup from ten paces.

His first attempt was too short, his second attempt much too long. The white chip caught an edge and rolled in a long curve to fall into the pit. It nestled among the coals at the bottom.

"Well, get it out, then," said Kumagai, smiling. He was squatting on his haunches on the edge of the fire's light, his face orange.

"It's just a stone," said the man who had spat. "I'll get it in the morning."

"It's clamshell that, it'll char," said Kumagai. "Get it out now."

The man knew he could not argue with his captain, and so he went and got a poker and tried to press the stone up against the wall and drag it upward and out. He did it at arm's length, the air shimmering with heat. Five times he tried, and five times the little white disk fell back.

"Looks like you'll have to use your hand," said Kumagai.

"What?" said the man.

"Use your hand," said Kumagai. He was very still, and the fire lit up the spark in his eyes.

"It's too hot, sir," said the man after a moment.

"That doesn't matter," said Kumagai. "Don't you understand that you have no choice in this? The world was written long ago, our names chosen, the color of our eyes. You were always meant to spit that stone. You were always meant to put your hand in after it."

"But . . ." said the man.

"What are you afraid of? Whatever will happen to you has already happened—how can you be afraid of that?" said Kumagai. "Don't you understand that your mother bore you burned? Don't you understand that your mother bore you *dead*?"

Kumagai stared at the man. The fire crackled. Frost wrote itself in spider's thread upon the blade of Bennosuke's spear. Kumagai and the samurai were of an age, but in that moment it did not seem it.

The man's throat tightened, and as quick as he could he thrust his hand down and grabbed for the stone. A shower of sparks and embers came with his hand as he flicked the white disk up and out, and then he swore and clutched his hand. But it turned to laughter because Kumagai was laughing, and he took the man's wrist.

"See! See!" he said, and showed the man his own hand. The flesh wasn't even blistered. "Enlightenment!"

They were all laughing then, save for Bennosuke in his dark tower. The men kept laughing, the spitter showing them his hand, and they did not stop as Kumagai walked away from them, spread his arms wide, rolled his head back, and gave a wordless snarl of a yell.

"My word, I'm bored," he said to no one in particular, and tottered off aimlessly into the night, clutching at the back of his neck.

Upon the paving slabs, the white stone cooled.

❄

The boy looked into Kumagai's eyes now, and he knew he would not be allowed to refuse. There was a crushing sense of isolation for a moment, surrounded though he was. Kumagai took his spear from him, still grinning behind his mask, and then the other samurai parted and cleared a way to the front for him. They looked at him expectantly.

Bennosuke saw Seibei too move to stand and wait at the mouth of the tunnel. He cut an imposing figure, perfectly still with his sword bloody, an oily, red sheen across the blade. A man, a proud warrior, a samurai—all the things Bennosuke knew that he was not. The knot was there, obscene and peristaltic and wrapping itself around his spine to the base of his skull. He knew he deserved oblivion, and so now that it was before him he should have been grateful to fate for arranging what he lacked the strength to do himself.

But he wasn't. He looked back once at the Nakata and the cluster of lords. Every eye there was upon him. There was no escape, nothing he could say or do. The tunnel waited, and so Bennosuke fought the urge to quiver and stepped forward into it.

CHAPTER SEVENTEEN

Seibei's composure was immaculate, his face like stone as Bennosuke approached him there in that little private chasm between two hordes. The boy was wringing the scabbard of his sword without realizing it, and Seibei's blade was so very still. The Yoshioka samurai bowed respectfully to Bennosuke, and the boy returned it.

"What is your name?" Seibei asked.

Bennosuke said nothing. His heart was pumping so fast with nerves he was worried his voice would crack. The boy kept his silence, drew his sword, and felt thousands of pairs of eyes upon him.

"What is your name?" Seibei asked again, and this time something broke across his face. It was impossible to tell what it was, whether it was pain, or anger, or confusion. His eyes bored into Bennosuke, beseeching, but Seibei saw only the cold metal visage of the facemask. No answer was coming, the Yoshioka samurai realized, and so with resignation he dropped into a fighting stance and moved forward.

Bennosuke began breathing slowly, the long exhalations seething and rattling around his helmet, trying to calm himself. He warily kept his distance, making no move to swing at Seibei. The other two samurai—*dead around your feet, stay clear of their corpses, do not trip on them*—had gone straight for him, and Seibei had thrived on it. He wanted to be attacked, to counter rather than lead. The boy would not give him such an opportunity again.

Moments passed as they weighed each other up, and soon Seibei realized Bennosuke's intention. Grudgingly, he changed his stance, raising his sword to a position to strike rather than to hover defensively by his side.

It became a test of nerves then. They inched slowly toward each other on agile feet shaking with anticipation, prepared to dodge or strike in any direction. Bennosuke heard his breath growing faster in his ears, but gradually he realized he could feel neither the surging of his lungs nor the pumping of his heart.

The more he focused on Seibei's sword, the more a serene detachment came over him. Closer still he drew, entranced by the blade, the blood upon it, the detail of the hilt's guard shaped like a dragon chasing its tail, the moment now was all there was and he was alive in that moment, and so death

could
never
find
him
in
this
void

and then Seibei snapped. The Yoshioka samurai lunged forward, swinging his sword down. Bennosuke ghosted to one side, the blade glancing off the armor on his chest, and before the man could raise his sword again Bennosuke grabbed his wrist and barreled into him with a speed free of the burden of thought. His weight and his strength separated man from sword, and Seibei staggered backward.

There was a heartbeat then, when Bennosuke found himself remembering Munisai's words of the honesty before death. Seibei looked Bennosuke in the eye with a proud dignity, no fear or anger there. Just an instant, though, so quickly gone—Bennosuke brought his longsword up, hands trained for years wielding a weapon refined over centuries, and in one great sweep took his head off.

He was surprised by what a small, sad, easy thing it was to do. Seibei was alive and proud one instant, and then he was two separate things of meat and bone and hair. The man's head bounced free, and his body crumpled onto the earth. In the silence that followed Bennosuke turned to Tokugawa's army.

"That's it?" he said in genuine surprise. "That's the Yoshioka school?"

As the sensation flowed back into his body, he looked suspiciously down at Seibei's remains. He felt almost guilty how easy it had been to beat the man. He had his answer quickly: blood was seeping out from under Seibei's waist, dark and arterial. The second challenger's spear thrust. The Yoshioka champion had been too proud to admit the wound, had chosen to face Bennosuke faint and lamed, and now he was dead.

He wanted to feel regret, but the cheers of Ukita's men reached him then. It warmed him, kindled something within him: the visceral thrill of victory. It surprised him, the magnitude of it, even though he had known this base pride in his swordsmanship had always been humming insidiously away beneath his higher sensibilities.

Sympathy vanished for Seibei, twisting into contempt for the man's idiocy. Behind his faceplate a skeletal grin broke across his face, his eyes glimmering far worse than Kumagai's ever had. He looked back across the army as they worshipped him. He was free of their burden now, the knot within him vanished. He was not some faceless part of it; they were they and he was he, an inferior whole and superior individual.

Bennosuke knew right then that he was worthy of everything, every adulation and glory that fate could bestow upon him. His eyes saw the burgundy banners, and he knew that whatever spirit that loved him had planned things out for him.

IN THE YEARS that would follow, he would think back to what he did next and his stomach would turn with regret, embarrassment, and fear. It was so stupid, and even as he moved to stand before Ukita's army he could hear the rational part of his mind screaming at him to stop. But his body was in the throes of triumph, and he knew with absolute certainty that at that moment he was invincible.

"Lord Ukita!" he bellowed, holding his sword above his head. The samurai thought Bennosuke's cry was merely honoring their lord, and so they howled along with him, repeating Ukita's name over and over.

"Lord Ukita! I have something to ask of you!" Bennosuke shouted over them to where the lord sat upon his horse.

Despite the din Ukita heard. He gave an order for silence, and then he whispered something to an adjutant. It was this man who called to Bennosuke; obscene for a lord to raise his voice.

"Who are you to make demands of your most noble lord?" the man called.

"My name is Musashi Miyamoto," he said. "But perhaps I am better known as Bennosuke Shinmen, the son of Munisai Shinmen."

With one hand he undid the helmet and tossed it to the floor, exposing his face to the nobles. Would they recognize him at this distance? They certainly tried to; there was a commotion beside Ukita, a frantic rearrangement of his bodyguards and attendants as two people pushed to the front. It was the old Lord Nakata and Lord Shinmen. Shinmen peered at him, struck dumb, while Nakata was frantically conversing with his retinue, his head whipping back and forth.

Slowly Bennosuke lowered his sword to point at him, and he froze in the saddle.

"This blade, Lord Ukita, is death to the Nakata," Bennosuke shouted. "Give me them now, Lord, or I join Tokugawa's army!"

Ukita did not offer instant dismissal. That alone was shocking. There were a few heavy, hanging moments when Bennosuke believed that he might have actually been considering it—certain, even at a distance, that he could see the lord's fingers drumming on his saddle's pommel—but whatever might have been was snatched away by the Eastern army.

Bennosuke had broken the cycle. Instead of facing another challenger from Tokugawa's men, he had turned his back on them. No one knew if this was an insult or not, because it had never been done before. But regardless, after they slowly realized they were largely being left out of matters of honor the thought of it had rankled, and that was the end of the diplomacy and etiquette of polite personal murder.

Behind him Bennosuke heard the yell as the Tokugawa spearmen began their charge, their feet thundering. He turned like an idiot, staring for a moment as hundreds of spearpoints leveled themselves at him. They were eighty paces away, seventy, and the vast wall of them stretched as far as the boy could see in either direction.

From behind them there was a sudden flickering that vanished upward into the mist. Moments later screams among the Ukita made Bennosuke turn once more. The arrows loosed by the Tokugawa were dropping out of the sky, expertly and sightlessly aimed to fall among the huddled formations, hidden until the very instant before they claimed their oblivious victims.

He gawped stupidly, still caught in the hollow aftermath that followed the adrenaline of his victory. The front ranks of Ukita's men raising arquebuses at the charging Eastern army and an officer raising his hand were almost meaningless to him, but something primal took charge of Bennosuke. It hurled his body to the ground just before the man slashed his hand down and barked the command to fire and the world exploded.

The bullets scythed through the first ranks of the Eastern spearmen. Men screamed and fell and a broad wave of them stumbled for a few moments, but those behind leapt over the fallen and still they came. The stink of the billowing gunsmoke was foul and acrid, making Bennosuke's eyes water as he rose to his knees, and when he looked next the arquebusiers were gone and Ukita's spearmen were charging forward to meet like with like.

There was nothing he could do but be absorbed into their number; they had kept their spears high to allow the arquebusiers to melt away through their ranks, and now he could either be trampled or scramble to his feet to be taken up among them. He did, and he was caught, and they thrust him forward as around him they lowered their weapons and the world became a thing of points and momentum.

Without a polearm, Bennosuke was a terrified passenger, pushed as much as he ran. He saw the coming spears of the Tokugawa and prayed for a gap among them, saw the frenzy written across the faces of the enemy ten paces away. In the next instant speartips were glancing off one another, pushed either skyward or into the ground to be snapped into nothing, and then the boy found himself twisting and sucking in his stomach as though that would somehow make his armor thinner in anticipation of what came next, for that was the impact.

It sounded like a great grunted wheeze, that moment before the screaming; hundreds of men slamming to a halt and finding themselves either impaled or trapped in a crush of blade and shaft and flesh. Bennosuke flinched as he felt a spear thrust rake itself across his stomach, but his armor held and the metal blade slid and stabbed past him, and then someone too close to him was gurgling and hot, wet liquid splattered upon the back of his neck.

There came a brief and uncontrollable flash of joy that he was not skewered, but it was all too easily dashed as he realized his situation; he was pinioned between wooden shafts, twisted like a dancer in the throes of some complex and angular pirouette, his feet barely on the ground and his cheek grinding up against the bowl of another man's helmet. Trapped, off balance, so close to death.

But he was not alone in this, and what awaited them all was the long, slow grapple. The fight stagnated into sporadic outbreaks of violence, whenever the space to draw a spear back and thrust it forward again could be found.

It was a test of endurance; either one side could break and cede a hole through their lines to the lords and missile troops behind, or they would hold on until their army could produce a maneuver that would turn the battle—flanking with cavalry, or a daring charge at a weakened point, or some improvised stroke of genius that would be remembered for centuries.

What did strategy or centuries mean to those men there, though? Nothing. There was only snarling and spitting and the taste of metal and the sound of curses growled from the very depths of lungs and the feel of the cartilage of noses crushed back and forth until they threatened to disconnect from the skull or rescind up into the brain.

The sword he still clutched in one hand was useless, much too short, and his arm pinned away from his body so that he could only feebly wave it with the power of his wrist alone. With his free hand Bennosuke did what he could and desperately grabbed at the Tokugawa spears closest to him. He tried to haul them away one-handed, wary of the blades splitting his palms open, but he may as well have tried to pull the moon down. The best he could do was cling tenaciously to them and glare hatred at the black eyes of the men opposite him.

A part of him remembered Munisai's words—about fighting for five minutes after fighting for five minutes. He was so surprised how quickly exhaustion crept through him. He had thought Munisai had meant swinging a sword, but here merely trying to keep his balance and pull or thrust with muscles he seldom used was making him dizzy with the effort.

How long they were there was impossible to gauge, but eventually something changed, some group of men finding inspiration and strength from somewhere. There was a huge push, the crowd twisted, and when it stopped the boy was crushed between men with both of his feet completely off the ground. He gasped for air, entirely helpless now.

Before the panic of suffocation could take him, something crashed down from the sky to strike him on the top of his bare head. He did not know what it was but it was hard and blunt and it knocked the senses from him, his vision turning white for a few moments, while some protected and fading rational part of him wondered if his skull was cracked.

Blood streamed freely down his face, his bared scalp lacerated. As if from far away he heard the incomprehensible sound of his own moaning. It vanished entirely as within his chest he became painfully aware of his heart beating, and to him the thump of it seemed to slow from frantic convulsions, calming, settling into a steady, faithful pulse that was overwhelming, lulling him down into nothingness.

THE SKY was there.

Bennosuke realized he had been looking at it for a long time before he recognized it for what it was once more. The morning fog had cleared; gray clouds were distant above him. He was on his back, earth cold and wet on the back of his skull. It hurt to look, he noticed, hurt to hear. At the back of his throat he tasted bile.

He sat up. One of his arms was beneath his body, and slowly, painfully he uncurled himself from the contortion into which he had fallen. If he had been capable of it he would have felt surprise to find his sword there still in his grip, the fingers wrapped tight around the hilt like prehistoric vines fossilized over rock.

Both his hands were sticky with blood, the flesh that emerged from beneath his gauntlets red. He remembered pain. Gingerly he reached up to his skull half expecting his fingers to feel whatever brains felt like, but he found only a long, painful gash. The boy probed it masochistically for a few moments until he convinced himself that the bone at least did not feel fractured.

He rose unsteadily to his feet, hauling himself up by his sword with its point in the ground. His hair had come loose and was matted with blood and dirt, half of his face caked in it. Over his right eye a filthy crust had formed, and he felt this crackling and breaking like a scab as he forced the lids open fully once more.

Bennosuke looked around; there were corpses at his feet. Men and beasts, hundreds of them twisted around him. Near to him sat the great bulk of a horse. Red, ragged bullet wounds passed through it, and its stomach had burst so that its guts had spilled upon the earth. But it was still mostly whole—and suddenly inviting to him. He was exhausted, the world was pulsing and untrustworthy and his armor as heavy as a glacier, and though he had been on his feet only moments now he felt the need to sit once more.

Like an old man he lowered himself onto the flank of the beast. As he put his weight on it, the horse's rib cage cracked and popped morbidly. So run through had it been by bullets that it simply gave up any pretense of structure and caved inward. Bennosuke sank into it, and he felt the rush of what was left inside the beast forced outward around his feet, the viscera still warm.

A carrion throne to look out across the battlefield from.

Battle. Soldier. Sekigahara. Only then did the reason for his presence here resurface in his mind, the logic linking sluggishly. Somehow the press of spearmen must have discarded him from their mass, expelling his motionless and filthy form like some queen hornet disgorging a stillborn larva before the fight moved on, driving and grinding the front line away.

That front line now was only a few dozen paces from where he sat, the interlocking spears and lances forming the skeleton of some demonic pagoda rooftop, and yet it seemed so impassably far to his torpid mind. Behind it he saw the full scope of the battle in the same manner, splayed across his vision like a great panoramic painting, all of it distant and unable to harm him.

He saw the banners of all the lords of Japan, the Western on the slopes and the Eastern in the basin, crashing midway like two waves;

the only way to tell who was on either side in that press of men was the direction of their standards. Arrows loosed, muskets fired, chevrons of horsemen wheeled and charged.

The idea of tactics and lordly strategy seemed as fanciful from here as it had been in the press of spears. But what Bennosuke could see now was the individual, the minor fates of the other thousands here, and he saw such little, pathetic things.

He saw two men circling each other, weary beyond endurance, the pair of them filthy and glistening with sweat, swinging wild, exhausted swipes and missing, staggering, one with a shattered sword and one grasping an arquebus by its barrel.

He saw the inverted eyes of a man on the ground, his mouth a black and red crescent moon as he mumbled a smiling farewell, seeing something or someone within his mind, remembering anything but this, head lolling in his helmet.

He saw a man sprawled with his armor spread open and his guts too, and a dog as black as coal was pulling on his intestines and backing away, and the man was mewling and pulling them back, and the dog's tail was wagging, the animal's eyes delighted at getting to play such a fun game.

Somebody grabbed the collar of his armor from behind, breaking his gaze. Bennosuke flapped numbly at it, his feet scrabbling in the horse guts like a newborn.

"Musashi! Up!" the voice was snarling. "Get up!"

It was Kumagai trying to haul him to his feet. The man's armor was dirtied, spear abandoned somewhere, and he was frantic with anger. The battlefield seemed to close in on Bennosuke, becoming not some remote theater but a near and tangible thing. There were other men standing there, wounded or dazed by terror or for whatever reason not fighting in the fierce melee of the spearmen. Kumagai was screaming to them, trying to rally them.

"Do you see? Kobayakawa is the traitor! Look!" he snarled and pointed to the slope along their right flank, one hand still wrenching Bennosuke by his scruff.

Like a bridge collapsing from one end, the formations and ranks of Kobayakawa's men were indeed turning around upon their former allies. That was the entirety of their flank, gone—the sheer number of them, a third of all the Eastern forces, still pristine and fresh and now the enemy. Tokugawa's men were letting them through their lines, falling in to march shoulder to shoulder with the Kobayakawa like old and trusted allies, and the united lot of them, unbloodied, unexhausted, were heading toward the frenzy in which Ukita and the other loyal lords had been embroiled for hours now.

"All of you, to me! Those dogs must pay!" spat Kumagai.

"What?" breathed one man, bent over double with blood streaming down his brow. "But . . . look at them!"

"On your feet, Musashi!" said Kumagai, but the boy remained anchored in and among the horse. Kumagai turned to address all the men around him. "We charge them! We must protect the flanks!"

"But—"

"Are you samurai?" said Kumagai, his voice low and cutting.

"That's—" began the man.

"Are you samurai?" said Kumagai again.

"Yes," said the man.

"Then why do you hesitate?" said Kumagai, and the man said nothing. He shook his head once, and then pulled himself up straight. Resigned determination came across his face. He knew what Kumagai said was the truth. Those around him, a ragged two score of men, knew so too.

"What about you, Musashi?" said Kumagai, looking down at the only one not yet committed. "Are you samurai?"

The boy said nothing.

"Are you samurai, Musashi?" said Kumagai, and he knocked him on the back of his head.

The boy did not move.

"Are you samurai?" snarled Kumagai now, and he bent low to speak face-to-face. "Or are you just going to sit here? You coward. What are you? You coward. You coward, *you fucking coward*!"

The boy met his eyes, and the emptiness in them infuriated Kumagai. He rose in one fierce movement, kicking Bennosuke in the chest as he did so, and then he drew his sword. "You fucking coward, Musashi! I always knew you were queer! You stay here, then! All true samurai, to me!"

He leveled his sword at Kobayakawa's men, and screamed until it became a bitter, choking hiss. Bennosuke watched as Kumagai ran in a stumbling charge, hopping over corpses and slipping in loose mud, and the other men went with him, a shabby sporadic line of men waving swords in desperate and ultimate bravado.

Kobayakawa's immaculate ranks raised their muskets and fired. The bullets that came from their guns were as big as eyeballs, and they punched Kumagai and his men to pieces in an instant. There was no agony, just eradication. The samurai fell. Only one tried to rise, muscle instinct alone pushing him forward a finger's length farther, and then he collapsed and was still.

No immortal souls fluttered upward.

An image came to Bennosuke. He saw the Buddhist mandala that hung upon Dorinbo's wall lit up in the morning sun. Enlightened white figures crawling up Mount Fuji, the condemning demons and devils under the world toying with the fates of men, and between them always that stratum of trapped, twisted corpses.

He saw those corpses now, on the slopes of the Sekigahara valley. But there was no devil here, no path heavenward either. There was just musket smoke and pageantry drifting above a carpet of those damned to nothingness.

Finally he understood.

He thought of Munisai, of the color of his blood soaking into white silk and the long, rattling moan that escaped him as his agony came to naught, and he understood.

He thought of Shuntaro, writhing, forever writhing in that bubbling oil with the men he thought he had saved dancing their ghastly terminal dance alongside him, and he understood.

He thought of Dorinbo, remembered his last words spoken before the burning pyre, and now, finally—*finally*—after years he understood.

Bennosuke picked himself out of the ruins of the horse. The battle still raged but he could not hear it. He had risen a child of Amaterasu and finally he made the choice to raise himself to where he wanted to be.

CHAPTER EIGHTEEN

When it ends it ends like a butterfly breaking out from a chrysalis, pushing outward from a vital point upon a central seam and the crack grows from there, and then there are two things—the magnificent color of new wings starting to beat, and a scabbed and decrepit husk cast aside and falling downward.

These are otherwise known as victory and defeat.

MARSHAL FUSHIMI STALKED behind the lines of spearmen, howling encouragement and slashing his sword through the air. They would not falter. They were samurai. They would hold. On and on he shouted, his voice growing hoarse.

What he bellowed would be unspoken fact at any other time, but the marshal knew deep inside that large-scale battles such as this removed from the world the laws of rationality and reason. When you got enough men together, fired enough arrows, and charged enough horses, it was as though any barrier of individuality ceased to exist and suddenly raw and thoughtless emotion could course through the whole of them as easily as blood through snow.

This had benefits occasionally, as when a rare band of honest men found sudden courage beyond what they knew they had, but what Fushimi knew as fact, why he had pursued zealous justice his entire life—why he *marshaled*—was that this world was inherently rotten. There were two villains for every decent man, five cowards for every hero, and so that meant that when enough men were together, such as now, there was a great looming contagion waiting to spread.

This was why Fushimi hated battle, and this was why he knew that he had to play the preemptive healer now; his was the task to remove the disease before it could claim anyone. With the flat of his sword he struck helmets he saw turning, he put a strong hand on the shoulders of men from behind regardless of which corner of the earth they had come from, and tried to speak as a father or brother would.

It had worked; the men of Ukita and the lords sworn to him had held like a cliff of stone, absorbed the fury of the Tokugawa charge stoically, and then they began to show the Easterners the quality of Bizen steel. Numbers had told, their skill had told, and they had begun the slow process of driving the thousands of the enemy back with spear and sword.

But that was half an hour ago; now Fushimi saw the treacherous horde of fresh Kobayakawa spearmen as they came, working their way methodically between and then replacing the tired Tokugawa troops. Ten ranks behind the main clash of spears, he turned to look for commands or reinforcements of their own, but neither the Lord Ukita nor any of his generals were anywhere to be seen.

None of the lords were. They had gone. Departed.

Fled?

The marshal could hear the ferociousness of the unwearied voices of the Kobayakawa as they began to engage, stabbing and slashing, and he felt a shudder of fear pass through even himself. He forced iron into his heart, clutched his sword tighter, and screamed until he thought his throat was tearing itself out.

His eyes caught sight of a spear falling, abandoned, and then someone worming away from the fight. He dashed across like a man seeing the ice crack beneath his feet, pointing at the samurai.

"You!" he barked with as much authority as he could. "Halt!"

The man showed no intention of doing so, and so the marshal stood in his path and put his hand on the man's chest. The other samurai did not meet Fushimi's eyes, and the marshal saw that the other's body was shaking with short little breaths. He tried to wriggle past, but Fushimi grasped his breastplate.

"We do not retreat," he said slowly and calmly over the din of the fighting. "Stand as one and we will not fall."

"Let me go," the man whimpered. "Please."

"You will go nowhere until ordered," said Fushimi.

"By who?" said the man. "Who's going to order us? They've gone! They've gone and they've left us!"

"Our lords are still here!" said Fushimi, but of this he had no proof.

"You lie! Let me go!" said the man, and he tried to squirm past once more.

"By my orders, then," growled Fushimi, and he moved his hand up to grab the man by the throat, trying to shock some wits back into him. "You will not—"

There was a sharp pain under his armpit, and then the man was pushing him back. Fushimi suddenly found he had no strength to resist, and then the man was withdrawing a bloody dagger from where he had stabbed the marshal beneath the armor of his outstretched arm.

"I'm sorry, I'm sorry, I'm sorry, it's not my fault," Fushimi heard him stammer, but he kept on going and did look back once as the marshal fell to the ground, no strength even to cry out.

Fushimi sat in the dirt with his legs splayed out before him, looking at the blood on his hands like a drunk counting out the last of his coins. The marshal felt a great and final hatred of the weakness of the world, and a bitter grin carved itself upon his face as around him the fading battle went on . . .

THE GREAT LORD Ukita had lost track of himself.

Oh, he knew exactly where he was, sitting at the edge of the forest stripped of all but the lightest armor on an unburdened and unremarkable horse, watching the battle unfold beneath him. He had no idea, however, where the man everyone else mistakenly presumed to be him had gotten to—the thrust and pull of combat had stolen his decoy from his sight.

When the Tokugawa spearmen had charged following the clash of champions, he and his retinue had slowly and calmly withdrawn to the rear of the fighting. There, among a carefully concealed huddle, the lord had dismounted and given one of his bodyguards his distinctive crested helmet and let the man take his horse. As the decoy had ridden off on the steed adorned so brazenly with the clan's banners and livery, Ukita had gotten onto this plain mare and then covertly fallen back to where he was now. His fifty finest cavalrymen waited with him, their horses pawing the earth between the trunks of the great trees.

This was not cowardice. Deception was a valid strategy, a logical one.

The proof of this was looming over the right flank of the battlefield—the coming of the Kobayakawa host proper. The first, most eager troops had reached the battle, yes, but behind them the rest were converging and advancing like the wall of a temple slowly crashing down. They were wheeling and arranging themselves, taking the time to best plot their attack, swords and cannons and horses maneuvering around one another.

Ukita took this in impassively, and then turned his eye to the mass of his spearmen and archers and arquebusiers below. He saw men starting to peel away and toss down their weapons. How quickly it unraveled—at first it seemed only a handful, and then it was a dozen, and then threescore, and then almost instantly the great lord saw entire formations of his men begin to scatter like leaves blown in wind.

Some loyal men stayed to try to hold the enemy back, and other bands stationed behind the line of battle charged downward attempting to fill the gaps that were being left, killing those of their own side fleeing if they could reach them, but these were rare outcrops of flowers among weeds. To look at the broad scope of it was to see a rout beginning.

Ukita knew what needed to be done. Seventeen thousand men he had brought to the fight, and now these men had the honor of becoming seventeen thousand martyrs to his cause. To some that number of men was a dream, an empire—to him it was a third. More fool the other lords if they had gambled everything here.

The great lord gave the signal, and then he and his horsemen turned and vanished into the forest, silent and unnoticed. Behind them the Tokugawa and the Kobayakawa pushed onward, rolling the flank inward, enveloping, devouring . . .

❋

Kazuteru wheeled in the saddle, sword in his hand and his horse skipping beneath him, trying to keep himself calm. Things had warped out of control, and it was hard to be a shield to his lord when the front of the battle was no longer clear. He had no idea what was happening—no one seemingly did—and all the while the young samurai had a dread sense of something closing around them.

"Hold here! Keep the banner high! Rally to us! Rally to us!" someone was shouting.

"We must leave! The lord must be saved!" yelled another body-guard, and all were screaming and all their eyes were wide.

Where was the Lord Ukita, where were his generals, where were the Nakata, the Uemura, or the Akaza? Their noble assembly had fractured like a shattered gem with the twisting of the battle, and any hope of reorganizing some semblance of an army out of this chaos had gone with them. It had all collapsed, they were gone, and he could see other men were fleeing now too, and what could they do? What could they do?

Kazuteru turned to Lord Shinmen. He alone was still, holding the reins of his horse tight, taking in what was erupting around him stoically. Did he have a plan, or was he just stupefied by the way the day had turned? The lord sensed Kazuteru looking at him, and their eyes met. They were lit with a grim and strange calmness.

What it reminded Kazuteru of was Munisai's expression as he had held before him the dagger he would thrust up into his belly.

It was a poor image to have in his head, a miserable memento of this harsh world. Kazuteru wanted to remember the kind smile of his mother, or the dignity of his long-dead father practicing the sword, or the hands of Fusako so soft and small and wonderful in his as they walked secretly beneath the Uji forests. But they were impossible to conjure. They did not belong here.

There came a swelling noise from behind them. They all turned to see an arrowhead of horsemen, fresh and unbloodied from battle, charging toward them. They wore the colors of the Kobayakawa, and the traitors came to claim the glorious prize of the head of a lord.

Kazuteru could see the faces of the leading men atop their mounts, the joy and the anger and the stillness in them. The foremost horseman seemed to hang in time. There was a savage glee in him;

bearded and scarred and carrying a huge two-handed sword that he had to stand in the saddle to wield, raising it above his head with deft and petrifying skill.

The man's horse never slowed from its gallop, his eyes never left Kazuteru, and all the young samurai could see, all he could think of was the elegant curve of that great, gleaming sword as it drew closer and closer to him . . .

ennosuke did not know that others were fleeing until he saw men overtaking him on the slope heading back to the forest pathways. They were panicking, sprinting wide-eyed, some even wailing in terror as they passed the boy who ran steady and silent; theirs was the animal decision to survive, whereas he did not run out of fear.

He felt that he was thinking clearer than he had in years, the air purer in his lungs. His had been a firm, rational choice to be here no longer, and he would have simply vanished if he could. But he was mortal—oh, how he knew that now, he wanted to laugh—and what awaited him now was the long slog back up the slopes and out of the valley.

As he ran he glanced over his shoulder. Things were disintegrating, the army dispersing second by second. Horns were being blown, futile commands given to groups of men who no longer heeded them. A captain was spitting at Bennosuke as he ran past, calling him a coward in much the same tone as Kumagai had. The man did not see his own standard-bearer behind him toss his banner to the ground and also start to run.

Into the forest once more, the trees enclosing him and funneling up the sound from below. The ground was churned horribly, and his run became a scrambling hop, passing men who had stumbled and twisted their legs and who were pleading from the ground for someone to carry them.

These men Bennosuke ignored, but eyes in the trees stopped him for a moment. He became aware of a gaggle of boys, perhaps two dozen of them peering furtively out from between the trunks.

The eldest could have been no more than ten, the youngest half that, and they must have been brought by proud fathers to watch the battle from what was thought a safe distance. But now the lot of them were standing in their little fine kimonos and their little swords, with their hair pulled up into childish tufts that must have delighted their mothers with the cuteness of it, and there was nothing but fear and uncertainty in their eyes.

Brought to bear witness, blooded before they knew any better— Bennosuke felt empathy for them lurch within himself. He looked the eldest squarely in the eye and told him: "Run."

He meant to speak warmly, but his voice hissed out as a panting snarl. What the boys saw was a heaving giant with a face half coated in blood, and at that they shrank farther back into the undergrowth.

There was nothing he could do for them. He pushed onward once more. Running uphill, the distance seemed so much longer than this morning, but eventually the slope leveled off. He realized this must have been close to where he had watched the hawk at dawn. He allowed himself a moment to catch his breath, and he turned to look down upon the valley spread before him.

It was clear to see the Western army was doomed; the Patient Tiger was closing his jaws around the jugular of Japan. Kobayakawa's army had swept across from the right, and his betrayal had sparked insidious inspiration in some of the other lords—or had at least put the desperate realization of defeat into them—and now the entire coalition was erupting into smaller battles as some lords tried to prove their worth to Tokugawa by smashing their former allies for him.

The honor of samurai. He wanted to laugh. Let them have it, let Tokugawa have his throne, and the crows and the flames can take those he crushed beneath him to fulfill his terrible ambition; Bennosuke no longer cared. He was leaving it all behind: the orders, the shame, the dogma, Ukita, Kumagai, the Nakata . . .

And yet, thinking that, Bennosuke found his eye drawn to burgundy amid the battlefield before him. One melee among dozens, a ring of banners slowly being driven inward by an overwhelming advance. The last stand of the Nakata, wrought so small at this distance. Little men flailing with little toy sticks, standards flapping like feathers on the smallest of birds. The nobles were there at the center, the old lord and Hayato too, he supposed, huddled together looking outward, trapped as the wall of men between them and the enemy grew thinner by the moment.

Bennosuke found himself filled with sudden regret that he was not down there ending them himself, but he knew that he had waived any right to do so when he had decided to leave the battlefield. The child of vengeance was dead and the child of Amaterasu ruled now, he told himself. That was the choice he had made—to be bound by no quest but that which he chose for himself.

But still that ache within him remained unanswered. He watched the last banners fall as the men in burgundy were overwhelmed, vanished beneath a host that screamed their victory for but a moment before turning to find a fresh enemy, and he wondered if Munisai was watching, wherever his spirit was.

His eye was drawn elsewhere; Sekigahara was lost, and if Bennosuke knew it, then the lords of the enemy knew it too. Forces could be diverted. From within the midst of the Eastern army, a band of light cavalry armed with bows began to peel away. They formed into a long ribbon of men, looped around their rear, and then started to race at a full gallop, heading up the slope already notching arrows on their bows. They came for those fleeing—this was to be a total victory, and Tokugawa was in no mood for mercy.

The wind was already howling through his lungs, but Bennosuke knew he would have to run a lot farther yet.

CHAPTER NINETEEN

As the horsemen began to gallop up the slopes, Benno-suke thought for a moment about stripping his armor from himself. He felt anchored by it, and he needed to be lighter, more agile, less exhausted. But there was no time, and in any case he doubted it mattered to a horse whether a man was naked or carrying a load of stone. Cuirass and guards rattling still, he forced himself to run once more. There was a pain in his side almost immediately—he shouldn't have stopped, he knew. To tease the body with the promise of respite only made it clamor for more, because flesh was ever weaker than the spirit.

Bennosuke breached the valleytop, and started to run downward. He was not alone, plenty of men before him. This side of the valley was not as heavily forested, yet the scattered outcrops of trees and wild bushes still funneled the panicked herd between them. It was chaos, dozens of them, perhaps even hundreds running blind, scrambling over brush and trampling long grass.

There was a cry of alarm from behind when the first of the arrows whipped down, fired blind from the other side of the ridge. Few were hit, but men cowered and yelped as the long shafts lanced out of the sky to impale the ground around them. Faster. Every man knew he had to be faster. They sucked air through gritted teeth, tried to put more earth beneath their feet.

Downhill, soft ground—this should have been an easy run. But other men staggered, and his own vision began to fade around the edges. Munisai's words taunted him once more—how many minutes had he fought?

At what he hoped to be halfway down the slope Bennosuke turned as he ran, and he saw the Tokugawa horsemen streaming down after them. They were far still, like little inked figures on a painted panorama, but even from here it was obvious how easy it was for them. A game almost, they were cantering, taking time to aim, and then an arrow lashed out straight and a man tumbled and fell. On they came, growing large, filling the space between the trees.

They could not enter those trees, though, and in them Bennosuke saw his escape. In the broad landscape before them was a mass of short, steep hills like the backs of great turtles in water, and when they reached the bottom of the valley they would have to find their way around or over these. To the right, heading inland to the mountains, the forest became much thicker, and in that cover he knew he could ghost away from the body of the men and go wherever it was that the forest led, safe from horsemen and whoever else might follow him.

But first he had to get there, and the distance shrank so very slowly. His body truly aching now, his ankles numb and bleeding from the chafing of his greaves, he felt phantom arrows pierce his back again and again, but none materialized and slowly the outcrops grew larger and larger and the safety of the forest proper grew closer.

It took his senses from him the closer he got, tantalizing him. He dreamed of finding a stream within that forest, his mouth dry and his throat raw from his skull to his sternum. He saw the trees, straight trunks that stood the height of fifteen men bare of foliage until the very top, no more than an arm's width between each of them, and they called to him, forty paces, thirty, twenty . . .

Passing a copse, the trees revealed to him a lone Tokugawa horseman. The man was a scout perhaps, a single outrider ahead of the main body of men, and the rider was wheeling his steed around a body run through with one of his arrows. There were two other men cowering on their asses in front of him, and as they looked at Bennosuke's sudden arrival the horseman too turned his head.

There was a moment of shock that both he and Bennosuke shared, and in that moment the boy realized that he was entirely exposed. No tree or bush to throw himself behind, he was at the mercy entirely of the bow in the rider's hand. There was no arrow notched to that bow, though, and those next instants as the rider reached to his quiver were everything.

Bennosuke moved for his weapons too. He drew his shortsword, took a staggering run, and then hurled the blade at the rider with such force that he almost tumbled over. But he was exhausted and the target was at a distance, and Bennosuke knew it was a bad throw as soon as it left his hand. The boy despaired as the wildly spinning sword veered hopelessly toward the ground.

The rider drew the string of his weapon back, and Bennosuke's eyes locked upon the rising arrowhead, body freezing with dread of the blow to come. He barely saw the sword bouncing off the turf. Wild though the throw had been, such was the strength behind it that it rebounded and shot upward, whipping around twice as ferociously. Caught in a fresh, chaotic arc, it rose to smash the rider's horse in the mouth. The beast screamed and began to buck and kick and the rider swore as his arrow loosed into the ground, and then the man was grabbing at the reins and fighting to regain control.

Bennosuke took the gift for what it was. He drew his longsword and charged, and the rider saw him coming with alarm in his eyes. The man dropped his bow and started reaching for something at his side, but he was too slow. The boy leapt like a savage hunter, holding the sword inverted above his head point-first, and his two-handed thrust pierced the light armor easily and stabbed through the man's rib cage.

The rider gave a cry and his horse bolted. Bennosuke's sword was torn from his grasp as he was knocked off his feet. The man managed to hang on for some distance, but from his knees Bennosuke watched his body go limp and fall from the saddle face-first. He did not get up, and as the boy scrambled for both of his swords where they lay, elation filled him.

The forest was his. Freedom.

"Thank you!" said one of the men. Bennosuke had forgotten they were there, and he turned to wave them away. But when he looked at them more closely, he found his body grew tense. The pair of them stared back awkwardly for a moment at the sudden change in him, before the second one grabbed at the first.

"Let's go!" he said, for all around them were screams and hoof fall. "No time! To the rally point!"

"To the hells with that! The lords're all dead!" said the first man. "Let's just go!"

"The heir lives! We have to protect him!" said the second, and he began to pull his companion away. They ran, the first man bowing to Bennosuke one last time in thanks, and he watched them go.

The forest was there, the safety that he had earned was there, and part of him begged to vanish into it. The pair of samurai were running farther and farther and he watched them, watched them, watched them, trying to convince himself that he could forget what they had said.

But he couldn't, because filthy though the pair were, beneath the dirt their armor was burgundy.

HE CURSED HIMSELF as he ran back up the slope through the same outcrops of trees he had just dashed through. They could be lying, the pair of them, or just wrong. This was battle—who knew the state of things? Yet still he followed. The two burgundy samurai did not look back, and up the valley slope he was aware of the shapes of horsemen through the trunks of trees, the mass of them ever present and scouring all before them like an avalanche.

The fleeing army ran their different ways, and the horsemen duly diverged to follow them. The chase had become separate contests, separate hawks swooping for separate mice through the weaving pathways between trees, sometimes intersecting like a wicker basket coming together. Men who thought themselves free would round a corner to find themselves suddenly beset by Tokugawa's men, and that was that.

A group of horsemen emerged ahead of Bennosuke, four of them cantering on some other trail, and they passed between him and Nakata's men for a few moments. Only the rearmost saw him, and on instinct the man lurched in his saddle and launched an arrow at him half drawn. The arrow flew too short, and it bounced off the ground before him, the length of it quivering in the air. It caught in his legs and he almost stumbled over it, but he managed to clatter onward, leaving it snapped beneath his feet.

Instead of notching another arrow the mounted samurai merely grinned and held his thumb and his forefinger a sliver apart at Bennosuke before he vanished between the trees once more. The horsemen did not stop, continuing down whatever path they were headed. Someone else would get him eventually—why bother with the minor inconvenience of turning when there was easier prey ahead of them?

The two burgundy samurai ran on, and their path twisted once more, leading downhill slightly. Ahead of them a grand burgundy banner fluttering above a small clearing soon became visible. Of course the Nakata would have a retreat planned. But it was a sad cluster of men beneath that standard, and even from a distance Bennosuke could see they were in total disarray.

There were no more than forty of them, and they were frantically scrambling around. As he and the burgundy samurai reached them, some were making a disjointed effort to place barricades of bamboo stakes facing uphill, but there were nowhere near enough to make a solid line. Rocks in a river, nothing more. Men held spears weakly, looking up at the coming horsemen. Not a single voice was giving commands.

Not a single man was checking friend from foe either; Bennosuke was let into their little encampment without hindrance. Men swarmed around him, and though most of them were fresh, enough had escaped the fight in the valley that he did not look out of place, covered in blood as he was. Each heaving breath a burn, Bennosuke put his hands on his knees as he looked around quickly, and there he was.

Hayato Nakata.

His armor was clean and fine, his missing arm artfully hidden. The lord's thin face was agape, his mouth flapping loosely. A horse was half saddled behind him, abandoned now in the face of what was coming. Bodyguards stood around him, but they were that in name only, staring helplessly at the horsemen who flowed down the slope and drew ever closer.

No time, no time, no time.

His mind was working quickly, deviously. Only one man stopped Bennosuke as he approached Hayato, the only one fit to be called a guard. He was a fierce man, and he looked familiar—his face was marked with a spattering of scars, the white flesh of old circular burns daubed scattershot across his cheek and neck. He halted Bennosuke with a hand on the shoulder, and for a heartbeat Bennosuke thought he had been recognized. Instead, the man leaned his ear in close and expectantly.

"I'm here for Lord Hayato, sir," whispered Bennosuke between pants. "I have an escape planned. There's no time to argue. We must go now."

The burned man nodded, and he looked relieved as he removed his hand and let Bennosuke approach Hayato. The boy dropped to one knee by the young lord's side, and kept his face down.

"My lord," he said, "we have to get you out of here. I have a route planned back to safety."

"We're going to die," said Hayato, hearing nothing but his own frantic heartbeat, his jaw quivering, his eyes locked on the approaching horsemen. "We're going to die."

"Listen to me, my lord. I can save you. I can get you out of here alone, secretly, but you must come with me now, through the forest," said Bennosuke. He gestured downhill toward the same trees through which he had planned to escape. "No horse can pass through that, my lord."

"Who—" Hayato began, his eyes flicking to Bennosuke for but an instant, but whatever he might have said was cut off by a scream and a crash nearby.

Horsemen had appeared from another direction, hidden through the winding of the trees, and now their beasts were rearing up against the bamboo stakes and their riders were cheering at their sudden discovery while launching arrows into the little Nakata encampment. The one-armed lord took a step back, horrified.

"We must go, Lord!" snapped Bennosuke. "Your father is dead! You are the clan Nakata now! Let your men serve you and lay down their lives in distraction, and come with me! You must live! That is all that matters!"

"He speaks sense, Lord," said the bodyguard.

Hayato said nothing more; he just turned and ran down into the thick forest. The only hesitation had been his terror-numbed mind comprehending the word *escape*. He went and he did not look back.

Bennosuke and the bodyguard nodded at each other, and then they followed him down into the trees, becoming nothing but indistinct splashes of color darting between trunks, and then they were gone. The remaining Nakata, too stupefied by their impending doom, did not notice.

ive minutes later, nothing in burgundy moved in the encampment. Corpses lay twisted clutching at arrows, and the hooves of Tokugawa warhorses picked their way between them. The main body of the cavalry had gone on, plenty more fleeing men and lords to hunt, but a few of them had been left behind to scour the area for anything of value. Two men were looking up at Nakata's banner from their saddles.

"That's nice," said one, eyeing the workmanship of the golden crest atop the frame appreciatively. He pulled his hand free of his riding glove and rubbed the material of the banner itself between his thumb and his finger. "Very nice. What are we supposed to do with it?"

"The command is to burn it," said the other. "Hills have to run with blood, the skies with smoke and all that."

"Shame," said the first, and replaced his glove. "Daughter's getting married soon. Wife needs a new gown. That's yards of good silk, that."

"You'd let your wife wear something you found on a battlefield?"

"I wouldn't tell her where I got it from."

"Savagery," said the second, shaking his head scornfully. "Such savagery."

A fire was struck, a lantern held to the banner until it ignited, and then when they were certain it was inextinguishably ablaze the riders left. The standard burned on for a few minutes until it collapsed unseen by any but the dead who had been left behind, and thus, in the eyes of the world, ended the clan Nakata.

This was wild country they ran through, picking their way through the trees and slopes, winding their way downward on unsteady ground. Autumn had not fully claimed it yet, patches of green remaining amid the encroaching gold. A deer froze as they passed, its antlers emerging nubs, its black eyes wide, glistening orbs.

Slowly the sound of the rout behind them faded, but never left quite entirely. Hayato did not look back—he was just determined to go, and so he barreled on without any concern for grace and decorum or waiting for his companions. Bennosuke shouted encouragement to him, offering advice and directions as though he knew where they were going.

His head throbbed, the wound there pulsing with every beat of his heart. He felt as though he wanted to vomit, his bowels tight and aching also, but he could not tell if this desire to expel everything was because of injury or exhaustion or because of what he now had within his grasp. Three years of suffering welling within him, and what he felt was terrible confusion and uncertainty.

What had moved him to come seek the lord out? He asked himself that question as they headed onward. Sitting in that horse's entrails down in the valley of Sekigahara, what he had realized—no, not realized, finally allowed himself to admit, for it had always been with him—was that death should not be cherished.

That was it. That was everything. It sounded so small and so stupid that such a thing should have to be stated. But this was what he had freed himself from. He wanted to ask, Who was the first man to see a corpse and consider it godly? How did he persuade others to feel the same?

Munisai the samurai had chosen it, yet he could not prevent the disgrace that Hayato visited on him, nor avenge it afterward because of his choice. Shuntaro the peasant had chosen it, but could not prevent his son and his friends from spurning his sacrifice by making exactly the same choice. No, death defined not samurai, but all men—and defined them only in that they could never define themselves again.

But Bennosuke had seen all that carnage and slaughter, and he had vowed that he was done with it all; from now he would define himself, by and for himself. The quest that Munisai had set him, the shame that followed—he no longer cared. He had thought it all obscene.

And yet, so quickly had he forgotten that. This opportunity had presented itself, and he had taken it.

Why?

If death should not be cherished, then surely neither should it be inflicted on others. That seemed logical.

Was it the instinct of years, driving his hand? He still wore armor, still carried Munisai's swords—did the man's ghost have some kind of hold of him?

No, he had chosen. To deny that was cowardly—he had chosen to leave the battlefield and he had chosen not to flee into the forest, and now he was here.

But you can still choose to let him go. Leave this all behind, return to Dorinbo and Miyamoto at last, just live for yourself . . .

The bodyguard was struggling, trailing red-faced behind Hayato and Bennosuke. He was not an agile man, and he was slipping and stumbling on hidden roots and mossy stone and earth. Bennosuke waited for him on top of a fallen log, and offered a hand down to help the man over.

The man took it, but rather than haul himself up he held it and looked Bennosuke squarely in the face, examining him. Recognition crept across his features, turning quickly to surprise, and he began to open his mouth. Before any sound escaped him the boy's hand lanced out and stabbed him in the side of the neck with the throwing dagger Tasumi had given him years ago.

The samurai made a desperate gurgling noise, and as the man died Bennosuke realized that the burns that marked him were each about the size of a lump of coal.

"What is it? What?" called Hayato, so far ahead he was almost out of sight.

"Arrows, my lord! An arrow has taken him! Go! Run!" shouted Bennosuke. "They're close!"

Hayato gave a yelp and ran onward, downward, not even bothering to check. The specters of assassins were in his mind already, probably flitting from tree to tree all around him like mountain demons. He grew smaller, his lopsided body weaving between the trunks.

Bennosuke let the lord run as he watched the bodyguard die, and then gently he lowered the corpse onto the log.

He followed Hayato at a measured pace, never letting the lord leave his sight. They soon came to a stream. Ten paces wide and barely calf height, clear, fresh water streaming over ocher stones. They followed it—easier to walk over wet rocks than scramble over brush—and gradually Hayato calmed down. His loping canter slowed into a walk. They went on silently for some time, the lord first and the boy a short distance behind.

Bennosuke ran his fingers along the wound on his scalp. Dull agony. The boy reached down and scooped handfuls of the water from the stream onto his head. He half hoped it would clear his head as much as it would clear his face of blood.

Hayato did not look back once. Bennosuke could just vanish into the woods, and the lord would be left utterly alone. The water was cold on his brow, an autumn chill in the air. *Wake up,* he told himself, *this is not your world any longer.* But still he followed, a gore-streaked somnambulist.

He asked himself, Do you hate this man enough to kill him? How long have you actually spent in his presence? A handful of hours? He made you endure nothing—you forced all this upon yourself.

Go.

Leave.

Be a child of Amaterasu. Go back to Dorinbo, lead a good life helping others.

"How much farther?" Hayato asked, again not turning his head.

"Not much, my lord," said Bennosuke.

"My father is truly dead?"

"Yes, my lord."

"How?"

"Surrounded and overwhelmed on the battlefield, my lord."

"How unfortunate," said Hayato, and on the side of his face Bennosuke saw the dimple of a malicious, triumphant smile.

So small a gesture, but Bennosuke found clarity within that smile. Something within him hardened.

To Hayato, death was something others offered for his benefit—Arima, the men in Aramaki, the thousands on that battlefield, the bodyguard, even his own father. Death to him was a boon, a convenience, an expedient end to his own betterment. Death should not be cherished, but equally it should be understood. But this lord did not, and never would. Men may all be trapped in that little stratum of corpses between the heavens and the hells, but on the wave of those bodies men like Hayato were borne aloft. Why would they ever look downward?

Let him go, walk away, and how many more would have to throw themselves into oblivion to keep the clan Nakata buoyant, to sate their regal and bloody maw?

Do not hate him as an individual; hate him for all that he represents.

Was Bennosuke to be a child of vengeance, or a child of Amaterasu? He thought, Why not both? Why not use the choice Amaterasu gave him to enact this vengeance because he, as a human, *chose* to do so?

As right as banishing the dark with fire, as natural as the thaw of rivers in spring, it could be the act of a conscious being thinking for the first time for himself—and that perhaps was as saintly as men could ever be. Bennosuke licked his lips, tasted the dried blood there.

"You haven't looked at me once this entire time, have you, my lord?" he said to Hayato's back.

"What are you talking about?" said Hayato, irritated. "Who do you think you're talking to?"

"Are you samurai, my lord?" said Bennosuke.

Hayato stopped and turned at that, and then he saw.

"No," Hayato breathed. "No."

He did not go for his sword. Instead he turned and ran. Bennosuke chased after him, kicked his legs out from under him, and then Hayato was on his hands and knees scrabbling in the water.

"No," said Hayato, his voice breaking. "Oh no no, you're dead, you're dead, they said you were dead, they told me they killed you, they showed me your arms, no no no . . ."

Bennosuke grabbed the lord by his armor, hauling him over so he lay on his back looking up at what stood over him. Water soaked into the fine threads that coated his armor. Bennosuke drew his sword, and Hayato flinched pathetically.

"Do you remember how my father died, my lord?" said Bennosuke.

He began to cut the thick cords that bound Hayato's armor

together, wrenching it away piece by piece. The lord fumbled backward when Bennosuke's hands left him for an instant here, a heartbeat there, a crab slowly being stripped of its shell. But he hadn't the wit to bring himself to his feet, and always Bennosuke caught him, always another layer went.

The lord was soon in his underclothes, and Bennosuke slashed them open too so that his torso and the sad stump of his arm were revealed. The boy picked Hayato's shortsword from where it had fallen beneath the water—never once had the lord gone for it—and tossed it to him in its scabbard. It bounced off his chest and was submerged once more.

"On your knees," Bennosuke said. "Perform seppuku and I'll take your head in an instant."

"Please, let me go," said Hayato. "I'll give you—"

"I don't want anything," said Bennosuke.

The tip of his longsword was in the water, a little chevron of a wake forming around it. Hayato stared at it, watched as an auburn leaf caught upon the current brushed up against it and spiraled away past them both. Tears formed in his eyes as with his one hand he picked up his shortsword, and rose unsteadily into a quivering kneel.

What to say now to Hayato? Bennosuke was no great orator, young still, unable to construct some grand speech. All he could do was spread his arms wide and say what he felt.

"It's all of it shit," he said. "I see it now. It had to be written so large for me, but I see it now. All of it a death cult built to serve men like you. And people just assent to it . . . just tread the same paths that have been trodden a million times before."

He laughed, once, as he realized he was quoting his uncle Dorinbo, imagined his face. Slowly Bennosuke moved to stand beside Hayato. On the lord's shaven scalp beads of water shivered a glimmering constellation.

"What happens when one man doesn't assent?" said Bennosuke. "I suppose that makes me a bad samurai. I suppose that doesn't make me a samurai at all. So what am I? I don't know, but I really, really don't care. I'm alive. And as far as you're concerned, I am going to live forever."

Hayato was sobbing, the shortsword feeble in his grasp. The stars upon his pate were dashed as the lord looked up, pleading. Bennosuke tapped him on the stomach with the flat of his blade.

"Do it," he said. "Do it, samurai."

WHEN IT WAS done, Bennosuke walked upstream looking skyward. Somewhere behind the clouds was Amaterasu. Around his feet darted the fingerlings of fish. Hidden by grass, cicadas sang their song. A swallow dived into the boughs of a tree, autumn leaves falling. The water and the clouds flowed on, ever on. It was all imperfect and wonderful. Tears streamed from his eyes as he realized it was over, and that of all this he was still a part.

He stripped off his gauntlets and beheld his hands; a dragonfly, mottled black and jade, settled on his wrist.

EPILOGUE

The clouds gathered and darkness fell, and on the corpse-strewn slopes of Sekigahara great bonfires were lit, lighting the faces of the dead and the living alike. The only men who rested were those who slept the slumber from which there was no waking. For the thousands still breathing there was work to be done through the night, for their Lord Tokugawa wanted to make a tower to commemorate the great victory he had won today.

He was lacking stone and mortar, so he had decided instead to use the heads of the enemy.

It was a command ghoulish only in the sheer scale of the work imposed on exhausted men. Other lords had been known to make far more capricious and macabre displays of might—stripping the enemy of their eyes, or their hands, or their manhood, or even all three, and then leaving them alive as an enduring, shambling warning. Tokugawa was indeed magnanimous in this, and so the men went about the task with a sense of pride at their lord's virtue.

Indeed, they were making a celebration of it. Men sang the old songs as they searched in packs, smiling and passing bottles of sake among themselves, turning over corpses where they lay to see whether they were friend or foe. Friend they revered and shed tears for, foe they severed the head, stripped the body of armor and valuables, and then bore the cadaver to one of the bonfires. This was war—no time for priests or corpsehandlers.

The captured survivors of the Western army were rounded up beside the tower, more being brought in all the time as stragglers were caught in the hills. These men looked at their guards with hatred, for many of them had been their allies in the morning. For them, though, there was to be no mercy—either a dignified seppuku or a blubbering decapitation.

Fifty men waited to behead them, famed swordsmen all. The soil around their feet had grown marshlike with blood, the hair upon their arms and the back of their necks burned away by the sheer heat of the fire they stood next to, but still their strikes were perfect, clean. There was no hesitation, no pause as they whittled down the thousands; a great machine into which the cowards and the unfortunate were fed.

Three of these swordsmen were of the Yoshioka school.

An enemy samurai was led up to them. He was calm, unafraid, and he dropped to his knees smoothly. He bowed to the Yoshioka, pushed a dagger up into himself, and then the leftmost one slashed his sword down and took his head.

"In another life, we shall be friends," he said to the corpse, as he and his comrades bowed respectfully.

Lesser samurai bore the head reverently to the tower, placed it face outward so that all might look upon and know the image of a brave man, and his body was added to the pyre behind them where space could be found. The Yoshioka swordsmen watched the body ignite, consumed and quickly hidden by the well-stoked flames.

The rightmost of them turned away first and pinched bloody fingers to the bridge of his nose. He was a gruff man, short and compact, and now he was scowling, angry. He had been muttering for some time.

"That's it—that's the Yoshioka school?" the man growled in imitation. "I cannot believe Seibei fell to that dog. What was his name?"

"Musashi Miyamoto, I believe he called himself to his own army," said the centermost man. He was calm, his voice gentle, a young man of slight build and sharp cheekbones. "That whole series of events was very strange, wasn't it?"

"Is it any wonder we won, with behavior such as that among their ranks?" said the leftmost. He was the eldest of the group, hair starting to gray, eyes sunken and narrow. "The first rule of constructing a house states . . . Well, I suppose that's a simile rather too morbid to continue, given the circumstances."

Another samurai was brought before them with tears streaming down his face, begging incoherently to be spared. He squealed and raised his hands as the blade came down. The rightmost samurai kicked the head toward the tower desultorily. It was hurled to the top of the pile, where soon the man's cowardly visage would be buried, hidden and forgotten from the world.

"Bastard," the rightmost man said. He picked the severed fingers from the earth, the product of the man's futile attempt at defense, and tossed them one by one into the fire. "Have they found Miyamoto's corpse yet? I feel the need to shit coming on."

"No," said the leftmost man. "Seibei's has been found, thankfully—both the head and the body, I might add—and it is on its way back to the school with some of the students. We'll pay our respects to him soon. But this Miyamoto . . ."

"He was caught in the charge of our spearmen," said the centermost man. "He'd have to be lucky to survive that."

"He had to have been lucky to have beaten Seibei. Really—wrestling like that? How crude."

"A strange one, indeed."

"But the spirits sometimes smile on those kind of men," said the leftmost, nodding. "Something tells me he survived."

"Well, I don't care how strange or how lucky he is," snarled the rightmost. "He insulted our school in front of every samurai in Japan—we're adding him to the list, right?"

"Oh, naturally," said the centermost man.

"Good," spat the rightmost. "If he ever comes to Kyoto, I'll spill his guts across the street and leave him for the crows."

"We all will," said the leftmost. "We are of the Yoshioka."

Yet another samurai was brought before them. The ranks of the captured did not seem to diminish. The rightmost man blinked as a rain drop splashed upon his brow. He looked up, eyes squinting, as above him and the dead and this newborn country of Tokugawa's Japan, the clouds began to burst.

The pyres burned on regardless.

ACKNOWLEDGMENTS

I am greatly indebted to and would like to thank Ayako Sato, who not only helped with translation and research but also endured increasingly ludicrous questions about Japanese culture and history with a patience and grace worthy of any samurai. She also kicked my arse into gear as and when it was needed with a ferocity to match.

DAVID KIRK
Glowing faintly with Cesium-137,
Sendai, Japan, March 2012

Printed in the United States
by Baker & Taylor Publisher Services